Prophet of Eden Park

Vivian Catfield

CATFIELD
PRESS

Prophet of Eden Park

By Vivian Catfield

Published by Vivian Catfield on her imprint, Catfield Press

2692 Madison Rd.

Ste. N1-354

Cincinnati, OH 45208

www.viviancatfield.com

www.catfieldpress.com

First Edition, Published 2025.

eBook ISBN: 9798992771558

Paperback ISBN: 9798992771541

Printed in the United States of America

Reader Advisory

This novel is a work of fiction that explores mature and emotionally intense themes. The story involves a series of violent crimes and follows both those who commit them and those affected by them.

These themes include:

- Trauma and abuse (including references to past sexual violence)
- Psychological manipulation and mental illness
- Death, grief, and brief mentions of attempted suicide
- Substance abuse
- Violence involving people and animals
- Strong language and adult situations

These elements are presented in service of the characters and their stories, with great concern taken to avoid unnecessary detail.

Please take care while reading. If you are a survivor of trauma, know that your experiences matter. Your well-being is important, and you are never alone in your efforts to recover.

If you or someone you know needs support and/or wishes to report abuse or assault, confidential help is available 24/7 through the resources below.

- RAINN (Rape, Abuse & Incest National Network – U.S.): www.rainn.org | 1-800-656-HOPE
- SAMHSA (Substance Abuse and Mental Health Services Administration): www.samhsa.gov | 1-800-662-HELP
- 988 Suicide & Crisis Lifeline: www.988lifeline.org | Call or Text 988
- Crime Stoppers (U.S.): www.crimestoppersusa.org | 1-800-222-TIPS

For David,
Who asked me to write something that felt real

Contents

Friday, October 6th, Morning

S hiloh Foley loved the fall.

The soft, sighing air as every living thing seemed to exhale.

Shuffling through the heaps of crackling red, orange, and yellow leaves on that quiet October morning, Shiloh remembered a field trip from high school. With public school budgets slashed, teachers had to get creative. That year, her teachers led their classes on a mile-and-a-half walk from Holmes High School to Linden Grove Cemetery for a history lecture among the graves of notable local people buried there.

Strangely, Shiloh recalled that trip more than any other. Perhaps it was the rarity of how they walked to the cemetery almost in total silence. Speaking only in hushed whispers, as if they were afraid the dead would hear them. A hundred tenth graders were never so quiet.

After arriving, they all settled down on top of the fallen leaves. The students remained as still as the stone angels surrounding them. A host of gray-haired librarians shared the stories of the cemetery's inhabitants. They were swaddled in vintage clothing reminiscent of the various eras they described. The silence was so complete that when a pair of squirrels scurried down from a nearby tree and started scratching among the leaves for acorns, chattering to one another, every kid's head turned toward them. Some even shushed, which made the librarians chuckle.

It was just as quiet on the morning of October sixth. Shiloh Foley, age forty, observed two squirrels frisking among the heaps of leaves that the previous night's wind had blown into mounds against the curbs and fences. As she walked to get her Friday morning pumpkin spice latte at the Bow Tie Cafe, she thought about driving over to visit her husband's grave at Spring Grove Cemetery.

It was part of her routine. Sure, Shiloh could make coffee at home and drink it sitting in her favorite chair by the fireplace with her cat in her lap exactly like she used to. She could also take out her tarot cards and do a morning pull to guess the day's fate, just as she had for years. Yet, since Ethan's death, Shiloh found it hard to linger at home in the morning, and she didn't really care about discovering whatever small mysteries the day might bring. However, getting up early so that she could be the first person through the door when the café opened each morning at seven gave Shiloh a reason to shower, put on clothes, and leave the house instead of staring at the empty spot in front of the house where Ethan had always parked his car. New routines were important, or so the grief counseling books that she'd read told her. The routine of getting up every morning to work through a list filled with little somethings, from sunrise to sunset, until the day was done. Checking off boxes attached to small, insignificant tasks was supposed to lead her back toward finding interest in accomplishing larger goals. To rediscover some sort of reason why the world continued to circle the sun without a certain person remaining in its orbit.

Shiloh's life was like that. A series of small, meaningless events, braided together into a lifeline that she hoped would lead out of the hole she'd been in ever since Ethan was killed.

Ethan.

Saying his name still made Shiloh close her eyes and catch her breath. But since she'd decided that she wouldn't dwell on it, that she would do as her therapy books told her and keep busy, Shiloh kept walking. Double-checking her earbuds to make sure they were secure, Shiloh turned up the volume of the music on her cell phone. Taylor Swift. *Folklore.* The best kind of album to get lost in.

Stepping up to the counter at the Bow Tie Cafe, Shiloh paid for her latte in cash. She settled down on a wooden stool by the front window to wait. Outside, she saw a young college-aged woman putting up a flyer. The flyer announced in bold, frantic letters: *Missing Cat!* Beneath the words was a full-color photo, depicting a large, fluffy cream-point ragdoll cat, whose name was apparently Muffin.

You look like a muffin, Shiloh murmured to herself, glancing over at the glass case of pastries. A barista handed her the pumpkin spice latte in a go-cup. Back out on the sidewalk, Shiloh scanned the flyer and took a photo with her phone. Muffin was last seen lounging by the window boxes of a porch on St. Gregory Street. Shiloh recognized the house number as being right across from her office on the way back towards her house. The coincidence made her uneasy; Shiloh double-checked the pocket of her hoodie for her keys. *Still there.*

I should go back and make sure that I locked the front door, Shiloh thought. Then, she reconsidered. *No, I shouldn't.* Checking and rechecking things that a person knew were already done was a sign of loss-induced anxiety and OCD. Concentrating so hard on the picture of Muffin that she could see each pixel of the grainy photo, Shiloh whispered to herself.

"I locked the door. I'm sure because I pulled on it three times." Even though she knew that creating such a ritual was a sign that her anxiety wasn't improving, it was one that Shiloh was willing to accept. It was the routine that calmed her. She needed the routine.

Nevertheless, Shiloh swung back by her house on the way to the park. *Just to peep in the window*, she reassured herself. Heading down St. Gregory Street past the brightly painted yellow front of her office, Shiloh considered popping in to check her email. Opening her clients' email account, especially on a Sunday morning, was an invitation to fall down a rabbit hole. At the bottom of which was likely to be at least one suspicious spouse or employer seeking to question a worker's comp claim and needing an immediate response. Deciding that if she didn't know of their urgent needs, she wouldn't feel compelled to respond to them so early in the day, Shiloh whistled past the window of Foley Investigative Services without touching the door.

Boundaries, Shiloh thought. That was another thing the stack of self-help books on her bedside table stressed was important in regaining a sense of control over one's life after a major loss. *Re-establishing boundaries.*

Rounding the corner, a block later, Shiloh passed in front of her house at 956 Hatch Street. From the opposite curb, she could see her enormous black smoke Maine Coon, William, sleeping soundly; his shimmering silver spine pressed against the warm pane above the sunny windowsill. The dark moon of his face turned away from her. Below the window, the black-painted inset was marked with an ornately sculpted ceramic letter *M*, custom-made at Rookwood Pottery. The initial was a wedding present from...

No, Shiloh willed herself not to remember who had given her—them—the letter. Turning quickly on her heel as she stuffed her fists into the pockets of her tunic-length olive green hoodie, Shiloh resisted the urge to cross the street and check the door. *Boundaries*, she thought again, as she hung a left and headed toward Eden Park.

Passing by the rows of historic townhouses as she sipped her latte, Shiloh congratulated herself on her restraint. Six weeks ago, she would have tugged on the door multiple times to make sure that it was secure. Then, she would have felt compelled to open it and to awaken William from his nap to make sure that the cat was still breathing before she could go on with her day. *Small steps*, she thought to herself. *Little improvements*.

The autumn sunrise was bright, but the wind was chilly as Shiloh started down the stone steps into the green bowl of Eden Park's main lawn. Walking around Mirror Lake in the middle of the park's upper tier first, Shiloh admired the orderly row of ducks standing on the water pipe leading to the fountain in the center. She raised her cell phone to take a picture of them and post it later on her socials, accompanied by some kind of witty caption.

"Up early this morning, getting my ducks in a row" would make a cute byline, she thought. Because that was what people did. Post happy pictures to social media in an attempt to confirm their happiness for the world, when most likely nothing was further from the truth.

About halfway around Mirror Lake, Shiloh peered over the massive rock retaining wall that separated the lake's main lawn above from the children's playground and basketball courts below. The lower space was once a water reservoir, long since drained and repurposed as city green space. Yet, the old steel pipes remained. Following one of these pipes over to the left with her gaze, Shiloh spied a pile of discarded spray paint cans in the underbrush.

Shiloh shook her head. *Kids these days*. She started around the far end of the retaining wall to pick up the cans. A volunteer in city cleanup programs for years, Shiloh hated to find trash lying around, especially when it was likely a remnant of vandalism. She'd seen plenty of graffiti in the park before. A never-ending battle between the park's maintenance crew, who had to wash and repaint over it, and the swarms of late-night teenagers, who scribbled it.

Months before, a maze of misshapen occult symbols appeared that were so disturbingly unintelligible, Shiloh felt compelled to leave them a note with pictures of correctly drawn figures. At the bottom, she signed it, *A Concerned Witch*, hoping that the kids who were dabbling with powers they didn't understand would get spooked and give up. The note worked for a while. Shiloh hadn't seen any new graffiti drawn on the wall since then.

Bracing herself against a tree as she climbed down to retrieve the spray cans, Shiloh stopped, horrified. There, lying on a broken concrete slab at the bottom of the wall, mostly hidden behind a curtain of overgrowth, was a cat. Or rather, what remained of one. The poor animal had been sliced down its belly and its skin removed, leaving only the exposed muscle, sinew, and bone beneath.

Tears of shock welled up in Shiloh's eyes as she forced herself to step closer. Whoever the cat's killers were had butchered the job. They left behind most of the fur on the animal's face, legs, and tail. Although the cat's head was covered in blood, Shiloh recognized the animal as the same one she'd seen less than an hour before on the flyer outside the cafe.

Muffin, Shiloh sighed, unable to stop herself from crying. *I am so sorry. What kind of monster did this to you?*

Knowing that she needed to call the authorities but not trusting her shaking voice, Shiloh looked away from the cat's ruined body and up at the walls. They were covered in newly spray-painted symbols. Lopsided triangles with lines through them. Then dozens of sigils that she recognized as those intended to summon wealth. One in particular caught her eye. It was a crooked sideways letter *M*, surrounded by a circle.

Mammon, Shiloh thought to herself, not wanting to speak the name. *The demon tied to worship of money in the Bible.* She reached for the phone in her pocket to snap photos of the drawings for the police. *They wanted money, so they made a blood sacrifice to try to summon the demon Mammon.*

As she turned, Shiloh glimpsed a larger drawing. Again, the figure was so poorly rendered in dripping red spray paint that she could barely discern what it was. It seemed to be a goat's head on a man's body, with the addition of women's breasts. One smudged hand with two fingers pointing skyward, while the other was meant to be an open palm extended toward the earth. An inverted pentagram with a circle drawn around it hovered between its horns. Shiloh recognized the drawing as a representation of Baphomet with the demon's hands in their signature pose.

Zooming in to capture the images, Shiloh froze. Sloppy globs of paint glistened at her, reflecting the morning sunshine that shone weakly through the cavern of overgrowth.

The paint is still wet. They could be close. Shiloh shoved her phone back into her pocket. Her gaze darting around in panic, Shiloh's pulse quickened. She could feel her heartbeat reverberating against the silicone cushions of her earbuds.

Completely forgetting her earlier mission of picking up the cast-off spray paint cans, Shiloh scrambled back up over the rock wall. She ran down the pathway toward the front of the park. At the entrance was a large gazebo. Painted green with a tiled roof, it was a relic of Eden Park's Victorian days. More recently, it was a place where high school couples gathered to take prom pictures. Finally feeling far enough away to be safe, Shiloh looked back over her shoulder.

Nothing.

Pulling her phone out of her pocket once more, Shiloh tried to decide whether to call 911 or the non-emergency police line. Then, she saw the bodies lying on the floor of the gazebo.

Two women. One older and one younger. Both with blonde hair and faces that must have been, in life, almost angelically beautiful. Their golden hair was twisted into long snakes that fanned out in grotesque halos. The women's jaws were agape. Their heads tilted back to expose the long gashes in their necks that sliced through to the bones. They were naked, and their backs arched unnaturally so that they formed a circle. Each had her right hand tied above her head to the left ankle of the other. Their left hands were extended downward toward their unbound right feet. In the center of the circle between them were four words rendered in the same irregular crimson strokes as the figures Shiloh saw painted on the wall. Only this time, the writing was in blood instead of spray paint.

Ut Supra, Ut Infra.

Even though her college Latin training ended decades ago, Shiloh knew the phrase's meaning.

As Above, So Below.

Friday, October 6th, Afternoon

S everal hours later, the ambulance carrying the bodies of the two dead women trundled slowly away toward Gilbert Avenue. Shiloh Foley and Detective Bruce Schultz stood on the steps of the Eden Park gazebo, watching the bands of yellow crime scene tape flap in the breeze. The EMTs and investigation team had cleaned up most of the blood, leaving behind damp, ominous, cloud-like shapes on the gazebo's floor. After their initial examination of the scene, Schultz and a forensics officer followed Shiloh down to the site where the cat was killed. There, the forensics officer tagged and bagged the cat for evidence. Then, he took down the number from the picture of the flyer on Shiloh's phone to call the owner. They agreed with Shiloh that the perpetrators of both crimes were likely the same suspects. Perhaps even more disturbing was their mutual, silent acceptance that the killer hadn't acted alone. It seemed obvious from the lack of a blood trail between both crime scenes that it was at least a two- or three-person job.

"I hate to say it, but this is probably the fastest missing person turned murder case I've ever worked on," Schultz said. He closed his small flip-top notebook and slipped it into his back pocket. "Got a call first thing this morning from Joe Arnold that his wife and daughter were missing. Dispatched a crew to his compound out past Indian Hill. They hadn't even gotten back yet from making the report when you called. I'd hoped it wasn't them, but..." Schultz shuffled his feet around in the gravel. "I've hoped for a lot of things. Real shame this time, though. I went to high school with Veronica, the mother, over at Withrow. Beautiful girl."

"Did you keep in touch?" Shiloh asked, keeping up the small talk to avoid awkward silence.

Detective Schultz grimaced and stuffed his large hands into the pockets of his goetta gray-colored jacket. Beneath it, he wore a wrinkled Oxford shirt with faint coffee stains that Shiloh felt sure Schultz's wife, Kaley, would pitch a fit if she saw him in. However, it was Fall Break. Shiloh knew that Kaley had taken the kids down to Louisville to see their grandparents. *Men really do fall apart quickly if left to fend for themselves*, Shiloh mentally noted.

"Nope. Ronni... She went by Ronni back in those days, instead of Veronica. She went on to Ohio State. I didn't go to college. Picked up a job as a meter cop straight out of high school. That's when Ronni met Joe, during college. He's one of *the* Arnolds. They all went to St. Aug's."

Schultz glanced over at Shiloh as if to suggest that she should know what he meant. The first question anyone in Cincinnati always asked a new person was where they went to high school. When Shiloh shrugged, Schultz continued.

"I keep forgetting you aren't from around here. Anyway, Veronica's husband was Dr. Joseph Arnold *Junior*," Schultz said, making air quotes with his fingers as he pronounced the last word snootily. "Third or fourth generation bigwigs from an old money family over in Hyde Park. They used to own a chain of those old-fashioned soda fountain-type pharmacies before CVS and Walgreens took over that whole business. Joe went kind of cuckoo a few years ago. He spent some time in a rehab facility. Probably because he was a pill popper—lots of those docs are. It was kept pretty hush-hush. Almost lost his license to practice pharmacy. Joe pulled through it, though, because of family money. That always helps. I just thought you might have heard of Joe Arnold because of..." Schultz stopped short.

"Because of Ethan, you mean," Shiloh finished. She sighed, noticing that Schultz still couldn't say Ethan's name. It was the reason Shiloh avoided her husband's former police partner. Ethan's death was especially hard on Schultz, his best friend on the force.

"Yeah, I know Ethan graduated from Saint Augustine's too," Shiloh added. "I could never keep all his old high school people straight. They're not my type of crowd."

"That's understandable," Schultz nodded. "It was a long time ago. Plus, I think Joe was a couple of years older than him anyway. Graduated the same year as Ethan's brother Roman."

"Do you think he did all of this?" Shiloh asked, bewildered. "Dr. Arnold?"

"Oh, God no," Schultz replied dismissively as his phone buzzed. He pulled it out of his pocket to read a text. "Joe was hysterical this morning when he came home to find Veronica and Savannah, that's their daughter, weren't there. I took over the call personally when I heard it was them. Hold on a sec."

Detective Schultz's thick thumbs flew as he returned the text. Then, he continued.

"Joe used to be a Grade A asshole. Now, he's just a little kooky. But he'd never do anything like this. Look, I'm sorry but," Schultz raised his phone. "I need to make another stop. They've located the owner of that poor cat. I'd like to explain the situation to her in person. We've got to keep the animal for a few days to make sure we've taken all the evidence we need before we return it to her for burial. After that, I have to call Joe and schedule a time for him to view the bodies. For the official record."

"I understand completely," Shiloh replied, as Detective Schultz turned to go. Opening the door to his police car, the detective stopped. He gave Shiloh a pained grin.

"I'm sorry that you had to be the one to find them. After all that happened."

Shiloh nodded.

"I hope you'll take Kaley and me up on that dinner offer sometime. Maybe next week, after she and the kids get back from Louisville? Or maybe come to the Policeman's Ball this December. Ethan talked about you non-stop. We all miss him. I hope you know that you're still welcome with all of us. Ethan was a great guy and a fine officer. That can't be said for many men I've known who grew up as he did. The Muellers were, well..." Schultz pushed a heavy hand through his salt-and-pepper hair. "They were like the Arnolds. Mostly above everyone else. Not Ethan, though. He was one of the good ones."

"I know," Shiloh sighed. "Thanks, Bruce. I've been meaning to give you a call. I truly have; it's just that..." She trailed off.

"It's hard," Schultz finished her thought. Smiling weakly, he added. "You'll get around to it eventually. When you're ready." Closing the door of his police cruiser, Schultz drove away up the street into East Walnut Hills.

Shiloh followed him at a much slower pace. She walked around the steep incline by the art museum and the amphitheater and finally back up the hill past Mt. Adams Bar & Grill to her office. Checking her watch, Shiloh saw that it was almost two. Suddenly, that bottomless pit of client emails didn't seem so difficult anymore. Instead, they were a welcome distraction. Settling into her office chair, Shiloh opened her laptop.

Clicking past the advertisements, Shiloh noticed a half dozen of the most common messages sent by potential clients. All suspicious married folks needing an investigator to capture some footage of their philandering spouses with their latest side pieces for use in divorce court. Then, the inbox signal dinged. Scrolling back up the page, Shiloh read the headline.

Requesting a Meeting Regarding the Arnold Case

"That was quick," Shiloh thought, clicking the email open.

Dear Ms. Foley, My name is Bernadette Jenkins, and I work for the Arnold family. As I have been informed that you are aware, the lady whom I worked for was murdered today, along with her daughter. Although I have no idea who their killer might be, I would like to schedule a time to stop by your office to discuss another matter of a more personal nature that may be connected. Please let me know, at your earliest convenience, when you might have time to see me. I am happy to come to your office and pay whatever you ask, within reason.

Checking the planner on her desk, Shiloh saw that she had no conflicts for the next day. She returned the email saying so and invited Bernadette to her office. Glancing out the window to see that it was almost dusk, Shiloh shut off the laptop and closed the lid. It was five o'clock somewhere, as Alan Jackson sang. Here that blessed hour had arrived.

Slipping into her usual seat at the very end of the row at Mt. Adams Bar & Grill, Shiloh ordered a Reuben sandwich and a pint of Rhinegeist Truth. In the background, an unhappy crowd of Bengals fans groused about the team's lackluster performance in last week's game. Slowly, Shiloh began to overhear a much more tense conversation unfolding near the patio door.

"Look, I'm sorry, but we can't let you in here anymore. Not after the last time," the manager's voice was tired, but his tone was firm. He stood with arms crossed across his chest and feet planted firmly in the doorway, listening to the other person's response. The muscles in the manager's jaw clenched and unclenched before he shook his head again. "No, like I've told you before. We don't sell bottles to take home. Just by the drink. And I'm afraid you're going to have to let a little more time pass. Allow people to calm down after your last visit before we can let you back in."

The manager hesitated a moment, then concluded. "Look, man, I don't want to have to call the cops on anyone tonight. The UDF is right up the street if you need a drink that badly. Why don't you get a bottle of wine up there to go?"

The mention of calling the cops seemed to have done the trick. Shiloh saw through a back window the briefest flash of an old, dirty black trench coat streaking around the corner as the manager shut the door.

"What was that all about?" Shiloh wondered aloud. Her favorite bartender, Fiona, brought her sandwich and beer to the counter.

"Oh, just the usual Friday night mayhem, you know." Fiona set down Shiloh's dinner and blew the grown-out fringe of lavender bangs away from her eyes. "Some homeless guy has been coming here pretty regularly, wanting to do shots of tequila. He's got money; I've seen it. Always pays cash. He keeps big wads of bills, mostly ones, stuffed in the pockets of that ratty long coat. No idea where he gets it, because he always looks like some stray cat that just crawled out of a sewer. Anyway, he came in a few nights ago and got plastered. Started shouting out to the whole bar that he was the Lord and that legions should bow to him. The boss had enough and 86'd him. Told him not to come back for a while. He's probably harmless, but he scared some of the regulars."

"Sounds scary," Shiloh replied, through a large bite of corned beef and sauerkraut. "Especially after the day I've had." Shiloh told Fiona about the gruesome scene that she'd found in the park. With the timeless patience given to all bartenders, Fiona listened. The snake sleeve tattoos on her slender forearms flexed as she polished glassware.

"That's horrible," Fiona replied. "Do the police have any leads yet?"

"Not that I know of," Shiloh replied, cautiously silent about the email request that she'd received that afternoon from the Arnolds' housekeeper. Even though she'd worked in the courthouse for over a decade as a public defender before picking up her private investigator license and hanging out a shingle, Shiloh Foley still knew how to keep a secret.

Sensing the need for a change in subject, Fiona poured Shiloh a double shot of whiskey and passed it across the bar to her. "On the house," she said. "After a day like that, I think you'd need it. Besides," she added, "Today's the anniversary."

"Anniversary of what?" Shiloh asked, picking up the shot glass.

"Of the day George Remus shot his wife on the way to divorce court," Fiona held up the bottle and used it to gesture toward the bar top. "This is a new brand of whiskey made in his honor, and this bar used to be in his house, or so the story goes. Surely, you've heard of him?"

"Maybe," Shiloh replied. "But I don't recall all the details. Fill me in."

Fiona stole a glance over her shoulder to make sure that the manager was watching her wipe down the counter as she explained. "I keep forgetting that you're not from around here. George Remus was like the King of Cincinnati bootleggers, or something. He's the dude Scott Fitzgerald based Jay Gatsby on. Anyway, he and his old lady, Imogene, were getting a divorce. Not sure why. I think she'd been running around on him with some G-Man while he was locked up. On the morning that they were both on their way to divorce court, Remus had his driver run Imogene's car off the road. Right by that gazebo, where you said you found..." Fiona widened her wing-lined eyes to indicate the obvious, "Those ladies. It's supposed to be haunted now. The gazebo. People come in here all the time, claiming they've seen her. Imogene Remus. Especially this time of year. On the anniversary of her death."

"That's quite a tale," Shiloh replied thoughtfully as she swallowed the whiskey. Although it was smooth going down, the whiskey hit the acidic sauerkraut in her stomach with a fiery burn that made her wince. Dropping an extra five on the bar over her usual tip, Shiloh slipped outside. She thought about going home, then became curious.

What if there was a ghost down there in Eden Park? One who had died on that same day. How many years had it been before the crime that she'd uncovered?

Shiloh pulled up the browser on her phone. When she put in Imogene Remus's name, Shiloh checked the result twice to make sure that her mildly intoxicated brain wasn't deceiving her. It was true. Imogene Remus had been murdered in the same spot where she'd found Veronica and Savannah Arnold's bodies. On this same day, a hundred years ago.

Now, I have to go back and look, Shiloh thought. She felt slightly guilty at her ghoulishness on one hand but encouraged by the spark of interest on the other. In her life before Ethan's death, Shiloh loved exploring places that were allegedly haunted. Back when she was in her sorority at the University of Kentucky, several of her sisters had a little ghost-hunting group that investigated supposedly haunted spaces around Lexington. Although they'd never seen anything that Shiloh could call, even in her wildest imaginings, definitive of a genuine haunting, she remained inquisitive. Since she'd lost Ethan, though, such mysteries were less intriguing, like everything else in her life. Still, her therapist kept encouraging her to get out of her comfort zone. *Just for a moment. Then I'll go home.*

Darkness had fallen completely as Shiloh descended the stone steps into Eden Park for the second time that day. A fog gathered from the riverfront lay just beyond the lower tier of the park. In and out of the gathering fog, a flock of little brown bats—the product of a breeding program started by the Cincinnati Zoo to increase their population in the area—swirled against the cloudy sky, obscuring the moon. Shiloh could see a standard-issue patrol car waiting on the other side of the gazebo. The entire scene where she'd found Veronica and Savannah Arnold was still encircled by police tape, warding off passersby.

As she observed the police car, Shiloh noticed two white dots bobbing through the woods. Her breath stopped. *Were they spiritual orbs?* Steadily, they came closer and closer. At last, Shiloh could see them for what they were. Deer. Two of them.

That must be the mother, Shiloh supposed, breathing easier as the larger one emerged from the forest. A gangly-legged, half-grown spotted fawn followed closely behind her.

So much for the ghosts of Eden Park. Kneeling for a better angle and pulling her phone camera up to take the picture, Shiloh saw the deer's eyes flash wide. Then, the doe and fawn darted off across the main lawn of the park, past the fountain, and into the woodline closest to her on the right-hand side.

Moments later, Shiloh saw another figure. A man in a faded black trench coat, clutching a bottle of wine in a paper sack. He stumbled out from the same thicket of underbrush from whence the deer emerged. Shiloh thought he might be the fellow who was 86'd at the bar. He squinted up at the sky. Shiloh realized that he was trying to see the moon. Even though he was on the other side of the park and much too far away to harm her, Shiloh crouched down behind some shrubbery. Instinctively, she didn't want the man to see her.

At the same time, the cop on the other side of the park spied the man in the trench coat too. The blue lights atop his vehicle flashed, and he tapped the siren. It gave out a few high-pitched yips. The man in the trench coat jumped and ran back into the undergrowth. The officer got out of his car and radioed for a relief deputy. Then, he followed the mysterious figure into the forest.

After the officer and the man in the trench coat disappeared into the darkness, the doe and her fawn stepped out again onto the main lawn. They sniffed the air and cautiously nibbled at the grass, inching closer and closer toward Shiloh. She could feel their intensely brown eyes studying her. When they were fewer than a dozen feet away, Shiloh was tempted to try to reach out and touch them. Suddenly, the deer changed course and bounded away through the fog, which continued to roll in from the riverfront.

Shiloh trudged back up the hill toward home. That night, she got out of bed to check the door three times and once more to locate her cat, William. He was safe under the sofa. When she finally slept, Shiloh dreamt of the deer she'd seen in the park, gliding soundlessly through the mist.

Saturday, October 7th, Morning

In her office the following morning, Shiloh sipped black coffee and reviewed her clients' billing statements until Bernadette Jenkins arrived for their appointment. Standing to welcome her, Shiloh noticed that Ms. Jenkins wore a smartly tailored, deep plum-colored skirt suit with a cream silk blouse and expensive-looking slingback heels. Her handbag Shiloh recognized right away as a Coach Tabby pillow.

Understated luxury, Shiloh thought. *The lady has taste.* When Shiloh offered her coffee, Bernadette shook her head and held up an insulated mug.

"Chamomile," Ms. Jenkins said. "I'm trying to avoid caffeine today. Couldn't sleep a wink last night."

"That's understandable," Shiloh said, refilling her own mug. "Do you mind if I record our conversation? It helps me remember things from our initial interview. Saves you money going forward with the investigation if I don't have to ask you for information more than once."

Ms. Jenkins removed her glasses and blinked her long, thick eyelashes as she considered Shiloh's question. "I'd rather wait until you hear all that I have to say first. Then, you can decide whether or not to take the case."

"Other than a possible conflict of interest, if I'm called as a witness to the crime scene, since I was the one who found their bodies, I can't imagine why I wouldn't," Shiloh replied.

Ms. Jenkins knit her brows together in a serious expression. Shiloh got the sense that Bernadette was thinking hard about what to tell her.

"Perhaps I should have explained a bit more in my email. I work for the Arnold family, but I am primarily concerned with a different matter. My sister is missing, and I'm worried the two might be related."

"Related how?" Shiloh asked. "I'm not following, Ms. Jenkins. If you're worried about confidentiality, please rest assured that I follow the same standards with my private investigation clients as I did when I was practicing law. We can go over the client agreement first if that would put your mind at ease."

"No, no," Bernadette replied. "That isn't necessary. I know that I can trust you, Ms. Foley. Although you might not remember me, we've met before. I'm Jasmine's sister. Jasmine Jenkins. We met that night at the hospital."

"Ohhh..." Shiloh breathed, realizing who Bernadette was. She took a sip of coffee, giving herself a moment to process the information. An image flashed across Shiloh's consciousness of a very different-looking Bernadette Jenkins on that night in June. The night when her whole world came crashing down.

While Shiloh waited to be brought Ethan's personal effects, Bernadette had flown into the emergency waiting room, begging frantically for information about the shooting. The duty nurse told her that Jasmine was being treated only for minor injuries and would be discharged after police questioning. Bernadette collapsed on the desk, sobbing with relief.

Unable to watch, Shiloh retreated to the elevator, riding it up through random floors. She wandered the corridors until she thought enough time had passed for Bernadette to calm down and leave. When she'd finally returned, Bernadette and Jasmine were still waiting for her. They'd expressed genuine gratitude and sorrow for Ethan's fatal decision to step between Jasmine and the gunman, but Shiloh couldn't remember a word of their conversation. Even in therapy, Shiloh struggled to recall anything that happened the night of the shooting after she saw Ethan's body. Grief had simply wiped the slate of her memory clean.

Breaking the spell of her reverie, Bernadette spoke. "I know it must be painful to talk about. I still miss my mother, and she's been dead for almost five years. It was cancer that got her. Lung cancer. She was a smoker. We had a long time to prepare for it."

Bernadette bit her lip. "Part of me hated to bring this to you. I wrestled with it for weeks. Filed a missing person's report. Did everything I could to try to take it up properly through the system. Then I walked in and saw Mr. Arnold's face yesterday. He told me that Ronni and Vanna were found dead, and you'd been the one who found them. That wild, lost look in his eyes made me know that he was worried about Jasmine too. So, I just thought, maybe it's fate. Maybe she's the one who has to save Jasmine again, like Detective Mueller did. Maybe she's the one who can help."

"Okay," Shiloh repeated softly, several times, more to herself than Ms. Jenkins. Her eyes scanned the surface of her desk, searching for something concrete to mentally latch onto. She tried to keep her thoughts focused instead of spiraling. The monthly desk blotter with all her client appointments and court dates written on it, double-recorded as a backup for the computer. A rabbit-shaped cup of pens that said *Welcome to Rabbit Hash, Kentucky* in cornpone lettering on the side. Finally, her gaze rested on the computer screen. The cursor blinked where she'd left it on the spreadsheet of client accounting. Shiloh grasped the mouse. It felt good and solid in her hand. Reassuring. She clicked open the document saved on her desktop labeled *Client Contract*.

Internally, a voice insisted, *Keep going. Little steps. You can do this.*

"I understand your reluctance, and I appreciate your thinking of me. We've both been through an ordeal." Shiloh pressed *Print*, and the machine obliged. She sniffed, a dry, rattling sound, as she took the paper off the tray and handed it to Bernadette with a pen.

"Regardless, I would like to help you as much as I can. If you are interested in hiring me, I'm willing to accept the case. Let's go over the agreement, shall we? Just so we're both on the same page with confidentiality, fees, our mutual rights and obligations, and all the usual things. Then we can begin at the beginning."

Going through the boilerplate contract language helped steady Shiloh's emotions so that she could begin asking questions about Jasmine's disappearance.

"There's no easy way to say this," Bernadette stated, easing back in her chair after signing the contract. "My sister, Jasmine, was spoiled. Part of it was because she was just such a beautiful child." Bernadette fished around in her tabby bag and pulled out a photo. She handed it to Shiloh. In the photo, a beaming, light-skinned Black girl stood next to a pageant trophy that was at least a foot taller than she. Her hair curled in soft waves, framing her perfectly symmetrical face. Jasmine's hazel eyes twinkled with excitement, bright as her crystal tiara.

"That was Jasmine when she was seven," Bernadette explained. "Her father and my father weren't the same man. My father Bernard, whom I'm named after, left when I was about five years old. He and Mom were sweethearts at Boone County High."

"You don't say," Shiloh said, studying the photo. "Kentucky girls. I graduated from Holmes back in 2000. Right next door in Kenton County. My father, P.J., went to Boone many years ago."

"Me and Jazzy, that's what we call her," Bernadette continued. "We were a good bit behind you. I was in the class of 2010, and she was in 2016. I took that photo at the first Little Miss pageant she ever won." Bernadette pulled another photo from her bag and passed it across the desk to Shiloh. "This one was taken the year after she graduated from Boone County. Jazzy ran track and was on the dance line at NKU before she dropped out. She won runner-up in the Miss Northern Kentucky University pageant too. People said she could have taken the whole state title before she graduated, but Jazzy didn't finish college. She dropped out after freshman year."

Shiloh looked at the second image. A tall, beautiful young woman in a sparkling teal dress smiled, cradling a bouquet of white roses in her right arm. Across her ample chest was a banner that read *Most Talented*. With her left hand, she steadied an instrument that Shiloh did not recognize. It had a long neck like an upright bass, but the spare, hollowed-out silhouette of the instrument's body was much smaller. This older Jasmine's almond-shaped eyes were fiery and defiant. Set against the cinnamon coffee radiance of her flawless skin and framed by the full halo of her natural hair, held in place by two glimmering crystal clips shaped like wings, she looked like a Greek muse brought to life.

"Why did she drop out?" Shiloh asked, half expecting the answer as she handed back the photo.

Bernadette shrugged. "Why do most young women quit college? It was a boy, of course. Summer between her freshman and sophomore years, Jazzy was seeing this fellow, Trip. Which was the right name. He certainly tripped her up. Trip was one of those wannabe music producers, if you know what I mean. He'd been in college for a while, dropped out, but still spent most of his time hanging around campus smoking weed and writing bad rap lyrics set to basic beats. He wasn't even good-looking. Skinny, with a scraggly beard. Our mom Destiny and I never saw what Jasmine liked about him. Anyway, Jazzy became pregnant. Mom told her that she would keep the baby if Jazzy chose to have it. Destiny knew that Jazzy always wanted big things out of life. Mom wanted her to have them. Jazzy was an accomplished vocalist and cellist and won a full ride to college for being on the dance team. Majoring in Communications with her sights set on moving to New York to become a news anchor. She could have made it too, if certain things had been different."

"What kinds of things?" Shiloh asked. "Did having a baby cause her to change course?"

"No," Bernadette said quietly, staring out the window. "Jazzy decided not to have the baby. Trip cut out as soon as he knew. Mom and I thought he would. But it wasn't just the pregnancy or Trip that caused my sister to take a turn. It was that other guy. She never told me his name. The one who was always at the club that Jazzy started dancing in after Trip left."

Bernadette sighed. "Jazzy told us that she was working the overnight shift at the television station as a switcher at WCPO. You know, the one next to the Elsinore Arch on the way into Eden Park? We should have known better than to think that a nineteen-year-old could have gotten hired without any degree, experience, or connections. We didn't question it because we knew she was in a vulnerable emotional state after the abortion. Jazzy didn't want us to be ashamed of her, so she lied and said it didn't matter that she'd quit school. She had her first professional job. In reality, she was dancing in a club down on the Newport riverfront called the Sizzle Spot. I don't think it's in business anymore. It was going downhill, and the pandemic finished it off. Jazzy knew better than to be in such a place, but what else could she do? Go to work at Walmart for barely above minimum wage?"

"A lot of people do," Shiloh said.

"Well, my sister Jasmine isn't a lot of people," Bernadette replied. "We were never wealthy, but Jazzy grew up thinking she was special. It was Mom's fault, partly. She felt worse for Jazzy than she did for me. Even though my father, Bernard, left us, he and Mom had been married. He, Mom, and I were all Black. I looked like I fit into the community. But Jazzy's father wasn't. Everyone knew Jasmine was different, with her lighter skin and hazel eyes. Mom didn't correct anyone when they tried to be polite and ignored it. She even gave Jasmine her married last name, Jenkins, but I don't think anyone was fooled. Folks we know count months."

"Who was Jasmine's birth father?" Shiloh asked.

"One of the doctors Mom worked for," Bernadette said, rolling her eyes. "He's Middle Eastern. Lebanese, I think. It was a typical hospital romance. Mom was an RN. For years she'd worked with a plastic surgeon, Dr. Khoury. I was in first grade when it happened, the year after Dad left us. It didn't last long. The Khourys were separated too at the time. I remember Mom telling me later, when I was around the age girls typically start dating, that the affair was a momentary lapse in judgment. They flirted for years. Things went too far a few times, and then there was Jasmine."

Shiloh looked up from her laptop screen where she was taking notes. "Did your mother tell Dr. Khoury that Jasmine was his? How did he respond?"

"That's the funny thing," Bernadette said. "Mom told him, and Dr. Khoury was supportive. Took complete responsibility, though he had to be quiet about it. I don't think his wife ever knew. They were Catholic, so divorce was out of the question. He felt guilty, I think. I believe he also really cared for Mom. They worked together for a long time. He admired her toughness at raising daughters alone. His wife came from a wealthy family and never worked a day in her life. Even before my dad, Bernard, left, he was gone most of the time. Dr. Khoury helped Mom move to another plastic surgeon's office in a different hospital for the same salary so that she wouldn't become the subject of rumors. He paid for all of Jazzy's expenses, even without a child support order—which was why Jazzy got the voice lessons, cello lessons, golf lessons, horseback riding lessons, and everything his other children got, but I didn't."

Bernadette pointed at the futuristic instrument in the photo. "That electric cello cost over two grand. Dr. Khoury bought her a horse too. Jazzy named her Lyra. Kept her out at a country club on the West Side. I guess she's still there, for all I know. Haven't seen her in years."

"Did you resent that?" Shiloh probed. "Your sister getting more attention and privileges? Did it ever cause tension between you, Jasmine, and your mom?"

"Mmm..." Bernadette mused. "When I was younger, yes. As I got older, I realized that it wasn't their fault. Mom gave me plenty. I painted a little, but I wasn't artistically talented like Jazzy. I didn't need all the extra lessons, instruments, or the like. I had nice enough clothes from the brands all my friends wore, my room, and a dog, a little Maltese named Sugarplum. Jazzy didn't go for dogs. She didn't like the responsibility. Mom used her nurse's salary to get me most of the things that teen girls wanted, within reason. It was plenty, since Dr. Khoury paid for everything else, even some of our rent. I was an easy and eager-to-please child. I read a lot, studied hard, got good grades, and earned a full ride to the University of Cincinnati. Probably should have taken a different major, but that's water under the bridge."

"What field did you go into?" Shiloh asked, continuing to type.

"English, with an art minor," Bernadette said, rolling her eyes. "The original *do you want fries with that* duo, if you can't get a teaching position. Huge mistake. The news always goes on and on about how there are all these teacher shortages. I don't believe it. If schools needed teachers that badly, then they'd start allowing people who have degrees in a subject to teach in public schools without certification. Perhaps with some sort of free training program or a supervised internship instead. Add-on teaching certifications take another year or two and cost twenty grand in addition to an already completed bachelor's degree. Since I didn't have twenty grand, and I didn't want to go into debt after I'd managed to avoid it through undergrad, my other option was to teach at a private school. It pays less, which is odd considering the high tuition. The bigger obstacle is that you have to know someone to get your foot in the door."

Bernadette sighed. "Most of the private schools around Cincinnati are Catholic. All of them are predominantly white. The parents shell out big bucks for the privilege of not having to mix with everyone else. Yes, in recent years, a lot of them have started trying to hire more faculty of color, but it's tokenism. I interviewed with several. They all seemed eager to hire me. Getting their DEI numbers up gives something for administrators to point at and say, *Look how inclusive we are!* However, when I did the walk-through days at the end, I seldom saw many Black students or faculty. Those I did meet were usually coaches or on some kind of athletic scholarship. They all ate together in the lunchroom, if you know what I mean. In the end, I decided it wasn't for me. I was looking for a place where I could make a difference."

"Unfortunately, I do," Shiloh said. "All the regulations in the world can't change the realities of how people think and behave. Only time and genuine interaction can do that."

"Agreed," Bernadette seconded. "Regardless, that's how I came to work for the Arnold family. My official title is housekeeper, but it's more of a blended role. I do all the homeschooling for their children, plus manage the staff and assist with grant writing and fundraising for the non-profit. If you watched *Downton Abbey*, I'm basically Mrs. Hughes with added educational duties. The place couldn't run without me."

"That sounds like a lot," Shiloh said. She'd begun to feel bad about quoting Bernadette the standard hourly rate in her fee contract. "I should hope that anyone who has the money to support a staff pays the manager well."

"They do," Bernadette nodded. "More than I would make teaching in a public or private school. Seventy-five grand a year, plus health insurance through the Foundation. A yearly bonus if we meet fundraising goals. Usually, we do."

"How did you get the job?" Shiloh asked.

"Dr. Khoury again," Bernadette replied as if the answer should be obvious. "He donates a lot of money to the Arnold Foundation. Mom's cancer was first diagnosed the summer after I graduated from UC. I was twenty-two, and Jasmine was sixteen. That year, he pledged an additional donation if Mrs. Arnold would take me on. Now and then he would do something for me too, if he thought it would help our family as a whole. He and Dr. Arnold both graduated from St. Aug's in the same year and still play golf together. Dr. Khoury knew Ronni would need extra help with Joe gone."

"I see," Shiloh said, trying to sidestep the discussion of the deceased Veronica Arnold and move on delicately to her next question. "I take it that was the year that Dr. Arnold had his... breakdown?"

"It's okay to say it, Ms. Foley," Bernadette acknowledged. "Dr. Arnold was an opioid addict. Oxy mostly, although he was starting to graduate up to other more dangerous drugs. I think that was what scared him. He went to that Asclepius facility in Switzerland. The one all the stars use, so that no one would know. Did the whole ninety-day program and came back sober. Completely a different man from who he was before, or so I've been told. That's why he started the Foundation. To fund similar efforts for recovering addicts in Cincinnati."

Shiloh could sense from the tension in Bernadette's voice that there was more to the story. "Did he stay sober permanently?"

"I... thought so," Bernadette ventured carefully. "At least, until last year's Christmas party for the Foundation. That's how it all started. When I got Jasmine a job as part of the catering crew. I walked in on her sitting in Joe's lap, doing lines in the indoor pool room."

Bernadette pressed her lips together tightly. "I thought I was helping her. Every year or two, Jazzy goes through these phases of trying to get clean. Usually, the holidays trigger it because that's when our mom died. When it happens, she comes to me and begs for help in finding some kind of job. I do what I can. Every time it gets a little harder. Jasmine never works more than a few weeks before she's back using again. But she's my sister, so I keep trying. I'll always keep trying."

"So, are you trying to say that Jasmine had an affair with Mr. Arnold?" Shiloh asked, piecing everything together. "They don't seem like a very likely pair."

"On the surface, no they don't," Bernadette agreed. "Emotionally, they're more alike than you might think. They both love to show out among beautiful people with beautiful things. They both swing low with depression, using drugs to try to cope when they think they've failed in some way to impress everyone. Jazzy's problem is that, because of her father, she was given the smallest taste of what the lives of people like Joe Arnold were all about. One little sip of the golden elixir of luxury. The thirst for more of it kills her every day. Jazzy finds people who live that lifestyle very impressive, whether they earned it or not. Joe has the opposite problem. He always had an overabundance of everything, but no one was impressed. That's why I think Joe Arnold was attracted to Jasmine. She was willing to be impressed in the ways that he wanted the woman in his life to be."

"I take it that Ronni, Ms. Arnold, wasn't sufficiently impressed?" Shiloh assumed.

Bernadette laughed out loud. One tense, harsh bark of a laugh. "Ronni? No. If anything, she thought Joe was a joke, with his private plane and his ten-car garage. She hated all of it. Ronni went to Withrow, the public high school. Came from a pretty basic family, I assumed, although she never said what they did. She met Joe in college when she was cheering. He sort of played football at Ohio State but mostly rode the bench. Ronni was a knockout from every picture I've seen. Once upon a time, she must have liked the idea of marrying into money. However, something shifted in Ronni's attitude toward Joe. I don't know if it was all the kids or his addiction problem, or how extravagant he got with displaying his wealth after they built that big new compound, or what. But Ronni is... she was," Bernadette corrected herself, using the past tense, "checked out of her marriage to Joe. She spent more time away traveling or at some kind of spiritual retreat over the past few years than she did at home. She'd only been back a few days when this happened."

"Veronica must have felt very confident with you to leave you in charge of her children for weeks at a time," Shiloh said. "What can you tell me about them? Especially Savannah."

Bernadette swallowed hard. It was obvious that she'd cared about the girl, as her words came out in a croak. "Vanna was..." she started, reluctantly. "Vanna was heading down the same path as Jazzy, unfortunately. Her parents couldn't see it, or else they refused to, but I could. Savannah was nineteen, their eldest. In the Arnold family after her were the two boys, then Scarlet. Savannah was her father's favorite, and she knew it. The boys are like looking at a pair of young Joe Arnolds. Conventionally good-looking in a cocky jock sort of way. Savannah looked just like her mother, as you know. Tall, willowy, and blonde. Scarlet's the only one in which I can't see either of them, which must be hard on her. Even though she'll only be fourteen next month, you can already tell she's not going to be as pretty as her mother and sister. But she's clever, in a way that forgotten little sisters are. Savannah never had to try to be smart, and she knew it. She had thousands of followers on Instagram. Kept insisting that she didn't need college because she was already an influencer. Savannah and her mother had a terrible fight about it in September. After Ronni got an early alert report from Xavier saying that Vanna was flunking every class, simply for not showing up."

"Do you think that Savannah was using drugs?" Shiloh inquired.

"Probably, but I can't be sure," Bernadette answered. "The last couple of times I saw her, Vanna's eyes had a wild, glassy look. I thought she might be smoking too much weed. I asked one of the maids to help me snoop around a bit when she spent the weekend of Fall Break in her old room at home. We didn't find anything."

"But you said that Joe was using again," Shiloh pressed. "With Jasmine. Do you think that might have been where Savannah was getting her supply?"

"I don't think so," Bernadette claimed. "I've been told that even when Joe was at his worst with his addiction, he was always careful to be discreet around the kids."

"If Joe were perfectly discreet about his misbehaviors," Shiloh rationalized, "then how did you find out about his ongoing relationship with Jasmine?"

"Jasmine told me afterward," Bernadette said. "I think she *wanted* me to catch her with Joe that night at the pool. She wanted me to know how quickly she could bend my boss's will to do whatever she wanted. Jasmine could be like that sometimes. Preening and spiteful. I love her, though, because I see through it. All Jasmine wants is for people to see her. It's like her whole life, she's been shouting with every fiber of her being, *Look at me! Look at me!*"

Bernadette stopped, as tears welled up in her eyes. She picked up her phone and opened the photo app, holding it out to Shiloh. "The problem is that I'm the only one who ever cared enough to *really* see her. Look at this, Ms. Foley. Look at these pictures and tell me what differences you see in my sister from the time she started seeing Joe Arnold until she disappeared last month. I know Jasmine wasn't an angel, but she wasn't… well, you'll see."

Shiloh scrolled through the photos. In the first one, taken at the Christmas fundraiser that they'd discussed, Jasmine wore an undersized sparkly Santa hat perched on a headband and a typical black button-down catering server shirt. It was unbuttoned strategically to show her large breasts at their best angle, with a hint of push-up bra peeping out around the edges. Jasmine made an exaggeratedly playful kissy face for the camera as she flashed a peace sign. Remembering her days waiting tables in college, Shiloh noted that Jasmine's blood-red, bejeweled nails were far too long for acceptable server length.

In the pictures that followed, Shiloh watched as Jasmine seemed to shrink and age before her eyes. By the time she got to the snaps from June, Jasmine appeared hollow-cheeked and tired. Her mischievous hazel eyes were death-staring and zombie-like, and her previously flawless skin was pocked with scabs. The one from June was especially difficult to look at. Jasmine had two black eyes and a busted lip. Shiloh winced as she remembered that was how Jasmine appeared on the one time she'd seen her in person—on the night that Ethan stopped the man whom Jasmine claimed was her pimp from beating her up. The night that Jasmine's pimp shot and killed him.

Forcing herself to flip through the last few, Shiloh saw that Jasmine's face never completely healed from the incident. In the final picture, although the swelling had gone down around her eyes, the sockets remained sunken and deep purple. The cut hadn't closed properly, leaving a scabby split in her cracked lips. Her hazel eyes, so bewitching before, seemed as if they belonged in the face of a dead fish, lifeless and too large for her head. The salacious woman from her sister's boss's Christmas party who had been Jasmine Jenkins stared into the same camera eight months later as an emaciated, wraithlike version of herself. After that, she was gone.

Shiloh closed the app and handed the phone back to Bernadette. "So, the picture that was taken on August first. Is that the most recent one you have of her?"

"That was the last day I saw her," Bernadette said, sniffling. "She had a little apartment where she was staying. I was going to take her some groceries, but she said she didn't need food because she let the apartment go. I asked if I could meet her somewhere anyway. I hadn't seen her in weeks. She said she'd stop by that afternoon. I said okay because the Arnolds were out. Joe was with the boys at the tennis tournament. Ronni had taken the girls to IKEA to look at things for Savannah's dorm room. I didn't see her drive up. She just walked to the door. We talked for about fifteen minutes. She was vague and jittery. Kept asking me for a cigarette even though she knew I didn't smoke. After we said goodbye, a black Mercedes van with dark tinted side windows came and picked her up at the end of the driveway."

Typing quickly again, Shiloh asked. "I know it would be too good to be true for you to have gotten the tag number of the van, but can you remember anything else about it?"

"Only that there was no tag on it at all," Bernadette said. "And that it was a man driving."

"How could you tell it was a man?" Shiloh pressed. "I thought you said the van had tinted windows."

"It did, but I could see him through the front windshield as he circled the drive to pick her up. He had a pale face with a high forehead. Hair swept back. He was wearing sunglasses and a surgical mask. One of the expensive kinds. I couldn't get a better look at him, though. I'm sorry."

"That's okay," Shiloh said, clicking save on her notetaking app. "You've given me a lot to get started with. A boyfriend that I didn't know about, a secret father figure, and so much more. As I think of other details that I might need, I'll call you. Your number's in the original email, right?"

"Correct," Bernadette replied. Thanking Shiloh for her time, she departed.

After Bernadette Jenkins left, Shiloh checked her phone. It was almost one o'clock. An unanswered text message blinked at her. *Thought we said noon at Pho Lang Tang?*

Shit, Shiloh breathed, texting back, *BRT—30 minutes. Grab a Thai tea; they're awesome.*

Saturday, October 7th, Afternoon

"You forgot, didn't you?"

"Nooo..." Shiloh drawing out the word. "I was just busy with a client."

"You totally forgot. It's okay, though. We've both been busy," said the slender young woman sitting across the table from her. She wore baggy nineties-style olive cargo pants and a cropped knit halter top. Two empty glasses of Thai tea sat in front of her. Her hair was in Ghana braids with three tiny wooden beads on the end of each strand that clicked as she moved. Seeing the girl's immaculate, milky pink nails as she played with her phone in its gold glitter case, Shiloh slid her hands beneath the table, hiding her close-bitten fingertips.

"Nadia, I'm sorry," Shiloh said. "Truly, I am. It's just been a long day."

"I bet," Nadia said. "The murders have been all over the news."

"Bad news travels fast," Shiloh said. "But I don't want to talk about it. I want to hear about something amazing. Tell me about Xavier. How's the first semester of college going?"

"Good," Nadia sighed as if she'd rather be talking about something else. "Classes are easier than I thought they'd be. All the professors seem like they're apologizing for giving us too much work. Which is weird because all our teachers at SCPA told us how college would be so hard, but it isn't." Nadia leaned back as the server delivered a plate of salad rolls to the table.

"It's always better to be over-prepared than underprepared," Shiloh replied, spooning out some of the peanut dipping sauce and dunking her salad roll into it. "Did you win the audition?"

Nadia breathed out a dismissive puff of air. "Of course. It was almost too easy." She swallowed her bite of a salad roll. Sliding into a soft, perfect falsetto, she placed a finger over her lips and sang, "They're gonna love me."

"I have zero doubts," Shiloh smiled. "You're going to make an amazing Effie White in *Dreamgirls*. Are you sure it isn't too much? Rehearsals as the lead and eighteen hours' worth of classes for the double major. It's a lot."

Nadia cocked her head to the side and gave Shiloh *the look*. Shiloh knew *the look*. She'd seen it many times. The look that meant *really?*

Shiloh became Nadia Haas's Big Sister through the program after her father, Denis, applied. His wife Zuri was local. A talented Black girl from Walnut Hills who grew up singing in the church choir. Her singing voice won her a scholarship and made her the first in her family to finish college. Nadia's parents met while studying opera at the University of Cincinnati. Denis was a lyric tenor on a student visa from Ukraine. They married right after graduation, partly so that Denis didn't have to return, and bought an old house in Northside that Denis was constantly working on. His father in Ukraine was a carpenter. Then, Zuri died in a single-vehicle car accident the Christmas after Nadia started sixth grade. Zuri was on her way home from a late shift at her second job. Her car hit a patch of black ice, spun out, and slammed into a tree.

Overwhelmed as a father of a biracial tween girl in another country while trying to hold down two jobs himself—one with the opera and another serving tables to make ends meet—Denis enrolled in the program to hopefully find a Big Sister for Nadia. Shiloh was the mentor who matched. The friendship had stuck for almost seven years. Longer, Shiloh realized, than she'd even known her husband, Ethan. Once, Shiloh considered asking Denis Haas out on a date but decided against it. Although very handsome and hardworking, Denis always seemed aloof, as if searching to be anywhere else. Still, they'd bonded over a mutual sense of pride in his daughter Nadia. Shiloh was the one who'd recommended that he enroll Nadia in the School of Creative and Performing Arts, where the shy girl blossomed into an exemplary student. Talking about his daughter, Shiloh noticed, was the one time that Denis Haas seemed happy and at ease.

"Well, I bet your dad is beside himself," Shiloh said, then changed the subject. "Say, you didn't happen to know Savannah Arnold, did you? The girl who was killed. She went to Xavier."

Nadia frowned. "No. I don't think so. Was she a freshman?"

"Yes," Shiloh said. "I don't think she went to class that often, though. At least, according to her housekeeper. I might be picking up the case."

"Was that the client you met with this morning who took so long?" Nadia asked.

"Mmm... sort of," Shiloh returned through a mouthful of salad roll. Nadia always asked about Shiloh's work, which wasn't unusual. Depending on which day it was, the idealistic girl vacillated between claiming that she wanted to be a lawyer or on Broadway. Her double major was in vocal performance and legal studies. Seeing no reason to crush her dreams, Shiloh tried to encourage both disparate paths. Although Nadia volunteered to work in her office for free many times, Shiloh always turned her down. There were some parts of her life, she thought, that were better kept mostly separate.

Still, it was important to be honest. "The housekeeper seems to think Joe Arnold had nothing to do with the death of his wife and daughter."

Nadia studied her closely. "I feel like there's a *but...* about to drop here. Do you think there's something more to the story?"

Shiloh weighed the possibility of giving Nadia a quick summary of what Bernadette had told her. She settled for the most basic solution in the interest of confidentiality. "All I can say is that the lady who was their housekeeper came to me this morning with a new wrinkle in the case. One that may involve her sister Jasmine. She's missing."

Nadia's lips formed an *O*. Shiloh could almost see the wheels of the girl's brain turning as she considered the myriad of possible implications. The waiter returned with their main meals. Large steaming bowls of *pho ga* into which they mixed liberal quantities of bean sprouts, lime juice, cilantro, and jalapeño. They ate hungrily, saying little else, until the end of the meal when Shiloh asked about Nadia's father, Denis.

"Dad's decided to sell the house," Nadia said, as the server carried away their bowls. "He's been offered a singing role with a company in New York. Someone fell through for a big Christmas Pops extravaganza. Dad's agent put him up for it. He got the part, so he leaves tomorrow for rehearsals. It lasts until the first week of January."

"Wow!" Shiloh exclaimed. "That's impressive. I wasn't aware Denis was looking for anything like that." Denis Haas had sung with the local Cincinnati Opera company for years. Shiloh hadn't heard of him auditioning out of town since she'd known the family.

"Yeah, he was kind of waiting for me to start college and be more independent," Nadia said. "Between his local singing gig and serving, Dad made just enough for the house payment and the basics of what we needed, but maintenance on the old place was eating him alive. When he got a crazy high offer from an investor looking for places to flip, he couldn't say no. Also, he had a low-key mid-life crisis around the time I started applying to colleges. That's why we decided for me to live on campus, even though I chose to stay in the city for school. Dad felt more secure with me that way, about taking chances to audition for roles further away."

"That makes sense," Shiloh said, pouncing on the unsplit receipt before Nadia could protest. Handing the server her credit card, Shiloh asked whether Nadia was going to spend the holidays with her father in New York or Cincinnati.

"Well, I was thinking about half and half," Nadia answered. "Dad will only have Monday nights off when the show is dark. Christmas Day is on a Monday this year, so that works out. We figured I'd fly up a week before that, so we'd have the Monday before Christmas too, for shopping and whatnot. I can kick around New York during the week. See the sights while he's at work. Fly back sometime the next week, on one of the cheaper days before New Year's. I'll have a little over a week to kill before dorms open again."

"Any special plans for that time?" Shiloh asked, feeling as if there was a question waiting in the way the girl's explanation stopped abruptly.

Nadia sat twisting her straw paper into a tight spiral for a few seconds before she asked it. "Dad's thinking about going to visit with some of his Ukrainian family that week. They all have lived in Germany since the war. He wants me to come, but I'm not really into it. I don't speak German or Ukrainian, and I've never met any of them before. Dad said he understood and would pay for a hotel if I wanted to go home early instead. I'd hate for him to spend the money. He has another show starting in February too. He won't say it, but that money would help bridge the pay gap as he moves short-term rentals from New York to Boston. Dad got a good price for the house, but I don't want him to have to dip into that money either. He's going to need it as a down payment for wherever he settles next. So, I was thinking about asking to stay with you. It's just for about ten days, but I understand if it's too much trouble."

"Of course, it's no trouble. You're more than welcome," Shiloh replied, a little surprised at the request but happy. "The house has four bedrooms. I only really use three. One to sleep in, one for my study, and one for storage. My cat William claims the bed in the one I keep ready for company as his own. I'll do my best to de-fur it and have everything clean, but don't be surprised if the little rascal decides you're his new best friend. All his toys and climbing trees are in there."

Nadia smiled, relieved. "That's no trouble at all. William's a cutie pie, and I love cats. If we could have one in the dorm, I would, but it's dogs only. They're way more upkeep." She paused, then added hopefully, "If it would be any help, I could work around the office a bit too. Maybe you might decide you'd like an intern after all."

Shiloh dodged the question by pretending to be occupied with her cell. She sensed where the discussion was going, but she didn't want Nadia to feel bad for asking by turning her down directly. It wasn't that she distrusted Nadia to be responsible. It was the opposite. Although she tried her best not to be a dream killer or discourage Nadia's interest in law or detective work, deep down she wished the girl would choose to pursue her other interests in music. In Shiloh's opinion, the law was not a kind profession. Especially to women who tended to take on too much too easily.

After lunch, Nadia asked if she could hang out in Shiloh's office for a while until it was time for her to go back to afternoon rehearsal. Seeing no reasonable way to avoid it, Shiloh agreed. When they walked through the front door, Nadia chuckled a little.

"Where are the Venetian blinds?" she asked. "I thought that all private investigators had to have them. And like an old electric fan too. This place is way too chill. All ferns and crystals."

"You watch too many old movies," Shiloh said, rolling her eyes. "I assure you that in real life, the job isn't the least bit glamorous. Mostly, it involves eating a lot of cold Taco Bell in the car. Trying to stay awake long enough to take pictures, discreetly from behind a hedge, of people doing things they shouldn't be doing at three in the morning. Kinda like being a paparazzi, but without all the intrigue of star-watching. And believe me, most of them are *ugly*." Shiloh pulled a face as she drew out the last word, sending both of them off into a gale of giggles.

They hung out, riffing off one another for about half an hour until a call came in. It was Shiloh's brother-in-law's wife, Kimberly. Sensing that Shiloh was going to be on the phone for a while, Nadia reached to pick up her tote, knocking it over accidentally. The contents of Nadia's bag spilled onto the floor. Multicolored pens, lip gloss tubes, and all the other usual flotsam that live in the bottom of young women's handbags rolled out in every direction. Bending over to pick up a small amber pill bottle, Shiloh had just enough time to read the label on the side before Nadia snatched it away.

Pulling the cell away from her face as Kimberly kept talking, Shiloh mouthed, "Since when did you start taking Adderall?"

"I'll tell you later," Nadia whispered. "I'm going to be late for rehearsal." Quickly, Nadia stuffed the rest into her bag and scurried out the door. In her haste, she let the door slam shut behind her, making the chimes hanging above it sound more like breaking glass than music.

"Shiloh, are you still there? What was that?" Kimberly asked. The last words of each question were drawn out into two syllables. *Thay-re. Thay-t.* Although Shiloh was from Kentucky, her sister-in-law's Tennessee drawl was much more pronounced. It made Shiloh wince every time she heard it. Not because of Kimberly's voice itself, but because of how Kimberly's husband Roman made fun of it. Like all the Muellers, Roman and Ethan's parents made them take accent training to remove any hint of Southerness from their speech. Ethan never made a big deal about Shiloh's accent, other than to say occasionally that it was cute. However, Roman was a different story. He made fun of both his wife's and Shiloh's Southern accents ceaselessly.

"Oh, just a friend of mine leaving," Shiloh replied, trying to sound nonchalant. The pill bottle worried her. Nadia never complained about her hectic schedule, but Shiloh knew the girl was taking on a lot, and her father was moving half a country away. Nadia had never been diagnosed with ADHD that Shiloh knew of. Even if the medication was a prescription, the fact that Nadia might be seeing a doctor for anxiety concerned her.

"Oh, okay," Kimberly said. She sounded confused. Mild confusion was Kimberly's natural state. Although she hated to stereotype, Shiloh knew her sister-in-law was exactly the sort of person for whom all the dumb blonde jokes were made. She wasn't a bad person, or even unintelligent, Shiloh knew. Just ditzy.

Taking a few moments to regain her train of thought, Kimberly finally remembered the question she'd called to ask. "Roman and I wanted to know if you still wanted to ride with us out to the home-coming bonfire tonight at St. Aug's. You know? The one before the football game? We talked about it a few weeks ago."

"Oh right," Shiloh said hesitantly, checking her desk calendar. She hadn't written the event down on purpose. Since Ethan died in June, Kimberly had been turning up the pressure steadily for Shiloh to con-tinue spending time with the rest of Ethan's family. It was a nice ges-ture, but it made Shiloh uncomfortable. Mostly because the Muellers were more welcoming to her after Ethan's death than they ever were during his life. Shiloh had been hoping that Kimberly, in her usual absentminded way, would forget that she invited Shiloh to accompany them to the reunion weekend festivities at St. Augustine's.

In theory, it would have made the perfect excuse. To say that she'd meant to go, she'd *wanted* to go, but she'd been so busy with work that it just slipped her mind. Asking Kimberly to be her human wake-up call was the perfect cover if Shiloh had zero intentions of attending the reunion. Sadly, Shiloh thought, Roman must have reminded his wife. Her cover was blown by answering the phone without readying the slightest excuse.

"What time did we agree that I would be out there?" Shiloh asked, trying once more to cause enough confusion to allow an escape.

"Mmm, Roman?" Shiloh heard Kimberly call out to her husband. "What time did you say you wanted to leave?"

"Bonfire's at seven. The game starts at eight. Tell Shiloh she needs to be here by six so that she'll be here at six-thirty," Roman yelled back.

From the way his voice echoed, Shiloh knew Roman must be some-where far away in their enormous house. Still, his gruff vocal fry carried the message loud and clear. Shiloh resented Roman's pointing out what she always tried to play off comically as her chronological im-pairment. It was one of the many reasons Shiloh finally decided to quit practicing law. After Roman was elected judge, he made a constant sport of it, along with many other things about Shiloh's legal practice.

Shiloh glanced at the clock and sighed. It was almost three. She still had some work to do on Bernadette's new client intake paperwork before she could head home to shower and change.

"Tell Roman I'll be there at six-thirty. Not six."

Saturday, October 7th, Evening

At precisely six twenty-nine, Shiloh pulled up in front of Roman and Kimberly's house on Camargo Road. Driving through the scrolling iron gates that announced she was on the grounds of the East Riverside Country Club, Shiloh marveled at how many new McMansions continued to spring up every time she visited. With their curiously asymmetrical high-pointed roofs, tall arrow-slit windows, and random stone turrets, all the homes in the neighborhood looked sadly unoriginal. Ethan used to say that they made him think about what it would have looked like if minor lords in medieval times had built a prefab model home village. Shiloh agreed. Neither she nor Ethan ever saw why his older brother passed on so many unique historical homes for sale all over the city to spend his money instead on a cookie-cutter new build. She and Ethan had often shaken their heads at the choices Roman and Kimberly made.

Parking her Subaru Forester next to Kimberly's Land Rover, Shiloh went up to the front door and rang the bell. Inside, a cacophony of excited barking erupted from her in-law's pair of Portuguese water dogs, Pearl and Shadow.

"Y'all, cut that out!" Kimberly hollered at the dogs from somewhere inside the house. Shiloh could hear the clip-clop of Kimberly's high heels as she ran for the door. Opening it with one hand while she held a large diamond stud earring threaded through her ear with the other, Kimberly beckoned Shiloh in.

"Them damn dogs!" she exclaimed. "I love 'em, but they barked so loud they scared me. Dropped my earring back in the bathroom. Of course, it bounced off to God knows where. Wouldja help me look for it? I'd ask Reece and Riley, but they're off somewhere. S'posed to be here any minute now to watch RJ. I'd ask him, but you know how well that would go."

Kimberly waved dismissively at her ten-year-old son Roman Junior, who was glued to the screen of his Nintendo Switch. Reece and Riley were Roman and Kimberly's twin daughters. Both were seniors at Xavier. They majored in marketing, but Shiloh knew the real reason they were there was the lacrosse team. Growing up, the twins did everything together and had to have everything the same. The habit continued into their young womanhood. When they'd turned sixteen, they'd demanded matching white luxury SUVs.

"I thought I didn't see the Volvos out there," Shiloh noted. She followed Kimberly down the hall to her bathroom to look for the missing earring back. "They'd better hurry up. Where's Roman? I'm shocked he wasn't here waiting to pounce on me if I walked in a second late."

"Oh, he's down the street at Joe's," Kimberly said. "We're s'posed to call him when we're ready to go. I think Joe's gonna ride with us out to St. Augustine's. Joe wasn't gonna go at all, with all that's gone on. Roman talked him into it. You know how persuasive Roman can be. Here, help me look for this earring back," Kimberly finished.

Shiloh got down on all fours next to Kimberly to search. After a few minutes of running her hands across the gray slate tile floor, Shiloh's fingers closed on the back. Kimberly did a little celebratory dance as Shiloh handed the finding to her. Then, she dropped it again as the dogs began barking once more. Giving up, Kimberly stalked off to the bedroom to retrieve a different pair of earrings from her jewelry cabinet. Shiloh opened the door for Roman and Joe.

"Well, well..." Roman began, glancing at his watch as he entered. "Surprised to see you made it here on time. I thought I told the wife to call me when you guys were ready to go."

Shiloh suppressed a smart remark about where she thought Roman could go. "Yes, she told me you'd gone to pick up Joe. We were trying to find her missing earring back first."

"Women," Roman shook his head at Joe. "Always losing stuff. Hope she finds it. Otherwise, she might try to pull out those ghetto-fabulous door knockers again."

"Whadja you say about knockin', Roman?" Kimberly asked, walking into the living room. She was wearing a very expensive-looking pink printed mini-dress with a pair of thick gold hoop earrings the size of tennis balls. Shiloh glanced at Roman and burst into giggles.

"There, you see!" Roman blustered. "You look ridiculous. Even she can tell. Take those awful things off. They make you look like you should be standing on a street corner somewhere after midnight in OTR, picking up johns. Especially in that dress."

"What's wrong with my dress?" Kimberly said plaintively. "It's Dior. That's classy." She turned to Shiloh. "Doncha think it's a classy dress?"

"I think you look beautiful as usual. Very youthful," Shiloh replied. It was true. Kimberly was one of those people who could look good in a plastic bag. The Dior belted wrap with its whimsical pattern of pink elephants and tigers made her appear especially fresh and girlish.

"It's too short," Roman growled. "Go change. And for God's sake, put on some smaller earrings. Quickly, so we can get to St. Aug's before the game."

Kimberly looked crestfallen as the rims of her eyes began to redden. "But I bought it 'specially for tonight. It's from their collection that was inspired by the Barbie movie. I thought it would be a fun conversation piece. Doncha you like it?"

"No," Roman replied harshly. "It wouldn't contribute to any conversation I'd like to have, especially while I'm trying to spend time with some of the most influential men in the city. Why can't you just wear black, like any normal woman? Where'd you get your dress?" he asked Shiloh.

"Oh..." Shiloh stammered, not expecting the question. "Um, I'm not sure. Saks Off Fifth, I think, but it's been a few years. It is Ralph Lauren, though."

Roman's eyes quickly scanned over Shiloh's body like an estate appraiser surveying property. "Really? Green, Black, or Purple label?"

Stunned that Roman was blatantly asking how expensive her dress was, Shiloh took a few beats to respond. "I think it's a Green label," she said finally.

"Oh, well, you still look nice in it anyway," Roman replied condescendingly. As he turned back to face his wife, Kimberly fled into the bedroom suite, sniffling loudly. Ten minutes later, a much more subdued and drab-looking Kimberly re-emerged, wearing a simple sleeveless black sheath and tiny, gold-beaded huggie hoops.

"See now," Roman said, taking Kimberly by the shoulders and steering her into place in front of a long mirror in the foyer. "Don't you think that looks better?" Kimberly grudgingly agreed. Shiloh could tell that in reality, her sister-in-law was seething.

While Roman and Kimberly bickered back and forth about how long they should wait for Reece and Riley to arrive, Shiloh began to notice Joe Arnold's silence as he lingered in the foyer. Although she'd seen Joe several times at barbecues Ethan dragged her along to, usually at Roman's house, Shiloh had never actually spoken to the man whose wife and daughter she'd found dead in the gazebo. When he attended Roman's parties, Joe was always alone, and he conversed primarily with men. Shiloh tried to say hello, but Joe did not respond. He stood with his hands shoved into the pockets of his wrinkled khakis, staring blankly out the window.

Seeing him ignore Shiloh's attempts at polite conversation, Roman whispered loudly as if Joe weren't there. "He took a sedative about an hour ago. The man hasn't slept in two days. It takes a while to level off. Should be okay by the time we get there."

Just then, a white Volvo SUV swung into the driveway, careening dangerously close to the mailbox. Riley Mueller jumped out, already apologizing. Her eyes were wild, and she was sweating profusely. Shiloh wondered if the girl was high. "Sorry, I'm late. Reece should be coming. She's still... um, at the library."

"On Saturday night?" Kimberly questioned, clearly unconvinced by her daughter's lie. "I would think that college libraries closed early on the weekends."

"Don't start!" Roman barked at Kimberly. "We're late because of you." He pointed an accusatory finger at Riley, who stared shamefaced at the concrete driveway. "I'll deal with you and your sister when we get back. Let's go!"

Shiloh got into the back seat of the Muellers' Land Rover opposite a still-silent Joe Arnold, who moved as if he were a zombie. Her inquisitive mind bored and already regretting the missed opportunity to speak with

Joe due to his incapacity, Shiloh pulled up the hours for Xavier Library on her phone. Kimberly was right. It closed at five on Saturdays. Shiloh said nothing about it though, not wanting to raise the palpable level of tension in the vehicle.

Half an hour later, they pulled up to the imposing gates of St. Augustine High. The school emblem, a flaming heart pierced with an arrow, was emblazoned on everything, from the wrought iron archway topping the gates to the sea of red polos worn by every man in attendance, including Roman and Joe. The Tudor-styled campus buildings, constructed uniformly of pale gray granite, resembled a village of old English manor houses surrounded by meticulously maintained gardens, tennis courts, and stables. To Shiloh, the whole scene seemed orchestrated to announce what everyone in attendance knew. St. Augustine was an exclusive club for the chosen few; the most expensive private high school in the city.

The bonfire was already alight. High flames leaped against the gathering darkness. A banner proclaiming St. Augustine's to be a place *Where Real Men Are Made* hung over a long open bar. Several attractive female bartenders dressed in all black mixed cocktails and took turns tending to the bonfire. The school mascot, a knight, was sculpted in swiftly melting ice that dripped steadily into the perfectly checkered lawn in front of the fountain by the main hall. Dozens of alumni and their wives milled about, drinks in hand, among the topiaries in the garden. Scanning the crowd, Shiloh determined she was one of the few non-blonde and non-surgically enhanced women in attendance.

Feeling a mild wave of panic at her obvious lack of belonging, Shiloh steeled herself by thinking about what a perfect opportunity it was to learn more about the circle in which the murdered women, Veronica and Savannah Arnold, lived. A circle that might also lead her closer to an answer about the disappearance of her client's sister, Jasmine Jenkins. Alcohol loosened lips. From what Shiloh had seen at past St. Augustine's events that she'd reluctantly attended with Ethan, it should be in ample supply.

Roman whisked Joe away to a group of old football cronies as soon as they got out of the car, leaving Kimberly to introduce Shiloh around. Quickly losing track of who was whom among the sea of heavily Botoxed and spray-tanned women surrounding her, Shiloh's interest waned. At last, one name caught her attention.

"Excuse me, did you say your name was Helen Khoury?" Shiloh asked.

"Yes," the woman replied. Shiloh noticed that Helen had a slightly more detached air than the other wives. She was different-looking too. Olive-complected, shorter, and much heavier set than most women in attendance. Perhaps even more noticeable, Shiloh couldn't tell if Helen had any cosmetic enhancements. Still, she was impeccably dressed and carried a handbag that Shiloh was certain cost more than her first car.

"My husband is Dr. Akash Khoury," Helen said, gesturing toward a trio of men standing by the outdoor bar. "The plastic surgeon." Here, she paused. Shiloh got the impression that Helen was waiting for her to be suitably impressed.

"Oh, of course," Shiloh replied, recognizing the name. *Dr. Khoury.* Jasmine Jenkins's father, according to her sister Bernadette. Glancing at the tall man from a distance, with his thick mustache and curly black hair just beginning to gray at the temples, she realized that he looked like a Mediterranean version of Tom Selleck in his prime. *No wonder Destiny Jenkins lost her head over him*, Shiloh thought.

The women stood in awkward silence for a moment. Shiloh grasped at passing thoughts to explain why she knew Dr. Khoury. She finally settled on the excuse that she'd seen his advertising billboards around town. The response amused Helen, who went to retrieve her husband so that Shiloh could meet what she called half-jokingly, *the man behind the billboard.*

Returning with Dr. Khoury and his friends in tow, Helen introduced the other two men as Rafferty Purcell and Kyle Lang. Purcell was slender, with a long, weasel-like nose and beady black eyes. The only man there wearing his red polo with a suit instead of khakis, Purcell introduced himself by handing Shiloh his business card, proclaiming him to be the CEO of Dynamic Investments Group. As Purcell reeled off his elevator speech, Shiloh figured that it must be one of those predatory real estate companies that bought up poor neighborhoods to gentrify.

The other man was exceptionally tall, standing several inches above Dr. Khoury. Lang's eyes were a piercing shade of blue, and his enormous biceps bulged at the sleeves of his red polo as he reached for a handshake. Shiloh marveled at the size of his hands, feeling like a child as his firm grip made the bones of her much smaller palm grind together.

"Didn't you used to play for the Bengals?" Shiloh asked.

Kyle Lang smiled with what Shiloh felt certain was an expression carefully practiced for press conferences. His blinding white veneered teeth gleamed as he ran his other giant hand through his layered dirty blonde hair. "Guilty as charged," Lang said, trying to appear charming. Shiloh cringed, remembering vaguely the messy divorce the Langs were involved in a few years back. Tabloid fodder involving Lang cheating on his model wife with a much younger actress, but Shiloh couldn't recall the details.

Purcell, mistaking Shiloh's lingering gaze for attraction, slapped Lang on the back. "Look at this fella, wouldja? Ladies are still falling all over him, nearly ten years after retirement. We should all be so lucky."

Shiloh got the impression that Purcell was trying to flatter Lang. *Little weasel is probably scouting for more investors to fleece.*

"Ms. Mueller?" Helen interrupted. "I asked if you and Ethan had any children."

"Oh, it's still Foley, and no. We didn't. We'd only been married for a few years."

Helen Khoury looked disturbed. "Oh, my mistake. I didn't know you still used your maiden name. How very progressive of you!" Shiloh could tell from her fixed mask of a smile, which needed no surgery to seem creepy, that Helen Khoury was not a woman who leapt willingly on the bandwagon of women's rights. Cocking her exquisitely coiffed head to one side, Helen added in a patronizing tone, "Don't worry. There may still be time for children if you're able to find someone. I had my second one at thirty-eight. Such a joy and a blessing."

Shiloh didn't have time to consider whether Helen's last comment was sarcastic or sincere because at that moment, Helen pitched forward into the grass.

"Oh my god!" Joe Arnold exclaimed, struggling to keep his balance after knocking Helen down. "I didn't see you standing there. Here, lemme help you up."

Shiloh noticed that Joe's speech was heavily slurred. She figured he must be drunk. They hadn't been there an hour, but if what Roman said was true about Joe taking a sedative beforehand, it made sense. After some struggle due to her tight-fitting pencil skirt, the group had Helen back on her feet again. Joe Arnold's beer must have been almost full. Helen's back was soaked. Kimberly snagged a stack of white cloth napkins off a passing server's cart. She and Shiloh went to work, patting down Helen's dress. Shiloh noted that the job would have been much easier with regular paper towels. The heavy starch on the napkins had the undesirable effect of being liquid-repellant rather than absorbent.

After proclaiming a perfunctory apology, Joe resumed his drunken yammering to anyone within earshot. Joe seemed not to care that he'd wandered away from one group of people and blundered into another. He continued telling the same story where he'd left off previously, without any background or introduction.

"So then I said to the little fag, do you honestly think that I care about Honor Codes?" Joe asked. "I gotta keep my stats up, or those scouts will never look at me twice."

"I'd appreciate it if you didn't use that term to describe a human being, please," Shiloh responded, continuing to blot Helen's back. "I prefer to hear that word used only as working-class British slang for cigarettes."

Joe glared at Shiloh from beneath heavily lidded eyes. The beads of sweat running down either side of his flushed face flickered in the light of the bonfire. Shiloh could see now that Joe Arnold was *very* intoxicated and that he likely didn't recognize her.

"Oooh... the woke police!" Joe mocked. "Don't get all bent outta shape, honey. I'm just calling people like I saw them." The direction of Joe's response shifted abruptly as he spied Roman Mueller sprinting toward him across the front lawn. "Hey Roman, don't you agree this one should lighten up on defending fags? Not like it's her war to fight anyway, is it? That is, unless there's something about her we don't know."

Joe paused, leering at Shiloh with a greasy, presumptive look before continuing at an ever-increasing volume. "What *was* that little fag's name again? The one who used to hang with your little brother all the time? I thought he mighta been kinda sweet on Ethan to follow him around like he did. Man, I taught him not to mess with my shit, didn't I, Roman? Doncha remember? All of us taught him about how the world really works after he ratted me out!"

"Joe, I think we'd better get you home," Roman said calmly. "Maybe this wasn't such a good idea. It's too soon. You've had a bit too much to drink. I don't think it's settling well with your medication."

"Aw, Roman," Joe Arnold whined. "Not you too. I was just starting to have a good time finally. It's been such a long time since anything's been a good time for me, yanno? What's with everybody tonight?" Joe glanced at the group around him tightening their circle, as if waiting for a dangerous animal to spring. No one answered him. Joe asked again, this time so loud that he was almost shouting. "You didn't answer me, Roman! What was the little fag's name?"

"Simon," Roman whispered venomously through clenched teeth. "His name was Simon. Now, shut up, Joe. I'm taking you home, and I don't want to hear any more about it. You can't be saying hateful shit like that around here. I've got too much at stake. This is an election year."

Roman reached to grab Joe by the elbow, but Joe twisted away. Stumbling again, Roman attempted to catch him before Joe could fall. Joe pushed Roman, his bloodshot eyes filled with distrust bordering on anger. Shiloh feared that the two were about to come to blows when a loud shriek rang out over the hum of the crowd. It came from one of the bartenders.

"There's someone in there!" the bartender screamed, pointing at the pyre of burning wood. "Somebody on fire!"

Sunday, October 8th, Early Evening

Curled up on her sofa with a cup of cocoa and her cat William in her lap, Shiloh Foley was exhausted. The previous night, after the bartender's panic alerted everyone at the reunion to the body in the bonfire, the administration at St. Augustine immediately went into damage control. While the fire continued to burn, the President of the Board of Trustees shuffled the bartender off quickly into a secluded office. After the bartender assured him that she was certain it was a body that she'd seen and not a figment of her imagination, he returned to the crowd to claim it was all a misunderstanding. Then, he opened the stadium gates and pushed the homecoming processional to start half an hour early. Thinking that the excitement was over, most of the drunken crowd filtered into the stadium oblivious to what was happening.

Catching Roman on the way into the stadium, the board president told him the truth. Roman advised him that he would handle the situation with minimal sensationalism. Giving Kimberly the keys with instructions to drive Joe and Shiloh home, Roman called the police.

The police arrived within minutes, followed by a single ambulance. They'd both been instructed by Judge Roman Mueller to turn off their lights and sirens so as not to cause a panic. They were a single pair of rookie cops, who normally would be stuck with Saturday night after-hours bar patrol duty. Taking no special pains with the scene because they assumed that the charred remains were those of a homeless person who'd crawled into the woodpile and died, the cops doused the bonfire with water. Believing the potential public relations damage contained, Roman left for home.

It was only as the paramedics were removing the body that the officers began to realize they'd mistaken its identity. In its position beneath the stacked-up kindling, the body was sitting on a fireproof lockbox. A key was sticking out of the lock as if intended for easy opening. When the paramedic opened the box, there was a woman's purse and a scroll of paper tied with twine inside. Protected by the firebox, the paper was intact.

On it, a Bible verse was written in a scrawling, irregular hand: *Isaiah 47:14-15.*

Surely, they are like stubble. The fire will burn them up. They cannot even save themselves from the power of the flame. These are not coals for warmth. This is not a fire to sit by. That is all they are to you—these you have dealt with and labored with since childhood. All of them go in their error. There is not one that can save you.

Realizing at last that they had an active crime scene and not just a tragic accident, the officers began taking greater care in preserving evidence. Paramedics took the body to the county morgue. An overnight forensics expert was called in to examine it, along with the contents of the box. After looking into the purse and then double-checking with dental records, they determined the body's identity.

When Judge Roman Mueller received their call just after eleven the next morning, he was sitting beside his wife Kimberly at Mass. He didn't answer the phone right away. Having missed her fun at the post-game party, Kimberly went home and invited a group of alumni wives from St. Augustine's out to Sunday morning brunch to compensate. She reserved almost the entire dining room of the downtown location of Maplewood. Roman Mueller was drinking a second Bloody Mary with his eggs benedict and mentally calculating how much this impromptu soiree was going to cost him when his cell buzzed again. This time, it was accompanied by a text message saying that the matter was urgent.

Frowning at having the situation disturb his expensive brunch, Roman returned the call outside. What the forensics examiner told him made Roman cover his mouth and swear. The dead person in the homecoming bonfire at St. Augustine High was thought to be one of his twin daughters, Reece.

Roman returned to the restaurant and handed Kimberly his credit card. Claiming that he had an urgent matter come up at work, Roman told Kimberly to catch a ride home with a friend. Sensing nothing wrong, Kimberly resumed her conversation.

After positively identifying the remains as Reece's, Roman called Shiloh first, before Kimberly or his other children. He wanted to tell them in person. Roman explained to Shiloh that he didn't want to leave Kimberly alone after breaking the terrible news, but he needed to get a statement out to the media before the press took control of the story. The murder of a local judge's daughter was sure to make headlines.

Roman asked if Shiloh would stay with his wife, Riley, and RJ until Kimberly's family arrived from Tennessee. It would take them at least four or five hours, perhaps six in Nashville Sunday traffic, to drive up. Both knew without explanation why Roman didn't call his parents to sit with his family. Horace and Sarah Mueller weren't the type of people whom anyone would summon for compassion or sympathy. Shiloh agreed, and Roman told Shiloh to meet him at his house at three that afternoon. For once, Roman did not chide Shiloh about her timeliness.

The remainder of the day was an emotionally draining disaster. Kimberly broke down sobbing immediately when Roman told her. She was still crying when Shiloh arrived. After Roman left to meet the press, Riley confessed to her mother that she hadn't seen her sister Reece in over a week, even though they shared an off-campus apartment. When asked about why she'd kept it a secret, Riley said that she was covering for her sister.

"Reece hasn't been okay for a while," Riley said tearfully. "It all started in August when she took that marketing internship with DIG." When her mother and Shiloh looked confused, Riley elaborated.

"Dynamic Investments Group. You know, that company Dad's friend Mr. Purcell runs? They own a bunch of old industrial buildings in gentrification zones that they're trying to rehab. Anyway, we both have to have an internship as part of our credits to graduate. Reece thought she'd do hers in the fall so that it wouldn't interfere with lacrosse season in spring. She wanted me to do it with her, but I told her it was too much. I'd rather wait until summer and just graduate late. Well, you know Reece. She threw a huge fit and accused me of not being supportive. All semester, she'd been avoiding me, but I could tell something was wrong. We stopped going to the gym together, which was always our thing. I didn't think that much about it at first. Just that she over-scheduled herself like I knew she would. Then, she started acting all jumpy when I would bump into her. Her face got thinner, and I could tell that she was losing weight. I thought that maybe she was on something, but a lot of girls take Addies–Adderall–when they need a little boost for a while. It can do that." Riley shrugged as if the casual drug use was no big deal. Kimberly stared at her, horrified at both her daughter's confession and her indifference.

"When did you last see Reece?" Shiloh asked.

"Like I said," Riley replied. "About a week ago. Last Friday, I think. She's been in and out a lot without saying where she was going on the weekends for the last couple of months. I didn't think anything about it until, like, Monday."

Riley glanced at her mother guiltily. "That's why I lied when you called last week and asked if one of us could come watch RJ on Saturday night so that you and Dad could go to the reunion. I told you that both of us were coming because I hoped that Reece would show up by then. I thought that being alone together with RJ would force her to talk to me finally, without causing a scene. She'd never get rough with me in front of RJ. She loved him too much. It would worry her to scare him by fighting."

"Did Reece get physical with you before she left?" Kimberly asked, regaining her ability to speak as the initial shock of her daughter's lies wore off.

"Yeah…" Riley sniffled, looking as if she were about to start crying again. She was sweating. Her face was pale and her voice was shaky. "I tried to confront her about why she was gone all the time. She acted like a total bitch. Slapped me a couple of times and warned me not to go ratting her out to you. Then she left. That was the last time I saw her."

As the conversation devolved more into a mother-and-daughter talk, Shiloh excused herself to go outside. Riley's mention of Reece's using Adderall, off-prescription, to help her manage a hectic schedule concerned Shiloh.

Was Nadia doing the same? Shiloh worried. And if so, was Nadia at least getting the pills properly with a doctor's prescription? Shiloh knew that any kind of pills bought on the street claiming to be one drug might contain many others. *That could account for the weight loss and Reece's strange behavior too*, Shiloh thought. *Getting a bad mix of something else that she thought was Adderall.*

Knowing from her years as a public defender that the worst way to confront a teen about anything was to ask them directly, Shiloh decided to play it cool. With Nadia, the better approach was to be discreet. Nadia was always hinting at wanting to work with Shiloh in the office. It would be easy enough to give her a stern lecture on confidentiality. Then set her on some busy work tasks, like typing client meeting notes or auditing billing and payment spreadsheets. Any kind of monotonous chore would do really, possibly even better than continuing to refuse Nadia's requests to work with her. Observing the girl regularly could open a door to having a conversation about the pills, which could put her mind at ease. Plus, it might have the bonus of making Nadia realize that a lot of legal investigation work was boring. *If that part worked*, Shiloh reasoned, *Nadia might lose interest in the law on her own.*

With those ideas in mind, Shiloh sent Nadia a text, requesting to meet. Then, she returned inside. A few hours passed, mostly filled with Shiloh trying to distract Kimberly from her grief by asking relatively innocuous questions about people they'd met at the reunion bonfire. Riley and RJ played a video game. After Kimberly's parents arrived, Shiloh said her goodbyes and headed home.

As she drove, other questions plagued Shiloh. Bernadette Jenkins's account of her sister Jasmine's decline in the weeks leading up to her disappearance was eerily similar to what Riley Mueller described about her sister Reece. Shiloh wished that Joe Arnold had been sober enough to talk about his daughter Savannah's behavior in the weeks preceding her murder. If Savannah was also withdrawing and acting hostile, Shiloh felt a case could be made that Savannah, Reece, and Jasmine were on the same drug. Making that assumption, it wouldn't be a stretch to assume they had obtained the drug from the same dealer, who might be the one to blame for what happened to all three.

Back at her own house, Shiloh sat down and began to make a chart. She compared and contrasted the three young women, Savannah, Jasmine, and Reece, side-by-side with Joe's wife Veronica, whom Shiloh had originally found dead in the Eden Park gazebo with her daughter. When the chart was complete, one fact stood out clearly. All three girls were daughters of men who were in the class of 1998 at St. Augustine. The sole outlier was one of their wives.

Sensing that this was more than a coincidence but having trouble remembering everyone's names from the blur of humanity at the re-union, Shiloh went upstairs to the attic. She knew that she'd seen a box somewhere labeled *Yearbooks* when she and Ethan moved in several years ago, right after their wedding. Like most of Ethan's high school memorabilia, Shiloh figured the box was still up there. After a quick search through the dusty stacks, she found the box and brought it downstairs.

Inside, the bright red yearbooks with silver lettering on their spines were packed neatly in order up to the year 2000, when Ethan graduated. Pulling out the 1998 volume, Shiloh turned to the senior class section. Sure enough, there were the portraits of three young men whose lives would become intertwined once more twenty-five years later by tragedy: Joe Arnold, Roman Mueller, and Kash Khoury. Flipping through the pages of organization photos and candid shots, Shiloh saw that the two other men she'd met the night before, Kyle Lang and Rafferty Purcell, were together there too, in a picture labeled *Senior Football Stars*.

The photo was awkwardly staged. Rather than having Lang, clearly the tallest, stand in the center as was most common in school group pictures, he was on the far left. The rest were in descending order toward the right by height: Khoury, Arnold, Mueller, and Purcell. Four of them assumed a typical parade rest-type stance, with hands clasped behind their backs and feet spread shoulder-width apart. Their faces bore serious expressions as they gazed off into the distance. Only Joe Arnold stood at ease in the center, hands on hips and grinning at the cameraman impatiently, as if to say, *Take the goddamn picture already*.

Continuing to turn the pages slowly as she jotted down names, the *Senior Who's Who* seemed scarily accurate. Lang was named *Biggest Flirt*, while Khoury was deemed *Most Handsome*. Arnold was declared *Class Clown*. Rafferty Purcell won no title that Shiloh could see, which seemed consistent with the man she'd met briefly at the reunion. Apparently, Purcell had always been a hanger-on with the popular crowd. Shiloh knew without looking that her brother-in-law was voted *Most Likely to Succeed*. Her husband Ethan's parents had never let their younger son live down the fact that his older brother was the best at everything. Ethan told her that was the biggest reason why he'd taken a gap year and then joined the Army instead of going directly to college after graduating high school. He had to go halfway around the world to Afghanistan before he could escape the shadow cast by his brother long enough to create an identity of his own.

As she sat skimming through each of their biography paragraphs searching for further connections, Shiloh recalled the confrontation between Roman and Joe the night before. The outdated, offensive slur that Joe used and Roman's reply haunted her.

What was that little fag's name again? The one who used to hang with your little brother?

Simon, Roman had said.

Simon who? Shiloh wondered. She couldn't recall Ethan ever mentioning a boy named Simon when he spoke about his high school days.

Skipping to the back of the book, Shiloh perused the index for mention of anyone named Simon. Nothing in the alphabetical listings for a last name, but when she backtracked to the top of the order, a first name caught her eye.

Simon Bowles. No middle name was listed. Just a single page number for a member of the sophomore class.

So, Simon would have been in the same year as Ethan, Shiloh rationalized, fluttering pages back to the correct one. Finding it, Shiloh pressed the yearbook flat to examine the picture.

Simon looked different from the other boys in his class photo. Rather than wearing the usual red polo of St. Augustine High School, Simon had on a black dress shirt with a black jacket over it. No tie. Simon's eyes were the palest of blue. His hair was dark and curly, surrounding a slender face with high cheekbones, a pointed nose, and an elfin chin. He did not smile but looked straight into the camera with an expression almost of despair. In his biography paragraph, Simon listed only three activities, rather than the usual dozen or so, followed by a Bible verse. The activities were Math Team, Interfaith Council, and Football Team statistician. The verse was not one that Shiloh recognized. *Isaiah 66:15-16.* Looking it up online, Shiloh read it aloud to herself:

See, the Lord is coming with fire, and his chariots are like a whirlwind; he will bring down his anger with fury and his rebuke with flames of fire. For with fire and with his sword, the Lord will execute judgment on all people, and many will be those slain by the Lord.

Shiloh could understand why Simon had only put the book, chapter, and verse number in the annual. *What kind of high school sophomore cited*

Bible verses like that? Any kid who referenced such passages nowadays would be considered crazy, possibly another Unabomber in training. Still, the ominous words rang in Shiloh's ears as she read them over a second time. Information began to slide into place within her mind like tumblers moving a lock to open. *Had Roman told her which verse was on the scroll found in the lockbox with Reece's purse?* If so, Shiloh couldn't remember it. She made a note to ask.

Forcing herself to look at one more page, Shiloh searched last for a photo of the entire football team. Finding it, she scanned its many faces row by row until finally, she saw what she was searching for. A likeness of Simon Bowles, with the same dour expression as in his portrait, stood at the very end of the second row. Shoulder to shoulder between Simon and the rest of the team was Shiloh's husband, Ethan.

Seeing a photo of Ethan at fifteen made Shiloh's stomach feel as if it were tied in knots. His sandy brown, side-swept hair and hazel eyes were confident in his youthful face. A close-lipped smile barely turned his mouth up at the corners. Shiloh knew that look. Ethan had his game face on. Strangely, Shiloh noticed that Ethan's name and position were there along with everyone else's. However, Simon's name and role within the team were not included. His image was there, but his name was erased.

Slipping the yearbook back into the white cardboard file box, Shiloh spied the distinctive marbled pattern of several old composition notebooks lying in the bottom. Beneath the annuals, as if someone were trying to hide them. Curious, Shiloh pulled out one of the notebooks. On the cover, in precise, all-capital, royal blue-inked letters, it read: *Ethan Mueller 2003.*

Scanning the contents briefly, Shiloh realized that it was her husband's journal, written during the time he was in the Army. She felt a wave of guilt crash over her. These words that she was about to read were Ethan's most private thoughts. Written down while he was a soldier in Afghanistan. Those who'd served often told horrific stories. She knew that Ethan had some of his own. Although she never pressed him for details of his time overseas in the war, he told her bits and pieces occasionally. She could tell it was painful for him. Stories about bodies mutilated by landmines and airstrikes. Even after Ethan's death, Shiloh wasn't sure that she should read his words. It seemed too invasive. Still, her intuition told her that something was in there. Something important.

Opening the notebook, Shiloh saw that the date for the first entry was October 8th. Her throat grew tight as she saw Ethan's familiar, forward-leaning cursive pressed heavily into the narrow-ruled pages, which were smeared with red clay dust.

That's today, Shiloh realized, *exactly twenty years ago*. This coincidence was the tipping point. Intuition prevailed over guilt, and Shiloh began to read.

8 October 2003

Wednesday

2300

SPC-4 Ethan Mueller

Have you heard the old Army saying, There are no atheists in foxholes?

Well, I'm not in a foxhole. I'm above ground. In a Comm Center near Kabul, which is about as precise as I can be about my location, just in case this is ever found. And while I'm not quite an atheist, I wouldn't exactly call myself religious either. I'm not even sure God exists, to be honest. I went to a Catholic school, but that's about the extent of my belief.

Still, that was enough for me to know the feeling of when I needed to confess something.

Our sergeant was killed today, along with half a dozen other men. Sadly, I knew all of them. I can't say who or where exactly, but it involved a land mine. Damn things are everywhere around here. I heard that some field promotions are coming through tomorrow. I'm up for one. I've been in the Army for over two years now, so I guess it's time. To be honest, I'd prefer to stay at SPC-4 and keep operating Base Comm. Not for any honorable reason. I'd just like to keep living longer. Going out in the field isn't exactly the best way to make that happen. But I'll do whatever I'm told. That's what I signed up for, and I've got two more years left.

That isn't what I'm writing tonight to confess, though. If I were unfortunate enough to get sent out and I die soon, I'd be proud of it. At least I would have died protecting people and their freedom. That would make my life worth something. Right now, I'm not sure that it is.

What I need to confess is about a time when I did nothing. If I were going to psychoanalyze myself, I might say that's how I ended up here, in this Hellscape of sand and death. In a way, this desert is my Purgatory.

Enough of that. I've got to go on watch in less than an hour, so I'd better get on with it.

Forgive me, reader, if you can, for what I didn't do. I've never confessed it to anyone else.

When I was fifteen years old and a sophomore in high school, my older brother Roman convinced me to go out for the football team as a kicker. I was on the soccer team already, and I was pretty good, so I wasn't really into picking up another sport. However, Roman can be pretty persuasive when he wants to be, which is probably why he's following Dad into the family law practice and I'm out here. One thing led to another, and I joined.

There was this kid who was always hanging around the practice field. Skinny, awkward, the all-around nerd type. A sophomore, like me. He'd tried out for the team but got knocked out cold during the first scrimmage. Still, he wanted to fit in so badly with the rest of the popular guys that Coach made a place for him as our Statistician. I heard he was really good at math, some kind of prodigy. Our school, St. Aug's, was a feeder for Ohio State and a lot of the other football colleges in the Big Ten. So it kinda made sense to have someone staying on top of everyone's stats up to the minute, in case some of the scouts wanted to know. That's how he came to hang around the field with a clipboard at every game and practice.

It seemed like an okay arrangement, except for some reason all the seniors hated him. Especially my brother Roman's best friend, this dude named Joe Arnold. Joe was the quarterback, and his dad was loaded. Joe kinda sucked, but everyone just assumed his dad made big donations, so that meant Joe could play any position that he wanted. Joe thought he was hilarious, always clowning around at practice. Really, he was a douchebag. The guys tolerated it, though, because Joe always threw these insane parties every time his folks went out of town. It seemed like every hot girl in the city rolled up to them.

Joe was the one who gave this skinny kid the nickname "Toilet Bowls." The kid's real name was Simon Bowles, which was bad enough on its own. Word was that he'd had some kind of really messed-up life too, before he came to St. Aug's. I never knew all the details.

Anyway, Joe didn't just give him a nickname. He called him other bad names too. Fag was the least mean one. Joe seemed to truly enjoy terrorizing the kid. Pretty soon he had all the other senior guys on the football team doing it too. They would wait for him to go into the bathrooms and then grab him and shove his head down in the toilets. They wouldn't let Simon up to breathe until they'd made him lap water out of the bowl like a dog.

As you might imagine, Simon hated Joe and those guys, but he was also scared to death of them. Simon was taller than Joe. Almost as tall as our other friend Lang, who was like a giant. Only Simon's was a rangy kind of height. Not a muscle on him, even though he tried to lift weights with the rest of us. He just never made any gains, so he wasn't big enough physically to fight back.

I felt bad for the kid, so I started trying to make a point of being nice to him. Little stuff like bringing him extra snacks because he always gobbled up food like a hungry animal. Watching him eat was sad. I think that wherever he came from before he started at St. Aug's, he must have been really poor. Once I tried to take him some of my old clothes so he wouldn't look like death warmed over, but he wouldn't take them.

Simon always wore all black, even on the hottest days. I asked him if he was, like, a goth or something. He just laughed and started quoting lyrics from this old Johnny Cash song. Claimed he dressed in black for the poor and the beaten down. It was pretty weird, but I guess everybody has to have some kind of a hero. Simon had an odd, high-pitched country twang, so I thought he must be from somewhere south, like Kentucky or Tennessee. He wasn't a dumb redneck, though. When I told him I was doing badly in Geometry, Simon offered to tutor me.

We started studying together during our free period in the library, and it did help. Simon had a way of explaining things and writing out all the steps very plainly that made sense. I felt bad at first for taking up his free period, but Simon told me that he enjoyed having someone to talk to who listened to him. I could tell that he was lonely.

Our studying together went on for about a month when Roman pulled me aside. He told me that he'd asked Dad to hire a real math tutor for me so that I wouldn't have to associate with Simon anymore. When I said that wasn't necessary and that I was doing better already just studying with Simon, Roman said that didn't matter. Other guys at school were starting to talk about me because they'd seen us hanging around together. If I didn't want to get labeled as a fag, I had better cut it out.

I hate to admit it, but I did what Roman said. I started avoiding Simon because I didn't want the other guys on the team to start calling me a fag too. It was stupid, but fifteen-year-old boys can be pretty stupid. In hindsight, I wonder if it wouldn't have happened if I'd told Roman to eff off instead. I think about that a lot late at night when I'm on watch.

Would that have stopped it? Or would I have ended up like Simon too? I hate to think that Roman would have let that happen, but Roman surprises me sometimes with how cold he can be. When he's around Joe and those guys, it's like hive mentality. He becomes a completely different person.

That's how Roman was the night that it happened. When they did what they did to Simon.

It was the first week of October. College scouts were swarming around all the big prep school games, looking to snap up scholarship recruits. Sports scouts loved St. Aug's because they knew our academics were tough. Most of our guys could make grades high enough so that they wouldn't flunk out and wreck their retention numbers. Kyle Lang, the best player on the team, got multiple offers and was already signed. Roman and this other friend of theirs, Kash Khoury, were offered scholarships to play college ball too. They turned them down because they knew they had good enough test scores to get free rides on academics alone. Even Rafferty Purcell, the senior kicker who got bumped down to second string after I got on the team because he was so terrible, got an offer from some little religious college upstate because his grades were really good.

Joe Arnold was the only senior player who hadn't received any offers yet. It made him furious. Part of it was because he was a terrible quarterback, but the other part was because he goofed off in class all the time too. His grades were barely C's. Teachers passed Joe with the bare minimum only because the administration made them. Otherwise, Joe's dad would have quit donating to the school. Joe made a big joke of the SATs, bubbling in stupid pictures on his answer sheet instead of trying. Of course, his scores there were awful too.

Not all of the scouts came to our games in person, which made sense because there are only so many game nights in a season. A lot of the ones from out of state just relied on stats alone to make offers. Some colleges, especially down South, didn't care what kinds of grades a player made. Joe got the idea he could trick one of those Southern scouts into giving him a deal if he paid Simon to change his numbers.

The problem was that Simon wouldn't do it. Not for any price. Roman told me that Joe started out offering Simon a thousand dollars, then five, and finally ten thousand. Joe thought that it was just Simon wanting more money, causing him to hold out, but it wasn't. Simon said he wouldn't do it because, to him, it was the principle of the thing.

Finally, after Joe had been pressuring him for weeks, Simon went to our coach and told him what was happening. The coach told Simon he was caught between a rock and a hard place because he couldn't discipline Joe or take him off the team. Joe's dad was the school's biggest donor, so Coach's hands were tied. In the end, Joe got kicked off the team regardless, through no one's fault but his own. Punching a referee in the face during a game tends to make that sort of thing inevitable.

Joe loved to argue with refs after pretty much any close play. That night, we were down by four points, with only a few seconds left on the clock. The coach called for a shuttle pass around the end to Lang, who was the biggest guy on the team and had the best chance of hammering it in. Joe wouldn't have it. There were several scouts in the stands, so Joe was trying especially hard to look like a hero. Rather than going through with the play as called, Joe tried to do a quarterback sneak and run the ball in himself. Naturally, being the terrible player he was, Joe dropped the ball when he got hit. Another player from the other team fell on it. When the ref ruled it a fumble, Joe lost it and punched the ref in the face. As a result, Joe got ejected from the game. The following Monday morning, Joe found out that the league stepped in and made the school suspend him for the rest of the season.

When Joe tried to show up to practice like nothing had happened on Monday night, Coach had to get tough with him. He told Joe to come back later and clear out his locker. Joe cussed Coach out and left. I thought that would be the end of it. Turns out I was wrong.

That night after practice, I realized that I must have left my graphing calculator in the locker room down in the basement. I would have just picked it up the next morning, but I didn't want it to walk off, if you know what I mean. Plus, I needed it to do my Geometry homework. So, I went back to look around for it. That's when I heard them.

Thinking back, there were a lot of other things that I could have done, even though I couldn't have stopped them all by myself. When I saw what they were doing, I could have run straight to Coach's office for help. I could have run into the shower room screaming my head off. Maybe that would have scared them away if they thought I was crazier than they were. But I didn't do either of those things. Instead, I just walked around the corner holding my calculator and froze.

There was my brother, Roman, and all his buddies holding Simon spread-eagle against the wall. Roman and Lang pinned his arms, while

Khoury and Purcell held his legs. Joe Arnold had both hands wound in Simon's hair. He was slamming Simon's face hard on the tile wall of the shower room, calling him every name in the book. Simon pleaded to be let go. With each blow, I could hear something cracking. I wasn't sure if it was Simon's skull or the wall. Simon had a towel tied around his waist. It fell onto the floor, leaving him naked.

Then, I couldn't help but see then why guys kept calling Simon a fag. Although I don't know how they knew unless they'd watched him pee or something. Simon didn't have a dick or balls or anything. Just this little knob. Everything else down there was smooth like an alien.

For a second, Joe stopped and let go of Simon's hair. I think it surprised him to see what Simon was missing. Joe started laughing, this evil, guttural sort of laugh. He slapped Simon hard on the ass and told him that he knew he was a pussy, but not that kind. Now that he did, though, he was going to treat him like one. Really eff him over, just like Simon tried to do to him.

I don't think the other guys knew what Joe meant when he said it, but Simon did. He started screaming and fighting to get away. They just held him down harder. It all happened so fast. Joe grabbed Simon around the waist, pulled down his sweats, and pushed himself in. Joe raped Simon.

Realizing what was happening, Roman let go of Simon's arm with one hand and tried to push Joe back. Simon wriggled free from my brother's grip and twisted around. His face was covered in blood. I could tell that his nose was broken and all his front teeth were gone. Seeing me standing there like the dumbstruck idiot I was, Simon screamed my name.

Everything stopped. They all turned to look at me. Roman yelled for me to get out of there. Terrified, I turned and ran. Being a soccer player, I was much faster and had a lot more endurance. I didn't stop to look back until I no longer heard footsteps pounding behind me. By then, I'd run almost a mile. It was only then that I realized I'd dropped my calculator.

I don't know what happened to Simon after that. Whether they went back and hurt him again or what. When Roman got home later that night, he knocked on my door. I pretended to be asleep. I knew what he wanted. He wanted to tell me to keep quiet about what I'd seen. He didn't have to. I was in too much shock to say a word.

The first thing the next morning, I got called into the office. The head-master was there, along with two nuns. One old one I'd never met and one young one. The old one introduced herself as Mother Gertrude. She said she'd worked at Simon's former school. Typical stern-looking ancient German woman. The young one was Sister Frida, a novitiate from somewhere in the Southwest, I think. She looked Latina. I'd seen her around campus. She ran the writing center at St. Aug's. Sister Frida went back to her office late that night for some reason and found Simon crying in the shower room. The writing center was on the first floor right next to the stairwell. I guess that's how she heard him.

The headmaster asked me if I'd seen or heard anything happen in the locker room the night before. When I told him that I hadn't, he reached into the top drawer of his desk and pulled out my missing calculator. The screen was cracked from where I'd dropped it on the tile floor when I ran away. Even so, there was no denying it was mine. I'd written my name on the back of it with a silver permanent marker. He told me that Simon said I'd seen what happened and could confirm his account of the abuse that occurred.

Sitting there staring at my broken calculator, it was clear to me what would happen to my brother Roman if I told the truth. My dad, Horace, was a lawyer, so I knew how that sort of thing usually played out. Roman and all his friends would be charged as accomplices to Joe's crime of beating and raping Simon. Every one of their lives would be ruined because, in Ohio, accomplices are sentenced the same as the primary offender. They would all be not just felons but convicted sex offenders. I didn't care so much about the other guys; they were all jerks anyway, especially Joe. And I was mad enough at my brother too for being part of it that I considered ratting them all out.

However, it was thinking about my dad that stopped me. My dad, who was one of the most well-known and respected attorneys in the city. Having it splashed across the front page of the Cincinnati Enquirer that his oldest son was on trial for being an accomplice to raping another boy at his prep school would destroy his practice. Dad was old-school, with a lot of old-money conservative Catholic clients, who, if I had to guess, were mostly homophobes. If they so much as suspected that Horace Mueller's son was not only a rapist but a queer rapist, it would mean the end of his career. My dad could be an asshole, but he didn't deserve that. Even though I knew that Roman had always been his favorite, I couldn't let that happen to him.

So, I lied. I told them that I hadn't seen anything. That hadn't gone back to the school that night. That I had no idea how my calculator ended up broken on the locker room floor.

Mother Gertrude sprang to her feet and began screaming. She said that God would damn me and my family for lying. That someday St. Aug's, the City, and the Church would have to answer in the Final Judgment for all the things that were done to Simon over his whole life that had been covered up. Then, she snatched my calculator up from the headmaster's desk and stormed off, slamming the door behind her. Getting up quietly, Sister Frida followed her out.

Seeing my surprise, the headmaster tried to explain away what Mother Gertrude meant. He said that Simon had always been a troubled young man with a tendency for bending the truth, ever since he was taken from his mother for neglect when he was a child and placed in a group home run by the Church over on the Westside. When he was ten, Simon was selected as an altar boy for Our Lady of Perpetual Help in Sedamsville. Not long afterward, Simon began making allegations to Mother Gertrude, who oversaw the group home in which he lived, that a priest named Father Eckhardt was making improper advances toward him. The Church made an official inquiry but found no evidence of wrongdoing. However, because Simon and Mother Gertrude continued to insist that something had happened and justice must be done, it caused a lot of gossip in the parish. Eventually, Simon was moved to a different group home and then enrolled at St. Aug's. Father Eckhardt was reassigned to another church. Our Lady of Perpetual Help closed shortly thereafter due to lack of attendance.

I didn't believe most of what the headmaster told me. All my life, I'd heard rumors about the Church in Sedamsville. How terrible things went on there with poor kids and bad priests, and why it closed. How the Rectory was supposed to be haunted because of it. I wanted to yell at the headmaster like Mother Gertrude did. For being a liar, for not standing up for Simon, and for giving me no choice but to continue the lie or to see my family ruined. I wanted to scream at him, why did Simon just have a little knob instead of regular parts if nothing horrible had ever happened to him over at Sedamsville?

But if I questioned him, especially if I said that last part, the headmaster would know that I had been there. He would know that I had seen what happened to Simon. Then, if he thought that I would try to go around him, to try to take him down as part of the cover-up, he might try to destroy me too. If the headmaster, St. Augustine's, and the Church were willing to turn their backs on Simon, on all the wretched abuse that he had suffered, how easy would it be for them to turn their backs on me too?

Too easy. I wasn't even my father's favorite son.

So I didn't say anything more to him. I pretended like I accepted the headmaster's explanation. When he gave me the non-disclosure agreement to sign, I signed it. When I mysteriously got straight A's on all my Geometry homework for the rest of the year, despite my papers being full of red marks, I accepted them without comment.

I did quit the football team, though. I told the coach that it was just too much to handle, two sports at once. The truth was that I simply couldn't look at any of those guys anymore without remembering what they'd done to Simon. Roman didn't say anything about it. Dad made jokes about how I couldn't hack it at a real man's sport. He'd always made fun of me playing soccer anyway. For the rest of the time I was at St. Aug's, I always changed clothes in one of the men's restrooms upstairs before soccer practice and showered at home. I couldn't make myself go back into that locker room.

Sister Frida quit that year over Christmas break. Not just St. Augustine's, but the whole thing of being a nun. I heard she got married and moved out West somewhere. I never saw Simon or Mother Gertrude again. I have no idea what happened to Simon either. I hope they got him some help, but I kind of get the feeling that Simon's someone who's never going to be okay. Maybe he could have been before what happened at St. Aug's, but not anymore. He was trying hard to put whatever had already happened behind him, but the past is like an old dog. It has a way of following people around, perpetually hungry, until they finally feed it what it craves.

So that's my confession. There's nothing left to tell because nothing else ever came of it. The same old machine keeps churning out the same old douchebags, generation after generation. My brother Roman is a first year in law school. He's a clerk with my dad's firm and will join as soon as he passes the bar. Khoury's in medical school just like his dad. Purcell's getting his MBA in finance, also just like his dad. Of course Joe's in pharmacy school, to keep the Arnold's Drugstore chain going into the fourth generation. Lang's a little different because he got drafted by the Bengals, which saved him from a lifetime of hawking cars like his old man. At some point, I'm sure he'll inherit the dealership, though.

And then there's me. Sitting here in this goddamned sandpit. Hoping not to get blown up, but knowing that if I did, I'd kind of deserve it. If by some miracle I do make it through the next two years alive and intact, I plan on doing something better with my life than just making money. I want to change the world for the better. I just haven't figured out the best way to do that yet.

So please, God, I know I started this confession by saying that I didn't think you were really out there. If you are, and you're listening, please allow me some time to do that first. Just a little bit more time to straighten some things out. That's all I ask for. Just a little more time.

Monday, October 9th, Morning

After reading the entry in Ethan's journal, Shiloh found it impossible to go to sleep. For a while, she just sat and cried.

She'd often wondered why Ethan rarely spoke about his high school years, when everyone else in the city was so obsessed with them. Ethan usually claimed it was because being around people who peaked in high school made him sick. Also, Shiloh had been perplexed by why such a gentle, easygoing man as Ethan would have chosen to join the Army and then later to pursue a career as a police detective. Neither seemed to fit his personality. Ethan always brushed off such questions lightly. He said the Army gave him the best reason to escape right after high school, and that becoming a policeman was the number one way he could think of to continue pissing off his greedy family by voluntarily being an underpaid public servant for the rest of his life.

In a way, it was the truth. Not the whole truth, Shiloh knew, but part of it. He died without telling her the rest. Shiloh could understand why. Ethan found it difficult to cope with the guilt around what he witnessed. He made it his life's mission to compensate by intervening whenever possible. After so long, Shiloh didn't know what to do with the knowledge of the assault either. The Ohio statute of limitations for reporting such a crime had long since passed.

Should she go to the police? Confront Roman directly? Her mind reeled with the possible consequences of both actions. The least of which would probably be that Shiloh's investigation into the disappearance of Jasmine

Jenkins would be severely delayed by the fallout. Ultimately, Shiloh decided to wait to disclose what she'd found in Ethan's journal until the time was right. Her legal instincts told her that time would come soon enough.

At sunrise, Shiloh showered, dressed, and made a list of people and places to visit based on what she'd read in Ethan's journal and learned over the past few days. Shiloh knew that, despite everything else, her primary focus should be on determining what might have happened to Jasmine Jenkins. First, she needed to reach out to Detective Bruce Schultz to see if there had been any breaks in the murder cases for Veronica and Savannah Arnold or the missing person's report filed on Jasmine. If Joe had been officially eliminated as a suspect in both incidents, it might be easier to get him to talk about his alleged girlfriend Jasmine, because he might not have lawyered up. Hopefully, Shiloh thought, Joe would have had time to start cutting back on the sedatives. That would make it easier to interview him. If Joe did happen to have any ideas regarding Jasmine's whereabouts, that might be a good place to start. Even so, Shiloh knew she would have to steel herself to speak with Joe, knowing what she did now about his violent past.

Next, she needed to call her client, Bernadette Jenkins, to pick her brain for more details about her sister's life. Details such as Jasmine's last known address and the names of specific people whom she'd spent time with would provide further insights into where to find her. Glancing through the notes she'd typed into her laptop, Shiloh knew why there were so many blanks. Normally she'd have already asked such questions in the initial client interview. Bernadette's visit and her sister Jasmine's unexpected connection to Ethan's murder had thrown Shiloh off her standard procedure, even though she'd tried to downplay it.

Shiloh remembered that the police report never named Ethan's killer. During the questioning that followed, Jasmine claimed she didn't know her pimp's real name. Ethan had been alone that night, driving home after working the second shift, when he'd randomly seen the pimp beating Jasmine. He'd radioed for backup before engaging, but by the time they arrived, Ethan was already dead. Jasmine's pimp had fled the scene. In the official inquiry, Jasmine said he was a new white guy she'd just started working with to try to get better, higher-paying clients. Jasmine claimed the other girls called him The Prophet, but Shiloh knew that Jasmine might have been lying. Although Shiloh thought Bernadette would have told her the identity of this mysterious prophet if she'd known it, she wanted to make sure.

After she made the rounds of checking out any possible leads based on this information, Shiloh supposed that she'd better call to check in on Kimberly too. Since further forensic examination of Reece's body was going to delay the funeral at least a week, Kimberly's folks were planning on heading back to Tennessee. Roman was likely going to be spending as much time as possible hounding the detectives downtown and drumming up media support in a manhunt for Reece's murderer. Given the nature of both crime scenes and the fact that the families were so close to one another, the news was already starting to use the term *serial killer*.

Checking over the list as she tried to think if there was anything else she'd have time to look into that day, Shiloh's mind drifted back to a particularly haunting line from Ethan's journal. *I kind of get the feeling that he's someone who's never going to be okay.* Certainly, neither Roman nor Joe Arnold would ever be okay again. Not after what had happened to their families. As Shiloh knew all too well, there would always be a *before* and an *after* in their lives. The years before their murders would be viewed through a rose-colored lens of nostalgia as the time when their lives were whole. In the years afterward, there would always be an emptiness. That emptiness would become a bottomless pit of questions, echoing *what if, what if,* in constant refrain. Shiloh knew because she heard those endless reverberations spiraling down into the depths of her soul every time someone said Ethan's name.

What if Ethan hadn't stopped to help Jasmine that night?

What if Jasmine hadn't needed help because her life had turned out better somehow?

What if Ethan hadn't become a detective in the first place?

What if Ethan hadn't gone back for that calculator and seen Simon being assaulted?

What if Simon hadn't been assaulted by those bullies at St. Augustine's?

What if Simon hadn't been sent away to St. Augustine's in the first place?

What if Simon hadn't been assaulted the first time at Sedamsville?

What if, what if, what if...

"I've got to get out of here before I go crazy," Shiloh said to her cat, William, who was looking at her with a concerned expression. Shiloh realized she'd been talking to herself, as well as automatically writing down her spiraling questions at the end of the page.

Slipping on a navy blazer to look more professional with her white button-down and dark jeans, Shiloh examined the list that she'd made once more. Seeing how many times his name appeared on it, she added one more item. *Background check Simon Bowles.*

Monday, October 9th, Noon

"Nothing new, I'm afraid," Detective Bruce Schultz said to Shiloh. They met over what for her was a late breakfast and for him an early lunch at the Sleepy Bee Cafe in Oakley. He chided Shiloh good-naturedly about ordering the stereotypical millennial avocado toast. She countered by noticing that his Beekeeper sandwich also had slices of avocado. Bruce, his wife Kaley, and their children had eaten brunch together there with Shiloh and Ethan countless times. Although she loved the place, with its bright, hippie decor, Shiloh hadn't been in since Ethan's death. Without him, the whimsical decor seemed hollow and contrived.

Schultz confirmed that Joe Arnold was cleared as a potential suspect in the murder of his wife and daughter. Judging from the stage of their bodies' *rigor mortis*, the toxicologist found that Veronica and Savannah were killed between six and twelve hours before the initial field examination.

"That evidence puts their time of death somewhere between midnight and six in the morning," Schultz said, taking a sip of diet soda. "Joe's paranoid about security. He's got cameras all over the house. The one at his front door showed Veronica leaving a little after midnight. According to the one pointed at the gun cabinets in his home office, Joe was passed out on the couch drinking whisky and watching old Western reruns by eleven. None of the other cameras show anyone entering or leaving the home until Joe wakes up to go golfing. The garage camera shows him getting on his cart and leaving at six-thirty. He met Roman and the guys right when they opened around seven. The country club confirmed their reservation. A big group of five men. They normally don't allow more than four unless folks get there at the butt-crack of dawn. It was a regular thing for this bunch. First Friday of every month. All of them except Lang. He's out of town a lot for appearances and television stuff. The club lets them bend the rules when he plays."

"That sounds familiar," Shiloh mumbled to herself as she swallowed a bite of egg. "Two questions. First, what time did Joe Arnold put in the initial missing person's report? And second, where was Savannah during all of this?"

"Ah, see, that's the weird thing," Schultz said, pointing at Shiloh with a chunk of sweet potato speared on the end of his fork. "Joe and Veronica filed the missing person's report for Savannah together the day before. Nobody had seen Savannah since the previous Friday, which would have been the 29th. Her roommate on campus at Xavier had been covering for her since her mother called on Sunday when she didn't show up for a family dinner. Veronica finally drove over to campus on Thursday, and that's when the roommate fessed up. Savannah left her phone in her room and never came back for it, which, according to her roommate, was super unusual. Savannah Arnold was like every other teenager in the world, glued to her phone most of the time. Joe claims that he didn't notice Veronica hadn't come home the night before because he'd been passed out in the office and then rushed to meet his friends for golf first thing in the morning. When he got home from golf to find that Veronica still wasn't home and that she'd left her phone too, Joe called the police immediately to report her missing in a second report. Our guys had just returned from taking Joe's statement when the bodies were found."

"Do you think Veronica went looking for her daughter?" Shiloh asked. "And then something happened to her too?"

"That's what we're going on at the moment," Schultz replied. "Our boys already interviewed the roommate. She said Savannah's been acting sketchy for weeks. Always been a big partier and weed smoker. However, the roommate thought that she had been taking something harder lately from the way she'd been acting weird and skipping classes. Said she was all sweaty and glassy-eyed, which is consistent with speed drugs. What's strange to me is why a girl with a new drug dealer would leave her phone behind–I mean, that's pretty essential to coordinate a drop."

"And then her mother left her phone too," Shiloh added. "It's like they wanted to make sure that no one could use their location to find them."

"Exactly," Schultz agreed. "We're also thinking that both must have known where they were going too. Otherwise, they'd have needed a GPS. Whatever it was, they didn't say a word about it over text message. Joe handed over both phones, and we've gone through them. Zero leads. It appears that both mother and daughter knew something was going on, but that Dad was clueless."

"Isn't that how it is in every family?" Shiloh quipped sarcastically, then changed the subject. Cautiously, though, because she didn't want to spill everything she knew. "So, I've seen on the news that they're starting to think it might be a serial killer, considering how close the three victims' families were. Do the police think there's any truth to that?"

"Maybe," Schultz replied, his detective's curiosity piqued by the question. "Being a Common Pleas Judge isn't exactly the best way to make new friends, if you know what I mean. Especially in the drug community. They're trying to keep it hushed up because of Roman. There's suspicion that Reece might have ended up in that bonfire because she didn't pay her dealer. If so, she won't be the first judge's kid who's gotten on the wrong side of the law. Final toxicology reports aren't back yet, but preliminaries say there were substances found among her remains. They're thinking it might be multiple things. With Savannah Arnold, they've found several. Including some new mixes that we haven't seen before. It seems to be steroids, probably dianabol, plus phentermine and a few different amphetamines."

"Jesus!" Shiloh exclaimed, trying to wrap her mind around the combination of drugs. "That sounds like it would turn somebody into the human equivalent of a velociraptor. Skinny, sleepless, jacked up, and ready to snap at any moment."

Schultz snorted, almost spewing coffee on his shirt. "You're probably right. We see new combos of shit like that on the streets all the time nowadays. Kids can't seem to get enough of finding new ways to kill themselves."

"About that," Shiloh had been waiting for the right moment to tell Schultz that their visit wasn't just her finally making good on her promise to get out and see some of Ethan's old friends again. "I have a new client. Bernadette Jenkins hired me to look into the disappearance of her sister,

Jasmine. She was the one whose pimp, well... you know." Shiloh was grateful that the server's retrieval of her plate spared her from having to meet Schultz's gaze as she trailed off.

"Yeah, I know," Schultz replied, watching the server too. "I didn't know she was missing too, though. It's been really busy the last few days. To be honest, keeping track of girls like her isn't exactly a priority when other high-profile cases are going on."

"Girls like her?" Shiloh replied, knowing full well what Schultz meant.

"Oh, don't act offended. You know how it is. I didn't mean anything by it. I was just stating the facts. The department has limited resources. A college girl—two college girls—and a mother from good families are found dead and the whole force goes all out in droves. A no-name girl from who-knows-where goes missing not long after her pimp shoots and kills one of our own while he's trying to keep the thug from beating the pulp out of her, and the general attitude is like..." Schultz shifted uncomfortably in his seat. He lowered his voice to a whisper as he leaned across the table. "It's like—good riddance. She had it coming."

"How do you know that Jasmine Jenkins didn't come from a good family too?" Shiloh asked, peering at Schultz skeptically over the rim of her coffee cup.

"Pfft..." Schultz exhaled. "Shiloh, I know you used to be a public defender, but can't you give it a rest with all the anti-stereotyping rhetoric for once? We all know what kinds of backgrounds are most likely to produce drug-addicted prostitutes."

Shiloh set her cup down and met Schultz's stare. "A former college athlete and beauty queen with a sister who's a teacher who also runs a nonprofit, a mother who was a nurse, and a father who's a well-known plastic surgeon in this city?" she asked with exaggerated innocence.

Schultz rolled his eyes. "Okay, you got me. So not all prostitutes are the same, and we should do better as a department following up on all cases equally. I'm guessing her sister, who hired you to find out what happened, told you all that?"

"And more," Shiloh replied, as the server returned. She already had her credit card in the check holder before Schultz could reach for his wallet. "Jasmine Jenkins's father was Dr. Kash Khoury. She was the product of an affair between him and her mother, Destiny, who was his nurse. From what her sister Bernadette tells me, Jasmine grew up pretty spoiled. Possibly because Dr. Khoury felt guilty and didn't want her mother to spill the beans to his wife. The pimp wasn't the only man in her life either. She flew pretty high, so far as women in her profession go. Joe Arnold was her alleged boyfriend."

"Get out of town!" Schultz exclaimed. "I don't believe it. With his money, Joe could buy off half the gold diggers in this city. Why would he choose her?"

Shiloh shrugged. "Like minds, her sister thinks. Bernadette works for the Arnold family and saw them together on at least one occasion. Plus, Jasmine told her all about it." She could almost see the wheels in Schultz's mind turning beneath the silver spiked crew cut of his hair as he processed this information.

"What if that's the connection?" Schultz asked, thinking aloud, his expression becoming more flabbergasted as he spoke. "If what you say is true, then it seems possible that Jasmine's entry into Joe's life might indicate who-knows-what was going on. That Joe might have fallen back off the wagon. That his daughter might have a hookup to get higher-powered illegal drugs? That her mother might have discovered all of it and went in search of her daughter because she didn't trust Joe anymore?"

"And don't forget that Reece Mueller, daughter of our very own Judge Roman, grew up right across the street from the Arnold family," Shiloh added. "How easy would it have been for Reece just to wander across one night to hang out with her neighbor Savannah, who goes to the same college, and then one thing led to another. It would be too ironic, don't you think?"

"Please don't tell me that you just quoted song lyrics at me in the middle of a serious conversation," Schultz said, rising from his chair and putting on his jacket as he prepared to go. "I need to get back to the office and start following up on some of this." He shook his head. "You millennials never know when to turn off those pop culture references. Who was that anyway? Morris Allset or somebody?"

"Close enough," Shiloh replied, following Schultz to the door. "It's been good talking to you again. Oh, and if you're heading back to the station, could you do something for me?"

"Name it," Schultz replied.

"Send me everything you can on Jasmine Jenkins. From everything I've learned about her so far, she seems like a woman who's capable of anything."

Monday, October 9th, Afternoon

After leaving brunch with Detective Schultz, Shiloh returned to her office. She called Bernadette Jenkins to see what time would be best to interview both her and Joe Arnold. Bernadette claimed that she had an Arnold Foundation meeting that might last all afternoon and then a personal errand to run, but that they could grab dinner together that evening. Then, they could compare notes on what the official police record of Jasmine's disappearance stated with what Joe said and what they already knew. When Shiloh questioned whether she thought it was unusual or suspicious for the headquarters of a non-profit to be located inside the founder's home, Bernadette just chuckled.

"I take it you've never been to the Arnolds' place before," she said. "It's not exactly just one house. More of a compound. The building that faces across the street toward Judge Mueller's home is the Arnold Foundation House. The much larger Arnold family residence is on the other side of the property. You only see it if you follow the curved road around like you're heading towards the golf course. It's not very tall, only two stories, but it sprawls out wide across the land. The sort of thing you'd see in Texas rather than Ohio. There are three elevators too, one in the center near the main entryway leading to the indoor pool and the other two at each end. Joe Arnold built it that way when his father was still alive. The old man was confined to a power chair in his final years. They designed the house with wider hallways to make it easier for Old Mr. Arnold to get around. They just left it after he passed away."

"That's logical," Shiloh replied. "Everyone gets old someday, even rich people."

"Sad but true," Bernadette agreed. "Regardless, Mr. Arnold is home right now. I saw him go by on his golf cart a few moments ago. Unless the weather is bad, he goes to the golf course every morning. Then he comes home to take a nap in his home office. If you want, I can tell Joe you're on your way out here to try to help us solve the mystery of Jasmine's disappearance. Then I'll head out for my meeting a little early so that you two can have some privacy to talk. I will warn you though, depending on what mood he's in, Mr. Arnold tends to rattle on. Some of it might be helpful, but a lot of it might not."

They agreed on a time and place for dinner, and Shiloh hung up the phone. Gathering her interview microphone and checking her laptop battery to make sure that she had a full charge to run the recording app, Shiloh glanced back at her list of to-dos. The last note about needing to background check Simon Bowles nagged at her. Since she'd already packed up her laptop, Shiloh thought she'd do that after she returned from interviewing Joe Arnold and Bernadette.

Also, she still needed to call Nadia and see if the girl wanted to come in to work part-time as an intern. Shiloh figured the answer would be positive, so she sent a quick text. Immediately, Nadia's reply was *yes*, accompanied by the little thank-you face emoji. Shiloh breathed a sigh of relief, taking it as an excellent sign that her concerns about Nadia's bottle of Adderall might not be connected to the other girls after all. *So glad I'm not a mom, except for a cat. Can't imagine worrying like that all the time.* Shiloh thought, pocketing her phone.

Half an hour later, as she drove past the Arnold Foundation House, Shiloh realized that she'd always assumed it was the Arnolds' actual home when she'd seen it across the street from Roman's place. It was certainly impressive enough to be, with its imposing columns completely encircling the two-story red brick walls on all sides. The lawn was manicured into that perfect checkerboard pattern that wealthy people's homes always seemed to have.

As a small child, Shiloh remembered asking her dad whether rich people bought special grass in different colors so that their yards would look that way. Her dad just laughed and said no, they just trained it. For years afterward, Shiloh's active imagination worked out all sorts of schemes about how rich people trained grass until finally she gave up and forgot about it. That was, until the first time she'd gone to Ethan's parents' house and endured her first evening sitting on their veranda. Carefully moderating every word to downplay her Kentucky accent lest it immediately become a topic of conversation, Shiloh remembered meditating on their checkerboard grass. Finally, she reached the conclusion that had eluded her since childhood. Rich people trained their grass in the same way that they trained people—by applying pressure repetitively until both conformed in the ways they desired.

Following the road around the backside of the property to a dead-end cul-de-sac, Shiloh arrived at the front of the Arnold compound. She was unsurprised to find the perimeter was skirted by a black wrought iron fence. The gate had a large letter A in a script font at the peak of the archway, which spanned over the brown sandstone columns. Although the gate was closed, there was a call box with a button. Pressing it, Shiloh was immediately greeted by an automated female voice asking her to state her name and purpose for the visit. Shiloh gave her information and waited for a few moments. A chirping sound like the bell of an old-fashioned cash register dinged, and the gates swung open. The digital greeter instructed Shiloh to pull around in front of the fountain by the main entrance. There, someone would let her in.

Obeying these directions, Shiloh passed by the tennis court on her right and the greenhouse on her left as she arrived at the front door. Getting out of the car, she was tempted to take a picture of the house but decided against it. Partly because doing so would make her feel awkwardly touristy. Also, she doubted that her cell phone camera could capture it all from so close up. Even with the wide-angle landscape feature, the house was much too long to take in with a single photo. Hovering near the front door, Shiloh sized up the design. Eight to ten windows down each side, culminating in a round turret on either end. The style reminded her of the Victorian Gothic sandstone mansions that she'd often seen in the old money section of East Walnut Hills downtown, only on a much larger scale. She vaguely remembered Ethan pointing out to her a few times that one of them had belonged to Joe Arnold's family. It was built several generations before when the Arnold's Drugstore chain had initially become a tri-state area staple. Considering that, the old-fashioned style built within a newer estate community made sense. The Arnold compound served as a reminder of an even greater amount of new money, paying homage to the roots of its generational wealth.

From inside, Shiloh could hear two young male voices shouting back and forth to one another. Eventually, they made it to the entrance. The door swung open to reveal an extremely muscular teenage boy. Wearing low-slung swimming trunks and flip-flops, his dirty blonde hair was wet and tousled. He looked like a model from one of those nineties-style Abercrombie & Fitch catalogs. Shiloh attempted to introduce herself but was interrupted by a flurry of foam darts shooting from somewhere inside the house.

"Dude, I told you to cut that out! Can't you see I'm trying to answer the door? Why don't you go down to Dad's office and tell him that I'm bringing the lady over there, like he said?"

Another boy, shorter but almost identical to the one who answered the door, stared at Shiloh warily. His blue eyes were wild and unblinking. He looked exactly like his brother, except for a thick white scar cutting through one eyebrow. As his younger brother took off running, the catalog-perfect older brother opened the door for Shiloh to enter.

"Sorry about that. Little brothers can be a pain sometimes," the boy said. He flashed a blinding fake smile of perfect teeth that caused Shiloh to wonder how much his orthodontist bill was. Reopening the door, he extended a hand for her to shake. Taking his hand, Shiloh felt that his palm was weirdly clammy with sweat. His face dropped the forced expression of welcome. "I'm Jefferson. People call me Jeff. That other clown was Jackson. Come on in. Dad's been expecting you."

Following Jeff down the long corridor to the left, Shiloh could see a sweeping round sandstone staircase leading to the upper floor. Beyond that, the back wall was almost completely glass. It looked out onto an atrium with what appeared to be an Olympic-sized pool inside, complete with a pair of diving boards. Seeing her notice the pool, Jeff commented. "Jack and I are competitive swimmers. Vanna was too, before..." The boy cleared his throat.

"Well, you know, I guess. Mom thought it was like a good family activity for everyone. Except Scarlet, but she's not really into anything." Jeff shrugged. "Mom had Dad add the atrium over the pool about ten years ago so that we could all swim year-round without having to walk up to the club. It's pretty sweet." This time, his smile seemed even more obviously false.

"I can see that," Shiloh replied. Sensing Jeff's discomfort at mentioning his sister and mother, Shiloh told him that she was sorry for their loss.

"We're dealing with it as well as people could expect, I guess," Jeff said, in a way that told Shiloh the opposite was more likely the truth. "Jack's taking it pretty hard. He's just sixteen. Dad is struggling too. He's hired a therapist. She came out the day after it happened to do a group session with all of us. We're supposed to go every day individually for a while."

"What about Scarlet?" Shiloh inquired. "I'd think it would be difficult for her too, especially now that she's the only girl left."

"Oh, Scarlet already had a therapist," Jeff answered. "Mom and Dad have been making her go to one for as long as I can remember. She seems the most okay of any of us. You can't ever really tell with Scarlet. She's, like, always sad about something." They'd arrived at the end of the corridor. Jeff opened the door to his father's office for Shiloh, then left to go back to the pool.

Inside, Joe Arnold's office was filled with highly polished, dark mahogany gun display cabinets and heavy maroon leather furniture. Behind his desk were built-in, lighted plexiglass cases filled with expensive-looking signed sports memorabilia. From between the shelves, heads of long-dead big game animals—a cougar, a bighorn sheep, and a moose—glared down at her with their unseeing glass eyes. Just to the left of the door, an enormous full-size grizzly bear stood on its hind legs, snarling at all who entered. On a big flatscreen television as long as a small car, an old Western movie played.

Wondering whether Joe remembered her from the alumni event, Shiloh introduced herself. Remaining on the leather sofa, Joe left the volume up and never took his eyes from the screen as he motioned for her to sit down. He did not object when Shiloh asked if she could record their conversation. As Shiloh unpacked her laptop and set up the microphone, Joe took a long sip from the cut-glass tumbler that he'd held protectively with both hands as she walked in. Draining its contents, he rose to get a refill. Shiloh noted that he did not offer her a drink.

"Bernie tells me you're here to talk about Jasmine," Joe said loudly, over the dialogue on the television, as he sank back into the sofa. "Whaddaya wanna know?"

Surprised by the bluntness of his question, Shiloh stammered. "Um... anything you have to tell me. If you've spoken to Bernadette, then she probably told you that she's hired me to look into her sister's disappearance. Hopefully you can forgive me for speaking freely in light of everything else that has happened—please rest assured that I am not judging you for it—but I understand that you and Jasmine were romantically involved."

"Yep," Joe said simply, taking another long sip of his drink. From the smell, Shiloh thought it was scotch. Then, Joe's blank expression twisted into a sneer that Shiloh recognized from the old photo she'd seen in Ethan's yearbook. The cocky look that said, *Hurry the hell up.*

"And please *feel free*," Joe leaned on the last two words. "Judge me all you want. I'm a rich guy whose girlfriend went missing and whose wife and daughter were murdered, all within a couple of weeks. Roman said you used to be a public defender, but you quit after Ethan got shot. If you're some bullshit, half-assed PI now, I'm sure this must be like Christmas for you. So please, *feel free* to allow your imagination to run wild. Just remember," Joe leaned over to growl hoarsely into the microphone. "If any of this shit ends up on one of those goddamn true crime shows, I'll have Roman hang your ass. He might have been your brother-in-law once upon a time, but he's been my best friend forever. Got that?"

Refusing to allow Joe the satisfaction of feeling as if his demeanor intimidated her, Shiloh merely nodded in acknowledgment and pulled out a notepad from her bag. "Mr. Arnold, I assure you that I'm only here to get as much information as I can that might help us to find Jasmine Jenkins. A cause I understand that even you support. So, I'd like to begin at the start of your relationship with Jasmine. How did the two of you meet?"

"Hasn't Bernie already told you?" Joe replied. "It was at that Christmas fundraiser for the Foundation. Jazzy came on to me first. Putting her tits in my face as she reached across the table, rubbing her ass against me as she walked by with a tray. She's an eye-catching woman, and I could tell she was trying to get my attention. Toward the end of the night, I followed her into the pool room, which was empty by then. We did a couple of shots and flirted. She had some blow on her, and we did a couple lines of that too. One thing led to another. She ended up calling the guy who was supposed to be her ride home. Said she'd met someone and decided to stay over."

"The guy that Jasmine called," Shiloh said. "Did she ever mention his name?"

"Not that night," Joe replied. Shiloh felt his initial hostility ebbing somewhat as Joe realized she'd been truthful about her intentions for their meeting. "Later on, after we got to know each other better, she'd talk about this guy she called The Prophet. Said he was her dealer. I didn't think that much about it. Everyone's gotta get their supply from somewhere. Most of those dudes on the street have weird nicknames. Jazzy only fessed up after Ethan was shot that this Prophet dude was her pimp too."

"Did that bother you?" Shiloh continued, choosing to ignore Joe's casual mention of her husband's murder. "That Jasmine was a sex worker? Were you concerned that she was only into you for the money?"

Joe let out a deep-throated squawk of a laugh. "Hell no! I mean, I was surprised at first. Went to the docs to get tested. When everything came back okay, it wasn't a big deal to me. Especially because she never charged me a dime. I gave her a lot of stuff, though, just because I wanted to. A beautiful woman should have beautiful things. Isn't every woman after every man in this world for that kind of stuff in some way or another if she's hot enough to pull it off?"

"No," Shiloh said, deadpan. It was getting harder not to let her revulsion for Joe Arnold show with every passing minute of their conversation.

"Well, maybe that's a slight exaggeration," Joe answered, taking another sip of his scotch. "Perhaps it's only 99%. Anyway, that's how it's always been for me. Shit, even with Veronica in the early days, I knew why she was there. I mean, look around!" Joe gestured with his tumbler to include the room. "Ronni went to public school at Withrow and grew up on the wrong side of Dana Avenue before it gentrified. When we finally crossed paths at Ohio State, I could tell she almost came in her pants when I told her who I was. Later on, it was a different story. But I think having kids does that to some women. Messes up their female hormones or something, and they just turn into complete bitches. They've been doing a lot of scientific studies. I see new data coming out all the time about it on Fox News."

"I'm sure you do," Shiloh said, trying not to let her tone of voice express sarcasm. "Getting back to Jasmine, did she ever tell you she was the daughter of your old high school football buddy, Dr. Kash Khoury?"

"Whaaaat?" Joe's glassy eyes grew wide as he drew out the word before erupting into another loud cackle. "Who told you that shit? Kash only has two kids, a boy and a girl!"

"Her sister, Bernie," Shiloh replied. "Their mother, Destiny, was working as a nurse for Dr. Khoury when Jasmine was conceived. They were having an affair."

"Oh man," Joe sighed, as the information sunk in. "No, I didn't know that. Jasmine never told me. I can see why she'd keep it a secret, though. Helen's claws would come out if she knew. That old bat's loaded, which was why Kash married her in the first place. All the Altmans were. It was one of those business merger marriages, if you know what I mean. Helen can be vicious when she wants to be, in a stealthy sort of way. Did Kash know?"

"Yes," Shiloh said. "Bernie said Dr. Khoury supported Jasmine financially all her life. He helped their family from time to time, even recommending her to you for the job she has now, teaching your children and working with your Foundation."

"That makes sense then," Joe nodded. "Back in the day, I'd wondered if Kash was pushing me so hard to hire Bernie because she was his younger squeeze he was trying to offload. Never occurred to me that..." Joe trailed off, sneering to himself as he drained the remainder of his glass a second time. "Kash is a slyer old bastard than I gave him credit for. Jasmine's mom must have been a real looker for him to take the risk. It's always the quiet ones."

"It does seem that way, doesn't it?" Shiloh asked patronizingly, glancing at the antique mahogany grandfather clock in the corner. She needed to hurry the discussion along if she was going to meet Bernie for dinner in an hour. "I don't want to take up your whole afternoon, Mr. Arnold, so just a few more questions. Could you tell me about the last time you saw Jasmine? What did she look like? Was there anything different about her personality, or was she associating with anyone new?"

Instantly, Joe's demeanor grew serious and more guarded. "Bernie said she'd already explained to you about this part."

"Yes, she did, but I'd like to hear your impressions of it too," Shiloh said, then added reassuringly, "for confirmation."

Joe swirled the large, swiftly melting single spherical ice cube around in the bottom of his glass. He began pacing around the room, pointing out various small abstract paintings on the walls that Shiloh had barely noticed because they were beneath the animal heads. When he spoke, Joe did not answer her question.

"It's no secret that I've had some issues with addictions through the years," Joe explained. "Kind of a cliche, isn't it? A pharmacy chain owner gets addicted to his own shit. But I've always found my way out, one way or another. Painting helps. I picked that up on my last trip through rehab at that Asclepius place over in Switzerland. Golfing always helped too. Anything that makes my mind focus on one thing at a time. The last time it got really bad was ten years ago. That was about the time Ronni and I started having real problems. Before, I'd always been very careful around the kids. They'd seen me drunk, but not the rest of it. That time, though, I got sloppy. Usually, I kept my stash in here, with the door locked. The kids were warned never to go into Dad's office unless I was there, but you know how kids are. One day, I left the door open. When I came back, Vanna and Scarlet were sitting right there on that rug."

Joe nodded at the floor as his eyes started to go red. "They'd found a bunch of pills in the desk drawer and thought they were candy. In a panic, I grabbed Savannah up by her arm and demanded to know if they'd eaten any of them. She told me yes, and that she was sorry but not to worry because they must have been stale. They didn't taste good anymore. We took them both to the ER and had their stomachs pumped. Luckily, we made it in time."

"Oh my God," Shiloh said, truly shocked. "You were very lucky. What were the pills?"

"Some oxy, some Percocet," Joe replied. "Whatever I was taking at the time. There were always plenty of drug rep samples available so that I never had to overstep my real prescription. And samples of a lot of new derivatives for other drugs that were big movers. Independent labs were always sending me samples to review because they knew getting on with a chain was a big boost to sales. Mostly things that had just gone out of patent and into generic, but sometimes entirely new products that were still in the provisional approval phase."

Joe sat back down on the leather sofa. "That was the last straw for Ronni. She demanded a divorce. I'm Catholic, so I didn't want one. Of course, she knew that I had Roman and Horace Mueller on my side, so she couldn't get custody of the kids. Ultimately, we agreed that I'd go away to rehab. When I came back clean again, we would remain married but live separately. We never put the agreement in writing. If it went public, I could lose my license, and it would mean the end of Arnold's Drugs. Instead, we agreed to hire a live-in tutor and nanny. That way, Ronni could live in a separate household but feel better that the kids were still being watched over. She no longer trusted me. I'm not an easy man to scare, but that scared me. I could have lost Vanna that day. And now..."

Joe Arnold raised his hands in frustration toward the ceiling as tears began to well up in his eyes. "Now I've lost Vanna in this horrible way. Despite everything I've tried. The drugs still found her."

"So you knew Savannah was using before she went missing," Shiloh said softly. Although she detested the man, it was hard to watch anyone clearly in so much pain.

Nodding, Joe sniffed deeply and began massaging his temples with both hands. "Ronni and I both knew. My wife's always been a health nut. Organic this, vegan that. Before she moved out, Ronni even had a yoga and meditation room set up on the other end of the house. No one has gone in there since she moved out, except Scarlet. She's the one who misses her mom the most. They were both into all that new-age bullshit. Vanna was her Daddy's girl, but Scarlet?" Joe shook his head. "She's all Ronni, except for the looks, which were the best part of her mother. Poor kid."

Avoiding comment on Joe's blatant favoritism, Shiloh waited patiently for Joe to gather his thoughts enough to continue.

"To get back to your main question, though, I'm sure you're thinking the same thing that I did. That Vanna got in too deep with a dealer, and he killed her. Vanna and I kept no secrets from one another. I knew that she liked to party, but what pretty girl her age doesn't? Sure, I worried about her, but she was smart enough to take care of herself. Or so I thought. She told me that she smoked weed and did a little Molly or a bump of Adderall now and then. I didn't think anything about it. Her mother, Ronni, went through the roof when she found out, though. Blew it way out of proportion and demanded that Vanna quit immediately. Which I think created the whole situation. Vanna got scared of pissing off her mom, stiffed whoever she was buying from, and whoever it was killed her. And when Ronni went looking for her, they killed her too."

"That's an interesting theory, Mr. Arnold. And I don't disagree with you about the possibility," Shiloh said. She couldn't tell if Joe was really distraught and just rambling as he tried to shift blame for his daughter's death onto his dead wife, or if he was deliberately avoiding answering her actual question about the last time he'd seen Jasmine. She decided to attempt one more time to get a straight answer by trying a different angle. "So if you think that there might be a dangerous dealer on the loose who is willing to kill women who don't pay, do you suppose that might have been what happened to Jasmine too? Did you say when the last time you saw her was?"

Sensing that his evasion wasn't working, Joe's mood became defensive. "Who do you think you are, anyway? Worming your way into a man's home and asking all sorts of these personal questions when you know two members of his family have been murdered. You're not a cop, and you're not a real lawyer anymore. You're not even a PI trying to figure out who killed my wife and daughter. You're just somebody my housekeeper hired to find her whore sister. How the fuck am I supposed to remember the last time I saw Jasmine after all I've been through? Maybe a couple of months ago? She always showed up and left whenever she pleased. Sometimes in the middle of the night. To be honest, I was thinking about ending things between us because she got weird. She never wanted to hook up anymore and was starting to look a little ragged. I could tell something was wrong, but I didn't want to get into it. When we first got together, we promised each other that there were no strings attached and no stories to be told. No baggage. It was just about having a good time. We were both down with that, so when she stopped showing up, I figured she'd just moved on. That's what gold diggers do, right? From time to time they just find another old man to mooch off. It was only when Bernie brought it up that she hadn't been in touch with her for over a month that it started bothering me at all."

"But you are worried something has happened to Jasmine too," Shiloh insisted. "Haven't you wondered, Mr. Arnold, why three women close to you, four if you count the daughter of your best friend across the street, have turned up dead or gone missing recently?"

Joe Arnold sprang to his feet and hurled his crystal whisky tumbler across the room. It hit the wall and shattered, spraying bits of glass. "I've had enough of your goddamned questions! Get the fuck out of my house!" he roared.

Grabbing her laptop and bag, Shiloh bolted across the office. The microphone fell off the coffee table, trailing behind her by the cord attached to her laptop. Snatching it up, she blundered through the heavy oak door. On the way out, she bumped into a petite teenage girl with long, curly black hair and dropped the mic again.

"Oh my god, I'm so sorry!" The girl exclaimed. Shiloh noticed she was accompanied by a skinny, nervous-looking black dog wearing an emotional support animal vest. The girl wore the stereotypical uniform of goth girls everywhere. A dark plaid mini skirt, a black tank top, clunky black leather engineer boots, and deep purple lipstick that contrasted dramatically with her pale skin. Her fashion choices couldn't have been more opposite to those of her Abercrombie model brothers' style if she'd tried. When the girl picked up the mic and handed it over, Shiloh could feel a piece of paper folded into the collapsible stand. She saw the panicked expression in the girl's small, dark eyes as she whispered two words. *Call me.*

"Scarlet, what are you doing?" Her father demanded. "I thought you were supposed to be in your piano lesson."

"It's after five. The tutor just left," Scarlet replied, her voice unnaturally calm.

"Then get out of the way," Joe sputtered, clearly agitated at finding his youngest daughter eavesdropping. "I need to show Ms. Foley to the door."

"That's okay," Shiloh replied curtly, giving a quick nod that she hoped communicated her thanks to Scarlet. "I'll find my way out."

Monday, October 9th, Evening

B y the time Shiloh got out to Mazunte in Madisonville for her dinner meeting with Bernadette, it was almost eight o'clock. While they were waiting on the deserted patio for their orders to be brought out, Shiloh filled Bernie in on the details of her meeting with Joe Arnold.

Taking a long sip of her margarita, Bernie sighed and rolled her eyes. "Typical. I'm sorry you had to go through with all that. Perhaps it gave you a clearer perspective of what Joe's like and the kinds of relationships he has with women. He flies off the handle at me over the slightest problems with his kids' homeschooling and minor issues at the Foundation all the time. I've always chalked it up to drug use making his personality volatile. Joe's an old burnout with a short fuse. I've never thought that he was the one responsible for Jazzy's disappearance though. Sadly, he'd never go to that much trouble, particularly for a woman who for him was just another fling. What I was hoping for was some kind of insight into who this Prophet person was. I think he's probably the one who's responsible for whatever happened to my sister."

"I was too," Shiloh agreed, as the server set down their orders. She'd gotten her favorite fish tacos, and Bernie ordered chicken. After they'd each had a bite or two of what Shiloh always mentally referred to as the good white cheese dip, she continued. "Unfortunately, Joe seems as clueless as we are. His hostility was a mask to cover up his embarrassment at his affair with Jasmine being called out, I could tell. But I didn't get the feeling that he had any animosity toward Jasmine at all. Joe wanted no strings attached.

With her disappearance threatening to uncover an entire web of lies that he'd rather keep hidden, especially now that he's under media scrutiny because of the murders of his wife and daughters, Joe's in panic mode."

"Understandable," Bernie replied, covering her mouth politely with her hand as she chewed. "Rich old white guys are usually the villains in pretty much any American missing person's narrative nowadays. I'm sure Joe's scared to death that he'll become a suspect, and life as he knows it will be over in a heartbeat."

"Well, from what I understand, Joe's not exactly a saint," Shiloh replied. "Even if he's not responsible for Jasmine's disappearance, he's certainly hurt at least one person in the past very seriously. Judging from the lavish lifestyle he's living now, I doubt he's ever been called to answer for it."

"Oh?" Bernie looked up from her meal. "What happened?"

Shiloh hesitated a moment, weighing whether or not she should tell Bernie what she'd found in her husband Ethan's journal. She studied the woman sitting across the table from her. Flawless hair and makeup, even late in the evening, had been applied over an intelligent, attractive face bearing no semblance of guile. Navy blazer, crisp silk blouse, highly polished simple gold hoop earrings—she'd thought out every element of her outward appearance with great care. Probably the same degree of care that she'd taken in each step of her strategically planned professional life. Shiloh knew Bernie's story, where she'd come from. The question was whether she could trust her with information that she was not quite yet sure she could process herself. Discoveries that she'd felt uncomfortable disclosing to her husband's police partner, Bruce Schultz, earlier that day. Shiloh looked at Bernadette. At her open, inquisitive expression. She considered the totality of all that she knew about her family and her past. Then, Shiloh told her everything.

"Jesus!" Bernie breathed. She pushed her plate aside. "I... I had no idea."

"No one did," Shiloh replied. "As I said, Ethan told no one what he'd seen. The only reason I knew about it was that I went looking through a box of his old yearbooks when I was trying to remember the names of some people whom I'd been introduced to at the reunion. That's when I found the journal."

Bernie took a long sip of the margarita she'd been nursing. "I knew that the Arnold family kept a lot of secrets but would never have suspected that Joe was capable of... that. It's too horrible to even imagine. That poor boy.

I wonder what happened to him." Here, Bernie paused for a moment, as if she were trying to decide whether she could trust Shiloh too.

"Joe Arnold is a man of many secrets," Bernie continued, contemplatively swirling her straw around in the almost empty glass. "Secrets that would humiliate him if they came to light. For example, did he say anything about Veronica's affair?"

"No," Shiloh replied. "But I can understand why. Not only would it be embarrassing to admit, but it could be construed as a motive in her murder case."

"Mmm," Bernie mused, cocking her head to one side. "I wouldn't say that, because they stayed married for so long afterward. When you said that you bumped into his youngest daughter in the hallway, did you get a good look at her?"

"Not really," Shiloh said. "Enough to see that she was different from the others. A goth kid in a house full of preppies, but that's all. I figured it was just a rich girl's rebellious phase."

"Well," Bernie continued. "I'm sure if you looked more closely and considered the resemblance, you'd have noticed that Joe Arnold's second daughter bears a striking resemblance to Joe's old buddy, Rafferty Purcell."

"Wait... what?" Shiloh stammered, trying to wrap her mind around the idea.

"It's okay. I was just as confused by it as you were when I first found out," Bernie replied. "Veronica was unhappy in her marriage to Joe for a long time. From what I've come to understand, they were just two very different people who happened to meet in college. Veronica was a cheerleader and in a sorority, and Joe..." Bernie shrugged. "Joe at least hung around as a third-string alternate on the football team. He threw great parties, though, with his daddy's money, and that's what caught Ronni's eye. After college, they were all still close friends. Joe's guys from St. Augustine's and their wives. They were close enough that when Ronni initially thought that she wanted a divorce, Rafferty Purcell was the first person she called. Purcell was newly divorced from his wife, Francine Altman, who is Helen Altman Khoury's sister. Rafferty agreed to help Ronni split her investments off from Joe's as part of the divorce settlement. One thing led to another, and somehow Veronica and Rafferty became lovers. About a year or so after Scarlet was born, it became impossible to deny that two blonde-haired, blue-eyed humans like Joe and Ronni could have given birth to a dark-eyed daughter with black curly hair like Scarlet. However, Joe Arnold chose to deny it anyway. The insinuation would have been more than he could bear. To save face, Joe always tried to treat Scarlet the same as his other children. Still, if you've met Rafferty and the girl, it's normal to at least suspect who her birth father was. Their resemblance is uncanny."

"Now that I think about it," Shiloh replied. "It makes perfect sense. In our conversation, he implied that Ronni chose to leave after Savannah and Scarlet accidentally took some pills from his office stash. He seemed scared that Vanna could have died, but not Scarlet. To a man obsessed with keeping up hyper-masculine appearances, a near-miss scare like that would play better to his buds at the golf club than having to admit his wife ran around on him. Although, what puzzles me is why Ronni went back to Joe after her initial affair with Purcell. Given that she ended up leaving anyway in the end, what made Veronica return?"

"Appearances again," Bernie replied. "Joe's not the only one who would have been embarrassed by his wife's affair with Purcell. When Scarlet was born and the resemblance was so immediately striking, rumors began to fly around the club. Rafferty's always been viewed as a sort of hanger-on in their set. Ronni might have been down to spite fuck him to piss off Joe, but she'd never dream of actually continuing the relationship. Raff wanted that, I'm sure, but it would have been too much of a blow to her pride. The easiest way out for Ronni was to retreat into her marriage to Joe. Cover it up by spending her life and his money at one spa retreat or another, and the whole thing just got smoothed over as another bump along the rocky road of their relationship."

"Wow," Shiloh sighed, taking it all in. "Rich people and their image obsession. I hate to say it, but if Ronni were so embarrassed by the accidental pregnancy, why didn't she just have an abortion? It would have been so much simpler to not bring an unwanted child into the world."

"You forget," Bernie replied, pushing her empty plate away. "The Arnolds are Catholics. Both of them, although Joe's always been more into it. Regardless of whether rich or poor, they don't do abortions and will try almost anything to avoid divorce. Ronni got into all the New Age spirituality stuff as a way to cope after she realized Joe would never give her a real divorce without taking everything away from her. Not just custody of the kids, but the house, the money, everything. Her whole lifestyle. I'm sure Joe explained that Ronni came from a basic working-class family. He loves to brag about it. How his family money helped him bag the hottest babe on the Ohio State cheerleading squad." Bernie rolled her eyes as she put air quotes around the last phrase. "Joe's words, not mine."

"What a stupid thing to be proud of," Shiloh said, shaking her head. "I don't think Joe Arnold's mind ever left high school. Which is super weird, considering the rest of it."

"I agree. It's very disturbing," Bernie seconded. "But actually, I don't think many of those guys from St. Augustine truly ever left. Your husband Ethan seems to have been an anomaly. If you'd spent as much time around that bunch as I've had to, working with the Arnolds and their foundation, you'd know. They're almost like some kind of underground cult."

"I don't see how you stand it," Shiloh said, as they gathered their things to leave. "You must have the patience of Job. After Ethan died, it made me take a really hard look at what my life had become, working within the justice system. I realized that if I hadn't made any positive changes in over a decade at the public defender's office, I wasn't ever going to. It was just an idealistic dream that was well past the expiration date. I couldn't deal with the charade of the justice system anymore. So I gave up and opened a PI office."

"That was probably a wise choice. I've always joked that it should be called the injustice system if people wanted to be accurate." Bernie said. "Getting back to your other statement, though, I'm actually on the verge of accepting a new fundraising position with the Cancer Society. They've been reaching out to me for over a year now, begging for an interview. That's where I was this afternoon, after the meeting. They made me an offer. I told them I'd have to think it over. It doesn't quite match what the Arnolds are paying me, but it doesn't include the double duty of homeschool teacher and Foundation manager either. Although it would be nice to have some free time on my hands, I don't know what I would do with it. Plus, if I'm going to make the move, I'd want to be sure that Scarlet's situation is resolved first."

"What kind of situation?" Shiloh asked.

"Oh, it's just that I want to help her see through her application to boarding school," Bernie answered. "She's applied to Interlochen. It's the top arts high school in the country and super competitive. Joe's boys would be fine with any tutor. Neither of them is especially academic. Jackson has some musical talent, but he wastes it by not practicing, and Jeff's just a typical jock. However, Scarlet's extremely bright, and her musical skills are the best I've ever heard for her age. Even so, I've warned her that she might not get accepted and that she should apply to other schools as backup. That way, when she presents the idea to her father, it will come off as well-reasoned. Joe's going to fly off the handle regardless. He's convinced that almost all schools nowadays, public and private, are full of woke rhetoric and teach nothing but leftist indoctrination. That's the whole reason he chose to homeschool them in the first place. I can only imagine what he'll say when his daughter announces she wants to go to some hippie performing arts high school up in Michigan. It's not going to be easy. I want to be there in case Joe needs someone to point the finger of blame at. I'd much rather have him vent his frustration by firing me than take it out on the girl."

"That's very kind of you," Shiloh said. "Hopefully, Scarlet will appreciate what you're trying to do. Boarding school sounds like the best option. With her mother gone and you possibly leaving too, she's lost every support system she has."

"True," Bernadette said. "According to what Ronni told me, Rafferty chose not to acknowledge Scarlet after Ronni decided to get back together with Joe. That's kind of where the girl's name came from. Ronni named her after *The Scarlet Letter* but covered it up by telling Joe it was from *Gone With the Wind*. He likes Old South names."

"Why am I not surprised?" Shiloh replied, shaking her head as she recognized the theme of the names of Joe Arnold's other children. Savannah, the daughter who'd been murdered, had a typical Southern name. Jefferson and Jackson were both slaveholding Southern presidents. Having been named by her own mother after the place of one of General Grant's bloodiest Civil War victories, Shiloh was surprised that she hadn't made the connection sooner. So many things in the region went back to that period if one dug deeply enough.

"One more thing," she said, pulling the folded piece of paper out of her pocket that she'd retrieved from where it was wedged into her mic stand. "As I was leaving Joe Arnold's, Scarlet gave me this and told me to call her. I'm assuming it's her cell number. I haven't called it yet, but I wonder what she might know about her mother's and sister's murders that she seems so reluctant to talk about in front of the rest of her family. Since Scarlet doesn't go to regular school, I didn't know if there was a best time to get in touch so that we could speak privately. Any ideas?"

Bernadette glanced at the paper. "Yes, that's Scarlet's cell number. As for what information she might have, I'm just as clueless as you are. I'd love to find out, though I wonder why she hasn't said anything to me about it." Bernie paused, thinking. "Anyway, the next best time to catch her alone is Tuesday night, when she practices with the youth orchestra at Music Hall. She plays flute there, in addition to piano at home. I usually drop her off around six. They finish at nine. I can stall picking her up for half an hour to give you two an opportunity to chat."

"Guess I'm going to the symphony tomorrow night," Shiloh replied as they exchanged goodbyes.

Monday, October 9th, Late Evening

B ack home in Mount Adams a half hour later, Shiloh found herself restless. She knew it was because she hadn't been to the gym since the day before finding the bodies of Veronica and Savannah Arnold. Knowing that the gym was already closed but that she needed to expend some pent-up energy to be able to fall asleep, Shiloh decided to take a walk around Eden Park. On especially stressful days, she liked to go up to her favorite spot overlooking the Ohio River to meditate. Often, she took a small pouch of crystals with her to set out in a grid, if she found the place empty of other visitors. It helped to support and clarify her thinking. Changing out of her blazer, blouse, and loafers into a t-shirt, hoodie, and sneakers with her dark jeans, Shiloh put her velvet pouch of crystals into her crossbody bag and gave William a quick belly rub before heading out. The large gray cat purred loudly as a lawnmower engine.

The waning crescent moon hung low in the sky, offering minimal light. Shiloh walked swiftly around the Playhouse in the Park and the outdoor Seasongood Pavilion amphitheater. Passing a couple of dog walkers making their last rounds before tucking in for the night, Shiloh tried to acknowledge them but was met with indifferent stares. Growing up in small-town Kentucky, she'd always been taught to at least smile and give a nod to passersby. Even after almost fifteen years on the other side of the Ohio River, Shiloh still couldn't get used to how rarely people spoke to strangers.

Perhaps that's one of the reasons why they keep the same friends they've had since high school, she reasoned. *If you never pay attention to strangers, they can never become friends.*

As she followed her usual path to the higher of the park's two overlooks, Shiloh contemplated the many differences between her upbringing and Ethan's. Shiloh's father, Peter James Foley Jr., or P.J., as everyone called him, ran the Treasure Chest Pawn Shop in the blue and white building at the corner of Main and Ninth Streets in Covington for as long as she could remember. Her mother, Amelia, was first diagnosed with breast cancer when Shiloh was eight. She passed away when her daughter was twelve, at the age of forty-four. Although she'd been terrified to go in for her first mammogram and genetic testing the week of her fortieth birthday in January, Shiloh was relieved to learn that not only was she completely healthy, but that she lacked any of the markers predisposing her to cancer.

Sadly, Shiloh remembered little of life with her mother before Amelia's diagnosis, other than the fact that she often seemed tired all the time. It was ironic because, in her early years, Amelia Gaines's life was a whirlwind of activity. A professionally trained ballerina, Amelia toured with several companies before semi-retiring and returning home to Northern Kentucky. There, she quickly met and married P.J. Foley. Initially, Amelia planned to open a dance studio for children in one of the many fix-and-flip buildings in Covington that P.J. seemed to be constantly acquiring in his daily wheelings and dealings. However, Shiloh was born a little over a year later. Just before Shiloh began kindergarten, her younger brother Peter James Foley the Third, or Three-Pete, as Shiloh dubbed him, followed. Thus, Amelia Foley's ambition to open a school of dance was delayed a second time. A few more years passed, and Amelia's declining health made it impossible.

After her mother's death, Shiloh became the *de facto* head of the Foley household. She learned to cook at an early age. Within a year, Shiloh told her father straight up that he needed to hire a housekeeper to come in once a week because she couldn't deal with school, cleaning, and watching over Three-Pete simultaneously. Deciding that the family would benefit from some quiet time together out in the country, her father bought an old farm dirt cheap in Boone County. It was down the road from the regionally famous Rabbit Hash General Store. P.J. Foley never remarried. Instead, he spent most of his time either hanging out with his friends from the Treasure Chest back in Covington, dabbling in local conservative politics and eventually serving on the town council, or out tinkering in his woodworking shop on the farm in Rabbit Hash.

Father and son bonded over working together to restore old furniture. In turn, that resulted in Three-Pete's eventual career path as an antique dealer and creator of new antique-inspired reproductions, primarily for commercial use in hotels and restaurants. Over the years, Foley's Furnishings continued to grow. It eventually encompassed an entire city block of downtown Covington in the Mainstrasse District. Through shrewd maneuvering, P.J. Foley and son bought the derelict warehouses out of foreclosure sales for pennies on the dollar. It had become one of the signature businesses in the area. Foley's Furnishings was written up in all the local home and style magazines. It had even been depicted on several streaming network decor and picker-themed television road shows. Like all the Foley men, neither Three-Pete nor his father P.J. ever attended a day of college. Instead, they preferred to tout the virtues of being self-made owners of independent businesses who were always their own bosses.

Growing up, Shiloh knew that nothing would have made her father happier than for her to come up with some kind of business selling something. According to P.J., all the Foley men since their arrival in America from Ireland had been salesmen of one kind or another. However, Shiloh never possessed the sort of good old boy charisma that seemed essential for a career as a small-town business owner. Instead, while her little brother had been their father's shadow, an eager participant observer of P.J.'s endless dealmaking, Shiloh preferred to remain at home or in the library. Shiloh loved the quiet stillness and order of libraries. She spent a great deal of time there from the summer her mother died onward.

It was in the calm coolness of the public library that Shiloh first found her calling into her lifelong interest in metaphysics, where she read and contemplated the works of nature-based philosophy. At the urging of well-meaning relatives and grief counselors, she'd tried praying to the traditional Christian idea of God with a child's earnestness during the first days of her mother's illness. Yet, it seemed that the harder she prayed, the sicker Amelia became. Following Amelia's death, the Foley household was overrun with an outpouring of support from friends and relatives. Although Shiloh knew that these people meant well, as the weeks turned into months with every day bringing another person stopping to share a story or dropping some photo or trinket by the house, it became overwhelming. Plus, their attempts to engage often felt hollow and inauthentic, because so few of them really knew Amelia. Never a girl to seek attention, Shiloh longed for an escape from their suffocating sympathy, from being a sounding board for their grief. She needed a way to mourn her mother alone.

Ultimately, she found solace in what she had over the years come to call her natural rituals. Sitting alone in the woods with only the wind and the river for company, Shiloh found her gods in the forest. It was a relief to mentally converse with curious animals and silent trees. They always simply listened, without offering empty assurances of an afterlife. When Shiloh spoke to the river, she sensed that the river replied that nothing was eternal, except change. The only thing that could be counted on, the river said, was that mountains would be worn down to sand, and that sand would wash down to the sea. Then, the sand would gather and harden, growing into mountains once more, continuing the circle of life that was elemental and eternal.

Because Shiloh was just a girl then, and could only sense what the river was telling her without knowing its actual words, she sought out language to give voice to these feelings in the library. She found them first in a series of English books called *Man, Myth, and Magic*, and later in many works of New Age spirituality. There, she learned about the healing power of nature and her place within its cycles. She kept that knowledge secret, carried close to her heart like a necklace tucked inside a blouse. When she turned sixteen, she bought a silver tree of life necklace with a pearl woven into its branches at a Renaissance faire because it reminded her of those lessons. She wore it until the chain broke and she lost it, ironically, in the ocean during her senior trip to the beach. Then, she bought a gold necklace with the same symbol at an antique shop on Dixie Highway. She was more careful with the second amulet and continued to wear it every day afterward as a silent memento of her place in the universe, in the eternity between mother Earth and father Sky.

After high school, Shiloh won a full-ride academic scholarship to the University of Kentucky. An anthropology and sociology double major, she'd simply cycled back into law school out of sheer lack of anything else better to do. Unfortunately, like many first-gen attorneys, Shiloh had been under the mistaken impression that the law was a lucrative career path for all who entered. Being the first in her family to earn a college degree, let alone finish graduate school, Shiloh struggled in her attempts to find employment as a lawyer, even though she passed both the Kentucky and Ohio bar exams on the first try. Despite sending out over three hundred applications to law firms, Shiloh did not receive a single offer. Although her father tried to push her into hanging out a shingle, Shiloh knew better. Any potential clients recruited by P.J. Foley through his network of acquaintances at Treasure Chest Pawn were bound to be broke and need to barter legal fees for things like lawn care services or cut-rate auto repair if they made any effort to pay her at all. It was then that Shiloh began to realize that law, like most other supposedly prestigious occupations in America, was a field reserved for the intergenerational elite and their chosen few. Newcomers, especially from small-town backgrounds with few connections outside of the pawn shop crowd, need not apply.

It also didn't help that Shiloh graduated in 2008, the year the market collapsed, taking legal hiring down with it. Having a vague idea that she'd like to do something to advance the cause of social justice and lacking a book of paying clients or well-to-do relations necessary for admittance into what was still the elite old boys' club of big-name firms, Shiloh started putting in for government jobs. Eventually, she was hired as a Youth Defense Counselor in the Hamilton County Public Defender's Office across the river in Cincinnati. Her main function was to attempt to keep juvenile drug offenders and petty thieves out of jail. Instead, she tried to steer them toward various rehabilitation programs in which they could hope to build productive lives. Although certainly not the path to riches that law schools across the country touted, over almost fifteen years of service, Shiloh finally managed to work her way up from not quite forty grand a year to almost sixty. By 2015, the money was enough to keep her in decent-looking suits from Banana Republic, albeit from the company's outlet mall stores, and to pay the bills on a two-bedroom apartment in a repurposed elementary school building just off Eden Park, in the part of Walnut Hills that was trying to gentrify.

That was the year Shiloh met Ethan. He'd just come back from a second tour of duty in Afghanistan and was attending college online through the University of Akron while working as a patrol officer. Akron had a special accelerated program in criminal justice for former military personnel. Ethan zipped through in three years by going to school year-round to expedite his promotion to detective. They'd bonded initially over a shared interest in deviant psychology. That was what first tipped Shiloh off to the fact that Ethan wasn't just an average cop. He wanted to understand and help the people whom he arrested. It took Ethan almost a year of getting coffee together and talking theory before he'd finally asked her out on a proper date. He claimed the delay was because he was afraid she'd say no, and he didn't want to have to live it down in front of both sets of their colleagues. Once he did, though, they were inseparable in a matter of weeks. Before the end of the year, they moved into a small house Ethan bought on the border between Hyde Park and Oakley. It was just big enough to accommodate the two of them and William, who then was still a kitten.

However, it was another two years before Ethan allowed Shiloh to meet his family. At first, Shiloh worried that it was because he was ashamed of her background. Which held nothing truly dishonorable, unless one went back in time far enough to drag up the fact that her grandfather, "Perfect" Pete Foley Sr., was a part-time bootlegger who ran a cab company as a front to move Newport-made moonshine back and forth across the Ohio River. The old man's nickname came from the coded way he responded to greeting potential customers in search of liquor. Upon meeting him, the buyer was supposed to comment on the "perfect" weather, to which he would reply, "Yes, perfect, perfect," twice, whether rain or shine, to indicate that he had some hooch to sell. Considering the colorful history of Newport, Kentucky, as the booze-fueled boomtown it once was, most people found tales of Perfect Pete entertaining rather than embarrassing. In the two generations since, Shiloh's father, P.J., and her brother, Three-Pete, operated mostly above-board, prosperous businesses and served small roles in public service. That tended to make the Foley family viewed as respectable members of the middle class on their side of the river.

Later, after he reluctantly introduced her to them, Shiloh realized that it wasn't her family background that Ethan was ashamed of, but his own. The issue was that being an average, respectable person simply was not good enough for anyone hoping to be accepted into the Mueller clan. For them, being the best at everything wasn't an achievement but an expectation. Similarly, their wealth and the life of relative ease that it bought was not a reward to be enjoyed, but rather an ongoing enterprise to be perpetually expanded upon.

As she reached the upper overlook that marked the halfway point of her walk-in circumnavigation of Eden Park and glanced around for a place to sit and meditate, Shiloh recalled the first time Ethan took her to meet his brother Roman and sister-in-law Kimberly for dinner. Roman chose the restaurant, the Fourth Avenue branch of Jeff Ruby's Steakhouse, because he liked to smoke cigars on the patio. Shiloh had only eaten there twice before, with her father and brother once each after her college and law school graduations. The food was excellent, but it was a place that she associated with only very special occasions because of the expense. Roman waltzed in with the three of them in tow, asking for his usual table without a reservation. When the hostess knew immediately what he meant, Shiloh understood what Ethan had tried to very carefully conceal up to that point in their relationship. The Muellers were mind-numbingly wealthy.

To their credit, both Roman and Kimberly attempted to make overtures of friendliness at this initial dinner by bringing up things that they thought might create common bonds. Yet, it was apparent to Shiloh very early on that she was way out of her league. Before he was appointed a judge following the sudden death of one of his father's friends, Roman began his legal career with his father Horace in the family's corporate defense law firm. Before their appetizers hit the table, Roman had already humble-bragged his way through barely getting into law school as a legacy with lower-than-average grades and a substandard LSAT score. Over salads, Roman detailed his struggles with having to take the bar exam twice because he failed it the first time while nursing a hangover, only to step immediately into a six-figure per year part-time caseload with his father's firm. After extolling the importance of work-life balance in avoiding burnout among attorneys by capping billable hours at thirty per week to allow for plenty of recreation, Roman finally got around to asking Shiloh what kind of law she practiced.

When Shiloh told Roman that she was a public defender in juvenile court who routinely worked over sixty hours per week in the office and more at home, Roman was aghast. Then, he laughed and said Shiloh must be joking. She assured him that she was not, which was when Roman demanded to see her pay stub detailing her billable hours. Ethan was livid at his brother's rudeness, but Shiloh didn't mind. After pulling up her most recent pay stub on her phone and showing it to him, all color drained from Roman's face. He made a big production of lighting a cigar between courses so that he would have something in his mouth and could avoid further commentary.

At that point, Kimberly attempted to intervene by asking where Shiloh went to college and whether she'd been in a sorority. When Shiloh told her yes, that she'd been an Alpha Delta Pi at the University of Kentucky, Kimberly went off on a tangent about how she and her sorority sisters at Vanderbilt had such a great time the year before at their annual alumni retreat. Explaining that they tried to go to a different European country every year and that they were all looking forward to Switzerland later in the fall, Kimberly asked where Shiloh's chapter planned to hold their alumni retreat that year. Shiloh's reply was Memphis. This statement caused Kimberly to wax poetic about how much she loved ancient Egypt ever since doing her first study abroad trip to Cairo while studying art history at Vanderbilt. When she found out that Shiloh meant Memphis, Tennessee, rather than Egypt, Kimberly's filler-enhanced lips snapped shut like an overly large clam until their main courses arrived.

In Shiloh's eyes, the remainder of their evening was all downhill from there. Roman's humble bragging about champagne problems continued. Kimberly's enthusiasm for her long-ago sojourn to Egypt during college prompted him to describe in excruciating detail his leisurely six-year trip through an undergraduate degree in Philosophy at Xavier, during which time he did five summer study abroad trips to Italy, Greece, China, Germany, and France. Roman and Kimberly had met at some expensive private college exchange student mixer while both were spending the summer in Paris.

"We go back to France every year for our anniversary," Kimberly gushed over her third glass of organic chardonnay. "It's so important to remember the little things that brought you together in the first place when you're trying to keep that spark alive in your marriage."

"What's that?" Ethan teased his sister-in-law. "Mergers and Acquisitions?"

Not appreciating his brother's insinuation, Roman kicked Ethan's shin under the table. On the way home, Ethan explained to Shiloh that the prenup between Roman and Kimberly had been a sore spot with his older brother for years. It was negotiated predominantly between their fathers. Kimberly's dad, Cliff Tuttle, was an even higher-end lawyer than Horace Mueller. Cliff's firm handled mostly Nashville entertainment industry clients. Cliff only agreed to support the union if Roman pledged at least fifty percent of his billable hours would come from servicing The Tuttle Firm's clients in Tennessee. Roman hated the arrangement. Even though it earned substantially more than his usual roster of Tri-State area clients, it meant that Roman had to spend a lot of time around country and gospel music singers, whom he despised.

Nevertheless, Roman dutifully maintained this semi-indentured servitude to his father-in-law's firm of hillbilly millionaires for over a decade. Many years of enduring forced association with the bards of rural life caused Roman to view his wife Kimberly and anyone else remotely Southern with boundless condescension. Roman made sure that their three children took elocution lessons beginning in kindergarten, lest they should begin speaking with the horrible accent that he'd come to detest. Eventually, Roman found an escape hatch in the conflict-of-interest regulations that barred seated judges from also practicing law with their firms. Thus, even though becoming a judge was a substantial step down the financial ladder, Roman was desperate to hold onto the position for the remainder of his career. To Roman, continuing in the judiciary was his only option for freedom without losing half his estate in a divorce.

I guess everything has a price, Shiloh whispered to herself. Standing on the low rock wall of the upper overlook, she could see the moonlight dancing along the quiet ripples of the Ohio River below. No cargo barges stirred, and the water was almost still. From her vantage point, Shiloh could see the tourist riverboats docked on the Kentucky side. The thought occurred to her, as it often did, that she'd watched the boats go up and down that part of the Ohio River her entire life, yet she'd never set foot on a single one of them.

As she pondered this missing link in her common experience, Shiloh gradually became aware of someone singing. The voice was high-pitched and wavering, like the sound a drunken cat might make if it were able to form human words. Judging by the direction from which the warbling tune came, the source seemed to be on the lower veranda. Unable to make out the lyrics, Shiloh became curious. She decided to take the back steps down around the small children's playground to see what the person looked like.

Crossing on the path behind the Chinese cormorant fishing statue to the bridge spanning over the Twin Lakes, Shiloh peered between the oak trees. Dancing there along the stone perimeter wall, she saw a man wearing a long, filthy black trench coat. Beneath the coat, the rest of his clothes were black as well. She recognized the coat as belonging to the vagrant whom she'd spied several days earlier—first, when he'd tried to purchase a bottle of alcohol out the back door of the Mount Adams Bar and Grill, and then later as the police officer chased him away from the crime scene boundary around the gazebo.

Guess he finally found somewhere to buy a bottle of booze. Shiloh murmured to herself as she crouched down beneath the top ledge of the concrete banister. From the shape of the bottle, he seemed to be holding the largest-sized bottle of Patron silver tequila.

That bartender wasn't kidding when she said he had money, Shiloh mused. Pausing in his crooning to turn up the bottle of liquor, he chugged several gulps easily as water. The pointed Adam's apple in the man's skinny neck jerked with each hungry swallow. The angular silhouette of his face in the moonlight, complete with a broken-bridged nose and elongated, upturned chin, was like a sketch of Ichabod Crane from a children's copy of *The Legend of Sleepy Hollow*. Dragging the ragged sleeve of his wrinkled black shirt across his wide mouth, the man trilled his thin lips in satisfaction. Popping the round cork back in the bottle, he burst into song.

Watching the man between the steel bars of the railing, Shiloh could at last make out the lyrics of the melody. It was "One Piece at a Time," the old Johnny Cash tune. Fascinated by this eerily off-key and out-of-tempo impromptu concert, Shiloh kept listening as the man cycled through bits and pieces of other Cash songs, stopping between verses to fortify himself with additional slugs of tequila. "A Boy Named Sue" was followed by "Folsom Prison Blues," and finally, "Hurt."

His voice growing increasingly unsteady with each word, the man's attention turned to a large doe that approached him from the woodline. Shiloh encountered deer in the park frequently, yet they'd always maintained a distance of at least ten or twelve feet from her. Far enough away to dash away if they felt spooked. This deer, however, showed little fear. Extending her long neck toward the man, she sniffed the air, as if sensing his sadness.

The man's voice decrescendoed to the softest whisper as he murmured the song's penultimate question and response, *What have I become, my sweetest friend? Everyone I know goes away in the end.* For a moment, he paused, realizing that other deer had begun to gather around him in a half circle. Their obsidian eyes glinted in the moonlight as they studied him intensely. The deer were so close that he could have reached out to touch them. Shiloh realized that she was holding her breath in amazement at how the animals seemed drawn to his pain.

Then, like the shifting tide of an uncalm sea, the timbre of the man's voice changed. His light, warbling tone morphed into a hoarse, menacing whisper that crescendoed into a roar as he screamed the last lines of the verse. *Then you can have it all, this empire of dirt. I will let you down; I will make you hurt.* At the end of the last word, the man hurled the empty tequila bottle as hard as he could. It smashed into one of the oak trees several feet away from Shiloh's hiding place on the bridge.

Startled, Shiloh let out a choked cry and stumbled, falling onto her backside. The deer cut and ran, galloping past her to the safety of the woodline behind the perimeter of the park. Slowly, the man's gaze followed them until he saw Shiloh sitting there, staring at him. He studied her for several seconds, locking his ice-blue eyes with her hazel ones. A wave of mixed exhilaration followed by panic crossed over the man's face like fast-moving clouds. Then, he smiled. A tight-lipped, half-smile that twisted only half of his mouth, revealing gums, but no front teeth. In a flash, Shiloh recognized who he was, even though her mind refused to accept it.

Edging backward a few steps, when his heel touched the rock wall behind, the man spun around. Leaping over the wall, he tumbled down the side of the precipice into the dark undergrowth below.

Shiloh felt no need to run up to the wall and peer over the ledge to see whether the man was injured. Having walked around the overlook countless times before, she knew that jumping into the underbrush would have padded his descent, slowing him down enough to not fall out onto the parkway below. Still, part of her wanted to chase after him, to try to catch another glimpse of his face. *He couldn't be who she thought he was, could he?*

Freaked out by what she'd seen, Shiloh bolted back toward the upper trail that led past the standpipe and through the President's Grove of oaks. The grove was full of deer, night feeding on acorns from dozens of trees. Shiloh followed this path down and around Krohn Conservatory, not quite jogging but moving faster than she had on her way in.

Arriving home less than thirty minutes later, Shiloh was surprised to find a calculator lying on her doorstep. An old, nineties-style Texas Instruments graphing calculator, to be exact. Picking it up, Shiloh examined the tiny machine with a shaking hand. It had the same protective sliding cover that she'd had on her high school graphing calculator, but the reverse was different. On the back were four words written in faded silver waterproof marker. *Property of Ethan Mueller.*

Tuesday, October 10th, Morning

S hiloh's difficulty getting to sleep before her late-night stroll around the park intensified when she tried to lie down again around midnight. Even downing three shots of whiskey failed to induce any soporific effects. Red-eyed and unable to relax, she decided to fire up the laptop and began looking for any leads that she could find regarding Simon Bowles. It wasn't easy. Although her background check, paid for through an online on-demand service, reached a dead end, Shiloh did stumble upon an interesting lead when she searched for the names of teachers who were employed at St. Augustine's at the time of Simon Bowles's attendance.

The listing was for the Writing Center director, who had found Simon in the shower room. What Shiloh found online corroborated what she'd read in Ethan's journal. Sister Frida Jiminez not only left her job at St. Augustine High the following year, but she gave up the habit entirely. Court records stated that the former Sister Frida married a military pilot, moved to Phoenix, and then returned to Cincinnati to obtain an uncontested divorce less than two years later. Having reclaimed her maiden name, Frida Jimenez never remarried. She taught ninth and tenth-grade English at the public Gilbert High School for almost twenty years. Frida's Facebook page revealed a surprisingly youthful-looking Hispanic woman along with a cell phone number, email, and physical address in the Price Hill neighborhood on the West Side. Shiloh wrote down Frida's contact information before closing her laptop at three in the morning. Deciding that it would be more prudent to nap for a few hours and clear her head before firing off an email,

Shiloh swaddled herself into one of her many self-crocheted throws in her favorite chair by the living room window with William under her arm and drifted off to sleep.

At sunrise, Shiloh awakened to William's soft gray and white paws tapping her lips to alert her that it was time for breakfast. Dry-eyed from leaving her contact lenses in overnight, Shiloh struggled to the kitchen to tap out some wet food for William before toddling off to the shower.

By nine o'clock, refreshed from a breakfast of black coffee, yogurt, granola, and fresh blueberries, Shiloh dressed in a camel blazer and light blue blouse paired with dark jeans and her signature tree of life necklace before trekking up the hill to her office. Less than fifteen minutes after emailing Frida Jiminez, Shiloh received an invitation to meet during her last period prep at two that afternoon. Jotting down the address for Incline Public House as their meeting place, Shiloh spent the rest of the morning researching other potential contacts on the case until it was time to go.

Pulling up in the parking lot of Incline, Shiloh marveled at the gorgeous skyline views across the river. For the second time in two days, she wondered why she'd never spent much time exploring the neighborhoods along the Ohio River coastline.

Frida arrived while Shiloh was snapping photos of the fall leaf-peeping panorama that surrounded the pub's patio. Dressed in a pretty burgundy-colored autumn sweater dress with ankle boots and a cropped leather moto jacket, Frida Jiminez looked a lot more like a lady who would have a hip young mom-influencer page on Instagram than a divorced former nun turned public high school teacher with a six-course load of composition. After they'd both ordered pizzas—prosciutto fig for Shiloh and caprese for Frida—they settled into a table on the patio with a view of the riverfront.

"Simon Bowles?" Frida asked, with a puzzled expression. "Oh. Yes, I remember him. By several different names. He went by his middle name, Isaiah, and his birth father's last name for a little while. The Tierneys had a lot of money. Simon felt intimidated by a lot of the other boys' backgrounds, I think. He tried on Tierney because he thought it sounded classier, but it didn't stick. Simon was always struggling to find himself."

Frida picked the basil leaves off her first slice of pizza and chewed them thoughtfully. "Simon was, beyond a shadow of a doubt, the most intellectually gifted student whom I've ever worked with. Inquisitive. Intuitive. Willing to go beyond every lesson and more. He was more gifted in mathematics than the humanities, but he knew his weaknesses and worked diligently to remedy them. Simon was every teacher's dream. He was a once-in-a-career student. And not only that, he was humble. Made a point to speak to everyone, from the custodians to classmates. I don't know how much time you've spent around elite private schools and the kinds of students they enroll, Ms. Foley, but that's rare."

"I've been around more than you'd think," Shiloh said, taking a bite of her slice. The mix of savory and sweet flavors was beyond delicious. "What I'm looking for are a few insights into what might have happened to Simon after high school. I mean, with such a bright student, surely he would have had his pick of colleges? Or am I mistaken?"

"Oh, of course, yes!" Frida replied enthusiastically. "Simon got a full ride to the University of Cincinnati, right here in town. Majored in mathematics and then went to medical school. Everything would have turned out better for Simon, if not for..." Frida hesitated. "Well, I'm sure you know."

Shiloh studied Frida's face closely. "No, I don't believe I do," she replied.

"Oh," Frida cleared her throat. "Well, I'm sure it's on record somewhere. But..." She paused as Shiloh swallowed a bite of pizza.

"Oh, to hell with it!" Frida exclaimed. "I'm sick of all this obliqueness. What do you know about Simon and his father?"

"Um..." Shiloh hesitated, chewing a bite with her hand over her mouth. "Next to nothing?"

Frida laughed. "That's what I thought. About the same as everyone else. Well, get set. I'm about to blow your mind."

Taking a long sip of diet soda, Frida Jiminez began telling Simon's story.

"Simon was born in UC hospital, just like Charles Manson. Also, just like Charles Manson, Simon's mother was a sex worker. This becomes important later on. You'll understand the connections," Frida explained.

"When Simon was about school age, some social workers visited his mother and found that she'd been living in deplorable conditions. So, they enlisted state intervention. Simon's mother, Doreen, was sent to a mental institution near Columbus. Simon was put in boarding school. At that time, St. Agatha's had the cheapest tuition, so that's where they sent all the charity cases. It was over in Sedamsville. Unfortunately, Sedamsville was also the place where problem priests were reassigned after they started causing trouble. It was a poor parish, so the Church thought fewer people who mattered would notice. You know what I mean when I say problem priests, right?"

"Unfortunately, yes," Shiloh replied. "What I've never understood, though, is why the Church kept covering up for them. I mean, it's not like pedophiles stop just because their job warehouses them somewhere else."

"It's an image issue," Frida rolled her eyes. "The optics would look bad, and churches of any kind are all about keeping up appearances. They're cleverly disguised instruments of social control. Don't get me started."

Dismissing the tangent with a wave of her hand, Frida continued. "After Simon was removed from his mother's custody, he became a boarding student at St. Agatha's. It's closed now, but at one time it was one of several Catholic schools on the West Side whose students attended Our Lady of Perpetual Help. Although St. Agatha's started as a school for girls only, they tried to merge it with a boys' school that was also struggling to maintain enrollment, but it didn't work. By the time Simon started there, both the school and church had gone downhill. They'd stopped charging tuition entirely because most of the students were like Simon. Kids from bad families whom the Church took in as boarders to save them from going into the foster care system. His father, Ian, signed the papers as guardian for Simon to go there after his mother was institutionalized."

"Wait," Shiloh stopped her. "If Simon's birth father knew that he'd been abandoned, why didn't he take the boy in?"

Frida sighed. "Because Dr. Ian Tierney was already married. He'd been married and had a family with another woman over on the Kentucky side of the river for many years before he fathered Simon. From what their headmistress Sister Gertrude told me, Simon's mother, Doreen Bowles, was a student at St. Agatha's herself when she first hooked up with Dr. Tierney. Doreen came from a very large, poor, religious, conservative family. She met Ian Tierney when she was sixteen, waiting tables after school at a chili place downtown. Tierney was some kind of rich upper-level hospital administrator. They would meet in his office late at night after everyone had gone home. Both lied to their families about having to work late. The thing between them went on for almost a year until Doreen found out she was pregnant. At first, Ian just ghosted her. When Doreen asked her family for money to get an abortion, they kicked her out of the house. Desperate for help, she went back to Ian to beg for money to get an abortion, but he told her to get lost. Tierney was a big churchgoer too.

He was afraid that admitting to fathering a child out of wedlock with a teenage girl would cause a big scandal. So, Ian tried to ignore her for as long as he possibly could. However, Doreen was relentless and insistent for his acknowledgment. Ultimately, I heard Ian threatened Doreen with commitment to a mental health institution to get her to go away. That may have been their final break in contact."

"Ironic how people who claim to be such devout Christians can be so arbitrary with their compassion," Shiloh said, rolling her eyes.

"Mmm hmm," Frida agreed, taking another sip of diet soda. "After she had the baby, Doreen needed more money than she could make serving chili part-time, so she became a sex worker. And like most sex workers, Doreen soon picked up a drug habit. From pictures I've seen, Doreen was a very pretty girl in the beginning and able to pick up a lot of wealthy clients. However, as her addiction worsened, her clientele declined along with her looks. By the time she lost custody of Simon, Doreen was homeless, living in one of the abandoned subway tunnels that run beneath the streets on the West Side. That was where Child Services found Simon. Some bartender tipped them off that they thought Doreen left her child alone down there for extended periods while she tried to pick up men."

"That sounds awful," Shiloh replied. She thought about the man she'd seen in the filthy trench coat the night before and considered telling Frida about how she believed he was Simon. However, not wanting to interrupt the narrative, she decided to wait.

"It must have been," Frida agreed. "When Simon first came to St. Agatha's, Sister Gertrude said that he was far behind the development of most children his age. Unable to read and barely able to speak. However, they quickly figured out that it was because of neglect rather than a lack of intelligence. Some nuns who'd known and felt sorry for his mother made Simon their special project. Soon he was performing well beyond his peers. According to Sister Gertrude, he'd become sort of a teacher's pet before the incident."

"This Sister Gertrude whom you keep mentioning," Shiloh asked, hating to butt in but needing to know. "I'm assuming she's retired now? Would it be possible to speak with her too?"

"No. She's dead, sadly." Frida replied. "She was very old when I worked at St. Augustine's. Sister Gertrude was the real deal. A nun who truly cared about the well-being of children who'd been abused. She dedicated her life to it, which is what makes the end of the story that I'll get to in a bit even sadder. Sister Gertrude's dismissal after trying her best to help Simon was the last straw in what made me finally leave the Church. But I'm getting ahead of myself."

Frida took a deep breath and waited for the server who was refilling her glass of diet soda to leave the table before proceeding. "Simon was about ten when Father Walter Eckhardt was brought in. Allegedly, the staff and congregation were told that he was some kind of charismatic master at recruiting parishioners and filling pews, which was sorely needed. At the time, everyone knew that both the church and school were in danger of closing due to lack of attendance. That was back in the days before social media, so there wasn't any real way to get the scoop on anyone's reputation except by word of mouth. And since the Church was purposefully vague about where Father Eckhardt was from, or why he'd been placed in a backwater like Sedamsville if he were such a dynamic priest, there was no one to ask."

"Perhaps that's one good thing that the digital age has brought us," Shiloh commented. "Better transparency and public accountability."

"True," Frida seconded. "Anyway, it wasn't long before rumors about Father Eckhardt began to churn. Several boys in the youth choir complained to Sister Gertrude, who was the headmistress of St. Agatha's at the time, that Father Eckhardt made them feel uncomfortable. However, Sister Gertrude claimed that when she initially tried to confront him about it, Father Eckhardt brushed her off by saying that they were exaggerating. Eckhardt played to her tendencies of being a strict disciplinarian. He told her that the boys were just making up tales to get rid of him because he made them work harder than they were used to. At first, Sister Gertrude wanted to believe him. She was an old German nun who was known for tolerating no nonsense, and she loved the Church. But after what happened to Simon," Frida sighed. "It was undeniable. There was simply no other explanation for his injuries other than abuse. Sister Gertrude told me that Father Eckhardt tried to claim that Simon did it to himself. However, no child would mutilate themselves in that way. Even if they were mentally ill, the pain from all those cuts would have been too excruciating. He would have passed out from it and the loss of blood. Also, Sister Gertrude said that the surgeon who completed the amputation claimed that the angles of the cuts proved that self-infliction would have been impossible. Plus, there were other newly healed scars too. Proving that the abuse went on for some time. That poor boy endured more than we'll ever know."

Shiloh nodded. "I have something I want to show you when you've finished."

"Is it one of Simon's journals?" Frida asked. "I have some of them too."

"No, I didn't know he kept any," Shiloh replied. "This is a journal that belonged to my late husband. He was a friend of Simon's later on, at St. Augustine's. In it, he talks about Simon."

"Oh?" Frida said, her sad eyes brightening as she made the connection. "Your husband must have been Ethan Mueller. He was such a sweet boy. Good to everyone."

"Yes, he was," Shiloh answered. "And you have an excellent memory."

"The best students always leave an impression," Frida said. "Plus, it's hard to forget anything related to Simon. He was an excellent student, but such an unusual boy. Simon tried desperately to make friends but never succeeded. Ethan was the only student who ever even tried to reach out to him at St. Augustine's. Such a shame. For something that horrific to happen to a young man not just once, but twice."

Frida turned her gaze out over the river with a pained expression. The sky was gray, and a dense fog hung low over the water. "One always wonders if there was something more that could have been done. Something that should have been seen. But then you think, *How?*"

"No one ever wants to believe that someone they know could be a monster," Shiloh agreed. They sat in silence for a few minutes, watching the barges glide along beneath the series of bridges spanning the river. Uneasily, Shiloh twisted her gold tree of life necklace on its chain.

"That's what they were, though," Frida said at last. "Not just Father Eckhardt, but all five of those boys. The ones who hurt Simon the second time. And the Church too, for covering it up." Frida turned her dark eyes skyward, toward the hazy light barely visible between the ominous clouds. "They think that money gives them the power to influence people. To control any situation. But someday they'll pay for it. Everyone who knew about it had the power to hold Simon's tormentors accountable yet did nothing. Like Sister Gertrude said: Judgment always finds the guilty. I used to think that meant punishment in the afterlife, but now I'm not so sure. Nowadays, I think that what we think of as God's wrath might just be what happens right here on Earth. That we're all living out a purgatory of our own making. Even me."

"You don't blame yourself for not doing more to help Simon, do you?" Shiloh asked, already expecting the answer.

"How could I not?" Frida replied, meeting Shiloh's eyes across the table. "It's the other reason why I left the Church. Knowing what they were covering up, but also that I was too cowardly to push the issue. I felt like a hypocrite. I had no right to claim that I was wedded to the cause of Christ when I could not do something so small as picking up the phone and calling the police to report that a boy had been severely abused. Instead, I fled. Into a hasty marriage, for which I paid dearly. After I ran away from him too, I've come to think of those couple of years, during which I was beaten almost daily, as a sort of divine retribution for my silence. Catholics might call it penance. Other people might call it karma."

Frida shrugged. "Perhaps I completed my purgation and atonement by testifying on Simon's behalf at the inquisition. If nothing else, hopefully, it assisted him in getting some help with his mental health."

"What inquisition?" Shiloh asked, confused. "I thought there wasn't much investigation into the cause of Simon's injuries."

"Oh, it wasn't for his assault," Frida said. "It was because Simon killed his father. Allegedly, anyway. Remember earlier when I told you that Simon earned a scholarship to UC?"

Shiloh nodded, hiding her surprise at the way Frida casually mentioned this new information, as she tried to catch the server's attention to bring a pair of boxes for their leftover pizza. It had grown cold on the table after their first slices. They'd been too engrossed in conversation to eat.

"Well, Simon never went back to St. Aug's after the assault. His things were moved out of the dorms and put into storage while he took his GED and SATs. The following fall, someone anonymously arranged for him to be given a full ride to UC, including room and board with early admission. Simon flew through undergrad as a math major and medical school afterward. Then, when he was in his first year of residency, Simon's birth father, Dr. Ian Tierney, had a heart attack. As fate would have it, Ian ended up recovering in the ward where Simon was working as a resident. The day before Ian Tierney was scheduled to go home, he died under suspicious circumstances. A toxicology report introduced at trial said it was from a lethal overdose of some kind of injectable speed drug cocktail that made his already weak heart simply burst. They found a needle mark between two toes on his left foot. There was a video of Simon with his back to the camera hovering near the end of his bed and rifling around in the closet in his hospital room about an hour before Ian went into cardiac arrest. The evidence was circumstantial. Simon was never formally charged after the hospital inquisition results were inconclusive. That didn't convince his residency supervisor or Dr. Tierney's family, though. When she found out who Simon was, Ian's widow pushed to have Simon expelled from the residency program on grounds of gross negligence. The residency supervisor folded under pressure from the administration. All of them were golf buddies with Ian. They knew that without his widow's continued solicitation of donors after his death, the hospital would lose a ton of financial support. So, the hospital put Simon on leave. A six-month suspension with orders to undergo mental health treatment. When Simon tried to return, they used his psychiatrist's diagnosis to declare him unfit to sit for the medical board exams. Then, they formally dismissed Simon from the program."

"That's diabolical," Shiloh said. "Do you think Simon killed Ian?"

Frida pondered for a moment as she placed her leftover pizza in the box and tucked it in the corners. "It's hard to say. If he did, though, and karma is real, then someday I suppose Simon will have to answer for it."

"Perhaps he already has," Shiloh mused, gathering her pizza into a box as she thought about the drunken, toothless man whom she'd seen in the park the night before.

"Perhaps," Frida echoed. "Although last I heard, Simon was working as a pharmaceutical sales rep for some drug company, making big money. That must have been, gosh..." Frida trailed off, mentally tallying the years in her head. "Over a decade ago. Who knows what might have happened to him since then?"

As they stood to go, Frida reached into her tote bag and pulled out two notebooks. They were ordinary-looking dollar store volumes, with spiral binding and tattered paper covers. One faded red and the other green. The outer edges of their pages were warped and discolored, probably from old water damage. "When you emailed me asking to meet and talk about Simon, I brought these along. Someone left them on my doorstep not long after I moved back to Price Hill following my divorce. I'm not sure if it was him, but the handwriting is Simon's. He was ambidextrous. This one,"

Frida held up the red notebook, "was written with his left hand, and the green one with his right."

Taking the notebooks from Frida, Shiloh put them in her bag and pulled out Ethan's journal. She'd copied the pages containing his confession of guilt about having witnessed Simon's assault. "I copied these for you too. They're from Ethan's journal. His account of what happened when... you know."

Frida stared at the copies in Shiloh's outstretched hand but did not reach for them. "So Ethan did finally confess to witnessing it?" she asked. Shiloh nodded.

"I thought someday he would," Frida replied. "Is there anything else in there that you think I wouldn't know if Simon already told me what those five boys did to him?"

"Probably not," Shiloh answered.

"Then I don't need to relive it," Frida said, motioning for Shiloh to put the papers away. "Whatever I had to atone for regarding what I should have done years ago for Simon was hopefully satisfied when I testified as a character witness on his behalf at his hospital inquisition. I never followed up on him much afterward because some people are like black cats. The more you think about them, the more you see them around."

Shiloh tucked the copies back into Ethan's journal and then into her red tote bag. "I take it that you'd prefer not to see Simon again then?"

Frida blinked slowly. "I'd prefer to think that Simon is somehow okay, despite everything. However," she pointed at Shiloh's bag into which she'd put the two notebooks. "Once you read those, I think you'll come to the same conclusion that I did."

"Which is?" Shiloh pressed.

"That it's just wishful thinking of a guilty woman," Frida replied.

"I don't understand," Shiloh said. "I thought you felt that you'd atoned for not speaking up on Simon's behalf."

"I did," Frida said, opening her car door. "But as the good book says, judge not, so that ye be not judged. Everyone I've ever met is always guilty of something."

Tuesday, October 10th, Evening

Shiloh spent the remainder of the afternoon trying to confirm everything that she'd learned during her meeting with Frida Jiminez. Although the information was scant, she was able to find some vague coverage by searching local archives for a series of short reports about the investigation. Sources stated that Dr. Ian Tierney, a hospital administrator from Fort Thomas, Kentucky, had died, possibly due to the negligence of a UC Hospital resident. However, Shiloh noticed that none of the reports mentioned Simon by name. Like everything else in his life, it seemed that Simon's alleged murder of his birth father had been quietly swept under the rug.

As she pulled into the deck beneath Washington Park, Shiloh's cell phone dinged with a text message from Bernadette Jenkins.

Scarlet is waiting for you on the benches beside the Pavilion. I'll be back in an hour.

Without giving it much thought, Shiloh knew why Bernie sent the text rather than Scarlet. A fourteen-year-old girl with a father who was suspicious enough of regular schools to insist on homeschooling his children would be monitoring his daughter's cell phone usage.

The air was crisp with the early chill of an autumn night as Shiloh shuffled her way through the piles of leaves across the park. Dozens of couples strolled by hand in hand, sipping cups of coffee and hot chocolate. Seeing them, Shiloh winced, unable to keep herself from thinking about how she and Ethan were among them only a year ago, blissfully unaware that it would be their final fall together. Ironically, she remembered how they stopped by a trio of monuments dedicated to a lady who had died young and the forgotten love story surrounding her life. Feeling herself beginning to spiral down the rabbit hole of memory, Shiloh was relieved to see Scarlet waiting for her, alone on a bench beside the Pavilion, just as Bernadette described.

Dressed in a long hooded jacket over a black turtleneck, another plaid skirt, and heavily buckled engineer boots with her dark curly hair swept up in a ponytail, Scarlet glanced up from her phone guiltily as Shiloh approached. The thick black winged eyeliner circling her brown eyes, which were set deep in her pale face, made Scarlet appear much older than fourteen, Shiloh realized. The girl's unnervingly sharp gaze settled upon her. Shiloh felt the girl staring at her gold tree necklace. As Scarlet silently judged her appearance, the corners of the girl's gray matte lips turned up in the slightest hint of a smile, as if to say, *I know about you.*

"Am I interrupting something?" Shiloh asked, sitting down on the bench beside Scarlet.

"No," Scarlet replied. "I just, um..." she paused. "Well, I know it might sound stupid, but when I come to this park, I always have to check for ghosts. I have an app on my phone."

"Really?" Shiloh asked, somewhat amused. There was an app for everything. "Why?"

"Oh, don't you know?" Scarlet said, tucking her phone into the crossbody bag slung across her slim torso. "Music Hall was built over a graveyard for unclaimed bodies. A potter's field, I think it's called. Every time they do renovations, they find more bones. Mom and I did the ghost tour once. It's supposed to be one of the most haunted places in America. For a while, it was an orphanage. Before that, there was some kind of steamboat disaster. The Moselle, I think, was the name of the boat. Blew hundreds of people to pieces all around here." Scarlet motioned with her black nail-polished hand, indicating the grassy area around them. "We're probably standing right on top of a bunch of dead people right now and don't even know it."

"I think I remember hearing about that someplace," Shiloh replied. "Cincinnati seems to be a city haunted by a lot of buried history."

Shiloh was relieved that Scarlet had already mentioned her mother, Veronica. Although she was used to dealing with juveniles from her years in the public defender's office, Shiloh worried about the awkwardness of bringing up the situation that necessitated their meeting. Most of the kids she'd dealt with at her old job already had adult-sized drug habits and petty crime rap sheets to match. Experiences that usually left them as jaded as any adult to the tragic loss of a parent or sibling. Although her brothers seemed to be handling the death of their mother and sister surprisingly well, Shiloh hadn't known what to expect from a teenage girl who appeared to be more sensitive than the rest of her family.

Sensing Shiloh's wariness to say more, Scarlet continued. "It's okay, you know. To talk about them. Dad already had me at my regular counselor's office twice this week, and then I had to go to that pointless group session with him and my brothers." Here, the girl rolled her eyes in exasperation at what she thought was overkill. "It's not like I'm going to off myself. If anything, I was like, the most prepared of anyone, because I knew more."

"What did you know?" Shiloh prompted delicately. Although the girl was putting up a strong face, she sensed that Scarlet was using it to disguise more painful feelings.

Grimacing, Scarlet blew at her bangs as she crossed her pale, skinny legs. The teen bounced her heavily booted top foot up and down nervously as she leaned over, pulling her dark jacket closed and hugging her arms to her chest in a self-soothing motion. Straightening with her arms still folded, Scarlet asked with her eyes closed. "How much did my dad tell you about his business?"

"Not a lot," Shiloh answered, knowing that the girl was feeling her out for the easiest way to begin. "But I can promise you that whatever you tell me will remain in strict confidence until you tell me it's okay to say anything about it."

Scarlet's kohl-ringed eyes slowly opened. "Even to the police? I thought PIs didn't have confidentiality privileges like attorneys."

This kid is no dummy, Shiloh thought. "Technically, we don't. If I were ever called to the stand to testify, I would have to do so truthfully. However, since I was a lawyer for many years before becoming a PI, I decided that I would hold to the same confidentiality rules for my investigation clients as a kind of, *don't ask, don't tell* situation if you know what I mean."

"Yeah... okay," Scarlet answered warily. Still staring down at the leaf-strewn sidewalk as she curled back over into a protective posture on the park bench, Scarlet started to explain.

"So, I'm sure you know where Dad's money came from originally. Arnold's Drugstores. That whole thing," the teen waved her black
nail-polished fingertips dismissively. "A few years back, Dad started investing a lot of money into this new research and development startup here
in town called Zauber Pharmaceutical Labs. Over by Central Parkway, I
think. Raff's company, Dynamic Investments Group, owns the building
it's in. Ever heard of it?"

Shiloh shook her head *no*.

Scarlet paused to shut her eyes again and let out another exasperated sigh.
"Not surprised. Nobody else has either. It's pretty sketchy. Raff talked Dad
into the idea of investing in them as a favor. He needed them to keep paying
rent, but I think even he was clueless about what they did initially. Which
is kind of a bitch, if you think about it, because he turned Mom onto it
too, for her *portfolio*." The girl air-quoted her last word. Without needing
to ask, Shiloh could tell Scarlet's bitter use of the clipped nickname for
Purcell made her feelings toward her biological father perfectly clear.

"Anyway," Scarlet continued. "I heard they make a lot of stuff that's
considered cutting edge in the performance enhancement field. You know,
pills and injectables to make you stronger, smarter, thinner, that sort of
thing. Not all of it is FDA approved, but they get away with it somehow
by branding themselves as a compounding facility for individual patients."

"So, Zauber creates custom drug cocktails?" Shiloh asked. Scarlet nodded. "And I'm assuming their products were for the extremely wealthy?"

"Oh yeah, you have no idea!" Scarlet replied, curling her gray lips con-
temptuously at the suggestion. "Dad was in a shit ton of debt when he
came back from rehab. Once he agreed to invest in Zauber for a share of
their profits, though, he made it all back and then some, just like that."
Scarlet snapped her fingers for emphasis.

"Makes sense," Shiloh echoed. "How does all of that fit in with what
happened to your mother and sister?"

The girl looked at Shiloh deadpan. "You mean, why do I think they were
murdered?"

"Yeah," Shiloh said, a little taken aback at the abruptness of Scarlet's
counter-question.

Scarlet slouched back into the park bench, keeping her arms folded
defensively across her chest. "Because they were both on that Zauber shit,
and then something went wrong. Mom and Vanna were into all, you know,

the whole idea of having to be super glamazon women. Wanting to look perfect and be perfect all the time. She didn't need it, but Mom had already been to Dr. Khoury several times to get work done around her eyes and neck. Vanna too. She had that new buccal fat removal thing done last year. Part of that whole bullshit of bowing to the patriarchy by becoming their Barbie doll mindset that some women still buy into. But it wasn't enough. They started taking some of those new Zauber compounds too and talking them up to all their friends. Pretty soon, every woman I knew at Dad's country club was on them."

"How could you tell?" Shiloh asked.

"Because their eyes looked like something out of an anime," Scarlet answered. "Wide open, with huge pupils. And they're super jumpy and sweaty all the time. The weekend before Vanna disappeared, I was playing with some bubble wrap from a package. When I popped a bunch at once, you would have thought Vanna was going to bounce off the ceiling. If you went to the country club tonight, I'm sure you'd see a ton of women like that. Quite a few dudes too. You can't miss them. Whatever's in the mix, it's got to have some kind of steroids in it, because all of their muscles stand out super jacked. Vanna's abs and calves were hard as bricks after she got on it. Totally crazy."

"I'm still not following you though," Shiloh said, confused. "I understand that your parents were both investing in Zauber's custom compounding enterprise and a lot of people you knew were on the drugs they produced. How does that end up with Ronni and Vanna dead and their bodies placed in such a weird way at the gazebo in Eden Park?"

Glancing around furtively, Scarlet motioned for Shiloh to lean in closer. "Because I don't think that Zauber is really just a drug-compounding company. Neither of them ever said anything to my face about it, but I overheard Vanna in the locker room at the country club pool talking about it one night this summer to Reece and Riley Mueller and a few of the other supposedly cool girls they hang out with. About some guy they called *The Prophet* and this ritual that they were going to do. From what they were saying, it sounded like some kind of cult."

"Ritual?" Shiloh replied, incredulously. Then, she remembered the poorly drawn symbols that had been newly spray-painted on the wall that she'd seen just before she found the bodies. Not wanting to influence the girl's recollection, Shiloh played it cool. "Do you remember anything about the details of the ritual or the real name of this alleged Prophet person?"

Scarlet shook her head and shrugged. "No names. Just that he worked with Zauber and called himself The Prophet. As for the ritual, it was something about a judgment. That was the word that they used several times. The rest was all messed up. It didn't make any sense to me."

Just then, both Scarlet's and Shiloh's cell phones dinged. Their messages were from Bernie, and both contained only a single word.

Ready.

After exchanging goodbyes and thanking the girl for her information, Shiloh remained on the bench. She watched as Scarlet walked over to Bernadette's Kia. The hood of her knee-length black jacket pulled up to conceal her face and carrying her flute case tucked beneath her bony arm, Scarlet's silhouette cast a sinister shadow in the setting sun.

How ironic, Shiloh mused, *that the sister who looked as if she had the most to hide was the one willing to reveal everything she knew.*

Not ready yet to go home as she pondered how this new information fit into the case, Shiloh ducked into her favorite OTR bar, Sundry & Vice. Being a Tuesday night with no theatrical shows playing, the place was virtually empty. A few couples snuggled into booths created a low hum of conversation, while a lone businessman in a slim tailored suit sat at the end of the bar. He wore an old-style fedora pulled down over his forehead and a black disposable mask over the lower half of his face. From the edge of her field of vision, Shiloh could see him lifting the mask from the bottom periodically to take a sip of his drink. It was made with some clear spirit, probably gin or tequila, with a couple of squeezed lime wedges tossed in.

Ordering a Penicillin, one of their signature cocktails consisting of scotch, honey, ginger, and lemon, Shiloh sipped slowly as she typed up the notes on her tablet of everything she could remember from her meeting with Scarlet. Finishing, Shiloh then searched for the location of Zauber Pharmaceutical Labs on her phone. Finding an address of 2021 Mohawk Place, she noticed that it was across the street from what used to be the old Imperial Theater. One of those long-term community revitalization projects that never seemed to come to fruition.

From the street view photos on the internet, the anvil-shaped four-story brick Victorian building seemed abandoned. All the windows were covered with sheets of plywood freshly painted black, while much older layers of paint drooped like loose scabs from its elaborately scrolled Italianate cornices. Yet, white letters on a plain black sign over the door at the bottom tip of the wedge spelled out the word *ZAUBER* clearly in brushed script font.

As Shiloh took down the address in her notes, the man who had been sitting at the end of the bar bumped into her shoulder. Mumbling incoherently, the man then tripped over the straps of Shiloh's open tote bag, causing the contents to tip out onto the floor. Falling to his knees on top of the bag, the man hovered there for a moment. His long torso hunched over with his hands in his lap, the ends of his expensive-looking wool suit coat spread around him like wings.

All conversation in the bar stopped.

"Hey man, are you okay?" the bartender asked, dashing around the corner.

"I'm fine," the man replied sullenly. Springing to his feet, he was out the door in two or three long strides. Watching the man leave, the bartender shook his head as he helped Shiloh gather up her things that had fallen out of the tote bag. Once they had everything put back together, the bartender joked. "Just so you know, he's not a regular."

"I hope not," Shiloh replied. She motioned to her face to indicate the oddity of the mask the man was wearing. "He doesn't seem like someone who gets out much."

The bartender shrugged. "I've never seen him before, but then, this is only my first real night on the job. Just started training yesterday, when we were closed. My name's Laurie, by the way. Laurie Blake."

Seeing her puzzled expression about his name, he added, "Mom was a big fan of Alcott's *Little Women,* and my dad was an English professor. It's short for Laurence. Kind of like the author, D.H., but spelled with a U, not a W. Mom won that battle."

Shiloh could tell that he wanted to say more but was waiting for her to respond. Laurie's eyes were startlingly blue. Shiloh felt her face grow hot at the awkwardness of staring back at this handsome man smiling at her. From the dark brown curly hair that fell over his forehead to the day's growth of stubble tracing the perfectly shaped outline of his jaw, every feature was like something one might see on a movie poster, not standing on the other side of a bar in Ohio.

"That makes sense. I'm Shiloh Foley," she said, at last, gaining her breath. "I'm an invest..." she started to say, *investigator*, shook her head, and changed her mind. "Something tells me you're not just a bartender. I feel like I've seen you somewhere before."

Laurie laughed, a warm, chesty sound and narrowed his eyes. "If you have, then you've got either excellent eyesight, a great memory, or both. Yeah, I'm an actor too. So far, I've only done small roles in television and theater stuff in New York. Which is pretty sad, 'cause I've been there—was there..." Laurie corrected himself. "For over twenty years. I went there for my MFA. When I didn't catch a break right away, I hung around to teach. Funny thing about teaching high school theater, though. You stay so wrapped up in what the kids are doing that you never seem to find time enough to audition for anything yourself. You keep thinking that you will, next summer, but then that season goes by. Then another, and another, and then the rent goes up so you pick up a side hustle bartending and have even less free time. Before you know it, there you are. Turning forty years old in the middle of a pandemic, and school shuts down. Theaters stay dark for a year, and you find yourself in a full-blown midlife crisis. You start doing all kinds of crazy shit like letting your apartment in New York go and quitting your teaching gig just a couple of years short of retirement. You have no idea what you're doing with your life, and one morning, boom! You wake up like Rip Van Winkle and have a revelation. *Maybe I want to try some Shakespeare. I've taught it for years; why the hell not?* So, on a visit home to see your mom, you audition, you get booked for the season with the local company, and then there you are. Back in Cincinnati, where you swore you'd never live again in a million years. Pouring cocktails named after legacy medications in a speakeasy bar for beautiful investment bankers on a Tuesday night."

"Wow," Shiloh said, stunned at how easily Laurie's life story poured out of him like water. And at the fact he'd slipped the word *beautiful* into the end of his tale to describe her. "Okay, well... that's awesome. Great to see someone never giving up on their dream. But I'm not an investment banker."

"Sorry," Laurie laughed again, this time sheepishly under his breath. "I know that I can talk a mile a minute sometimes. It's just been super quiet here tonight. I can't stand dead air if you know what I mean. So, what *do* you do?"

"I'm an investigator—private investigator, not a cop," Shiloh replied hastily. "I used to be a lawyer—a public defender, but I hung that up. Guess you could say I had a midlife crisis too."

Laurie whistled softly as he began to wipe down the bar top. Picking up the twenty left underneath the suited man's old glass and ringing it through the register, he replied. "I bet that was depressing, huh? Seeing all those people go to jail every day."

"Yeah," Shiloh sighed. "Especially the kids. I worked with juvenile defendants."

"Oh man, that's rough," Laurie seconded. He reached for the remote control to turn up the volume on the television as the news came on. "You should meet my mom, Joanne. She was a social worker for, God... like forty years. So depressing that she couldn't even talk about it much at home. All the awful things that happen to kids. She went the other way, though. Got super obsessed with her job. She stayed until they made her retire. Now that she doesn't have hundreds of cases to look after, she doesn't know what to do with herself. She even bought season tickets to my company, even though she doesn't like Shakespeare. Claims that it's because all his tragedies resolve too neatly when real life is never that way. Guess she's just that much of a loss for something to care about, to tolerate watching it all season..."

"Or she's proud and happy to be able to see her son perform after he's been away so long. I'm sure you're excellent." Shiloh said. Laurie beamed. His smile was comforting and genuine.

"When does the run of the next show start? I'll have to come see you. I used to have season tickets, but I didn't buy any for this year because..." Shiloh trailed off with a shrug, not wanting to spoil the happy effect her enthusiasm for seeing his show had on Laurie by telling him the reason. *Because that was one of our things*, she thought. *Something Ethan and I did together.*

Not sensing her awkwardness, Laurie began fumbling around beneath the bar top as a news program's theme music on the bar TV drowned out the end of Shiloh's explanation. Slipping two rectangles of cardstock across the counter to her, Shiloh saw that they were a pair of tickets for a preview night with the Shakespeare Company across the street. A new adaptation of *Hamlet.* Deliberately avoiding eye contact as Shiloh picked up the tickets, Laurie motioned to ask if she needed another round. Shiloh nodded as the program began.

"Our breaking news story," the announcer read. A video of a large group of sobbing girls holding candles played in the background. "A candlelight vigil is being held tonight for two young women, college roommates and members of Pi Omega sorority at the University of Cincinnati, who were found dead this morning. Although police have yet to release full details, we have learned that the bodies were discovered near campus in a public space. They'd been left out at some point during the previous night. Police say that the bodies were placed in what is being called an unusual circular formation. After contacting their parents to identify the victims, it was confirmed that one of the young women was Jaya Khoury, an academically gifted pre-med major and the oldest daughter of prominent Cincinnati plastic surgeon, Dr. Akash Khoury. The other was identified as Lorelei Winter-Lang. Already following in the footsteps of her famous mother, German-born runway model Elke Winter, Lorelei appeared in her first series of shows during Paris Fashion Week three years ago, at the age of sixteen. However, after a very public split with British bad boy musician Robby Drystan of the band Cindervoid last summer, Lorelei explained on social media that she intended to take a break from modeling and public life to just be a quote, *normal college student*. Tragically, that was not to be. Lorelei's father was hometown football hero and former Bengals wide receiver, Kyle Lang. More on this developing story at ten."

As the screen displayed photos of the two girls side by side, Shiloh gasped in disbelief.

"Oh, that's horrible!" Laurie said. His eyes filled with concern as he studied the screen. Images of Jaya and Lorelei faded, and what appeared to be an overhead drone shot of where the bodies were found came into view. "That looks like the Campus Green just across from Burnet Woods. I wonder if someone attacked them while they were walking back from over in Clifton. That used to be one of the popular hangout areas back when I was an undergrad at UC. Those woods were always super dark at night. It was the quickest way back to campus, though, so we all took it anyway."

"I know those girls' families," Shiloh said, her reservation at speaking plainly about her life falling away with the shocking news. "Kyle Lang and Kash Khoury, they went to school with my husband and his brother at St. Augustine's."

"Your husband?" Laurie asked. His expression was a mixture of concern and disappointment.

"I'm sorry," Shiloh replied, not answering Laurie. "I have to go. I need to make some phone calls. How much do I owe you to settle up?"

Laurie placed the receipt on the counter. "Are you okay?"

"Not really," Shiloh frowned, pulling a credit card out of her red tote bag and swiping it as Laurie held the machine. Tucking the tickets into her bag, she added. "I have a lot on my mind right now. But I'll try to be there tomorrow night for your show."

Wednesday, October 11th, Afternoon

"**Y**ou forgot again, didn't you?" Nadia said as she stood in the doorway of Shiloh's office. Dressed in a crisp slate gray blazer and skirt with silver hoop earrings and a laptop case under her arm, Nadia looked every inch like a young lady showing up for her first day on the job.

"No, no..." Shiloh trailed demurred as she dabbed at the hot sauce on the corner of her mouth from the last bite of quesadilla she'd been absentmindedly nibbling from a near-forgotten late lunch order. Her cat William did not stir but merely switched his tail as he lay on top of her desk, contemplating whether or not to taste the last bit of sour cream left on the side. "I was just trying to grab a bite while I was waiting on you."

"Mmm hmm, sure..." Nadia dragged out the word. "I'm sure you've seen the news."

"Yes, I spoke with Bruce Schultz for the official police take on everything. They seem to agree with my initial intuition. The murders of Jaya Khoury and Lorelei Winter-Lang are likely connected to those of Reece Mueller, Savannah Arnold, and her mother Veronica. It seems that someone is deliberately targeting their particular group of old friends from St. Augustine's. There are some theories as to why, but nothing solid yet." Shiloh replied, glancing at the clock. "I've also talked to Dr. Khoury and his wife Helen, as well as Kyle Lang and his model ex-wife Elke Winter-Lang. Elke flew in from Los Angeles this morning to supervise the pickup of Lorelei's body to return home for burial once the police have finished the autopsy. They'll all be stopping by but at different times. I think that the disappearance of Jasmine Jenkins is connected somehow with all of it too, because of her relationship with Joe Arnold. That's why I asked them to meet separately, at different times. I wanted to hear all sides of the story. They all said yes. The Khourys will be here at four o'clock, then Kyle Lang at five, and his ex-wife Elke Winter at six. After that," Shiloh held up the tickets that Laurie had given her the night before at Sundry & Vice. "We're going to see some Shakespeare."

Nadia snorted skeptically as she settled into a leather chair beside Shiloh. "Not that I'm opposed to culture, but why?"

"Well, last night I met this guy at..." Shiloh began.

"About time," Nadia interjected.

"Excuse me?" Shiloh replied good-naturedly. "Since when did you obtain a license in counseling? Because that escaped my knowledge."

"I didn't," Nadia said, shooting Shiloh some serious side-eye. "But it also hasn't escaped my knowledge," she put air quotes around the phrase, "That you haven't been the same since Ethan passed. It's been five months, and you don't seem interested in anything but work."

"And here we have our four o'clock," Shiloh interrupted. The bell over the exterior door leading into her office chimed. Relieved to talk about anything else other than her sadness over Ethan, Shiloh invited the Khourys to sit down. She pulled up a note-taking app on her tablet. Settling into a nearby chair and pulling out her laptop, Nadia did the same.

Although Shiloh had met with countless concerned parents during her years as a juvenile defender, she immediately noticed that something was off about the Khourys. Most often, when a teen was killed unexpectedly, the parents moved slowly and delicately, as if merely breathing would cause something in the room to break. However, from the way that Kash slammed the door shut, and Helen refused her handshake while seemingly trying to make a point of dragging a chair over so that its legs squealed loudly before plopping down in it with a disgusted expression on her face, Shiloh could tell that both Khourys were angry. Their dour countenance and passive-aggressive body language gave every suggestion of a couple that had been arguing all day. The reason became clear moments into the interview. Shiloh asked about their daughter Jaya's friends and whether any of them had mentioned any possible suspects.

Helen Khoury wrinkled her nose and straightened the hem of her too-tight, but expensive, skirt suit as she replied, "Well, she had at least one *very close* little friend that we didn't know anything about."

"From the implications of that phrase, *very close*," Shiloh leaned on the word in imitation of Helen's inflection, "I take it you mean that Jaya had a boyfriend whom you weren't aware of."

Not answering, Helen stared at Shiloh coldly. Her coal-black eyes reflected the lamplight behind her with a look of accusation as if Shiloh caused her some personal affront by asking the question. Her posture stiffened as she smoothed her glistening, perfectly coiffed black hair.

In a very low, stern voice, Kash answered for his wife. "If only she had, Ms. Mueller." Shiloh did not correct him. Most people assumed that she'd taken Ethan's last name rather than continuing to use her own and would continue to do so months after his death.

"No," Dr. Khoury continued, nervously straightening his pale blue silk tie as he stared down at his reflection in the highly polished leather of his custom Italian loafers. The shirt that he wore had a sort of pearlized sheen to it as well, which reminded Shiloh of what she'd thought of the doctor the first time she'd met him. Akash Khoury always dressed like a *GQ* ad that had somehow come to life. "Even though I assure you we most certainly did not raise her that way, we found out from some of Jaya's other friends with whom we've been in contact that our daughter had a female companion."

Nadia Haas, who had been silent until then, glanced up from her laptop screen. "Do you mean to say, Dr. Khoury, that your daughter Jaya had a girlfriend? That she was a lesbian?"

"My husband means to say that our daughter was suffering from some type of mental illness," Helen replied. "In which Jaya falsely believed that she was improperly attracted to another young woman whom she'd known since childhood." Helen pursed her lips primly. "It would have been just a phase, I'm sure. Doubtlessly caused by all this left-wing indoctrination that kids are getting these days from the internet. We put Jaya and her brother Khalid in private religious schools specifically to avoid that kind of rhetoric, but it's like a virus. Sooner or later, everyone is exposed."

"Whoa," Nadia muttered under her breath. Shiloh glanced over to see the look of shock on Nadia's face and knew what it meant. Her generation wasn't used to hearing such blatant negative statements about a person's sexuality, especially from educated professional people. Still, Nadia maintained her composure as she continued to type furiously on her laptop.

Ignoring the increasing level of tension in the room that she'd caused, Helen trained her judgmental gaze on her husband. "If Dr. Khoury had supported me in encouraging Jaya to go to Xavier or some other Catholic college instead of that public university," Helen wrinkled her nose again with disdain. "Then perhaps such ideas wouldn't have infected her brain."

"Helen," Kash sighed with exasperation. "The other girl *was* a student at Xavier. A senior. I know you don't approve of it, and I'm not happy about it either, but we have to face the facts. Our daughter had a girlfriend, whom we knew nothing about. The Muellers are a good family too. I've known Roman my whole life. That's just the way things are now."

"Wait," Shiloh held up her hand to request silence. "Did you just say that Jaya's girlfriend's father was Roman Mueller?"

"Yes," Helen Khoury replied, her lush, plum, lipsticked lips tightening into an expression of disgust. "Your husband's brother." Helen cleared her throat as she paused to select her words carefully. "Jaya was seeing his daughter Riley. Apparently, everyone else knew."

At this revelation, Nadia Haas exhaled another quiet *whoa*.

"Not everyone, I don't think," Shiloh replied, trying to conceal her surprise. *So that's why Helen was staring at me so hatefully when she first came in*, she thought to herself. "I was unaware. Has Riley been in contact with you? I'm sure she must be devastated."

"No, she has not," Helen snapped, her tone growing icily more proper. "Which was one of the reasons we agreed to speak with you. We thought that you might have better access to information regarding Riley's whereabouts. After Jaya's friends told us about their relationship last night, I immediately called Riley's mother, Kimberly, to see if it was true. Such rumors can destroy a young lady's reputation and chances of making a good marriage. So, I thought that she should also be made aware of the situation. Unfortunately, Kimberly Mueller's character as a mother was not what I supposed it to be. She knew about their immoral relationship but had done nothing to correct it. This made it less surprising to me when I learned that she didn't know where her daughter Riley was last night either. I told her to call me the moment she got in touch with Riley. However, I'm not holding my breath. The fact that she conveniently disappeared on the night of my daughter's murder makes me more than a little suspicious that Riley Mueller has something to hide. Because she's already shown a willingness to confide in her mother about her shameless behavior, perhaps Kimberly is concealing something as well. One never knows," Helen concluded primly, "what people of such devious character might be capable of when they've been exposed."

Feeling her anger beginning to rise at Helen Khoury's increasingly bigoted tirade, Shiloh forced herself to remain calm by staring at her hands on the keyboard. "Ms. Khoury," she began, deliberately avoiding Helen's piercing gaze. "I understand that you've suffered a great deal of trauma over your daughter's recent death. However, I would appreciate it if you reined in your personal beliefs a bit for the remainder of this interview. We're both just looking for facts here, I hope. If Riley Mueller were an actual person of interest in your daughter Jaya's death, I'm sure I would have learned about it when I spoke with Detective Schultz this morning. However, she is not. Thus, I'd appreciate it if you took into consideration the personal nature of your insinuations regarding members of the Mueller family. Of which, as you know, I am a part."

"You *were* a part," Helen corrected her, emphasizing the past tense verb. "And for a relatively short time, Ms. Foley," she added, using Shiloh's preferred last name for the first time like an indictment. "I wouldn't expect you to understand my displeasure at learning of my daughter's indiscretions or how they reflect negatively on my family. After all, such matters are merely hypotheticals to you. You're not a mother."

"Oh, look at that!" Nadia broke in, trying to distract Shiloh before she could respond. "I think I see someone else pulling up. It must be Mr. Lang. I think he's a little early."

At the mention of Kyle Lang's name, Helen Khoury stiffened and picked up her expensive handbag. "We should go. We're wasting our time here." Taking her husband firmly by the arm, she pulled him out of the chair and toward the door. Kash protested that he knew it was a mistake to come.

Seeing that they were about to leave without answering the one question she'd hoped to get around to, but had known it would be difficult with both of them present together, Shiloh called out to Kash. "Dr. Khoury, wait! I was wondering if I could speak with you privately about the disappearance of Jasmine Jenkins. Her sister Bernadette hired me to…"

Kash Khoury's handsome, tan face blanched. He pushed past his wife on the way out the door. "If you've spoken to Bernadette Jenkins, then I'm sure you already know everything I would have to say about her sister. I know nothing more than the fact that she is missing."

Allowing the door to slam shut on its spring behind him without waiting for his wife, Dr. Akash Khoury hurried out, just as Kyle Lang walked in. Seeing Shiloh standing behind her desk, Lang's face lit up into the thousand-watt television announcer smile that Shiloh remembered from seeing him at the reunion bonfire several nights before.

"Hello Kyle," Helen said in a knowing voice as Lang strode past her into the room. "I didn't know you had an appointment here today as well, or I would have scheduled a more convenient time."

Lang spun around, and his face froze. He swallowed hard, and his eyes grew large with surprise as he attempted to speak pleasantly. "Helen! I didn't think I'd see you here again so soon after the identification. How are you holding up?"

"As well as one might expect under the circumstances," Helen replied through a false, tight-lipped smile as she readjusted her shoulder bag and reached for the door. "But one mustn't dwell on the negatives of life. It's better to be discreet when one is grieving or suffering some kind of embarrassment. Wouldn't you agree?" Helen's obsidian eyes were so intensely bright with obvious hatred that Lang retreated several steps.

"Yes, I would never dream of being indiscreet," he mumbled.

"Well, I wouldn't say that," Helen remarked over her shoulder, allowing her icy stare to linger on Kyle as the door closed behind her. "But now is as good a time to start as any."

Kyle Lang exhaled an audible sigh of relief as he sunk into the chair that Dr. Kash Khoury had recently vacated. Although it was a normal office-size leather seat, Lang's gigantic torso dwarfed the piece of furniture. He shifted around uneasily, crossing and uncrossing his long legs to find a more comfortable position. Dressed in old jeans paired with a black and orange Bengals polo that had his old number *21* embroidered over the left side of his chest and a day-old growth of gray stubble, Kyle Lang looked like what he was: an old jock who would never quite adjust to life after the game.

"What was all that about?" Shiloh asked. "I take it that the two of you know one another, but from her demeanor, it doesn't seem that the association was pleasant."

"No, I mean..." Lang trailed off as his eyes followed the Khourys' black Mercedes SUV out of the parking lot. "Yes. I know Helen. No, it hasn't always been pleasant. I mean, once it was very much, but now..." Lang stopped himself again, running his massive, wide-receiver hands through his close-cropped, corn-colored hair. "God, this is awkward. Can we just get onto talking about Lorelei? The police are saying that they don't have any suspects yet. I wanted to meet in hopes that you might know something more that they weren't telling me."

Lang's blue eyes were bloodshot as if he'd been crying, or drinking heavily, or both. The lines on his forehead and around his mouth seemed more pronounced under his spray tan than the last time she'd seen him, and his cheeks looked sunken above the sharp German edge of his jawline. For the first time, Shiloh felt a glimmer of sympathy for the man. Whatever beef he had with Helen Khoury notwithstanding, Kyle Lang was a father who was plainly in shock over his daughter's sudden death.

In as delicate words as she could muster, Shiloh repeated the main facts about the crime scene as Detective Bruce Schultz described it to her. The two young women were found just beside the main path through Burnet Woods. Naked, with their backs arched far enough so that they could be bound hand to foot in a circle. They were found in the same position as Savannah and Veronica Arnold. Both of their throats were slashed too. The only difference was the Latin phrase, inscribed in what the preliminary forensics report presumed was their blood. *Quod me nutrit, me destruit*, or *that which nourishes me, destroys me*.

"The ouroboros," Shiloh finished. "That's what the detectives seem to think the killer or killers, plural, are trying to suggest with the placement of their bodies. Creation and destruction together. They think it's connected somehow with Reece Mueller's murder too. Because, even though she was burned alone, the Bible verse found in the lockbox with her suggested some kind of divine retribution or judgment of sins. It's a dramatic statement, shaded with religious undertones, although they don't understand yet what it means. Do you have any ideas?"

"No," Lang replied quietly. Massaging his temples before covering his face with his giant hands, he added, "Lorelei wasn't religious. Her mother,

Elke, and I aren't either. I've thought all that crap about sin and punishment—you know, the kind of stuff they try to use to instill guilt into you at Catholic school—was just garbage since junior high. There isn't any such thing as sin or the judgment finding you or any of that horseshit. These messages," Kyle lifted his hands in frustration as he got up to pace around the room. "They're probably just the ramblings of some kind of religious nut who has it out for me and all the rest of us old guys from St. Aug's. Some random jealous asshole we'd never remember, who's decided to take it out on our kids and our wives, because we're successful and they're not. My morality runs more like that thing Hemingway said once, about how it feels later on."

"You mean that bit in *Death in the Afternoon.*" Shiloh recited the quote from memory. "*So far, about morals, I know only that what is moral is what you feel good after, and what is immoral is what you feel bad after.* Are you a fan of the author, Mr. Lang?"

"Yeah," Kyle said, watching the traffic go by outside the window with a faraway expression. "And I've read probably more of him than anyone else. He tells things like they are. Very straightforward, not trying to hide the ball of meaning like a lot of those others."

"Well, there are some who would say that Hemingway's work is much more layered than it appears," Shiloh said. "Have you ever heard of the Iceberg Theory, Mr. Lang? How many critics believe that there is much more under the surface of Hemingway's simple prose than readers can see unless they take the time to look beneath the water?"

"No," Kyle said, crossing his arms as he looked away from the window. He seemed annoyed at the direction the conversation was taking. "I don't see what any of this has to do with Lorelei's murder or those other women. What are you trying to get at?"

Shiloh took a deep breath, mentally preparing herself for one of the questions she'd wanted to ask the Khourys before they left. However, their argument distracted her. "What I'm getting at, Mr. Lang, is that I believe a lot is going on beneath the surface in the lives of all the young men who were on that football team with you and my husband Ethan back in the day at St. Augustine's. The more I think about it, the more I'm beginning to suspect that there was one incident in particular that happened a long time ago that might have caused your daughter and the daughters of Kash Khoury, Roman Mueller, and Joe Arnold, along with Arnold's wife, to become targets for a very sadistic person's revenge. Do you have any idea what that might be?"

Kyle Lang's bloodshot stare locked on Shiloh. "I don't have the slightest clue."

Shiloh closed her eyes and opened the top drawer of her desk. Carefully, she turned the graphing calculator so that Lang could see the name written on its hard plastic cover in permanent silver marker. As he bent over to read, Lang's left hand reached involuntarily to cover his mouth.

"Oh God," he whispered, the normally deep baritone of his voice quivering as he recognized the object. "Where did you get that? Did Ethan give it to you?"

"No," Shiloh answered. "It was left on my doorstep two nights ago. Not long after, I saw someone in Eden Park that I think you would recognize. Although from what I understand, he is very much changed now from the young man you'd remember."

"Oh God," Kyle Lang repeated. "I didn't know he was here. Or that he was still alive."

"Didn't know he was alive, Kyle, or hoped that he wasn't?" Shiloh probed.

The look in Lang's eyes was wild, like a scared animal. "How much do you know? Who have you told?"

"I haven't told anyone yet," Shiloh replied. "Other than you and my associate here, who's assisting me with a related investigation." She gestured in Nadia's direction. "And someone else who already knew, because she was there too. Sister Frida Jiminez. She was the Writing Center director at St. Augustine's at that time."

Lang swallowed hard. Beads of sweat began to form along the rugged lines of his face. "How much did Sister Frida tell you?"

"Nothing that I didn't already know from reading this," Shiloh answered, pulling the notebook from the same drawer and laying it on the surface of her desk beside the calculator. "It's one of Ethan's journals. From when he was a soldier in Afghanistan. Thinking that he might die any day, my husband wrote out a confessional. It describes everything that he saw that night in the locker room, what happened afterward, and the guilt he felt for helping to cover it up."

As his glance flickered back and forth between the calculator and the worn cover of the composition book, Kyle Lang's eyes filled with tears. "It all happened so fast. We never meant for it to go that far. Joe was furious about Simon getting him kicked off the team. All of us were. It was just a load of pretentious bullshit. How Simon refused to help a fellow out because he felt *superior*. That he had *principles*."

Lang emphasized the last word of each sentence resentfully.

"Simon was always such a pompous little prick. Thought he was smarter than everyone else. All the nuns acted like he was the Second Coming. That he was brilliant and could do no wrong. We were sick of it. So when Joe said that he wanted us to help catch him and hold him down so that he could show him who ran the school, we didn't think twice. Seconds before it happened, we were all laughing about it. Joe was spanking him like anybody would do to a bad kid, not hurting him. Simon was squealing like the little sissy he was. Then, for some reason, Joe just snapped." Lang raised his hands in frustration. "I've always thought that we would have let him go anyway, even if Ethan hadn't walked in and seen it. But I don't know if that would have helped anything. The damage was already done. We all knew that we had to keep it quiet, not just for Joe or the school, but for ourselves. Do you know what it would have done to my prospects of playing in college or the NFL if word got out that I'd been a part of something like that?"

Lang didn't wait for a response. "My career would have been over before it began. It would have cost me every scholarship offer. If it had come out later on, the Bengals would have voided my contract. I would never have set foot in a professional stadium, never met Elke, never become a father to Lorelei, never been hired as a commentator on SportsNet, nothing. It would have ruined my entire life. For less than a minute of a prank that went too far, it would have ruined all our lives."

"What about Simon's life?" Nadia interjected. Shiloh shot her a look.

"His life?" Lang snorted with contempt. "His mother was in the nuthouse, and he had no dick. I think Simon's life was already shot to shit long before he ever met any of us."

Growing serious again, Lang asked Shiloh, "So, do you think he's the one who did it then? The guy who killed Lorelei and those other girls? Because as much as I'd like to find out who it was, I'm having a hard time believing that he'd be capable. I mean," Lang scoffed. "I just don't think he'd have the guts."

"Some people change, Mr. Lang," Shiloh replied, growing weary of his condescending attitude. "Or rather, the world changes them. Bitterness and pain can make people very strong. They live just to spite those who wronged them. What I would be concerned about if I were you, Mr. Lang," Shiloh said, "is that the police don't believe Simon acted alone. They believe he had help. However, they have no idea who those accomplices might have been or where they might be hiding. For all we know, they could be right outside that door, watching us this very moment."

Lang's eyes flashed with fear as he jerked his head toward the door, considering the possibility. "What do the police plan on doing about it?" he asked, his voice rising.

"Nothing they can do," Shiloh replied, rising to show Lang to the door. "They can't just shoot into the darkness. If I find out any more details, I'll let you know. Thanks for coming in."

Wednesday, October 11th, Evening

After Kyle Lang left, Shiloh slumped down in her chair. She felt completely exhausted.

"Two down, one more to go," she said to Nadia. "What time is it?"

Nadia glanced at her smartwatch. "Nearly six. Do you think we'll have time to meet with Elke Winter and still make it to the theater?"

"Mmm," Shiloh mused. "We'll be cutting it close. You can take your ticket and go on if you want to. I can always sneak in during intermission."

"What?" Nadia scowled. "There's no way I'd miss out on a second of this master class in tactfully dealing with pure assholes. I don't think I could ever do it without giving them a piece of my mind," Nadia shook her head. "I mean, these people's daughters are dead. They're just sitting there saying all this awful, unrelated shit. Trying to cover their asses like they don't even care. Are all rich people like that? Do they even know how they sound?"

"Not all of them," Shiloh said. "But most of them, yeah. As for your other question, I think that the vast majority went deaf to the sound of their self-aggrandizing nastiness a long time ago."

"Well, I know it's horrible to say this, but if that's the case," Nadia reasoned, "then I can kind of see why Simon would have a motive to kill them. A sick and twisted motive for sure, one that proves he shouldn't be out roaming the streets because he's such a dangerous person, but still... it kind of makes sense."

"Are you sure you wouldn't prefer a career in psychiatry?" Shiloh whee-dled. "You'd still get to work on problems like this if you specialized in the deviant cases."

"Nice try, but I suck at math, and anything medical requires calculus," Nadia replied. "I know you don't like it, but I'm going to law school."

"Calculus?" Shiloh questioned. "For psychiatrists? That's pointless, isn't it?"

Nadia's response about how many useless STEM classes were included in the prerequisites for medical school was interrupted by multiple chirps of an automatic door lock in the parking lot announcing the arrival of their final meeting for the day.

"I will never get used to these clicky things for the doors," Elke Winter said in her thick German accent as she entered. Dressed in fitted dark jeans that accentuated her long legs and a half-tucked natural linen blouse left open at the neck to reveal cascading tiers of layered gold necklaces, Elke Winter bore an even more striking resemblance to Claudia Schiffer in person than Shiloh had expected. Her face was framed by golden tendrils cascading from her perfectly mussed chignon. Elke's eyes were the bright, innocent blue of a girl's. Her lineless face made her seem more like a woman in her twenties, even though Shiloh knew Elke must be at least her age. She'd seen her in magazine advertisements modeling for luxury brands her whole life. Hovering awkwardly near the door like a lost stork, Elke waited for Shiloh to invite her to sit and then said nothing. Although her facial expression was blandly pleasant, Elke's eyes were rimmed red from holding back tears, just like her ex-husband's.

"I saw Kyle leaving," Elke ventured finally, her accent making the ending of the word sound like "ink." Elke fidgeted nervously with the chain strap on her Stella McCartney bag, waiting for Shiloh to take the hint that she hadn't the slightest clue what to say next.

"Yes," Shiloh replied gently. "Kyle said that the police didn't have any new suspects. I'm afraid that I don't have much more to share, other than a few details regarding some crimes that might be related. We," Shiloh gestured to Nadia. "My associate and I were hoping that you could tell us a bit more about Lorelei's friends. To see if there is anyone else whom we might interview for leads."

Elke stared solidly at Shiloh during her explanation. Swaying a little in her seat, like a drunk person trying to steady herself by fixing her gaze at a point on the wall. "Kyle wants to blame Lorelei's ex-boyfriend, Robby Drystan. I know he does. But Kyle's never even met Robby. He's not a bad boy at heart. He's just got all these tattoos. What do you call them in English?" Elke's hands swept over her arms.

"Sleeves?" Nadia suggested.

"Yes, that's the word. Sleeves," Elke replied. "Kyle's always been very judgmental against young people wearing all black and going for that, how do you say it, gothic look? But there's nothing wrong with Robby. At least, that I could find. In Germany, darker industrial music and the aesthetic that goes with it are very normal. Robby was devastated when I saw him at Lorelei's viewing in the morgue. Poor boy. Lorelei had told him that they were just on a break until he was sober and that she might be willing to try things again. But she'd started dating Khalid Khoury at UC about a month ago, and well..." Elke rolled her eyes. "You know how it is with girls sometimes. Always trying to do something to please their fathers and gain their attention. It rarely works."

Shiloh glanced up from the screen of her note-taking app. "It makes sense that he'd be happier for his daughter to date the son of a doctor who was a long-term friend than a semi-rock star with an addiction problem. I take it that Kyle approved of Khalid more than he did of Robby. Because he knew Khalid's family?"

"Of course not," Elke answered indignantly. "As soon as he found out, Kyle told Lorelei why she had to break things off with Khalid, and she did immediately."

"Just one of those dads who's impossible to please, huh?" Nadia quipped. "Speaking from experience with my Dad, I know that's a thing."

"No," Elke hesitated. "This is... different. Kyle said that both he and the Khourys were stopping by to speak with you today. I'm surprised that neither of them mentioned it."

"Mentioned what exactly?" Shiloh replied, confused. "I must have missed something."

"Why, the reason that Kyle and I divorced," Elke said. "He was having an affair with Helen Khoury. Khalid Khoury is Kyle's son, not Kash's."

Shiloh heard Nadia inhale loudly behind her.

"Yeah, they both skipped over that part," Shiloh said, trying to mask her surprise at the revelation. "I'm going to need a bit more explanation."

"When I was pregnant with Lorelei," Elke began. "It was at the beginning of all that stuff with models taking nude shots of themselves while they were pregnant. Artistic. In all the fashion magazines. The whole *women's bodies are beautiful* type of thing. Kyle got very upset with me because I was doing quite a few of those types of shoots and also a lot of runway shows. But because my hormones were running wild, I'd lost all interest in sex. With me being away most of the time and constantly telling him no when I was home, Kyle felt rejected. However, at that time he was scared to get involved with anyone notable because it might end up in the tabloids. His contract with the Bengals was up, and he'd just started working as a commentator with SportsNet. Kyle didn't want to begin his career with a scandal. The way that Kyle explained it to me was that Helen knew her husband, Kash, was having an affair and that they'd discussed the possibility of opening their relationship."

Shiloh could hold back her surprise no longer. "Helen Khoury was okay with opening her marriage! The Helen Khoury I know?" Shiloh patted her hair, crossed her legs tightly, and pursed her lips, imitating Helen's unmistakably judgmental expression.

Elke snorted, recognizing Shiloh's imitation. The sort of sound a sad child might make if something funny caught them off guard. "At first, I couldn't believe it either. I mean..." Elke trailed off, twirling her wrists in a *What can you do?* motion that made the stacks of slim gold bracelets on her arms jingle.

"There we were, right? This picture-perfect couple. The model and the athlete. Yet the moment the model turns him down, the football star goes back home to bang his best friend's wife. A woman who'd had a crush on him since high school. Whom he'd never considered hot enough to give the time of day. In counseling, Kyle admitted that it was ego. He'd hooked up with Helen because he knew that she'd always wanted him, even though she'd married Kash. Because when they were young, it looked like Kash was the better catch. Nobody would have guessed that they'd turn out to be worth the same amount of money, which was all Helen cared about. Both of the Altman sisters were like that. They grew up with money and wanted to make sure they had even more of it. Helen married Akash Khoury because she knew he would become a surgeon. Just like her sister, Francine married Rafferty Purcell because she knew he was going into finance like the rest of his family."

"It seems weird though," Shiloh said. "Wouldn't Helen have everything to lose if Kash changed his mind when he found out that the man his wife chose was one of his best friends? What did she get out of the arrangement that made her ready to take that risk?"

Elke shook her head. "I don't believe Kash Khoury ever cared whom Helen slept with. Kyle told me that Kash married Helen Altman because her family was rich and well-connected enough to help him secure a top-notch residency in plastic surgery right out of medical school. As for Helen, she didn't care what their motives were. She was content to stroke her vanity by marrying the best-looking guy in the senior class at her high school and then having the second-best one, whom she preferred, come crawling back to her when his wife rejected him."

"I could see that," Nadia said thoughtfully. "Kind of like how it's easy for ugly girls to be judgmental of pretty ones for losing their virginity early and pretend to get on their religious high horses about it. When they finally do latch onto a guy to marry, they'll do anything to keep them. Let them cheat, or whatever. Because controlling their secrets makes them feel more powerful finally, over the men in their lives."

"So you're saying that's what Helen did?" Shiloh asked Elke. "She made Kyle feel like having an affair with her was safe when it allowed her some measure of control over both him and Kash."

"That's exactly right," Elke replied. "When Helen got pregnant, that sort of sealed the deal all around. Kash knew the baby couldn't be his, but he was afraid to speak up because then she'd bring up that affair with his nurse, Destiny Jenkins, and use her family's money to hire Roman Mueller as her lawyer to take everything in the divorce. Roman is anyone's friend who pays him the most. Kyle only told me about all of it because I confronted him in counseling right after Lorelei was born. I went into premature labor while I was in England for a photo shoot. He was back here in Cincinnati that weekend doing commentary on a Bengals game. I figured out he was with Helen that weekend because he accidentally sent me a text message meant for her. Stupid Kyle."

Elke shook her head. "We separated soon afterward, but still I felt sorry for him."

"Why?" Nadia asked. The girl leaned forward in her chair, wide-eyed and starstruck in equal parts at hearing such a confessional from a woman she'd watched on television for years.

Elke turned to her. "I feel sorry for anyone who grew up in this place, the way he did. Only knows one type of person his whole life. Kyle would have never seen anything of the world if not for football. My family was middle class, but I was raised in Berlin, going to public schools. My parents saved to take my brother and me to a different country each year on holiday because they thought it was important for us to meet people from everywhere and all walks of life. They thought that only hearing one rhetoric from one place over and over was not only stifling but also intellectually dangerous. A lot of Germans from their generation, growing up right after the war, felt that way. That it was important to see the world and to learn to think and reason for oneself. It's too easy to fall into... mmm," Elke squinted. "I believe in English it is called a feedback loop. A confirmation bias. If all one hears is the same old same. I think that is what happened to Kyle. He heard for years and years that he could trust the people here. The ones he went to church with and grew up with at that school, St. Augustine's. When in fact, the opposite was true. Those people were full of lies, and this place... this place is poison. The politics of Berlin or even Hollywood are nothing compared to here. There, you know who your enemies are; you can see them coming and be ready. But here, there is an illusion of trust. A false sense that you are as secure as royalty because everyone knows you and you think you know them too. Yet all along, someone follows along behind. Watching and waiting for a chance to poison the king's cup."

Elke closed her perfect blue eyes. "My Lorelei found that out too late."

Concluding the conversation by thanking Elke Winter for her time and reassuring her that she'd be in touch as new information came to light, Shiloh showed the model out and locked the door. She checked the clock on the wall above the door.

"It's six-forty," Shiloh told Nadia. "I think if we hustle, we should have just enough time to make it to the theater. You can ride with me. Grab your coat."

The pair hurried to the car. On the way across town to the Shakespeare Company, they dissected the trio of interviews from that afternoon.

"You know," Nadia began as they pulled out of the parking lot. "I know you're not crazy about my going to law school in general, but I think I've decided that if I do go, I'd rather pick a law school in New York rather than here."

"Oh really?" Shiloh answered, swirling down the hill out of Mt. Adams and onto Gilbert Street. "What prompted this decision? Did listening to all those sad parent interviews today make you start missing your dad?"

"That's part of it," Nadia explained. "But the other part is that the older I get, the more I feel like I need to branch out. Get some different perspectives on the world."

"That's natural at your age," Shiloh agreed. "What Elke Winter said resonated with you, I'm guessing."

"It did," Nadia replied. "What's weirdest to me is how Elke Winter was having the most normal reaction of all. I never expected her to be so down-to-earth and generally aware of her daughter's life. The more I think about it, the more I'm like, she's the only parent who was focused on her kid. Which is kind of the opposite of what you'd expect. People from less worldly places, especially if they're big churchgoers, tend to go on and on about the value of family and community, but from what I saw today," Nadia shook her head. "It seems more like they're just trapped here because it's the only place they feel like people will keep covering up for their lies. I didn't get the impression that anything they said or felt was genuine."

"Elke was the only one who didn't talk about herself the whole time." Shiloh agreed, frowning at the slowing traffic ahead. "But I've found that to be true with a lot of genuinely beautiful people. Especially if they're well-known. They're often kinder than you'd expect, usually because they're very lonely. Beauty intimidates a lot of people, and fame can be a curse."

"You must be right," Nadia replied. The traffic going into the Over-the-Rhine district had ground to a halt. Nadia held up her phone screen for Shiloh to see. "After she got rid of her official, professional accounts, Lorelei had less than a hundred friends altogether on any of her socials. And she's gorgeous! Look at her skin! She was like, glowing!"

Shiloh glanced over at Nadia's phone. Sure enough, Lorelei Winter-Lang's perfectly symmetrical, bronzed face radiated from her profile picture pretty enough for any beauty influencer profile. What caught Shiloh's eye, though, were the comments. Tributes from Lorelei's ex-boyfriend, Robby Drystan, including a special acoustic song dedicated to her memory, along with a couple of friends from Psi Chi. "She was an honors student in psychology? I wouldn't have picked that as the most likely possibility for her major."

Nadia examined the posts again and tilted her head to the side. "I can kind of see it too, though. Most psych majors I know pick that field because they're sort of trying to heal themselves. Becoming a model at a young age, especially with already famous parents, would be a lot of pressure. The constant expectations to look a certain way and be a certain weight, all that stuff. If Lorelei decided to take some time out for herself to go to college like a basic person, I could understand her taking a more normal kind of major for self-improvement."

"Makes sense," Shiloh agreed somewhat absently as she watched the driver in front of her shut off his car and get out to peer down the street. "I'm going to put this in park and see what's going on up there. It looks like someone may have had a bad accident that's going to jam things up for a while. Yell if anything starts to move, and I'll run back."

Leaving Nadia in her parked car, Shiloh jogged up toward a group of other drivers standing on the sidewalk at the corner of Central Parkway and Elm Street. Following the sightline of their pointing fingers, Shiloh spied what they were all gawking at.

A massive ball of flame right in the middle of Elm Street, in front of the historic Music Hall building. Hearing fire truck sirens squawking in the distance as they attempted to weave through the impossible traffic, Shiloh stared with the others in disbelief as she realized what the object on fire was. One of those antique horse-drawn carriages that often circled Washington Park. She'd ridden in one just like it on the night that Ethan had proposed to her.

"Did someone rear-end the carriage and set it on fire?" Shiloh asked a teenage boy standing in front of her.

The boy didn't answer her question. He kept staring at the flaming carriage. In a high, whining tone, he began singing under his breath, off-key and out of tempo.

Ezekiel saw a wheel. Way up there in the middle of the air. Now the little wheel runs by faith. And the big wheel runs by the grace of God. And a wheel in a wheel whirling. Way in the middle of the air.

As she stood listening to the eerie hum of his melody, Shiloh recognized the boy's profile. Dirty blonde, tousled hair. Pug-nose with a bare, white scar through one eyebrow. Muscular frame, plainly athletic. He was one of Joe Arnold's boys. Jackson, the younger one.

At last, the boy turned and looked at her. Sweat streamed down the sides of his face. Shiloh saw that the pupils of his eyes were dilated so much that she could hardly tell the color of his irises, a paper-thin ring of blue surrounded by bright red. The veins on his neck stood out like a bodybuilder's as the boy's song changed into a chantlike mantra. "I did what she told me, but I let her horse go. I would never hurt the horse. Never, never, never. I did what she told me, but I let her horse go."

"Did what who told you?" Shiloh asked the boy. "You're not making any sense. What did you see? Are you okay?"

The boy's eyes bulged even larger as it dawned on him that Shiloh could hear what he was saying. Before Shiloh could react, the boy grabbed her throat and began to squeeze.

"Get down!" Someone yelled from the group watching the fire. "It's going to blow!"

Instinctively, Shiloh fell to the ground. The boy let go of her throat and took off running down Elm Street back toward the parkway. As she lay coughing on the pavement, Shiloh heard the carriage explode behind her.

Thursday, October 12th, Noon

The preview night for Laurie's play that Shiloh and Nadia were on their way to see was canceled after the explosion. It was rescheduled for Saturday. Although a few people were struck by small fragments of flaming wood and metal when the carriage blew, no one was seriously injured. No one except the young man who was in the carriage at the time of the accident. Police speculated that he was dead already, several hours before the carriage fire. Few remnants of his body were left intact. Still, forensics experts were able to work overnight to match some of the blood, tissue, and bone fragment samples to a young man named Ellis Purcell, son of Dynamic Investments Group owner and St. Augustine's alum Rafferty Purcell. Ellis's mother, Francine Altman, the ex-wife of Rafferty Purcell, reported her son missing after he failed to return home following youth orchestra practice. Finding a fireproof lockbox very similar to the one tucked into the bonfire that became Reece Mueller's funeral pyre, the police opened it to find Ellis's clarinet with his nameplate inscribed on the handle. Along with a sheaf of papers, each containing cryptic Bible verses, the same two from Isaiah and another from the Book of Matthew, along with several crudely drawn sigils and depictions of Baphomet in red ink.

Sitting by a window facing Central Parkway at Coffee Emporium, Shiloh perused the color photocopied reprints that Detective Schultz brought along. She agreed to meet him that day during his lunch break to offer her advice on some symbols found at the crime scene. Although they'd never formally spoken about her spiritual preferences, Bruce knew from his partnership with Shiloh's husband, Ethan, that she was, in his parlance, someone "who was into New Age philosophy." Content that this descriptor raised no eyebrows in professional circles, Shiloh never corrected them. Being known as a witch won no one any friends in court. However, it became a fact universally acknowledged, if never voiced around the courthouse, that if anyone on the police force or in the D.A.'s office had a case in which the evidence included occult-themed evidence that required explanation, Shiloh Foley was their first call. She liked to think of it as keeping her broom in the closet until pulling it out was justifiable.

"There's no doubt about it," Shiloh said as she handed the photos back to Bruce Schultz. "Those are the same symbols as the ones in Eden Park. Even though whoever drew these was a little better artist."

Schultz put his glasses back on and squinted at the pictures. "How can you be sure? It all just looks like heathen gibberish to me."

"Mmm..." Shiloh mused as she drained the last sip of her honey and vanilla latte, aptly named "The Bee's Knees" on the Emporium's beverage menu. As usual, Schultz mocked her choice of beverage. "I wouldn't necessarily call it heathen, in the sense that the term can be used to mean people who have no religion at all. If religious belief is defined by worship, then whoever drew these symbols is using them to call attention to their idolization of a particular deity or deities."

Schultz screwed up his nose in disgust as he took a pronounced slurp of his plain black coffee. "Well, it certainly ain't any *deity*," he snarled as he repeated the word, "that this Catholic boy is familiar with. Enlighten me."

Shiloh sat her coffee cup down on the table and picked up one of the copies again. "This one," she said, pointing at what looked like a lopsided capital letter *B* in a circle, "is fairly straightforward. A symbol to summon Mammon. The demon people invoke with prayers for wealth and abundance. If I had my guess, it's also used here as a condemnation of people who place too much value on gaining or holding onto wealth at others' expense because of the verse that's cited with it."

"Matthew 6:19-21," Schultz read from the photo. "That one I am familiar with. About not laying up treasures on Earth and how one can't serve both God and Mammon. Or as that Latin part underneath puts it, *De solo Mammona cogitant, quorum Deus est sacculus.* Which Kaley translated for me as, *They only think of Mammon, whose god is the purse.*"

"Good Latin pronunciation," Shiloh smiled. "Did your wife coach you?"

"Don't rub it in," Schultz grumbled. "We both know Kaley's the brains of our outfit. Getting back to business, what about those other ones? That number doesn't correspond to any Bible verse I'm aware of."

"Me neither," Shiloh shrugged. "The figure is Baphomet. Goat-headed god with both male and female anatomy. Depending on who you ask and why they're trying to invoke the deity, he can be either an evil demon or a symbol of harmony and gender nonconformity. Darkness and light all in one. His hands are in the same position, suggesting the *As Above, So Below* graffiti message that we found on the wall in Eden Park next to the dead cat. The message usually signifies a microcosm. That one small thing or person is indicative of society as a whole and whatever is wrong with it. But that series of numbers," Shiloh shook her head. "III.IV.CXC. Those are Roman numerals for 3, 4, and... a hundred and ninety? It could be a date of birth, maybe, for someone born in the nineties?"

"If it were the date of birth of someone still living, shouldn't it be written as four numerals, not three?" Schultz asked.

"You'd think so," Shiloh agreed. "However, when you're trying to figure out the meaning of someone's intention who's working in occult symbols, there's often a lot of mixed messaging. It could be anything. A date of historical significance, perhaps, in redacted form. Some say that the history of humanity moves in cycles. One of those cycles, Uranus and Neptune, for example, orbits precisely every 172 years, bringing extreme social change."

"So, it could be one of those looney, radical left-wing groups then," Schultz posited. "Trying to say whatever goes around comes back around. If so, that fits with our theory that someone is targeting the old St. Augustine's bunch that Ethan used to run around with in high school. People are always after the one percent these days. Everyone wants to kill the rich."

Shiloh paused. This was the moment in which she could tell Schultz everything she'd learned. What she suspected about the boy who had been Simon Bowles. Yet, it was so circumstantial. A near-Dickensian level of coincidences pointing toward a man who'd already suffered so much. Judge Roman Mueller and all of Ethan's cop buddies always chided Shiloh about her hunches on whether an accused person was guilty or innocent. Even though she trusted that her witch's intuition was right most of the time, a wrong accusation toward a person who was as vulnerable as Simon could be a death sentence if they found him, whether he was guilty or not. The justice system, Shiloh knew all too well from having worked in it, was no place for the marginalized. Not to mention her lingering reluctance to believe that a man who was likely in fragile mental health could have orchestrated such a diabolical scheme on a grand scale. There was just one more thing that she had to see for herself before she felt confident enough to share her findings with the police. Anything less would make her feel guiltier than she would from waiting. Before throwing Simon to the lions, Shiloh had to be sure.

"Well, perhaps some of them deserve it," she replied. Seeing the stunned look on Schultz's face, Shiloh sensed the need to add something more to soften the abruptness of her response. "After all, what was it that Mark Twain said? History doesn't repeat, but it rhymes. I guess we'll see whether there's any justice, poetic or not, in this case soon enough."

Gathering her things to go, Shiloh noticed a text message from her client, Bernadette Jenkins. *Jackson didn't come home last night after rehearsal. No one has heard from Jeff since yesterday either. Joe is furious and also terrified. Police already know.*

If the police already know, Shiloh wondered, *why didn't Schultz say anything to me about it?* Feeling slightly better about not sharing information with Schultz right away, Shiloh exchanged pleasantries and left. Once she was safely out of earshot of Schultz, Shiloh attempted to call Bernadette. The call went to voicemail, but immediately a second text dinged on Shiloh's cell.

Can't talk right now. Scarlet knows something too but won't tell me alone. Insists on seeing you. Are you free to meet up again tonight in Washington Park at 6 pm? Woodwind sectionals are canceled, but Joe isn't aware, so I can still bring her.

Agreeing quickly to the meeting time and place with Bernadette, Shiloh checked her watch. Almost seven hours. Plenty of time to see what she needed to see and determine whether her intuition was correct. That Simon Bowles was a much more complex man than he appeared.

Setting the GPS on her phone for 2021 Mohawk Place, Shiloh turned right onto Central Parkway in the direction of Zauber Pharmaceutical Labs.

Thursday, October 12th, Afternoon

F ifteen minutes later, Shiloh pulled up parallel to the curb next to what used to be the old Imperial Theater. Having seen pictures of the dilapidated former movie house featured in numerous social media campaigns to *Save Cincinnati's Dying Landmarks*, she recognized the building right away. The location app on her phone and the Google Earth photos that she pulled up to double-check confirmed the location of Zauber Labs to be the anvil-shaped building across the street. However, there was nothing to indicate it as a place of business other than one plain black and white sign over the door. *ZAUBER*. Every first-floor window of the building was boarded up. Perhaps even odder was the complete lack of litter or evidence of homeless encampment surrounding the building, as with so many similar empty structures. Eerily, it seemed twice abandoned.

Nevertheless, when Shiloh walked over to try the front door, she could see that there were numerous handprints in the dust around the handle and muddy footprints still damp in the entryway. *Someone's been here recently*. Glancing up from the locked door, she could see one of the upstairs windows was open, as if for ventilation.

Her skin prickled as a wave of uneasiness hit her. She considered knocking but didn't. *Something isn't right here*, Shiloh thought as she backed cautiously away from the door. She grasped her gold tree necklace and ran it back and forth along the chain against her collarbone. Glancing from side to side down the cross street, Shiloh did not see a single other car. No traffic of any kind. Scanning the pavement of the surrounding streets,

Shiloh noticed that it was clean. Too clean for a street strewn with potholes in a deserted part of the city, so close to the Parkway. Having visited many of Cincinnati's poorer neighborhoods to meet up with clients and witnesses during her years as a public defender, the lack of trash indicating a normal level of random humanity passing by bothered her. *Someone is picking up trash but doesn't want anyone to know they're here.* Every instinct she had told her to leave. Feeling her heart rate growing faster, Shiloh turned around quickly and started back toward her car.

Halfway across the street and not paying attention to where she was walking, Shiloh tripped over a manhole cover and fell to her knees. That's when she saw it.

An expensive-looking silver charm bracelet was wedged in the groove of the manhole cover. Not a piece of cheap base metal from a chain store at the mall, which would have broken into a dozen pieces if the heavy steel cover had fallen shut on it. A thick-linked, shiny rope of pure silver, filled with too many charms to count, broken just at the clasp.

Struggling to her feet and picking the road grit out of her palms, Shiloh stared at the squashed bracelet curiously. It didn't belong there. A bracelet like that belonged on the arm of a young woman. The kind who would have friends and family who would give her a new little charm for every memorable occasion. Birthdays, Christmases, and each holiday were an opportunity to offer her a reminder that she was treasured. Not an extravagant sort of remembrance, but a consistent one. That sort of young woman had no business on a random, creepy street in a deserted part of town.

Shiloh bent over again and tugged first at the bracelet, then at the manhole cover. Finding that she could not free it with her bare hands alone, Shiloh returned to her SUV and pulled out the small crowbar that she always kept under the driver's seat as both a tool and a weapon. Afraid she'd fumble around and shoot herself in the foot somehow if she ever had to use it, Shiloh never felt comfortable carrying a pistol for protection while driving.

Holding onto the bracelet with one hand so that it wouldn't fall into the sewer and prying the cover up with the other by pressing her body weight against the crowbar, Shiloh managed to pull the bracelet free. Slipping the bracelet into the pocket of her blazer, Shiloh peered down into the darkness. Although the sun was still mostly overhead, the shadows cast by the sewer tunnels made it impossible to see clearly. However, there seemed to be a glimmer of something silver shining brightly at the bottom, like a coin deep in a well.

Flipping on the flashlight from her cell phone, Shiloh beamed it down into the hole as she leaned forward, trying to determine what the object was. More distinct handprints marked the slime on the rungs of the iron ladder bolted to the side of the manhole. Just then, her cell dinged with another text message. Almost dropping the phone in surprise as the sound startled her, Shiloh cursed her stupidity and scuttled back to the curb.

What was I thinking? What if a car had run me over, crouching like an addled stray cat, with no one to keep watch?

Yet, no car came. Possibly hours or even longer could pass on that deserted street without a single vehicle.

Catching her breath, Shiloh pulled up the text message. It was Nadia.

Where are you? I thought you said we'd meet at your office after your coffee with Detective Schultz. Did you forget again?

Shit, Shiloh swore. Of course, she'd forgotten. Still, should she tell Nadia about what she'd just found out? That the location of the so-called "labs" for Zauber Pharmaceuticals appeared to be a shady front for some other kind of secret operation? She hit the green call button and considered her options for an explanation as she waited for Nadia to pick up.

Not without better context, Shiloh thought, *and a plan for the two of them to return together for safety. Or perhaps not. Perhaps it would be better to tell Detective Schultz about what she knew at last. Have him come out with other officers and a warrant to search properly.*

There was something wrong about the place. Shiloh could feel it with both her witch's intuition and her attorney's instincts. This meant that the last thing that she should do was tell her college girl assistant about the whole situation. The temptation to explore on her own would simply be too irresistible. Sensing Nadia's concern from her probing tone as the girl answered and repeated the questions from her text, Shiloh quickly decided it was better to lie.

"Yeah, okay," Shiloh said, deflecting. "You caught me. I'm sorry. Got caught up thinking about case stuff. Still sitting in the parking deck over in OTR, looking up things on my phone. I'm on my way there now."

"I thought you said I could come with you if you thought of anything new to research or found more witnesses to interview," Nadia replied. Shiloh could hear the disappointment in Nadia's voice that the girl's good manners wouldn't let her admit to. It would seem too much like whining. *When are you going to start treating me like a real colleague whom you can trust?*

"I... I am going to let you come with me," Shiloh stammered, as she offered what she hoped would be an olive branch. "I'm supposed to meet up with Bernadette and Scarlet again at 6 pm. Why don't you pick us up a pizza from Firehouse to have ready when I get back to the office? That way we can eat and then leave to go over there together. I haven't had anything but coffee all day, and I'm starved. There's cash in the box in my top desk drawer. Use it to get whatever you like. You still have the key I gave you to the office, right?"

Nadia sighed heavily. "Yesss... I am capable of keeping up with a key too, you know. Stop acting like such a mom. You're not the only person in the world who's responsible."

"Okay, okay," Shiloh replied. "I'll do better, I promise. It's hard. It's not you. It's just that I'm used to doing everything on my own. See you in a few at the office."

After they exchanged goodbyes, Shiloh returned to pick up her crowbar that she'd left in the street. She used it to pull the manhole cover back closed. Sitting down in the car, Shiloh pulled the bracelet out of her pocket to examine the charms before leaving for the office. A tiny cello with four wire strings. A miniature horse with dainty wings that still moved. A polished heart crushed flat, most likely from getting stuck in the groove. Then, an empty jump ring next to the spot where the bracelet snapped just beside the catch. Shiloh wondered what charm had been there and how it had been lost.

These final observations took Shiloh about five minutes. Nadia Haas was aware of that because she didn't leave for the pizza place until she saw Shiloh's little blue tracker dot on the location-sharing app begin moving back up Central Parkway toward her office in Mt. Adams. Like most technical things, Shiloh promptly forgot how to turn the app on and off after Nadia showed her several months before. In the days following Ethan's death, Nadia realized what her very independent friend refused to admit: Shiloh was depressed. The trauma of losing her husband in such a sudden and random way, especially after having grown up mostly without a mother too, was a little more than a person could cope with on her own.

Nadia understood that feeling. Losing her mother so young had taught her. That sense of waking up in the morning and those first few glorious seconds before you thought about it. Before the weight of absence settled onto your day like a hangover. But because Nadia couldn't ever seem to find that elusive combination of the right time and the right words to express this bond of sadness with Shiloh, she just showed her how to use an app instead.

An app that would always tell her where her friend was going. When she stopped, and where. If she was running late or forgot a meeting they'd planned entirely. If she was safe.

What Nadia Haas couldn't understand is why Shiloh Foley would lie to her about something as inconsequential as stopping by an abandoned warehouse across Mohawk Place from the old Imperial Theater. It must be something about the case. Something that Shiloh couldn't or didn't want to share, for one of two reasons. Either she didn't trust Nadia to keep a secret, which seemed unlikely after she'd already sat in on all the witnesses and was scheduled for another meeting that afternoon, or she didn't think Nadia could handle what she found.

Deciding it was the latter, Nadia saved the location from the app into her phone. If Shiloh needed proof that she was up to the task of being treated like a real partner, Nadia planned to offer that proof very soon by doing some investigation on her own.

Thursday, October 12th, Evening

T he smell of fresh-cut grass, likely the last of the season, mingled with dusty leaves and orange-muddled bourbon cocktails wafting through the air as Shiloh Foley and Nadia Haas sat on a bench with their backs toward the outdoor porch bar in Washington Park. They watched as a group of hand-holding couples followed a tour guide, who stopped in front of Music Hall to regale them with ghost stories. The police had completed their preliminary investigation already, carrying away for evidence every scrap from the carriage explosion. Only the circle of bricks burnt black beneath where it had been remained as a testament to the tragedy.

Shiloh tried not to think about her first actual date with Ethan, which had started at the Cincinnati Zoo and ended precisely where those couples were standing. Ethan chose both locations because he knew Shiloh loved animals and also anything spooky. Shiloh still had a printout of the selfie they'd taken with Music Hall in the background tacked to the corkboard over her desk. It was strange for Shiloh to think about how something so ephemeral as a piece of paper could have outlasted him. Her Ethan, who seemed so straightforward, calm, and constant.

"Do you think it's haunted like everyone says?" Nadia asked abruptly.

"Everything becomes haunted if it survives long enough," Shiloh replied, her reverie broken. She nodded in the direction of the underground parking deck as she saw Bernadette Jenkins and Scarlet Arnold approaching. Scarlet had her flute case tucked dutifully beneath one arm of her black turtleneck sweater, which she'd paired with another dark plaid skirt, fleece-lined tights, and Doc Martens. Bernadette was dressed more casually than usual, in a fitted camel sweater dress and suede slouch boots with a long, lightweight wool coat.

"How was woodwind practice?" Nadia grinned conspiratorially as Scarlet approached.

The younger girl's dark eyes narrowed suspiciously until she realized that Nadia was joking with her about pretending to go to rehearsal so that she could come to the meeting. They all exchanged pleasantries and sat down at a table just outside the porch's overhang. The presence of a person closer to her age seemed to put Scarlet more at ease. Shiloh noticed as Scarlet shared what she knew about Ellis Purcell, she directed most of her story towards Nadia.

"Ellis and Jackson had been together like forever," Scarlet began. "Ever since they hooked up at Crosswalk Ignite last summer."

"What's Crosswalk Ignite?" Shiloh asked.

"Church camp," Nadia interjected. "A mix of Catholics and all other kinds of random Bible beaters from a bunch of different Protestant denominations. Kind of an outreach thing."

"Huh. Church camp has become a lot more interesting since I was a kid," Shiloh said, jotting down the details. "Continue."

"Wait," Bernadette stopped her. "Your brother hooked up with his boyfriend at church camp?" She took a deep breath. "Not that I have anything against love wherever anyone finds it, but I'm just glad it didn't happen on my watch so that your father could blame me."

Scarlet rolled her eyes and turned back to Nadia. "He always finds someone to blame besides the boys, but whatever. As I was saying, Ellis and Jackson were hooking up for about a year when Jackson got kicked out of the percussion ensemble here with the youth orchestra."

"Why did he get kicked out?" Nadia asked.

"Um, because that's what happens when a dude shows up to rehearsal high and smells like weed. They've got a no-tolerance policy," Scarlet said, cocking her head to one side.

"Did your dad get upset about that?" Nadia pressed. "He seems pretty strict, with the homeschooling, church camp, and the rest."

Scarlet shrugged. "Not really. Dad's pretty *laissez-faire* when it comes to drugs. Weird, I know, but not really if you think about it. Drugs are kind of our family business. Anyway, when Jackson got kicked out, Ellis quit too.

But because going to orchestra practice was the only time both of them had to meet regularly each week outside of the house without anyone getting suspicious about their being together, they just lied and pretended to keep going."

"Did you know about all of this?" Shiloh asked Bernadette.

"Not all of it," Bernadette replied. "I knew Jackson and Ellis were a thing, but I didn't know how it started. And I knew that Jackson wasn't going to orchestra practice anymore, but I didn't see how anyone would be helped by outing him. It would just cause him to argue with his father. With less than two more years left before he went off to college, it didn't seem productive. Jackson had talked about going to a school in New York to swim competitively on a scholarship somewhere, so I figured the whole thing would just run its course."

"You're probably right," Nadia seconded. "I mean, why out him if it would only start a fight?"

"That was kind of what I thought too," Scarlet said. "Not just about his relationship with Ellis, but getting kicked out of the orchestra and the whole weed situation too. We both just wanted some freedom from that place, yanno? Savannah and Jefferson were Mom and Dad's golden kids. They could do no wrong. But since Jackson and I were both kind of mistakes who probably shouldn't have been born to them, why start anything?"

"Are you and Jackson close?" Nadia asked, wincing a little at Scarlet's self-dismissal.

"More so than I was with the older two," Scarlet replied. "Jackson was my favorite."

"This is what bothers me," Bernadette whispered to Shiloh. "She keeps talking about Jackson in the past tense."

Shiloh furrowed her brow. "I can see why." Looking up from her notebook at Scarlet, she asked, "Do you have any reason to suspect that your brother isn't just missing but has been hurt in some way?"

"Mmm..." Scarlet crossed her skinny, awkward legs in their overly large boots and hunched over protectively. "Hard to say. If Jackson and Ellis had just stopped smoking weed, I'd say he was okay. He just got pissed off and went somewhere. He and Jeff both do that occasionally. For the past few weeks, though, they've both been super weird. I think Jefferson started getting high on the same shit that Savannah and the Muller twins were on, which isn't surprising really. Jeff would have done anything to get back with Reece Mueller after they broke up, and ugly Allen Purcell has followed Savannah around basically since the moment they started college. Whatever the girls were doing, the boys were doing too, to try to impress them."

"So, what you're saying is that you think your older brother, Jefferson, and Ellis's older brother, Allen, got their younger brothers, Jackson and Ellis, started on this new harder drug?" Nadia asked.

"Yeah," Scarlet said. "All of them are kind of tangled up together, relationship-wise. I mean, Jeff and Reece were a thing for a long while, and Riley was with Jaya Khoury. Everyone knew about them. They weren't as careful as Jackson and Ellis. Allen thirsted for Savannah, but she wanted Khalid. Mostly because Dad hated him, but that was Savannah. She was like that. She did anything she could to rile Dad up because she knew that she was his favorite and he'd never punish her. If it were me though... pfft." Scarlett paused to blow her bangs out of her face dismissively. "I'd be like, disowned."

Nadia wrinkled her nose. "Sounds pretty incestuous. There's no way I'd ever consider getting with one of my Dad's friends' kids. It would just be too weird."

"It's gross," Scarlet agreed. "Which is why I can't wait to get out of this place. The key is that if you make it out, never come back. Lorelei Winter-Lang came back, and we all know what happened to her."

"The problem is," Shiloh interjected, "we don't know exactly *who* killed Lorelei or the others. That's what we're trying to figure out. Go back to the part about why you think Jackson and Ellis were getting into harder stuff. Are you certain that they got their supply from their older siblings? Do you know for sure that the drugs they were taking were cocktails from Zauber Labs?"

"Like I said, I'm not sure about that part," Scarlet answered. "Could have been how they got their start. They were always hanging out down by the corner of Liberty and Elm. That's a pretty regular pickup spot for anyone looking to buy. It wasn't long after they started kind of disappearing down that way for hours at a time that Jackson started coming home all glassy-eyed looking, just like Savannah and Jeff."

"What's at the corner of Liberty and Elm?" Bernadette asked, her face lined with concern.

"A whole lot of nothing," Nadia interjected. "It's just a corner of, like, empty warehouses and overgrown lots. Past where all the cool bars are in OTR, but still several somewhat shady blocks before you get to Findlay Market. It's been a dealers' drop spot forever."

"How do you know?" Shiloh asked, shooting Nadia a look.

Nadia met her gaze. "Because it's common knowledge. That's where all the loser skater kids hung out when I was in high school. They talked about it all the time. There's nothing there except people lurking around trying to buy drugs on the down low and the entryway to some closed-off old subway tunnel. They went to skate and left tags everywhere."

"An old subway tunnel?" Shiloh asked. Her eyes grew large. "Oh," she breathed. Then, Shiloh began scribbling on her notepad.

It was Nadia's turn to be suspicious. "What do you mean by *Oh?* Do you know something about the subway tunnel? Are they connected somehow to the murders?"

Shiloh paused. She knew that she needed to be careful and try to change the subject, or Nadia would suspect she was hiding something. "What I meant was, oh, isn't that the way the carriage horse ran after the explosion? I was just wondering if it ran down into the tunnel somehow. I don't know if anyone found the horse yet; do you?"

"Not a clue," Nadia replied testily.

She knows I'm hiding something, Shiloh thought.

Sensing the tension between the two, Bernadette tried to intervene. "Changing the subject, but did you learn anything new about Jasmine's case when you met with Detective Schultz?"

"Not especially," Shiloh shrugged. "The police seem more preoccupied with this evolving serial killer case. They've started calling him the Prophet of Eden Park, after the place where I found the first two bodies and the religious-themed notes left at the crime scenes. I must admit that I have been too. I was just at a location related to that case a few hours ago. Picked up the strangest thing while I was there." Shiloh fished the charm bracelet out of her pocket and held it out to Bernadette in her open palm.

Bernadette stared at the bracelet in disbelief. "The Prophet of Eden Park," she whispered, her voice quivering. "Where did you say that you found this?"

Shiloh could feel Nadia and Scarlet watching her, but she was stuck. There was no choice but to tell the truth. Dodging it again would seem even more suspicious and intriguing.

"After the meeting with Detective Schultz, I decided to do a little drive-by of Zauber Pharmaceutical Labs. It's the name of a business that's associated with the Prophet in the killings of Veronica and Savannah Arnold, but the building is rented out by Rafferty Purcell's holding company, Dynamic Investments Group. I'd been working out possible connections among the deaths of Reece Mueller, Jaya Khoury, Lorelei Winter-Lang, and now Ellis Purcell. When I got there, it was all boarded up. Yet, I could tell someone had been there recently. I found the bracelet wedged in a manhole cover in the middle of the street. It was ajar too, as if someone climbed in not too long ago. It seemed very out of place, so I picked it up."

"She was *very* out of place," Bernadette said softly, reaching for the bracelet. "May I?"

Shiloh tipped the broken silver charm bracelet into Bernadette's open hand. Bernadette turned over the crushed silver heart and studied the back. Then, she shut her eyes, clutching the bracelet tight in her fist. Tears began to well up in her eyes.

"Bernie, what's wrong?" Scarlet asked.

Bernadette began to cry softly. "This was—is—oh, I don't know... my sister's bracelet. Jasmine." Touching her fingertips lightly beneath her eyes to wipe away the tears, she explained. "Our mother, Destiny, bought it for Jasmine the Christmas she started high school. At first, Jazzy didn't like it because she thought silver was cheap. She'd seen a gold one in the window at Richter & Phillips downtown. It was the first thing at the top of her list that year. Jasmine always wanted the best of everything. When Mother showed her it was from Tiffany's, she perked up."

Bernadette turned the broken heart over so that the others could see both sides. Although the engraving was distorted where the metal was crushed, when Shiloh looked closer, she could see it. The capital *PLE RET*, and *TIF* on one side indicate the company logo, and on the reverse, *JAS* and *JEN*. The first few letters of Jasmine Jenkins's name.

"They usually cost over $500, but Mom got it on sale when they moved out of the Fountain Square location and over to the Kenwood Mall. The first Christmas, she didn't have enough to get any charms on it. Every Christmas and birthday afterward, Mom tried to get something relevant to what Jasmine was doing that year." Bernadette carefully spread the broken bracelet out in her palm, pointing out the charms one by one.

"This boot was the year Jasmine started on the dance squad. The sneaker with wings from the summer her track relay team placed first at state." She smiled sadly, touching the little cello and horse. "Mom and Dr. Khoury had kind of a fight over these two. Jasmine's father wanted to buy her two that year because he'd also bought both the actual instrument and the animal. Paid for music and riding lessons too. But that would have left Mom with nothing to choose from, so she beat him to it. She bought this little horse with wings instead. Dr. Khoury had already purchased a plain one, with no wings. Jasmine liked Mom's charm better, so her dad had to take the other one back." Bernadette gave a little half laugh. "Why would anyone want to stay grounded, Jazzy used to say, when they have a chance to fly?"

Scarlet leaned over to examine the bracelet more closely. "What was there, where that space is?" she asked, indicating the space where the tiny silver jump ring was pulled open, just before the break.

Scanning the line of other charms, Bernadette replied. "I believe that was where the initial J charm that I gave her for graduation was. She needed one more to finish it out next to the clasp. By then Mom was sick, so I bought it for her. I guess it must have broken off."

"Are you absolutely sure that's Jasmine's bracelet?" Shiloh asked, ignoring Nadia, who continued to stare at her accusingly. "Do you have any idea how it might have gotten stuck in a manhole cover outside of the address for Zauber Labs?"

Bernadette leaned forward and handed Shiloh back the broken bracelet, hissing bitterly. "If I had any idea where my sister was or what she was doing, then I wouldn't need you, would I, Ms. Foley? Bringing me my sister's jewelry that she dropped in the street like trash."

"I'm afraid not," Shiloh said, feeling the tension growing from Bernadette too. She attempted one last time to change the climate of the conversation. "For that, I'm sorry. I know this must be hard, but I'm trying everything I know. I'd hoped to be further along by now. Which reminds me," Shiloh glanced down at her notebook, then up at Scarlet. "I wanted to double-check something. Which one of your older brothers has a scar through his eyebrow?"

"That would be Jackson," Scarlet said. "He got an eyebrow ring like the day after he got his driver's license. He and Dad got in a huge fight when he came home with it. Dad was drunk, and he yanked it out of Jackson's face. Dad gets that way sometimes when he's drinking."

"Scarlet!" Bernadette said reproachfully. "Do you have to tell everything you know?"

"If Joe Arnold is regularly violent toward his children, Ms. Jenkins..." Nadia began.

"Please," Shiloh intervened, waving Nadia off, hoping to avoid upsetting Bernadette further. "Can't you see that..."

Bernadette stood up. Dabbing at the corners of her eyes, she picked up her purse and motioned for Scarlet to follow her. "I'm sorry for snapping at you, Ms. Foley, but today just made me realize something I've been trying not to accept." Bernadette shook her head. "Something I've been trying to avoid for half my life. The next time I see my sister Jasmine, she's not going to be alive, is she?"

Shiloh swallowed hard. Blinking, she shook her head slowly from left to right. "Probably not."

"I understand," Bernadette said. "Not what I was hoping to hear, but I'd appreciate it if you kept trying anyway. To find out what you can." She turned to Scarlet. "Is there anything else that you feel like you need to tell Ms. Foley?" Scarlet shook her head.

"Actually," Nadia started again. "I was hoping that I could ask you one more thing about Jasmine's..."

Shiloh glared at Nadia to stay silent. "I'm sure it can wait until next time. This is an ongoing investigation."

"Thank you," Bernadette replied. "Come on, Scarlet."

Nadia and Shiloh stood in awkward silence behind the chairs on the porch until the other two were out of earshot. As Shiloh picked up her bag to go, Nadia spoke.

"Are you just going to leave without any explanation or apology for lying to me?"

"Nadia," Shiloh sighed. "It's not a big deal. I decided to drive over there to check out the Zauber location on a whim. Didn't find anything very exciting, except that bracelet that I told all of you about just now. I swear, you know everything I do."

"Why didn't you tell me the truth on the phone then?" Nadia insisted. "I thought you were going to let me be your assistant. To get some real experience. How can I get any experience if you don't trust me?"

Shiloh rolled her eyes. "I don't expect you to understand this, because you're young, and young people never see danger. Even when it's right in front of their face. I chose not to tell you about the Zauber trip because I didn't want you going over there. It's in a bad neighborhood, and even I was a little creeped out by it. Something is going on that doesn't feel right. Whatever it is, it isn't a normal research lab that's on the up and up, that's for sure."

"So why couldn't you just tell me that?" Nadia pleaded. "Why do you always treat me like a child?"

"Because sometimes you act like one," Shiloh snapped. Nadia's mouth fell open. "Like just now, when you kept pushing Bernadette to answer questions. The woman needed a moment to gather her thoughts."

Shiloh pulled the silver bracelet out of her pocket once more. "I'd just shown her a piece of very intimate evidence belonging to her sister, which probably means she's dead. If that's true, then it's okay if a cold case like Jasmine's takes one more day to be solved. It isn't going to bring her back anyway. Why traumatize her sister with pushy questions when the result is going to remain the same? Jasmine Jenkins is probably dead. Just like all those other people. And there's nothing you, or I, or her sister Bernadette can do about that. Other than trying to let the truth come out in the kindest way possible."

Nadia crossed her arms. "Who are you to talk about what's kind? Is allowing someone to learn to depend on you and then continuing to forget they exist kind? Is misleading them into thinking that they were your equal your style of kindness?"

"Nadia, if that's how I'm coming across, I'm sorry," Shiloh said. "It's just... It's just been hard to hold everything together since..."

"Since Ethan died, I know," Nadia finished. "I understand that. Of all people, I know what it's like to lose someone close to you suddenly too. But that doesn't mean you have to start shutting everyone else out. The world goes on, Shiloh. It's okay to still care about the people who are left behind, even if the one you care about most leaves you. You can't be everything and do everything by yourself forever. Sooner or later, you have to remember how to let people in. How to listen."

"I am listening!" Shiloh insisted. "Come on, let's not argue out here. Let's go back to the office and get a cup of coffee or something. You can tell me all your ideas about the case there. Where we have some privacy."

"Not now, okay?" Nadia said, the anger inside her subsiding as she struggled into her sweater coat. "I just can't right now. I've got somewhere else I need to be." Leaning down to rummage through her bag for her car keys, Nadia smirked.

Straightening, she held up Scarlet Arnold's flute case. "Guess she left this."

Shiloh reached for the instrument. "Here, give it to me. I know where the Arnolds live. I'll run it out there before I go home."

Nadia tucked the case beneath her arm. "Nah, I got it. I need to head out that way for a show choir costume fitting tomorrow afternoon anyway. A lady out there is going to re-hem some things for me. I can take the flute to Scarlet if you give me the address. That is," Nadia paused for effect. "If you trust me to handle a dangerous errand like band instrument delivery."

"I trust you," Shiloh said, reaching for her phone. "I'll text you the address now."

As the text dinged through, Nadia turned to go. "One more thing," she said over her shoulder. "I wanted to ask Bernadette if she knew whatever happened to Jasmine's horse."

"Oh," Shiloh said. "Bernie told me about it in our first meeting. That Dr. Khoury kept Lyra, I think she said the horse's name was, in some stable situation out on the West Side. But that was ages ago. People buy horses for their kids, put them out to pasture, and then forget about them all the time. Hate to say it, but Lyra's probably glue or dog food by now. Even if somebody had Kash Khoury's type of money, who would keep up a horse that no one rides or even visits anymore indefinitely?"

Nadia considered this. "Maybe. But you never know. Horses live a pretty long time if they're taken care of. Plus, if you've ever read *Black Beauty*, you know horses can have as many different lives as the number of owners they have. I just thought it was worth checking out, considering there wasn't a horse recovered in the police report."

"I have to admit that I'm not up on my classic Victorian equestrian novels," Shiloh said. "But good on you for reading the whole police report before I even got around to it. And you do make a good point. Horses don't just disappear into thin air. If there wasn't one recovered into evidence, then it's got to be out there somewhere." Shiloh paused. "You aren't suggesting that Jasmine's horse, Lyra, might be the one that was pulling that carriage?"

"How would I know?" Nadia threw up her hands as she spun around to leave. "All I know is that we have a horse unaccounted for and a person who used to own her unaccounted for under similarly strange, possibly interconnected circumstances. If I were a detective, I think I'd want to follow up on that. But I'm not a detective; I'm just an innocent little college girl." Nadia stuck out her bottom lip in a pout and cinched her long cardigan sweater tighter as she concluded in a sing-songy voice. "And when you are young, they assume you know nothing."

"Oh, you did not just quote Taylor Swift lyrics against me!" Shiloh called after her.

"I most certainly did!" Nadia called back playfully. "Go do your job, woman. Find that horse!"

Watching the girl walk across the park in the gathering darkness, Shiloh shook her head. Half at herself for missing the obvious fact that Nadia picked up effortlessly and half at Nadia for simply being that age when one could be so cavalier about anything.

Not ready yet to go back home and begin working, Shiloh decided to duck into Sundry & Vice again. Although she didn't want to admit it to herself, Shiloh was hoping that Laurie would be there. Seeing his handsome, friendly face would be an even better relief from her stressful day than the drink.

Inside, the bar was humming with patrons. Shiloh could hear all their conversations buzzing about the news of the most recent murders. Yet, Laurie spotted Shiloh right away as she slid into the last open seat at the bar.

"Hello, beautiful! What can I get for you?" Laurie asked, smiling warmly as he tossed a towel over the shoulder of his fitted vest. For the first time, Shiloh noticed how strong his biceps looked. They flexed beneath the crisp fabric of his white shirt, which he wore with the sleeves rolled up and his subtle, sable-colored diamond tie loosened at the throat.

"Surprise me," Shiloh sighed. "I'm too brain-dead to make such a complicated decision."

"Long day, I guess?" he asked, whisking ice into a shaker.

"Yeah," Shiloh sighed, setting her red tote bag on the floor. "At what age do we stop being the cool kids and start being the old people that cool kids quote song lyrics at?"

"Sounds like you're having a *parents just don't understand* kind of afternoon to me," Laurie quipped, his blue eyes gleaming mischievously.

Shiloh rolled her eyes as she caught the reference. "Not you too, Fresh Prince. The fact that you even made that joke proves that you're old like me."

"I prefer to identify as vintage," Laurie replied. "That way, I seem more distinguished."

"That's fair," Shiloh replied. "I just hate how I keep missing all the little things that kids around me pick up on so easily. I mean, isn't that how almost every horror movie starts? With some dumb grown-up not listening when a much smarter kid tries to tell them something?"

"I believe so," Laurie mused, scanning the top shelf behind him and reaching for a bottle. "Do you drink gin?"

"I drink everything," Shiloh replied. "Except Cabernet and Chardonnay. Too many tannins. The joys of middle age and dry skin, you know."

"I hadn't noticed," Laurie replied, already stirring in the other ingredients. "Gin, elderflower, a little vermouth, and a little cucumber. See what you think of the Drops of Life." He tipped the cocktail into a glass and slid it across to Shiloh. She took a sip and brightened.

"Refreshing?"

"Yes. Just what I needed."

"Thought so," Laurie winked and spun away to attend to other guests.

For the next hour, as the number of patrons slowly ebbed away, Shiloh sipped her cocktail and ordered a refill as she reviewed her notes. She made a list of locations where each victim's body was found. Turning the page, she drew a rough map of their locations. The first two were at Eden Park in Mt. Adams. A third at St. Augustine's in Walnut Hills. Four and five across from UC in Clifton's Burnet Woods. The latest was right across Washington Park, only a block from where she sat. Studying the diagram, Shiloh thought it looked like a slightly misshapen horseshoe. She plugged the locations in order into the direction app on her phone, along with one more. 2021 Mohawk Place, the alleged location of Zauber Pharmaceutical Labs that she visited earlier that afternoon. Shiloh was surprised to realize that it was along the same path. Right up Central Parkway where it intersected with Linn Street. Finally, she added her address to the end of the list of directions. The horseshoe instantly closed into a circle.

"Holy shit!" Shiloh breathed, putting down her phone and pushing her cocktail glass away across the bar. "It ends with me."

"That's quite a dramatic announcement," Laurie said, picking up her glass and placing it in the sink. He glanced down at the list and diagram. "I take it you've been working on the big case. Figure anything out?"

"Yeah. It's super creepy," Shiloh replied, rubbing her eyes in disbelief as she peered closer at her phone screen.

"Oooh, I love creeps from way back," Laurie said, craning his neck to see the diagram right side up. "My first paid gig was as a scare actor at Dent Schoolhouse. Am I allowed to know, or is it confidential?"

"Mmm... this part is all over the news for anyone who chooses to put it together, so I guess I can tell you." Shiloh turned her phone around so that Laurie could see. "The scenes for each of the murders. When you connect them in order, they make a horseshoe shape. The last part follows right beneath Central Parkway. If you connect the ends, it comes full circle back to Eden Park. It's only about a seven-minute drive or a thirty-minute walk from where the carriage exploded to where I live in Mt. Adams."

"That is creepy," Laurie said, his playful expression growing somber. "May I?" he gestured as if to take Shiloh's phone. She handed it to him. Laurie zoomed the map in. Shiloh watched as he carefully followed the circle around with his finger before handing it back to her. "What do you think it means?"

"What I'm wondering," Shiloh began, staring into the screen again. "Is where someone would be able to hide a horse inside the perimeter of this circle without anyone seeing. It's the most densely populated part of the city. Surely, someone would notice."

"I don't follow you," Laurie questioned. "What does a horse have to do with it?"

"My associate read the police report and noticed that there was no mention of the horse that was pulling the carriage just before the explosion. It wasn't taken into evidence, and no one's seen it since. The last thing I saw before the explosion was..." Shiloh stopped short of saying Jackson Arnold's name. "This young man, who is also missing. He said he did what *she* told him, but he let the horse go."

"Now I'm even more confused," Laurie said. "Are you saying you were right there when it happened?" He pointed out the window across Washington Park toward Elm Street. "Were you on the way to our preview night?"

"I shouldn't have said that," Shiloh backtracked, feeling suddenly uneasy. "I should go. How much do I owe you?"

"No, wait, please," Laurie lowered his voice and motioned for Shiloh to lean in closer. "I know there are probably all sorts of confidentiality agreements and stuff you can't tell me because it's still under investigation," he whispered. "But you can't just drop half a story like that and walk out. Every person who's walked through that door tonight has been yapping nonstop about the murders. I've heard so many theories that I've lost count. You don't have to name names if you're not comfortable, but I'm dying to know what you saw. Can you just tell me that much?"

Shiloh relaxed a little. "Okay. I guess I can sketch it out for you without getting too specific. Last night, when I was on the way to your preview at the Shakespeare Company, I got stuck in traffic right after I turned off Central Parkway on Elm Street. I got out to see what was happening, and I saw a young man. A young man whom I had met earlier, as I was questioning someone else about the case. His eyes were doing weird things, and he was singing this old spiritual song. *Ezekiel Saw a Wheel*. Are you familiar with the tune?"

"Yes," Laurie replied, casting a glance at the last table of people remaining. Two couples, giggling and camping out. Completely lost in flirtation. "It's the one about Ezekiel from the Bible and what he prophesied would happen during the Final Judgment. Go on. What happened next?"

"Well, when he realized that I recognized him, the young man said something very strange. He said that he did what *she* told him, but he let the horse go. He used the word *she* specifically. And then he..." Shiloh trailed off.

"Then he did what?" Laurie rested both elbows on the bar.

"He tried to choke me," Shiloh finished.

"God, Shiloh!" Laurie hissed, trying to mute his reaction by covering his mouth. "Are you okay? Did you go to the police and report it?"

"I'm fine. It knocked the wind out of me, that's all. When the carriage blew up, we both fell. He let go of me and took off. I haven't seen him again. No one has seen him again. I met with his sister this afternoon in hopes of learning more. All I found out was that his father reported him missing. They don't know where his older brother is either. Their father was a suspect early on, in the first two murders, but was quickly cleared by multiple solid alibis. I haven't reported any of it to the police yet, because I don't want to scare off his sister. She's young, just a teenager, but she's the best witness I've got so far in this other missing person's case that I'm working on. The case that I think may tie all the rest of these killings together and might be the key to solving them. However, the lady whom I'm trying to find is the kind of person who can completely disappear off the face of the earth. No one would give a rat's ass about her except her older sister. The older sister is my client. And this sister works for the man with whom her missing sister was having an affair. The man who also happens to be the father of the boy who choked me on Elm Street right before the carriage exploded."

Laurie's eyes grew wide. "Wow. That is a very tangled web indeed. So, if you don't think that the kid or his father is behind all of it, who is?"

Shiloh sighed. "You wouldn't believe me if I told you. It's too bizarre."

"Try me," Laurie countered. "I've made a career out of Shakespeare, and my mother's a retired social worker. There isn't any family revenge plot that's too twisted for me to believe."

Shiloh met Laurie's eyes. They were earnestly, intensely blue. "I want to, but I just..."

"If you can't, you can't," Laurie said, dropping his gaze to the bartop as he took a step back. Then, he pulled out his phone. "You don't know me from Adam. And I understand you're trying to protect your client and the case. But what if I were to guess? The names of the people you're talking about, I mean. It's all over the news. I went to the School of Performing Arts down the street, and I grew up in this neighborhood. I don't know everyone who lives here anymore, because I was away for a long time, but I do know every street. I skated all of them. Maybe I could help."

"You were a skater boy?" Shiloh asked, surprised. "I would never have guessed. In this neighborhood?"

"Yeah, for years. Why?"

"This is going to seem random," Shiloh said. "But did you ever hang out down on the corner of Liberty and Elm Street?"

Laurie grinned and crossed his arms over his chest. "Are you asking me if I were a stoner? Well, I hate to break the stereotype, but not all skater kids are stoners. Some of us just enjoyed skulking around in black clothes with attitudes as bad as our haircuts." He turned in a three-quarter profile and made a Zoolander face.

Shiloh tried to stifle a giggle. "Somehow, I have a hard time believing that."

"It's true!" Laurie replied. "I mean, we weren't above spraying a few tags down in the old subway tunnels from time to time, but the crew I ran with at SCPA all thought we were destined for greatness. Our hubris kept us sober, most of the time."

"Interesting," Shiloh stopped laughing. "Seriously though, what do you know about Cincinnati's abandoned subway tunnels?"

"I know that they run beneath Central Parkway and then circle to..." Laurie trailed off. "Ohhh..." he breathed. The realization dawned on him. "You think that the boy who set off the explosion ran off with the horse down into the tunnels?"

"Wait, now I'm confused," Shiloh said. "Can you get into the subway near that corner of Liberty? Right down the street from here?"

"Honey," Laurie replied, picking up Shiloh's notebook and turning to a fresh page. "Let me draw you a map."

***

Three hours later, Shiloh sat in the green velvet chair downstairs in her living room on Hatch Street. She'd stayed at the bar until almost closing, switching to Sprite instead of gin. Shiloh told Laurie most of what she'd learned about the case, without naming names, and was pleasantly surprised that he didn't try to pry them out of her.

Instead, Laurie helped Shiloh decipher the seemingly random trio of Roman numerals found among the papers in the lockbox almost immediately. As it turned out, the numbers seemed to refer to a passage from *Hamlet*, Laurie's play that was set to open at the Shakespeare Company across the street on the night of the carriage explosion.

Heaven hath pleased it so. To punish me with this and this with me. That I must be thy scourge and minister.

When Laurie quoted the lines for Shiloh word for word, they made perfect sense with her theory of the case. Simon perceived himself to be some sort of self-appointed executioner, carrying out a kind of divine justice by killing the families of the men from St. Augustine who had assaulted him so many years before. The level of premeditation in it gave them both chills.

Laurie proved to be a wealth of information about the city and its history as well. According to him, Cincinnati had the longest set of never-used subway tunnels in America. They looked up an old map online of the abandoned tunnels and found that the system was planned originally to encircle the entire city. However, less than half of the system was completed before the city ran out of funding in 1928, on the eve of the Great Depression. In the decades that followed, the forgotten subway became a hideout for homeless people and bored, mischievous teenagers looking for urban adventure. Although Laurie never went more than a few hundred feet into the entryway near Liberty Street, some of his old friends who still lived in the city explored much further. They exchanged numbers, and Laurie promised to call her if he found out anything more after speaking with them.

Unable to sleep again when she got home, Shiloh pulled out the two notebooks that Sister Frida Jiminez had given her. The two notebooks that belonged to Simon Bowles. They seemed to have been part of a therapy journaling project of some kind. Doubtlessly prescribed by an unnamed counselor to whom Simon was assigned after moving to St. Augustine's School. Although the green-covered one started on the earliest date, Shiloh soon found that they weren't necessarily chronological. Flipping through the green notebook, Shiloh found the lonely ramblings of a gawky teenage overachiever.

After about a year's worth of weekly entries were recorded in the green notebook, the red notebook began. Its tone was much angrier. Rather than complaining about being ignored or bullied by his classmates, as in the green one, this red notebook was filled with Simon's fantasies about revenge. The two continued as if in conversation with one another for about six months longer, one whining and the other raging before the green one stopped abruptly. From that point on, there was only the red notebook. A few entries after the red one's narrative continued alone, the handwriting became too erratic to read. Over the last pages, it gave way completely to crude drawings that evolved into sigils. The same sigils that Shiloh had seen twice before. Once on the retaining wall of Eden Park and again in the drawings that Detective Schultz showed her. Those were among the papers recovered from the fireproof box in the exploded carriage.

Upon closer reading, the stories told in both notebooks were equally disturbing. In the green one, Simon described what he could remember of his life before he was removed from his mother's custody. A life spent in and out of various shabby apartments that he could only recall in flashes. The journal fluctuated between discussing Simon's vivid childhood nightmares and his actual life. Simon's first clear memory was of falling asleep, hungry and cold, while he waited for his mother to bring him food. By that time they were homeless, living somewhere that he referred to only as the Concrete Jungle. Shiloh wondered whether Simon meant the subway tunnels, from his descriptions of the damp gray walls. She couldn't be sure. At that point, the handwriting was so poor and the narrative so garbled that Shiloh couldn't tell whether Simon was talking about an actual place or another fantasy. The only parts of the story that she could make out were unbearable. Simon described with disturbing coherency strangling a stray cat who had gotten into a bag of leftover fast food that his mother left for him. The cat had eaten all the food, forcing Simon to starve for days. After that, Shiloh could read no more. Emotionally exhausted, she set the notebook aside and cried.

Eventually, she fell asleep in her favorite green velvet living room chair. When Shiloh awakened, her cat, William, was sitting in her lap, growling toward the large bay window. William faced away from her, with his long, brushy gray tail sweeping back and forth against her face. When Shiloh tried to get up, William scooted back against her. The large cat covered her in a protective stance as he growled menacingly, the hair prickling along his spine. William's alarm made her wary. Shiloh flipped on the floor lamp next to her and peered out the front bay window.

Nothing.

Easing out of the chair with William still swirling around her feet, Shiloh went to the broom closet and pulled out her shotgun. Patrolling the house with her gun in hand, she checked all the doors and windows. They were locked securely, with no signs of disturbance. Shiloh looked at the clock. It was after three in the morning. She thought about calling her father, P.J., or her brother, but decided it was too late. Anyone else would just make fun of her for being overly jumpy as a woman living alone. Instead, Shiloh took the shotgun upstairs to bed, along with William, and locked herself in.

Outside, across the street, a man in a long, dirty trench coat sat on a low stone wall, hidden by the shadow of the parking deck. He took a swig of tequila straight from the bottle as he watched the last light go out in Shiloh's house. Then, he shambled away down the sidewalk past Seasongood Pavilion, into the starless night bowl of Eden Park.

Friday, October 13th, Morning

W hen Shiloh arrived at her office at almost eleven the next morning, two emails were waiting for her. One was from Laurie, the bartender. The other was from his mother, Joanne Blake. Yawning through her tiredness, Shiloh smiled as she opened the one from Laurie first. He explained briefly that he'd been unable to sleep the night before too and had called his mother to share with her what they'd discussed. Laurie closed by saying to expect a message from Joanne, who wanted to help. Reading the email twice, Shiloh hated to admit that she was a little disappointed Laurie hadn't included a second invitation to anything unrelated to the case. Perhaps she'd read him wrong, and he was just flirtatious by nature. Hoping to push aside further speculation regarding Laurie's feelings about her, Shiloh opened the second email from Joanne.

In the opening, Joanne confirmed what Laurie told her. Joanne said that she was a career social worker and recently retired after thirty years. She claimed that Laurie came over to her house early with breakfast to make sure that she followed up on his message from the night before. Joanne recalled helping care for a woman named Doreen Bowles when she worked at the old Athens Asylum in 1993. Then, she'd been an intern fresh out of school doing her residency, so every case made a deep impression. At her son's insistence, Joanne looked up the case, and it turned out Doreen was released later that same year when the asylum closed. Since all the records kept at the Athens Asylum ended before 1996, none of them were protected by HIPAA. Joanne could access the entire file if Shiloh were interested and thought it might help her solve the case to know more about Simon's background. The email ended with an invitation for Shiloh to reach out. Shiloh called the number. Joanne answered on the first ring as if she'd been waiting. She invited Shiloh over to her house in Norwood for lunch.

When Shiloh arrived at Joanne's house on Park Avenue, she was slightly amused. Although the smallest on the block, Joanne's house stood out like a peacock among ducks in a row of otherwise solid, mundane Tudor houses. The deep navy-painted brick with emerald and burgundy accents reminded Shiloh of the old paisley print sofa from the seventies that had lived in the back office room of her father's pawn shop since she was a child. It was the first sofa that P.J. and Amelia bought when they married in '79. P.J. couldn't be made to part with it, despite Shiloh and her brother's best efforts. Pulling up in the driveway, Shiloh followed the solar light-lined, white pea-gravel pathway to the front door and rang the bell. Rather than a simple chime, Shiloh could hear Bob Dylan's "Like a Rolling Stone" echoing through the house. Then, the sharp barking and galloping feet of a dog made it to the door before his owner.

The woman who opened the door was small in stature but projected large. Her long, salt-and-pepper hair cascaded in voluminous curls over her shoulders, which were draped in a calf-length soft violet cardigan with fringed ends. She wore it over a silver silk tunic-style blouse, leggings, and stamped black leather clogs with the toes turned up in a way that reminded Shiloh of elf's shoes. Long peacock feather earrings hung to her shoulders on delicate wires. Her thin arms were stacked with wooden bracelets that clicked as she moved, and around her neck, she wore multiple loops of long beaded necklaces. Tortoise-shell, cat's-eye reading glasses perched on top of her hair, holding it in place like a headband. She had a charcoal drawing pencil tucked behind one ear. A reddish-blonde corgi in what looked like a children's Hawaiian shirt darted around Joanne protectively and continued to bark as she introduced herself to Shiloh.

"Gervais!" Joanne exclaimed. "Where are your manners? How many times have I told you not to bark at guests? No, no, no!" The dog went silent, and he looked up at Joanne sheepishly. "That's better," she said. Pulling a strip of dried beef jerky out of a pocket hidden in the folds of her cardigan, she tossed it to Gervais. The corgi caught it in midair and trotted back into the house, wagging his tail happily.

"Great choice of name," Shiloh said. "Corgis are the comedians of the canine world."

"He's a big fuzzy clown who likes to yap, so I thought it fit," Joanne replied. "Laurie bought him for me several years ago, when they started building that," she nodded down the street in the direction of the new Factory 52 development. "He worried bringing more traffic into a more affluent neighborhood might attract more prowlers. I didn't agree at first, but it turns out he was right. I've seen more suspicious characters around here than ever in the forty years I've lived here. It's like they've finally figured out there were things worth stealing in Norwood."

"I think that's the case with gentrification everywhere," Shiloh shrugged. "It brings all kinds of results that people never expected. Both good and bad, depending on your perspective."

"True," Joanne nodded, motioning for Shiloh to come inside. "I will say though, I've sold more paintings this year than ever in my life. All these people are renovating and wanting new art on the walls, in search of something local and authentic. I should have a gallery space already, but the waitlist at Essex Studios is still over a year long. Laurie gets onto me for inviting strangers over and showing new pieces in the living room, but I don't have anywhere else that's good to exhibit them."

"Oh, I didn't know you were a painter," Shiloh said. Joanne's living room was indeed filled, ceiling to floor, with paintings of every possible size. Abstract sunsets, dancing figures, whimsical animals. Their bright array made Shiloh slightly dizzy. The more she spoke, the more Joanne Blake reminded her of Lily Tomlin's character on *Grace & Frankie*. Verbally sharp, but an old hippie. Uncannily, Joanne resembled an older version of Shiloh's mother, Amelia. She also wore a silver tree of life necklace, Shiloh noticed, as she unconsciously fidgeted with the similar pendant she always wore. Although Joanne was engaging, Shiloh felt that it would be too easy to waste the afternoon on friendly chatter with a kindred spirit if she didn't make an effort to keep the conversation focused. "Laurie told me you were a social worker," Shiloh stated.

"I am, or rather, I was," Joanne replied. "For over thirty-five years. It's the kind of career that's not easy to walk away from if you know what I mean. That's part of the reason I took up painting again after I retired. I needed something to occupy my mind. Too many voices in my head of people who stuck out to me over the years. I still worry about what happened to some of the cases I worked on. Where those people are now. Especially the kids. It's kind of like being haunted, if you know what I mean, only by the living."

"I used to be a public defender, so I get it," Shiloh answered. She shuffled her feet through the deep green shag rug with tufts as tall as grass. "Not to be too abrupt, but your email mentioned that you remembered working with Doreen Bowles. That she was a patient at the Athens Asylum whom you cared for years ago when you were still an intern."

"Oh, yes, of course," Joanne said. Reaching into the large, crocheted satchel sitting on a floor pillow in the living room, she pulled out an expandable folder. "When you said that you were able to come today, I went ahead and pulled Doreen's old files. Printed everything out for you to look over. We can discuss it if you have questions about anything I remember. But I'll warn you," Joanne winced. "Doreen's life was difficult, and the end was especially brutal. It was hard for me to look back over her story, even after what I've seen through the years. It must have been tough on Simon to be her child. People like Doreen, who've never been shown love... well, it's hard for them to be parents. Knowing her story makes it easier to understand why she and, it seems, Simon too, turned out as they did."

Joanne sighed. "On a lighter note, you don't mind vegetarian food, do you?"

"Not at all," Shiloh replied. "I know I should be eating healthier than I do."

"Oh good," Joanne replied. "I've got a pot of tofu vindaloo on the stove, and I just put some fresh naan in the oven. I don't want them to burn. Why don't I go see about those, and you go ahead and look over the files? We can eat afterward if you like."

"Sounds great," Shiloh said, picking up the expandable folder from where she'd laid it on the coffee table—or rather, the short, fat Asian urn with a thick piece of glass placed on top that Joanne appeared to use as a coffee table. A nearly empty mug of what smelled like chamomile tea sitting on it was inscribed with a declaration that Joanne's other car was a broom. The room smelled of sage and lavender. Shiloh settled down onto one of the several round, brightly colored mandala floor cushions that surrounded the urn, feeling more at ease than she had in days. Over the next half hour, as spicy Indian food smells wafted through the house, Shiloh leafed through the pages of Doreen Bowles's tragic life.

The first document in the file was a copy of her initial patient evaluation form. It corroborated several facts about Doreen's story that Shiloh already knew, which she found reassuring because they confirmed Shiloh's understanding of the case, while adding a few more details. Doreen was born to a poor, strict Catholic family from the West Side. Her father was a factory worker who stayed drunk most nights and slapped around both Doreen's mother and their kids regularly. The youngest of seven children, Doreen began looking for an escape early. She started working as a server in a chili parlor downtown the summer after she turned fifteen. Not too long afterward, she met Dr. Ian Tierney, who was a hospital administrator in his late forties. Dr. Tierney showered Doreen with gifts—jewelry, clothes, and money—that she hid away from her family lest she be forced to share. After less than a year of secretly meeting Dr. Tierney at his office after hours to carry on their affair, Doreen found out she was pregnant. A rising high school junior, Doreen was expelled from the Catholic girls' school she attended, St. Agatha's, after the administration found out that she was expecting. Hoping for help from her family, Doreen confessed the affair with Dr. Tierney to them. However, Doreen's father kicked her out of the house too. By Doreen's admission, her mother "was too much of a scared cow to argue in any way."

By sixteen, Doreen found herself living alone on the streets. She tried to reach out to Ian Tierney by phone several times. When that didn't work, she showed up at his office, demanding to be seen. Through hospital security, Dr. Tierney had Doreen removed and restrained. He put her on a psychiatric hold in the suicide ward for twenty-four hours. Injected with sedatives, Doreen recalled waking up strapped to a gurney with Ian standing over her. Dr. Tierney explained that he had no intention of supporting her or the child. If it weren't already so far along as to have been a partial birth, he would have already ordered an abortion. Dr. Tierney claimed that if Doreen made any other attempts to contact or humiliate him in public or court, he would have her permanently committed against her will. Terrified at the prospect, Doreen promised never to reach out to Ian again. She kept that promise.

Having no other place to go and too scared to share her story at a women's shelter for fear of Dr. Tierney's reprisal, Doreen slept during the daytime in libraries, parks, and cemeteries. At night she walked to stay warm. She sold a few of the gifts that Ian had given her to buy food, a sleeping bag, and personal care items. However, she kept the jewelry for as long as she could, sewn into the lining of a trench coat that Ian had given her one night early in their relationship. The record said that Doreen thought that Dr. Tierney's choice to give her the coat "right off his back" because she was cold, "proved he was a real gentleman who would take care of her." Seeing the detail about Dr. Tierney's trench coat, Shiloh winced at how naïve Doreen was as a teenager and how bitter the woman must have been later, to have mistaken the small gesture as an indication of genuine compassion or chivalry. Then, Shiloh remembered the trench coat that she'd seen Simon wearing in the park. She wondered if it could possibly be the same one as she kept reading.

Sometime during the week of Christmas, Doreen gave birth while living as a squatter in Spring Grove Cemetery. She went into labor and passed out from the pain. Doreen had no recollection of how long she was out for because she'd lost track of days due to starvation-induced confusion. A groundskeeper found Doreen bleeding in the snow and called an ambulance. Paramedics took Doreen to the University of Cincinnati Hospital, where the delivery was completed on Christmas Eve. Miraculously, both Doreen and the baby survived. Afterward, she woke up delirious and for days said nothing intelligible, other than quoting random Biblical scriptures. Charging her nothing due to her circumstances, the hospital staff asked Doreen who she was and the identity of the child's father, claiming the need to put a last name on Simon's birth certificate. That was how Dr. Ian Tierney found them. He made sure that both mother and son were turned out of the hospital the next day, with all records of the incidents surrounding Simon's birth destroyed.

Back on the streets once more, Doreen began selling off the rest of the gifts that Ian gave her, including the jewelry that she'd initially tried to hold onto, to feed Simon and to buy diapers, a carrier, and other things that she and the baby needed. When that money ran out, she turned to sex work and began living among a group of similar women in the city's abandoned subway stations. Paying older sex workers whose clients had dwindled in fast food, alcohol, and drugs to watch Simon while she was away, Doreen managed to eke out a living until her drug habit became too much to handle. She stopped being able to pay Simon's babysitters, such as they were. By the age of four or five, Simon was left alone for increasingly long periods to fend for himself there in the tunnels. Doreen only stopped by to leave bags of fast food, as if she were feeding a random stray animal. Eventually, around the time Simon turned seven, this arrangement was discovered by some of the workers at bars Doreen frequented. They called Children's Services to come and take Simon away. Doreen fought with them, was initially charged with child abandonment, and then later moved to Athens Asylum after a suicide attempt in jail.

That was where Joanne Blake first met Doreen Bowles. Joanne's bubbly, girlish initials checked the corners on about six months' worth of status reports. She documented the sedative dosages that kept Doreen from attempting another suicide and recorded what Doreen was willing to eat at meals along with her sleeping patterns. All of them were erratic. Doreen also continued to preach whatever random bits of sermons entered her clouded mind to whoever would listen. Most of them were filled with prophetic verses and bits from the Book of Revelations about the Second Coming. Whatever happened to Doreen Bowles during those seven years after Simon's birth had done something to her mental state from which she never recovered. A series of monthly status update photos charted Doreen's increasingly rapid decline from a tired-looking, but still noticeably pretty, young sex worker to a completely gray, drugged-out, toothless hag in just a few short years.

"Sometimes I wonder if the way we do mental health in this country actually does more harm than good," Shiloh said, shaking her head. Joanne returned to the room carrying a tray with two bowls of tofu vindaloo and a basket of naan.

"You and me both," Joanne said. Craning over Shiloh's shoulder as she set down the tray, she continued, "That last photo was taken the week I finished my internship, just as the asylum was closing. If you look at Doreen's discharge papers, you'll see that she was released without supervision."

Shiloh glanced at the last pages of the file, which included an inventory of the belongings that Doreen was given upon her release. Her list of personal possessions was so few that a particular item stood out immediately to Shiloh from the record. *One black trench coat, used.* Making a mental note of this fact without mentioning it, Shiloh continued the conversation.

"So, you're saying that after years of being prescribed increasingly pow-erful medications and being completely confined in a psychiatric hospital, they just let her go?" Shiloh asked, somewhat shocked. "Right back out on the streets?"

"Sadly, yes. That's exactly what happened. Not just to Doreen, but to a lot of patients when the facility closed," Joanne replied, halving a piece of naan and handing it to Shiloh.

"What isn't included in those records is that Doreen was considered a problem patient, in more ways than one. Normally, a licensed physician would have been overseeing her care and signing off on all her checkpoints. By the time I arrived, all the doctors in Athens were afraid of her. Even when she was somewhat coherent, Doreen was an exhibitionist. She had a habit of taking off all her clothes and then throwing herself at any male physician who came near. Given her personal statement about how her only sexual relationship with a man not for profit was with Dr. Tierney when she was very young, I always thought it was like some sort of throw-back hallucination. In her heavily medicated state, Doreen's brain was regressing to a time when she was younger and having the affair. Similarly, I thought she was probably remembering scraps of sermons she'd heard preached at her when she was regurgitating Scriptures. Whatever it was, every physician on campus was terrified to be in a room alone with her. Since all the doctors were male, it fell to whoever was the newest nurse or intern to do her daily monitoring. Doreen had a kind of cycle with female staff she'd meet. She'd start out very friendly and almost pitiful, in a poor me, kicked dog kind of way. Then, if she couldn't get what she wanted, which was usually more drugs, she'd scream and start to become violent. That's why she spent so much of her time on suicide watch. She'd begin self-harming with anything she could get her hands on until someone gave her enough sedatives to knock her out. It's like she craved them. Those little spots of death were her only peace."

Joanne pointed to the last photo. "I remember the day she lost her teeth. It was about five months after I'd started working there. By then, Doreen figured out that she couldn't wheedle her way into getting what she wanted from me. She started resorting to other tactics to see if I could be intimidated. It worked sometimes with other younger interns. The girl before me was fired for throwing a bottle of pills at Doreen and bolting through the door after Doreen bit her. Doreen Bowles ruined a lot of careers before they even began. For me, it was a battle of wills. I was a divorced single mom, older and mentally tougher. She'd threaten that she was going to bash her teeth out, and I'd tell her to go right ahead. Make a move, and I'd call security. Turns out, that was exactly what she wanted. Doreen broke out every one of her front eight teeth by banging her face on the marble window sill because I wouldn't give her any more pills. It looked awful. Blood everywhere."

Shiloh winced. "My God! What did you do?"

"What else could I do?" Joanne asked, "I locked the door and called security immediately. Doreen broke her face up pretty badly that day. Fractured her maxilla and busted her lip too. You can still see the bruising if you look closely enough in the last picture, even though it's black and white."

Examining the photo more closely, Shiloh winced. Doreen's smashed face was painful to look at. "If Doreen was allowed to just leave on her own when the asylum closed in 1993," Shiloh said, still holding the untasted naan in her hand, "do you know what happened to her afterward?"

"As you might imagine," Joanne said. "It didn't end well. They put Doreen on a bus back to Cincinnati. From what I heard, she tried to go back to her old ways. Living as a sex worker, over in one of her old haunts near Linn Street. Although I'm sure you can see why she wasn't very successful in getting much new business. I heard through the grapevine that Doreen applied for some social services benefits but got denied. She must have had her wits about her enough to still try at that point. I called a friend who worked in that benefits office for years. She tried to pull the file, but the only thing in it was the initial application. It didn't say anything I didn't already know, so I didn't bother printing it out. After that, Doreen Bowles just sort of dropped off the map. For me and the rest of the world, it seems. I was working at UC by then full-time. I had my own son to take care of too as a single mom. Although Doreen's story was tragic, it wasn't unusual. To be honest, I might have thought about Doreen Bowles maybe two or three times in passing all these years until Laurie called me and told me about your conversation."

"Well, I appreciate your going to the trouble of looking all this up," Shiloh said, motioning toward the stack of papers on the table. "It can't have been a pleasant memory. I'm guessing you don't have any clues regarding what happened to Doreen's son Simon after her release though, do you? I'm not sure how much of our conversation Laurie told you, but I'm trying to piece together some details about his life. What might have triggered Simon to seek revenge on the boys who abused him all these years later? I'm wondering if his mother's reappearance might have anything to do with it. Maybe she re-entered his life, and it stirred up something that set him off. Otherwise, I can't figure out why he would wait so long."

"The killings of those young people," Joanne said, shaking her head sadly. "Yes, Laurie told me all about it. Unfortunately, I don't have any insights to offer there. People don't realize how easy it is for a child to get lost in the system if they have no one to advocate for them. I guess that Doreen didn't live very long after her release from the asylum. A few years, at most, given her level of instability. But that doesn't explain the lapse of time between then and now. Twenty years? Pfft..."

Joanne waved her hands, making the carved wooden bracelets on her arms clatter. "Anyone can become a completely different person in twenty years. Hell, even in five. Look at me. At twenty-two, I was on top of the world. New bride, full of hope for a promising art career. Not a worry in the world. Then, ten years later, wham. Divorced. Single mom of a small child. Basically no child support because my ex made so little money. Byron left his teaching position the year after he finally earned tenure to join the Peace Corps! What a cliché!"

Joanne snorted in disgust. "Who does that? Running away allegedly to find himself and save the world while leaving his own family behind. But that was Byron, though. Laurie's father. Spoiled rich boy. Hopeless romantic, until he wasn't. So there I was, with a completely useless art degree and no means of support. Byron's family took pity on me and paid for me to go back to school to get another degree and a master's. At least they were supportive, and that helped me to keep going. Got my MSW, made a second career, and now here we are. Almost four decades after Byron left me, I'm finally getting back to my art. If you look at it one way, I lost a lot of productive years in which I could have been building a reputation for myself as an artist. But if you look at it differently, I did a lot of things during that time too that were productive in other ways. Saved a lot of kids, including my own. Who do you think helped pay for Laurie's apartment all those years in New York? Because I assure you, one cannot afford to live alone even with a full-time teaching job in Brooklyn these days."

"I'm guessing you did," Shiloh agreed. "That was good of you to make the sacrifice."

"Being a good parent is the essence of self-sacrifice," Joanne replied. "However, some people sacrifice the wrong parts of themselves for the wrong reasons. Like in Doreen Bowles's case. Pearls before swine. A lot of people simply have no help. My parents didn't have the money to send me back to college a second time, but they were emotionally supportive. My mother watched Laurie a lot when he was young, and Byron's mother did too. It takes a village to raise a child. Especially if that child is a boy whose father just up and leaves. But we did it, and I'm proud of the man my son became. Even if he didn't make a go of an acting career exactly as he planned, he's still doing it. I'm happy to have him back here, closer again too, now that he's chosen to do so. I don't think any of his efforts were wasted either. Maybe he inspired the next Robert De Niro or Al Pacino up there in Brooklyn when he was teaching public school."

Sensing their meeting was nearing the end, Joanne added, "He really is a good person, my son, but he's lonely being back here with just me and his work, I can tell. Most of his old friends have moved away. Most creative people who grow up here do. It's not a city for the open-minded. People here lack imagination. If I'd made more money, I would have left long ago. Maybe now that I'm retired..."

Joanne trailed off with a dismissive wave of her hands that made the stacks of bracelets on her arms jingle. "But all of that's bygones. Here in the present, I just try to do what I can for my son to make him happy. Which is why, even though I know it really isn't my place, and you might think I'm one of those typical meddling mothers, I have to say that I could tell Laurie was interested in you when we spoke. He has pretty good instincts, but he's always been slow to act on them. Especially in relationships, he always second-guessed himself and thought he wasn't good enough."

Joanne chuckled softly as she touched the tree of life necklace at her throat and then motioned to the similar one that Shiloh wore. "I know we've just met, but I have a good feeling about you too. Perhaps, you might give him a call sometime, when you're ready."

Shiloh started to speak, then stopped. Joanne was a sweet lady, and she *had* thought Laurie was handsome. They were both easy to talk to, and she felt that even from what little she knew about the two of them, it seemed like it would be easy to fit into their family. Still, the timing was off, and Shiloh felt it. She simply wasn't ready to begin a new relationship, especially after all of the new insights that working the case had brought to the surface about Ethan and his alienation from his background. There was so much left to process, Shiloh couldn't even begin to explain it to Joanne. Perhaps on a different afternoon, she reasoned, but not that one. So, she simply changed the subject, hoping that leaving Joanne's suggestion dangling there didn't come across as too awkward.

"I guess every life's path all just comes down to a person's individual circumstances," Shiloh said, polishing the bottom of her vindaloo bowl with the last piece of naan. "Thank you for your time, Joanne. And for the food. It was delicious."

"My pleasure," Joanne returned, indicating only by a slow blink of her eyes and a sigh that she intuited it was best not to drop any further hints about Shiloh calling Laurie. Instead, Joanne helped Shiloh up from her seat on the floor. Shiloh gathered the papers back into the expandable file and tucked them into her red tote bag to go. When they got to the door, Joanne lingered with her hand on the knob.

"After so many years in social work, I know a lot of who a person is comes down to just what you said. Circumstances. Who has privilege and who doesn't. Many times, that determines who's successful. Yet, there are still the Dolly Parton's of the world. The Oprah Winfrey's. The Ralph Lauren's, Eminem's, and Nicki Minaj's. Right here in Cincinnati, Sarah Jessica Parker. In between their level of success and others' failure is a sea of mediocrity filled with people who grew up hard and turned out just okay. They achieved a moderate level of success. Nothing great, but they added something to the world despite their backgrounds. People like that are everywhere. Quiet heroes, who overcame so much just to be ordinary. And then you have people like Doreen Bowles and perhaps, if what Laurie told me you suspect is true, her son Simon."

Joanne opened the door. "On some days, I think that the only person to rightfully blame when monsters like them are made is us. All of us. A society that has simply failed that person in some truly wretched way. It's our penance to suffer through the destruction that they leave in their wake. If you really think about it, it wouldn't take much for any of us to turn out that way, given their range of limited options. Then on other days, I wonder if there wasn't something emotionally or spiritually wrong with them all along. Like an incurable disease that festers inside a rotting corpse for decades until someone digs up the coffin and lets it loose upon the world."

Shiloh stepped through the door and turned back to face Joanne. "Nature versus nurture. The age-old question of what makes a person good or evil. So as the expert, tell me, Joanne. Which one do you think it was with Simon then? Nature or nurture? What made him start all this? And perhaps more importantly, is there any way to stop it?"

"That's the most insidious part of it all," Joanne said as she shut the door. "I think with Simon Bowles, it's both. And that's why there's no way of stopping him until he's finished."

Friday, October 13th, Early Afternoon

After leaving Joanne Blake's house, Shiloh called her father, P.J. She was supposed to meet her father and brother's family for dinner at Otto's in Covington. It was their Friday night ritual. They all loved their fried green tomatoes. However, Shiloh knew she was too full of tofu vindaloo to want to eat again at the stroke of five, which was when her father always dined.

She was happy to learn that both had completely forgotten about their usual arrangement. A long-awaited truckload of fresh antiques had just arrived from Maine to be refurbished. Father and son were both elbows deep in measuring and planning. Still, Shiloh wanted to pick her father's brain about the underground geography of the subway tunnels. She remembered P.J. once talking about how her grandfather, the original Peter James "Perfect Pete" Foley, had used the tunnels to help move illegal liquor undetected. Perhaps knowing more about whether or not any of those old hideaway spots still existed could help her make an educated guess about Simon Bowles's location.

When she pulled up to the loading dock behind Foley's Furnishings, Shiloh's father and brother were sweating through their matching company navy polos and khakis. They were attempting to wrestle an antique swan-necked sofa out of a box truck.

"Dad, how many times have I told you that you shouldn't be lifting heavy things like that anymore?" Shiloh called as she climbed out of her vehicle. "And you!" she yelled at her brother. "Why are you letting him do that? Where's your loading crew?"

Three-Pete set down his end of the sofa on the loading dock and mopped the sweaty hair out of his eyes with the back of his arm. "Shi, you know very well that I can't tell Dad when to do nothin'. He does whatever he wants. Besides, I'd done let the loading guys go home for the day when these showed up."

"What's goin' on?" P.J. yelled. His voice echoed from inside the almost empty box truck. "Why'd we stop? Don't give out on me, boy, while I'm still holdin' the end of this thing!"

Three-Pete tapped his left ear. "See? He left his hearing aids out at the farm this morning too. There's been no telling him anything all day." Sighing, Three-Pete picked up his end of the sofa again and staggered backward with it. Shiloh held her breath as her seventy-five-year-old father stumbled over the gap between the back of the truck and the loading dock, caught himself, and, with a torrent of swearing, stepped over safely to the other side.

Pulling the Kentucky Wildcats ball cap off and fanning himself, P.J. noticed Shiloh standing there for the first time. "Shi, I didn't know you were here! When did you come up?"

"Just now," Shiloh said, shaking her head and smiling at her brother, who stifled a laugh. It was a running joke between the two of them about how their father knew absolutely nothing going on around him when he didn't have his hearing aids in. Shiloh reached to hug him, but her father backed away.

"Naw, don't hug me. I'm sweaty," P.J. said. "Your brother has had me slavin' away all afternoon haulin' this load of old Duncan Phyffe. Phew," he whistled, still fanning his cap at his face, which was flushed with exertion. "This fancy shit's always heavy as lead. Come inside where it's cool. Let's have a Coke and maybe some chocolate for strength."

"Now, Dad," Shiloh nudged. "I thought your doctor said you were supposed to be cutting back on sugar."

"What's that, darlin'?" P.J. asked, cupping a hand around his ear. "I can't hear you."

"Selective hearing," Three-Pete mouthed at Shiloh from behind his father. He opened the cooler on the loading dock and handed P.J. a bottle of water. P.J. frowned at his son but took a swig anyway as they headed inside.

After they'd all settled into the back office of Foley's Furnishings, Shiloh explained why she'd come.

"Awww, yeah!" P.J. replied over tented fingers as he leaned forward in his chair. "Pop and them buddies of his had all kinds of underground hidin' places. Every bar that sold bootleg hooch back in the day had 'em, on both sides of the river. Whether or not any of them were connected to those old subway tunnels or if any of it's still there is a mystery to me. Although," he paused, massaging the day's gray stubble on his chin, "I do think I have something that could give you a place to start lookin'. Hold on a sec, and let me run across the street. I'll be back."

"Save yourself the return visit," Shiloh replied, rising to follow her father. "I'll come with you. Three-Pete?" She glanced at her brother, who was staring at the screen of his laptop at the website for another furniture store.

"Naw, y'all go on ahead," he said. "I'm still workin' on an email that I promised to send to this designer from Wilmington I met last summer down at the Southern Home Show. Nora Hewitt. She's got huge orders in the works for big-money restoration projects in several old mansions down in Charleston, Savannah, and Nashville. Been waitin' on this shipment for a while. I'm tryin' to see if I can get in on a collaboration deal down there through her connections. The Southern real estate market has just gone wild. She's got more business than she can handle."

Leaving her brother to finish his business, Shiloh followed her father, P.J., across the street to Treasure Chest Pawn. Inside, she waited while P.J. fumbled through the drawers of filing cabinets that lined the back wall. The shop looked the same as always. A hodgepodge of collectibles, musical gear, jewelry, and antiques for sale that people had pawned and left. Shiloh thought that there were many good novels to be written about the kinds of things that people left in pawn shops. There was a melancholy quality about it, she thought, of a person leaving behind something that had once been very valuable to them in an act of desperation. Before she'd gone to law school, Shiloh thought that she'd be the one to write those novels. Every once in a while, she still thought so.

"Here it is!" P.J. said, sliding a drawer shut with a clang. He waved a manila folder triumphantly in the air. "I knew I still had it somewhere."

"Had what?" Shiloh asked, stepping up to the glass display case of old watches as P.J. unfolded a large sheet of paper on top of it. The sign behind her father had a black and white cartoon drawing of an old miser on it with a caption that read, *I made my fortune fixing clocks.*

"Pop's old map of all the moonshine drops," P.J. said. "Look here." He pointed at a spot on the map marked *Race Street Station.* "Do you know who the contractor was for the first stop on the Cincinnati Subway Line?"

"I have no clue, but I'm sure you're going to tell me," Shiloh responded, yawning. She'd long grown accustomed to her father's opening a long-winded family story with a question as if he were casting out an enticing lead for the nightly news.

"None other than your great-uncle, D.P. Foley," P.J. said smugly.

Shiloh stifled the yawn. "Really? I never knew any of our bunch were in with the powers that be on the other side of the river."

"We weren't," P.J. said. "Pop told me that his uncle won the bid the right way. Because he was the lowest bidder. However, a lot of the other builders in town got wind of what a massive project it was. So they all started submitting their plans for higher prices."

P.J. rolled his eyes. "All the usual Cincinnati crowd's cronyism kicked in. They pushed him out. It's one of the reasons they never finished the subway. D.P. was too cheap and efficient. Everyone else wanted a bigger dip from that well of money, which ran dry too quickly to complete the project. This is a copy of D.P.'s original map, showin' how the whole system was originally intended to connect to other existing underground spaces for repairs and ventilation. It has every ground-level access point proposed as an entryway to the main tunnel in the fall of 1919. Of course, with the end of the Great War still causin' rampant inflation and Prohibition cutting out a lot of revenue, there simply wasn't enough left to complete the railway. That was why it got scrapped. However, I wouldn't exactly call those tunnels abandoned. They were greatly utilized by Pop and his pals to get plenty of Kentucky corn whiskey where it needed to go. Because wherever there is a demand, a supplier will appear pretty quickly," he winked.

"I bet," Shiloh said. She studied the map. Even with what little knowledge she had about city planning, she could tell it was destined to be a complete disaster.

The track loop started at the corner of 4th and Walnut Street near Fountain Square. Then, it ran north along Walnut Street to the canal, beneath Central Parkway, up through the Mohawk and Brighton areas to Ludlow Avenue. Stopping just above the Western Hills Viaduct, the last part marked to be below ground on the West Side went under Hopple Street. From there it went above ground along what became Interstate 75 to Saint Bernard on the East Side, where it again went under the business district, only to take a turn into Norwood's Montgomery Road. From there, it was almost like a rollercoaster, down under Harris Avenue, up through Waterworks Park, dipping south along Beech Street toward the old U.S. Playing Card building to Duck Creek Road. The last leg to close the loop followed the present-day Interstate 71 to Madison Road, going subterranean at Owl's Nest Park one last time before culminating in the grand finale of an elevated railway trailing down Columbia Parkway back to Fountain Square.

"What a mess!" she exclaimed. "No wonder they couldn't finish it. This thing was like Zillow Gone Wild for road construction."

P.J. laughed. "You ain't kiddin'! Look closer, and you will see nearly every block has some kind of access point marked where it goes underground. Those are the spots where Perfect Pete used to drop his whiskey."

"Where did they end up?" Shiloh asked.

"All the most convenient places for a bootlegger," P.J. said, leaning back in his chair. "Underneath bars mostly. Pop told me a lot of them had sewer main access too. Made it handy for him and the other boys to run off if they caught word that the heat was gettin' too close while they were makin' a delivery."

"Did those sewers lead back into the subway tunnels?" Shiloh asked, even though she already knew the answer.

"Yep," P.J. replied. "Every one of the tunnels that was finished at least. They only got around to eleven of the sixteen miles you see on that plan. But you know," he leaned forward toward Shiloh again conspiratorially. "Pop used to say that there were even more tunnels than what you see here. He claimed there was one that even went all the way underneath the Ohio River and came out on the Kentucky side. He was usually high as a kite when he talked about that part though, so I don't know if I'd believe him that far."

"Jesus," Shiloh breathed, her eyes going wide as they raced over the map. "He could be anywhere at any time. Spy on anyone he wanted and then just vanish without a trace."

"Who you talkin' 'bout, darlin'?" P.J. asked.

Shiloh paused. *Should I tell him?* She wondered. *Probably not.*

Her father had always been uneasy about her safety working in the public defender's office. P.J. made Shiloh accept his gift of a shotgun and lessons on how to use it when she opened her detective service. Shiloh knew her father would discourage her from continuing to work the case if he thought she would follow Simon down into the tunnels alone. Where she knew he would be. And where she hoped that she would not find whatever remained of Jasmine Jenkins.

"Oh," Shiloh hesitated, avoiding her father's eyes. "I just heard a courthouse rumor that the man who's the main suspect in that killing spree of those college kids across the river might be hiding in the abandoned subway tunnels. Possibly even living there."

"Baby doll, look at me," P.J. said softly. Shiloh looked. "When are you gonna learn that you can't lie to your Daddy?"

Shiloh felt guilty as a girl. "Who told you? Was it Three-Pete?"

"No," P.J. said. "You ain't the only one in this family smart enough to put two and two together. I've been watchin' all the news reports about those murders. Seein' where the bodies were being left was kinda makin' a ring around the city. I didn't know they had a solid suspect. Police on the news haven't said anything about that yet."

P.J. studied his daughter's reaction calmly. "However, I do know that my daughter is a private investigator who's all of a sudden developed a keen interest in hearin' one of her dear old daddy's long-winded tales about the historical geography of Cincinnati and its subway. So... did I give you the information you needed?"

His deep blue eyes twinkled with intrigue. "Enough to tell me who you think this monster is, and who you predict he'll kill next?"

"Are you going to try to talk me out of following up on it? Of doing my job?" Shiloh deadpanned.

"Not if you promise you'll take a whole gang of cops with you for protection when you go," P.J. smiled. "Plus yours truly. Because I'm a much better shot than those clowns."

"Okay," Shiloh sighed. "I've been waiting to be sure before I said anything because I know how the police tend to railroad people who are already marginalized, but yeah. I think I know who it is. His name is Simon Bowles. He was the illegitimate son of a hospital administrator named Dr. Ian Tierney and a teenage sex worker, Doreen Bowles. He used to be a boy who went to school with Ethan at St. Aug's a long time ago. Something terrible, unforgivable, happened to Simon there, with some of the other boys. Now I think he's gone over the edge. He's out for revenge, trying to kill all their families."

"The families, but not the men themselves," P.J. said, contemplatively. "That's quite a punishment. There's nothin' worse for a father than to know that his child died because of something that was his fault. That's worse than Purgatory. It's Hell on Earth."

"I know," Shiloh replied. "I think that's his intention. One of the notes found with the boy who was killed in the carriage explosion quoted Shakespeare's *Hamlet*. A friend of mine who's in the theater said that the lines he wrote, *Heaven hath pleased it so. To punish me with this and this with me. That I must be thy scourge and minister*, means that Simon sees himself as the hand of God's vengeance on Earth. That when no one else stepped up, not at his school, or the church, or the court, to stop what was happening, he decided to do it himself."

"A religious fanatic on a mission," P.J. said, nodding. "They're the most dangerous kind. Those who think their vendetta is justified by the will of God. As the sayin' goes, the Devil himself can quote scripture for his purposes."

P.J. closed his eyes slowly. "How in the world did you get wrapped up in all this mess? Was it Ethan? Was he one of the boys who did this?" P.J. shook his head. "I never did believe that whole tale about him gettin' shot by some random pimp, and then the police couldn't find the guy. It's fishy. Especially for a fella whose choices in life don't square right to start with. People from families like Ethan Mueller's don't become cops. They become lawyers, judges, and politicians if they're interested in government. People with real power. Not ticket writers. What did Ethan do to piss this monster off?"

Shiloh was taken aback by the directness of her father's questioning. It forced her to consider something that she'd tried to push out of her mind. "Nothing. Ethan did nothing. He walked in on the other boys in the locker room when they were assaulting Simon, but he did nothing. He ran away. He refused to report it, even when the school questioned him about it. He didn't want his brother to…" she trailed off, realizing she'd said too much.

"So it was Roman," P.J. said. "I never liked that jerk. Nor his Daddy Horace either. Ethan was okay," he shrugged. "I tolerated him because he was good to you, but I knew what kind of man Ethan was, deep down."

Shiloh couldn't believe what she was hearing. She could feel angry tears of shock welling up. "How could you say such a thing?" she hissed.

"I don't mean it like that," P.J. whispered. "All I mean is that no matter what a person tries to become, who they are and where they came from is what they return to in the end. Ethan was a Mueller. Yes, he was better than the rest of 'em, but when it came down to it, to the choice of doin' the right thing or the wrong thing, he chose the wrong thing. Because that's what the Muellers and all the rest of their class do. They close ranks. They protect their own. And now, many years later, it seems like they're paying a price for it."

P.J. sighed. "I'm just sorry that you're having to pay for it too."

"How's that?" Shiloh replied, sniffling.

"You've always been a smart girl," P.J. said. "Smarter than me or your brother. You must have gotten it from your mother. You know what happened to Ethan. You just don't want to admit it. I'm sorry that you have to hurt like this because of it. From losin' him, because, like I said, Ethan grew up to be a pretty good man. He just made a terrible mistake a long time ago. Of coverin' for his no-good family. And now, a lot of people are paying for it."

Shiloh couldn't help herself. She reached out for her father and hugged him tight.

P.J. hugged her back. "Do what you have to do to finish out the investigation. Help the police catch this bastard if they can. But promise me something."

Swabbing away tears with her sleeve, Shiloh asked. "What's that?"

Her father held her by her shoulders. "That you won't go down into those tunnels lookin' for him alone. Generations of bad men's schemes have grown like cancer down there for over a hundred years. It's all fine and good to tell stories about it now because, from the safe distance of history, we feel like we've put the past behind us. It's like old Bill Faulkner said, *The past is never dead. It isn't even past.*"

"Okay," Shiloh said. "I'll call Detective Schultz tonight and tell him everything. Hopefully, we can get a plan together to start a search party first thing in the morning."

She sniffled, feeling a little better. "Since when do you read Faulkner?"

"High School," P.J. shrugged. "Really though, I'm a Southern man with a memory. I don't need to read Faulkner. I've lived it."

Friday, October 13th, Late Evening

S hiloh Foley arrived home that night from visiting her father and brother in Covington to find her front door open. The brass handle had been pried off, and the heavy wooden door itself was broken at the lock. It looked as if someone used a crowbar. Immediately, her skin prickled. Someone was in her house.

Stepping warily back from her door, Shiloh pulled her cell from her pocket and thought about calling the police. She hesitated. Her first thoughts were for the safety of her cat. Like most childless women who owned cats, Shiloh considered William to be her furry child.

How long had the door been open? Shiloh wondered. *Was William still inside?*

Scanning the autumn-sparse backyard where she parked, Shiloh saw no sign of her enormous black smoke Maine Coon cat. If William attempted to run away from the house, he was nowhere to be seen within the perimeter of the high wooden fence that she'd installed specifically to prevent his escape. Shiloh thought about the night before when she'd dozed off in the chair by the window while reading Simon's journals. William awakened her by growling at the window. The cat saw something or someone, but when Shiloh went to look, whatever it was had vanished.

William wouldn't have run away, Shiloh knew. He was a cat who weighed almost twenty pounds and was over a yard long, nose to tail. The size of a bobcat with an attitude to match if he felt threatened, although he had always been gentle with her.

No, Shiloh thought. *William wouldn't have run from someone breaking into his house.* That worried her more.

Desperately wanting to know if her cat was safe, Shiloh stepped up to her door again. Her heartbeat pounded in her temples. She considered the best way to frighten off the intruder if they were still there. Turning sideways, she kicked the door open as hard as she could, then spun around into a crouch. The door hit the wall with a loud bang. Shiloh winced as she realized she'd probably just knocked a hole in the drywall.

Least of my worries, she thought. She stared at the open entryway.
Nothing.

Hopefully, they're gone. If I can just reach into the coat closet and get my shotgun. Shiloh took a deep breath, reconsidering. *What if the gun isn't there? What if the intruder has it and is waiting just inside the door?*

Her father's warnings about being careful about where she stored her gun echoed through her brain. She waited an agonizing minute as she watched the second hand make a complete sweep around the face of her stainless-steel Timex. Unable to wait any longer, she scurried inside.

The coat closet door in the entryway was open. The shotgun was still there, propped in the corner, exactly as she'd left it. *What kind of thief breaks into someone's house and leaves a closet door wide open with a loaded gun inside?* The consideration made the whole situation feel even creepier.

The kind of thief who was looking for something else or someone specifically. Shiloh grabbed the shotgun and pulled it up to her shoulder, putting her back in the corner of the entryway so that she could see both inside and outside at the same time.

"Is anyone here?" she yelled in her fiercest voice, hoping to sound like a police officer. "Come out with your hands up!"

Nothing. She yelled again, walking slowly into the living room.

This time, she got a response. A low, guttural meow came from inside the fireplace.

"William?" Shiloh called the cat's name, continuing to step cautiously across her living room. The green velvet chair where she'd fallen asleep by the window the night before was on its side. The little white marble end table where she'd left Simon's journals lay overturned by it. The top was cracked in half as if someone had kicked it over in anger. Scanning her living room, Shiloh could see that her collection of crystals—amethyst, quartz, citrine, and dozens of other geodes and pillars that she'd picked up over the years during her travels—was also scattered across the floor. Many of them were broken. It was clear that some had been thrown hard into the walls and rock fireplace. The small hydroponic herb garden that she kept in a glass cabinet next to the kitchen door was overturned and completely smashed. Shards of glass sparkled in pieces across the hardwood floor, which was littered with potting soil and broken plants. Written in red spray paint, the same kind of paint Shiloh recognized instantly that she'd seen scrawled on the retaining wall the day she'd found the first two bodies in Eden Park was a message.

The Prophet of Eden Park Sees All and Judges All.

It was him, Shiloh thought, her heart racing. *Simon. He was here. In my house!*

Her eyes darted around the living room. She realized that the red and green notebooks that she'd been reading from the night before, Simon's journals, were gone.

He was watching me read them through the window. Shiloh stared out the window at the parking deck across the street. *He was right there all along.* She lowered the shotgun. Her hands began to shake. Her palms felt wet with sweat against the steel and polished wood of the stock. Suddenly cold with shock, Shiloh began to shiver uncontrollably. She sank to her knees.

That's when she noticed the blood. A blotchy trail of it leading into the fireplace.

"William!" Shiloh cried. The cat yowled again. Scrambling across the floor on all fours, heedless of the broken glass, Shiloh peered up into the chimney. There was William. The walls of the chimney flue around the cat were smeared with his blood.

"My poor baby!" Shiloh exclaimed, reaching up into the chimney. The cat snarled and hissed a warning. She lowered her voice, faking a comforting tone in hopes of calming down the terrified cat. "Will, it's me. Mom. I'm so sorry, honey. Please, let me help you. It's going to be okay. It's all over."

The cat stopped hissing. He made a low, wet trilling sound, halfway between a growl and a purr. William curled protectively into a ball on the narrow ledge inside the chimney. As she reached up for him, that's when Shiloh saw it. William's tail had been cut off.

"Oh God," Shiloh sighed, continuing to shake as she cradled the injured cat close to her. William melted into her arms, purring nervously to soothe himself. His fur and paws were sticky and damp all over with blood. Shiloh brushed her hand against the few remaining inches of his tail. A tremor shook through the cat's body as he made the guttural trilling sound again. Holding her cat close to her chest, Shiloh picked up a throw blanket off the floor and wrapped it around William's midsection. Carrying him over to the kitchen counter, Shiloh sat the cat down so that she could reach into her pocket for her cell. Lying by the sink, Shiloh saw the meat cleaver from her block of kitchen knives. Next to it was a thick, matted rope of bloody silver fur. William's tail. The attorney part of her brain kicked in. Knowing better than to touch any of it because it would be crucial evidence, Shiloh dialed 911.

When the police arrived, Shiloh was sitting in her car, still holding her cat in the blanket. The blood on William's fur had dried, but the stump of his tail continued to ooze slowly, soaking through the blanket and onto her clothes. While she waited for the police to show up, Shiloh had called a 24-hour emergency vet in Hyde Park. He agreed to treat William immediately, with the police present to gather any available evidence.

Arriving in a patrol car flanked by two officers, Shiloh handed William over to the pet surgeon on night duty, who examined him gently. Other than his severed tail, William had sustained no other serious injuries. Noting that he'd lost a lot of blood but appeared to be stable if still somewhat in shock, the vet ordered an immediate sedation, x-ray, and prep for surgery. In the waiting room, Shiloh was just finishing up giving her official statement to the two uniformed officers when Detective Schultz arrived.

"Good Lord, Shiloh!" Schultz exclaimed as he saw the blood-crusted front of Shiloh's sweater and slacks. "What happened? Are you alright? I heard someone broke into your house and tried to kill your cat."

"I'm as good as I can be," she replied. "All things considered. The vet seems to think there's no saving William's tail." Glancing down at her gory clothes, Shiloh pulled her blazer closed and buttoned it up to cover her bloody sweater.

"Well, he's a lucky cat to be alive at all," Schultz said. "As he seems to be the only creature yet to be attacked by this Prophet madman who's survived. Too bad he can't talk. It would give us a break in the case."

"Actually," Shiloh replied, "I think I know who did this. It's a long story, but I meant to call you about it when I got home tonight."

"Well, if you're going to be up all night waiting to see how the cat pulls through, then I guess I can too," Schultz answered. "What do you know?"

Shiloh told Detective Schultz everything. From her meetings with Bernadette and Scarlet to the uneasy feeling of being watched she'd had the night before, reading Simon's journals. When she'd finished, Schultz eased back in the steel and plastic waiting room chair. "So you knew about this already, the day that we met for coffee?"

"Not all of it," Shiloh admitted. "Truthfully, I just wanted to be sure. After we spoke, I had a hunch to go down to the location of Zauber Labs, where I found this." Shiloh pulled the broken silver charm bracelet out of the pocket of her blazer. "My client, Bernadette Jenkins, said that it belonged to her sister, Jasmine. The lady I've been searching for in a case that seems to be running parallel to the Prophet's killings. I still don't know whether Jasmine Jenkins is alive or dead. Although I speculated about Simon's connections with the tunnels, it wasn't until I'd spoken with Joanne Blake about Simon's mother, Doreen, and then my father, P.J., who had that map of all the subway entry points, that I felt certain enough to point the finger at Simon for sure. I'm sorry to say it, Schultz, but I was on the defense side long enough to know that the first person accused is often the one found guilty. Whether they actually are or not is irrelevant. Simon had already been a victim so many times. I just didn't want to be one more attacker."

Schultz stared at the floor. "You know," he said after a long pause. "It's a damn shame that the police have come to be seen as just as dangerous as a mass murderer in this country, but what can I say?" He held up his hands. "We've brought it on ourselves. Just like Roman Mueller and those four other boys brought all this on themselves. I can't say I agree with what Simon's done or that I even sympathize with it. I wouldn't be a man sworn to uphold the law if I did. But I understand it. How could a person who's been denied justice so many times become so warped by all those experiences that they become a monster? There's madness in it, surely, but a sort of justice too. Old Testament justice. An eye for an eye, to replace the so-called civilized justice system that has done so much harm to so many."

As Schultz spoke, the emergency vet entered the room, carrying a round plastic cylinder. "Ms. Foley, Detective," he began, acknowledging the pair.

"What's wrong?" Shiloh asked. "Is William going to be okay?"

The vet nodded. "William is a very strong, very lucky cat. Unfortunately, I did have to amputate most of the remaining inches of his tail. It would not have healed properly. Almost every bone was crushed or dislocated. Regardless, even though he will be a bobtail for the rest of his life and possibly have some problems with balance as a result, William should otherwise make a full recovery. I don't believe he suffered nerve or spinal cord damage, which is sometimes the case with traumatic tail injuries. What I do believe, though, is that whoever broke into your house, Ms. Foley, grabbed your cat by the tail with the intent of killing him. Probably because the cat attacked him first. Male Maine Coons can be very protective and territorial of their home surroundings, especially when they've only come in contact with a limited number of other people or animals. William fought back hard. That's how the dislocations happened in the smaller joints of his tail. It was nearly pulled off him before it was severed. Judging from all the pieces of human skin tissue that I've harvested and preserved from his claws, I believe that William's attacker is certainly carrying some severe wounds from their struggle too."

Holding up the clear container to the light so that its contents were visible, the vet continued. "These are all the clippings from William's claws. It's standard procedure to trim them as close as possible to prevent the animal from scratching as their stitches heal. As you can see, there was a sizeable piece of skin and even a few eyelashes caught under his nails during William's fight to escape." The vet handed Schultz the container. "I believe that William clawed the eyes out of his attacker, and that's why he survived."

"That's some cat," Schultz replied. "I should take this to the crime lab immediately. Have the toxicologists run tests. See if we can confirm the suspect's identity."

Schultz turned to Shiloh. "I'd like you to come too so that I can get an official statement down for the record about everything you've just told me."

Shiloh glanced at the vet. "Would that be alright? To leave William here?"

"You should have plenty of time," the vet replied. "We'll be keeping William for a couple of days for observation. I'll have my team call you with regular updates if anything about his condition changes until he's ready to be picked up. Your cat is safe here, Ms. Foley. For William, the worst part is over."

"Okay," Shiloh nodded, adding to Schultz. "Then, I guess we're heading downtown."

***

When they arrived at the Hamilton County Crime Lab, Shiloh was surprised to see two people—an older, grouchy lead doctor and a tech—still working, even though it was well after midnight.

"We've had the team running pretty much twenty-four-seven since the second pair of victims were found in Burnet Woods," Schultz said, noting Shiloh's puzzled expression. "So far, nothing definitive. There hasn't been a single trace of evidence from which to draw DNA or prints on any of the victims until now."

Handing over the clear plastic container that the veterinarian gave him to the tox expert, who introduced himself as Dr. Offenbar, Schultz explained the situation. "You don't need to do a full workup at the moment," he concluded. "We're just looking for a quick match from our databases. Checking to see if it's anyone we already have on file as a victim or suspect in any other cases, open or closed."

Dr. Offenbar nodded and called his tech over. "Come back in a couple of hours. I can't make any promises if anyone whom we don't already have records on. If we do have a match, we'll be able to say that with some degree of certainty."

Leaving the sample of tissue and hair with the toxicology team, Schultz showed Shiloh to one of the lab's conference rooms. He took down her statement on video to keep as part of the official record. By the time they were finished, the assistant returned and was waiting by the door holding a laptop. Tall, thin, and bespectacled, the young man looked anxious.

"Well," Schultz asked, stashing the tablet and webcam in his briefcase. "I take it you've found something interesting."

"Very," the assistant replied, clearing his throat. "It appears that we do have a DNA match on file for the sample you brought us, only it can't be. Doc says there must be some glitch in the system or that I screwed it up somehow. He's re-running the tests himself now."

"Why's that?" Shiloh asked, pulling on her coat.

"Because dead men don't break into people's houses and attack their pets," the assistant said. Tilting his head to one side, he squinted at Shiloh in disbelief.

"I'm not following you," Schultz questioned. "I wasn't aware that we'd had any new bodies show up today. I checked the morgue records before I left. Neither our top suspects nor anyone among his suspected accomplices was there."

The assistant pushed his glasses up along the bridge of his thin nose. "That's because the match we found isn't for someone recently deceased. It's for a person who was suspected as a victim in a case over a decade ago. His name was..." The assistant paused as he opened the laptop and scrolled to the place in his notes where he'd recorded the name. "Ian Tierney. He was some doctor who allegedly died of a heart attack. Foul play was suspected, so his family requested a full tox workup. Ring any bells?"

"Holy shit!" Shiloh swore. "That's Simon's birth father!" She turned to Schultz. "Remember the doctor that I told you about that had an affair with Simon's mother, Doreen? The man who Simon was accused of killing while he was in the hospital recovering from a heart attack?"

"Yes, I do," Schultz replied, his brows furrowed. "But that still doesn't explain..."

Shiloh interrupted him with a question for the assistant. "Who has access to these records?"

"No... no one who doesn't have county or hospital clearance," the assistant stammered, caught off guard.

"That could have been enough," Schultz replied, catching Shiloh's insinuation as it became clear what she was suggesting. "Son, do you have any records listing all the doctors and techs who've had access to this database over the years?"

"Maybe?" The assistant answered, his voice rising with apprehension. "If you're suggesting that I messed it up somehow or that I breached security protocol..."

Shiloh interrupted again. "We're not suggesting anything of the sort. What happened to this victim's record must have been done a very long time ago. Very close to the time of his murder, most likely. Before Simon would have lost access."

Schultz again looked at Shiloh. "Lost access to this particular facility and hospital database, perhaps. Where everyone would have known and suspected him. However, in other parts of the world, other countries that didn't share information with the United States could have made everything else in his life very, very convenient."

Shiloh returned Schultz's glance as she realized the culmination of the scheme. "Simon killed his father to avenge his mother's mistreatment and abandonment. Then, he utilized his hospital resident access to steal Ian's identity and buy drug components from overseas. Probably from shady suppliers who asked no questions. That must have been how he started Zauber Labs without any prescription power. By using Ian's instead. Simon was only a few months away from becoming a licensed physician. He had all the knowledge he would have needed to compound the drugs however he saw fit to make whatever new cocktails he wanted."

"Then he sold them back to the families of the people who'd destroyed his life," Schultz finished. "From a compounding lab space that he rented in one of their very own buildings. The victim became the victimizer. First by poisoning their children, who came to him in desperation for some easy fix to pump them up so they could clear the too-high hurdles of their parents' unrealistic expectations in academics, sports, or whatever. After he was done being amused by watching them run around all hyped-up, paranoid, and crazy, he killed them. Simon created every parent's worst nightmare and is making them live through it, like some kind of Purgatory."

"What does all of that have to do with the man who broke into her house and tried to kill her cat?" the assistant asked, pointing at Shiloh.

"Everything," Dr. Offenbar said over his shoulder. He handed Schultz a slim folder of papers. "I just finished rerunning the tests. I wanted to double-check it myself because it seemed too crazy, but it's true. That tissue sample comes up as a DNA match for Dr. Ian Tierney. A man whom I know died in 2008 because I was working here then too. I was the doctor who found the needle mark between his toes and made the recommendation for further investigation. Simon Bowles Tierney killed his father; there was no doubt in my mind about that. I said so in my official statement, which should still be part of the police record. He was the only member of hospital personnel attending Ian Tierney after his heart attack who had both motive and access to the amount of propofol that I found in his system when I did his post-mortem workup."

Schultz opened the folder and leafed through its contents. "Rather than following up like they should have and arresting Simon for murder, the police department, and probably the D.A.'s office too, bowed to pressure from the hospital to sweep it under the rug. So that the hospital could spare its reputation from scandal, a murderer went free. Only to pop back up years later and go on a rampage." He sighed heavily, muttering under his breath. "Layer upon layer of corruption, over and over again, with the police complicit every time. It's a goddamned shame. No wonder people hate us."

"I just have one question left," Shiloh said to Dr. Offenbar. "I understand the hospital wanting to institute a cover-up to save its reputation. What I don't get is why no one among Dr. Tierney's family ever stepped up to push the matter further. Why none of his friends or colleagues demanded justice for his killing."

"Did you ever meet Dr. Ian Tierney, Ms. Foley?" he asked.

Shiloh shook her head. *No.*

Dr. Offenbar's mouth twisted up at one corner in disgust. "If you had, then you'd understand why. Everyone who truly knew him was probably relieved that he was dead. Dr. Ian Tierney was a predator. His wife and family tolerated his behavior for the money and lifestyle. It was common knowledge among women in the local medical community that it was best to stay away from him if you were young and pretty. Once he'd singled out a new nurse or tech who caught his eye, Dr. Tierney pursued them relentlessly. He wouldn't take no for an answer, and if a woman tried to say no to him, he would ruin her career. After a while, it got to the point where the hospital couldn't get any decent nurses to staff his offices because they would all quit within months. Outside the hospital, though, he was a big asset. Very charismatic and great at charming big donors. Eventually, the powers that were at the time did the only thing they could do. They promoted him to upper administration in charge of fundraising and assigned him only male support staff. Easier to keep him out of trouble that way, but inconvenient for Dr. Tierney. He had to resort to banging chili parlor waitresses."

Offenbar shrugged. "Which would be my best guess as to how he met and seduced Doreen Bowles, Simon's mother. Otherwise, someone of her lower social class would never have registered on the radar of a high roller like Tierney. Doreen looked like easy prey. But we all know how that turned out. Karma can be a bitch sometimes."

The skinny tech screwed up his face. "Ugh. The more I hear about working in medicine back in the day, the more I'm glad we're so beyond all of that. All those boomer coverups, protecting each other, even promoting men who were known sexual predators. It's beyond disgusting."

Schultz and Offenbar looked at each other and burst out laughing so hard tears came to their eyes. The young tech stared at them quizzically, not understanding the joke.

"I hate to break it to you," Shiloh said gently to the tech. "But corruption and coverups aren't just a boomer thing, and they're not just a medical thing. They still happen every day, in every industry you could think of. How long have you been out of college?"

"I've got one more semester," the tech replied. "This is my internship."

Shiloh took a deep breath and blinked slowly, trying to ignore her colleague's amusement at the tech's naivety. "You'll figure it out, soon enough. The best thing I can tell you until then is that the good news is that about half of what you've learned in college about ethics and how the world supposedly works is a complete lie."

"That's the good news?" The tech replied incredulously. "What's the bad news?"

"The bad news," Shiloh repeated, "is that you don't know which half."

***

By the time they finished up at the crime lab, it was almost morning. Shiloh and Detective Schultz agreed that the best approach was to go through all the proper procedures to ensure that the case was rock solid. Schultz said that he could get a bench warrant and assemble a proper team to search the Zauber Labs building and the tunnels beneath it that afternoon. Shiloh agreed with Detective Schultz's suggestion that it was best not to go home to sleep. However, she declined his invitation to have an officer escort her there to pack a bag so that she could stay with her father or brother across the river until she got the call that the police were ready to move forward with the full site investigation. Instead, Shiloh opted to go back to her office, hoping to catch a few hours of sleep on the sofa.

When Shiloh plugged in her dead phone, there was a message from Nadia Haas. She listened to it twice, trying to make sure that she wasn't hallucinating with exhaustion. Still working through the shock of disbelief at the content of Nadia's message, Shiloh called Detective Schultz and explained that she was returning to the station immediately.

From the dormer window in the slope-roofed attic storage space of Shiloh's house, a man in a filthy black trench coat with a bandage over his right eye sat watching as Shiloh pulled out of her office parking lot. Frantically engaged with her cell phone, she did not think to look up. Dropping the attic ladder, he climbed down, carrying a bottle of tequila and the thing he'd been searching for when he broke into Shiloh's house earlier that afternoon.

Although he'd intended to steal it when he'd taken his journals, Simon was forced to flee after his fight with the cat. By the time he'd finished bandaging what remained of his eye, it had been time for the ritual. Simon was not a person who adapted easily to any changes in plans, so he'd gone through with the ritual, only to be interrupted a second time. That was okay though. He'd left his followers to take care of that. Afterward, when he returned, Simon had to wait until Shiloh and the police left with the injured cat before he could search again. Another delay. Cats had always caused him problems, Simon thought. They were so hungry and unpredictable. He could not stand them.

Yet, this second search had paid off. Simon had known it would. He considered patience, persistence, and endurance of pain to be his three greatest virtues. Simon Isaiah Bowles Tierney was a man willing to play the long game in life.

The socket of his eye throbbed as Simon righted Shiloh's green velvet chair. He positioned it behind the noise-canceling curtains, so that it remained concealed in the shadow of her fireplace. A few minor disruptions, but everything was coming back into order. As Shiloh drove away, he took a long pull on the bottle, draining the last of the tequila. The liquor made his gums feel raw. He hadn't brought any denture cream, but that was alright. Just another minor inconvenience. Another discomfort, but any pain was tolerable once a person set his mind to it.

Simon pulled a blue plastic case out of his coat pocket, removed his dentures, and clicked them into place in his mouth. Sitting the bottle down on the hearth, Simon opened the cover of Ethan Mueller's journal and began to read.

Friday, October 13th, Late Afternoon, Across Town

When Nadia Haas pulled up to the Arnold family compound, she thought she'd made a mistake. Circling the neighborhood in her old turquoise Toyota Prius, at first she thought the Foundation House up front was the Country Club. Double-checking the address, she was on her second circle when she saw Scarlet Arnold out walking her dog. Nadia pulled up beside her and rolled down the window.

"Forget something?" Nadia said as she handed Scarlet the flute case. The dog, a slim black whippet wearing an emotional support animal vest, plopped its front feet up on the window ledge. Panting, the dog stuck its head over the window frame and whined.

"Nubi, get down!" Scarlet scolded," The dog gave her a guilty look and dropped to all fours on the ground. She opened the flute case, scanning its contents. "Whew, that was a lucky find! Thank you!"

"Don't mention it," Nadia returned. "Cute dog. Is he new?"

"Oh, no…" Scarlet replied, absentmindedly stroking the whippet's head. "It's not n-e-w-b-i-e like someone new," she explained, spelling out the word. "It's N-u-b-i, short for Anubis."

"As in, the Egyptian guide to the underworld," Nadia added. "Nice reference, but that's a pretty heavy name for such a sweet-looking dog."

"I got him when I was going through a rough time," Scarlet shrugged. She motioned as if to ask whether it was okay for her to sit down. Nadia unlocked the door. Nubi put his paws on the open window frame once more. Scarlet did not correct him.

"I struggled a lot when I started junior high. Before Dad started having Bernadette homeschool us, I mean. I've always been kinda, you know…" Scarlet gestured toward her clothes. "Into goth stuff. When I got to sixth grade, the girls were pretty mean about it. Started calling me Wednesday Addams, talking behind my back, tripping me, and pulling my hair. You know how girls are. Mom thought finally getting me a puppy for Christmas that year would cheer me up. And it did, some. Nubi's the best friend I have."

Hearing his name, the black dog began to bounce up and down, as if trying to climb through the window. "Do you mind if I just let him in? I don't want him to scratch up your car."

Nadia chuckled. "Go right ahead. Not worried about the old Prius. I love dogs. Wish I could have one. My dorm at Xavier allows it, but I don't have the time to be fair to one."

"Oh right, Bernie mentioned that you went there as we were on our way home," Scarlet said. The dog curled his long legs up in her lap, rested his head on her shoulder, and sighed, content to be close enough to her for comfort.

"Did you know my sister, Savannah?" Scarlet asked as she smoothed Nubi's silky fur.

"No, we didn't move in the same circles," Nadia said, noticing that Scarlet was avoiding eye contact and that her face had begun to turn red and blotchy. "Say, if there's something that you feel okay telling me, that you didn't say back when we met with Bernie and Shiloh, you can. I grew up as an only child. I know how it feels to not have anyone to confide in."

Scarlet sat silently for a moment, continuing to stroke Anubis's head. "Yeah," she said finally. "Yeah, there is something. I think I know where Jackson is."

"Okay, are you going to tell me or just leave me in suspense?" Nadia said, after a long pause, hoping Scarlet would say more without prompting.

"He's down in that tunnel," Scarlet began hesitantly. "I just know he is. That's where he and Ellis used to meet up, you know, to fool around. I heard them talking on the phone about it late at night when they thought no one could hear. I didn't say anything more before because I thought that maybe he just needed some time down there to, like, be alone for a while. To grieve and think things through before he had to come back and face all the embarrassing questions in front of Dad and the whole world.

Jackson wasn't ready to come out to everyone. Dad would have kicked him out if he knew. Jackson would rather kill himself than disappoint Dad any more than he already does, just by existing."

"Do you think that your brother would hurt himself for real?" Nadia asked, her face wrinkling with concern. "Or that he might have been capable of hurting Ellis if he thought Ellis was about to out him?"

Scarlet nibbled at her lower lip, thinking. "I don't think Jackson would ever harm Ellis unless he went completely out of his mind. The two of them were crazy about each other. Jackson goes off by himself a lot, especially since he's old enough to drive. Jefferson does too, and Dad says nothing about it because they're boys and can take care of themselves." Scarlet rolled her eyes and made air quotes with her fingers. "Jackson has stayed out overnight before, but never this long, into the next day. He knows that would make Dad ask too many questions that he doesn't want to answer. When he wasn't home after we got back from meeting with you guys, I started to get worried. That's why I was out walking the dog. I didn't want to linger around the house until Dad came home and asked me where Jackson was. I didn't trust myself not to say anything."

"I understand," Nadia said. "I know you don't want to bring the heat down on your brother if you can help it. What if we drove down again to where the tunnel opening is by Washington Park? Just to see if Jackson's vehicle is there. If it isn't, then maybe you'll feel more ready to speak to someone else who can help us find him, like the police. If it is, maybe we could just go in a little ways and call. See if he's camped out down in there, depressed about his boyfriend dying. Either way, we'll know something more."

"Okay," Scarlet said. Sniffling, she stared out the window of the Prius, back at the Arnold compound. "You know, everything on TV nowadays is so hateful about rich people. Everyone wants to eat the rich. Steal their stuff. And then be just like them, with all the fancy shit, only done the way *they* want it to be. The thing is though, that we're not all the same. We're not all monsters. Vanna could be snooty sometimes, yeah. So would any girl who was that pretty. But Vanna could be down on herself too. That's how she got on the Zauber shit, I think. Because she knew that she didn't have any real girlfriends and boys just wanted her for her body and Dad's money. Mom and Dad didn't help either. Yeah, she was their favorite, but it came with a lot of pressure. She had to get perfect grades, be the perfect athlete, and be the perfect weight. So many expectations, every second of her life. Savannah just wanted a little escape from it all. I think sometimes everything hurt her even more. With her, there was nothing wrong. She was like, flawless all the time. Not like..."

Scarlet trailed off as she covered her face in her hands, crying softly. "I'm just running off at the mouth. I'm so sorry."

"Hey," Nadia said, reaching into the console for some fast food napkins and handing them to Scarlet. "It's okay. You have nothing to be sorry about. You've lost your mom and your sister, and now your brothers are missing. The world kind of feels like it's falling apart. You've got to let it out somewhere, so go ahead. I swear, zero judgment."

Scarlet dabbed at her eyes, drying the thin rivulets of what used to be winged eyeliner as they trickled down her cheeks. When she finished, she wadded up the napkins and stuck them into the pocket of her tunic-length hoodie. Nubi whimpered and nuzzled at Scarlet's face.

Nadia started the car and turned down the hill toward the city. "Just for the record, everybody has problems. Plenty of them. The rich just have enough money to pay people off so that most of the time, hardly anybody notices."

She drove past Washington Park, allowing Scarlet to guide her close to the entrance of the Liberty Street tunnel. Surprisingly, there were quite a few cars parked along the curb across a trash-strewn empty lot from the tunnel's entryway. Nadia asked Scarlet if she recognized any of the vehicles as Jackson's or Jeff's, but she said no. They decided to get out and walk as far as the entryway so that they could call Jackson's name down the tunnel before turning back.

"Look at that," Nadia said to Scarlet, who held an anxious-looking Anubis close on his leash. She pointed at a line of marks on the muddy ground as the pavement gave way to dirt and scrub grass. "Hoof prints. I was just telling Shiloh this afternoon that I thought the key to figuring out what happened to Ellis Purcell in the carriage explosion was finding that horse."

Nadia knelt to examine the prints more closely. "The mud is still moist, which means they can't be that old. I think that whoever was waiting to catch that horse after the explosion took it right down into the tunnel. That's why it disappeared and never became part of the evidence gathered at the scene." Nadia stood and peered down into the endless depth of the tunnel. Then, she glanced up at the sky, as the last rays of sunset dwindled beyond the cityscape. "I think I'm going to run back to the car and get a flashlight. Just to check a little further inside before we call the police. Man," she added under her breath. "I can't wait until Shiloh sees this."

"Why?" Scarlet asked. Anubis struggled against his leash, sniffing the hoof prints and whining at the mouth of the tunnel.

"Because she always thinks that I can't handle things on my own," Nadia scoffed.

The dog began to bark and jump against the leash, his lean muscular frame pulling the light cord taut.

"Nubi, quit that! You're going to hurt yourself!" Scarlet pulled back sharply on the leash. She heard a soft "ching" sound as the metal D-ring holding the dog's lead to his harness snapped. In a flash, Anubis disappeared down the tunnel.

"Nuuuubi!" Scarlet wailed.

Having found the flashlight in the glove compartment of her Prius, Nadia looked up just in time to see Scarlet drop the broken leash in the mud and take off after her dog into the abyss.

Swearing, Nadia slammed the car door shut, flicked on the flashlight, and chased after.

Fifteen minutes later, they both stood panting before the open door of what looked like an old fallout shelter. The outside walls, like most of the rest of the tunnel, were covered in multiple layers of graffiti. Nadia noticed that the top layer, printed in red spray paint, was a quote from an ominous W.B. Yeats poem that she'd read in high school, *Surely, the Second Coming is at hand.*

Inside, someone had left the overhead lights on. They buzzed and flickered from the faulty current. Rusted metal bunk beds covered in buggy mattresses and what looked like piles of old blankets lined the walls of a long room otherwise filled with empty wooden crates. Most of the crates were overturned and positioned in a semi-circle as if people had recently been using them in place of a table and chairs. From the labels, Nadia could tell that the crates used to hold government C-rations. Having found what he smelled initially, Anubis eyed the entryway cautiously. He sniffed the air and trotted inside.

Nadia and Scarlet exchanged glances, asking each other without words whether they should follow. When Nubi returned to the entryway wagging his tail, Scarlet followed the dog. Wary of what or who else might be nearby, Nadia remained outside.

"They were here!" Scarlet exclaimed in a loud whisper, re-emerging from the shelter room with two blue warm-up jackets. She held them up for Nadia to see the monograms. On the backs of both were screen-printed white silhouettes of swimmers in mid-stroke, doing the overhand crawl. On the fronts were their names stitched in white thread: *Jackson* and *Jeff*.

Scarlet's face brightened with excitement. She pointed down at the mud-saturated concrete floor, following the track of hoofprints into the dark distance. "Do you think if we keep following these tracks, we'll find them?"

"Maybe," Nadia replied, feeling uneasy. "But there could be anything, or anyone, down in these tunnels. Now that we've found evidence that both of your brothers have been down here recently, I think it would be best if we called in reinforcements before going any further."

Scarlet's happy expression darkened. "So, you're saying that we've come this far and gotten this close, but now you want to quit? That I can't go?" Her dark eyes flashed. "What's the matter? You think I'm just a kid who can't handle it?"

"I'm not saying that at all," Nadia corrected herself quickly. "I'm just saying that I'm afraid if we continue by ourselves, we might be getting in a little over our heads."

Scarlet's matte gray lips twisted into a thin smile. "Do whatever you want. I'm going. Anubis!" she called. The dog pricked up his ears. Scarlet reached into her pocket and pulled out a small rubber ball. Leaning back, she threw it as hard as she could down into the tunnel. The dog sprang after it, disappearing into the darkness, with Scarlet right behind. Feeling as if she had no other choice, Nadia followed.

After what seemed like an eternity, but according to her watch was only about half an hour, Nadia caught up to where Scarlet and her dog had stopped. Sensing that Nadia was about to tell her off, Scarlet put a finger to her lips, whispering as she pointed ahead. "Not now! Listen and look over there."

Nadia listened as she shone the flashlight around, past a sharp bend in the tunnel. Surrounded by graffiti-emblazoned walls, she could just make out a sign affixed to the outside of what appeared to be an enclosed platform of the abandoned subway. *Linn Street Station.*

Just beside the sign, tied to a sewer pipe and calmly munching hay, was a horse. At first, Nadia thought the animal was covered with a very bright iridescent green blanket. Glancing down at where its hooves seemed to disappear into the concrete floor, she realized what must be true. The horse was painted with some kind of glow-in-the-dark paint.

Putting a finger to her lips in hopes of keeping Scarlet silent, Nadia crept forward slowly toward the horse. As she grew nearer to the enclosed station platform, Nadia heard the low hum of chanting and the sound of shuffling feet, as if people were walking around inside. Reaching the spot where the horse was tied, the animal snorted. Wary of an approaching stranger, it took a few halting steps backward. Nadia laid her hand on the horse's shoulder, just above its foreleg, and whispered, "Easy, easy girl. I'm not here to harm you."

The horse turned a skeptical eye toward Scarlet and Anubis as the girl and dog inched up behind Nadia but put its head down and continued eating. Nadia looked at the inscription on the horse's leather harness. In a scrolled, Western-style font, the animal's name was printed in all caps.

LYRA.

"Shit, I was right," Nadia breathed softly.

"What?" Scarlet said, in a whisper almost as loud as her normal voice. Nadia shushed her again.

"This is Jasmine Jenkins's horse," Nadia replied, in a much softer tone. "The horse everyone thought she forgot about and put out to pasture somewhere on the West Side. Jasmine's the lady we've been looking for. Her sister, Bernadette, is our..." She paused and corrected herself. "Shiloh's client."

Nadia motioned toward a vent from which thin bands of light streamed weakly across the dirty, broken concrete floor of the subway tunnel. The sounds of chanting and movement behind the wall had increased in volume. "I think that Jasmine may be in there," Nadia murmured, her voice barely audible.

Sensing the urgent need for silence in her friend's tense expression, Scarlet mouthed soundlessly, "Do you think Jackson and Jeff are in there too?"

Nadia nodded. Stepping gingerly up to the open vent, she peered through the slats. Instantly, she knew why their noisy approach through the echoing tunnels had not been detected.

The station platform was enclosed by cinder block concrete walls. Inside, the walls were covered with poorly drawn sigils and bits of Biblical verses scrawled in red. A group of people wearing masks were dancing in a circle. An eerie, heavy-footed sort of dance that kept time to their chanting. Their chant was not in any language Nadia knew. The masks were shaped like the faces of goats. All but two of them had horns. Their shoulders were covered in lumpy, misshapen fur cloaks that reached the ground and appeared as if they were made from randomly selected roadside carrion. The animals' heads and tails were still on. The garments looked as if they'd been hand-sewn by someone with very little skill. The smell wafting through the vent was nauseating, like rotten, uncooked meat. Nadia counted six dancers and one person in the middle, holding one hand up and the other extended down behind a fire in a small cauldron, which sat upon a large, inverted wooden star surrounded by a crude circle about knee-high. On top of the circle were several rusted metal coffee cans without lids. The wood was rough and warped. Nadia supposed it was repurposed from cast-off crates similar to those they'd seen in the fallout shelter.

"What do you see?" Scarlet probed, sticking a skinny elbow in Nadia's ribs to push her aside.

"Ow," Nadia mouthed, massaging her ribcage where Scarlet poked her. "All kinds of weird shit. Look." She slid away from the vent so that Scarlet could see between the slats.

The pace of the chanting picked up tempo, and along with it, the speed of the dancers' shuffling steps. The sound of their feet beating the crumbling concrete echoed like a set of otherworldly timpani drums until suddenly, everything stopped.

Scarlet sucked in a breath and ducked down. Nadia clamped a hand over the girl's mouth and edged her way back over to see what was happening through the vent.

From behind the goat mask with the largest horns, an unusually high-pitched man's voice rang out inside the chamber.

"Young brothers and sisters," he began. "Tonight, we stand on the eve of victory. For too long, we have been silenced. Oppressed by those who seek to hold power and control over us. Yet, in our Lord Baphomet," the man gestured widely toward a rough drawing in what looked like dripping red spray paint on the wall behind him. It depicted a goat-headed deity making the same gesture as he had behind the cauldron. "We have found the path to freedom. The keys that will release us from the bondage of expectations our captors made for us. The unrelenting pressure that has kept us cowed and meek, beholden to them for the nourishment of our lives."

A chorus of hisses sounded around the dimly lit room. The lead goat-man silenced them with a sweep of his arm, like a conductor before a symphony. "We need only complete our ritual of sacrifice to the great Lord of Darkness. His reward shall be riches untold, flowing down upon us like wine to do within our leisure as we will. For once this justice is done, there is no longer the yoke of expectation laid upon our shoulders. Only the pleasures of free will shall guide us. We shall face no judgment because we are the judges."

"We are the judges," the ring of dancers echoed in unison. Startled, Nadia dropped her hand from Scarlet's face as her skin prickled with goose-flesh. Sensing danger, Nadia leaned back as the leader beckoned the group to unmask. Scarlet placed her hands softly on the vent and continued to watch. Nadia scanned the surrounding area for an exit with her flashlight. About fifty yards beyond, where the track headed upward around a curve, she spied a metal ladder.

"That must be a maintenance shaft going up to street level," she whispered into Scarlet's ear. "We should go before they finish the ritual."

"Wait," Scarlet insisted. "I want to see if Jackson and Jeff are in there. We've come so close," she pleaded.

"Okay," Nadia said, resigned but also morbidly intrigued. She too wanted to see what would happen. "But as soon as we confirm it's them, we're getting the hell out of here."

The two girls peered once more through the vent. All the dancers had removed their goat masks except the leader in the center and one of the hornless females. She lay across the star with her arms and legs spread wide, like a sacrificial beast on an altar. The small iron cauldron was on the ground between the two points closest to her head.

Scarlet recognized all of them immediately. She pointed each one out to Nadia. Both of her brothers, Jackson and Jefferson Arnold. Ellis Purcell's older brother, Allen. Khalid Khoury. Nadia knew the last one without assistance as Riley, the surviving twin daughter of Roman Mueller. As Scarlet whispered, Nadia could feel the younger girl shaking beside her. Motionless until then, Scarlet's dog, Anubis, began to rumble with a low growl. Scarlet put her hand around the dog's long muzzle to quiet him as the hairs rose along his spine.

On the other side of the cinderblock wall, the ritual continued. They poured out the contents of the coffee cans, which smelled like gasoline, along the boards that formed a circle and lit it. As the flames licked toward the ceiling, the leader gave a command for the woman laid across the star to be disrobed. When the others peeled away her robe, Nadia could see that the woman's light coffee-colored skin was streaked with blood. Realizing that the pelts from which the robe was sewn must be made from animals freshly dead, Nadia clamped her mouth tightly shut and closed her eyes to keep from vomiting. Taking several deep breaths, she wondered if the figures on the wall were painted in blood, causing the putrid smell.

Drawing a long, straight-blade machete from inside his robe as he dropped it to the floor, the leader pulled off his mask. His face was covered in deep, inflamed red gashes. He wore a filthy, blood-soaked bandage over one eye. In his nakedness, Nadia could see his disfigurement.

Simon, Nadia thought, saying nothing for fear she would puke. *That must be Simon Bowles. What happened to his face?*

Simon gestured for the others to do the same. They obeyed. Each stood naked and wild-eyed, coated in dried blood at one point of the wooden star, holding identical machetes. Studying the piles of skins, Nadia could tell at last what kinds of animals they'd come from. *Cats*, she thought with revulsion. *Dozens and dozens of cats.*

Slowly, Simon reached down and removed the mask from the woman. The long braids of her hair tumbled out, touching the ground.

Nadia recognized her face and froze. The woman on the altar was Jasmine Jenkins.

Sensing the rising tension surrounding him, Anubis began to growl louder. The dog pulled his head away from Scarlet's grasp as the girl remained transfixed in horror.

"To give us the strength to see this justice to its end," Simon announced. "Let us drink the blood of our sister, then of one another, so that we may move and think as one." Simon raised his machete. Placing his blade along the side of Jasmine's neck, he made a small slit. Then, squeezing her flesh to make the blood flow, he lowered his head and drank. Jasmine winced but kept silent. Following Simon's lead, the others cut similar marks into

Jasmine's wrists, ankles, and abdomen. Unable to stand the pain any longer as they sucked her wounds, Jasmine cried out and writhed on the altar.

Hearing her, Anubis barked, spooking the horse. Rolling her eyes back in her head, Lyra reared on her hind legs, straining against the rope that tied her to the sewer pipe. Nadia jumped to her feet, pulling Scarlet up with her.

"Run!" Nadia commanded, thrusting her free hand toward the ladder as they took off.

Behind them, Nadia could hear shouting from Simon's cabal. Drugged by the stupor of their ritual haze, they fumbled confusedly to break out of the flaming circle and determine the source of the noise.

Reaching the bottom of the ladder with Anubis at her feet, Nadia saw a problem. Scooping up the squirming dog, Nadia handed him to Scarlet.

"Take him and go up first," Nadia said.

Scarlet wrapped her arm around her dog and started up the ladder. By the time she reached the second rung, it was clear that Scarlet couldn't carry Anubis and climb too.

"We can't leave him!" Scarlet cried. Her eyes pleaded with Nadia.

"Okay," Nadia said, casting a glance over her shoulder. Simon and the others were still out of sight around the bend in the tunnel. "I'll take him. You stay right behind me."

Nadia bent to pick up the dog. She noticed something shiny and silver on the ground. Instinctively, she picked it up and slipped it into the back pocket of her jeans, not paying attention to what it was. She stuck the dog's hind legs through the strap of her crossbody bag and wrapped his front legs over her shoulder. Awkwardly, she made it to the top of the ladder. Nadia pushed with one arm against the manhole cover. It didn't budge.

"It's too damn heavy," she said, trying not to panic. Scarlet stood beneath her with both hands resting on the ladder. Nadia unwound the dog from around her torso and handed him back to Scarlet. "Hold him for a second so that I can use both hands."

Scared silent, Scarlet said nothing. She took the dog in her arms as she stared anxiously back down the tunnel. In the distance, they could hear a rush of footsteps approaching.

Scrambling back up the ladder, Nadia hooked one leg through the rungs to brace herself. Using both arms, she pushed with all her strength. The manhole cover flipped off to the side as the gleam of early streetlights shone down into the tunnel. Grabbing the dog from Scarlet, Nadia struggled up the ladder again. At the top, Nadia pushed the dog through the opening and pulled herself up.

Blinking in the half-dark, Nadia glimpsed the sign for the old Imperial Theater. Realizing where she'd come out immediately, she turned around. There it was, right in front of her, with its boarded-up windows and suspiciously clean sidewalks. *Zauber Pharmaceutical Labs.*

"Hurry!" Nadia yelled back down into the hole. Crouched on hands and knees, she could see Scarlet climbing the ladder. Anubis's barking reached a fever pitch. The dog scampered in a circle around the manhole. Knowing she'd have to close it quickly, Nadia scrambled to push the heavy cover halfway back into place with her feet, leaving just a half-moon circle of opening. As Scarlet neared the top, Nadia reached down to help her. The younger girl screamed. Nadia saw her kicking wildly behind her with one leg. Frantically, Nadia grabbed for Scarlet's arms. The girl's thin wrists snaked through her fingers as she fell backward into the darkness.

Shining her flashlight into the hole, Nadia could see Scarlet fighting to free herself as Simon and the others, once more clad in their gruesome fur robes, wrestled her to the ground. One face, hawk-cheeked, sharp, and laser-eyed, shone up at her from the bottom. Jasmine Jenkins. She had seen her.

"Oh shit," Nadia yelled. Hearing Jasmine's hands hit the bottom rung of the ladder, Nadia dropped the flashlight and bolted up the steep street. Anubis darted ahead, the frantic dog tearing down McMicken Avenue in a burst of speed. Nadia stopped to catch her breath outside of Northern Row Distillery. She ducked inside, hoping to get lost in the crowd. The dog followed.

"Ma'am, can I help you?" The host asked, seeming concerned.

"Yeah, um…" Nadia stammered. Knowing that her clothes were dirty and disheveled and it would sound like she was out of her mind if she tried to explain, Nadia quickly decided a half-truth was best. "I was planning on meeting someone, but I got kinda scared that someone else was following me. So I ran away, but I fell."

"Say no more," the host replied, showing Nadia to a seat at the corner of the bar facing the door. She glanced down at Nubi's service animal vest and nodded. "Happens all the time. Young ladies really shouldn't be out late at night in OTR alone. You can wait here and call your friend. Have a drink if you like, but," she paused. "I'll have to card you first." The host stood expectantly with her hand out.

"Oh, yeah, sure..." Nadia replied, trying not to panic as she fished around for her wallet in her crossbody bag. Remembering the fake ID she'd gotten for her Spring Break the year before, Nadia pulled it out. She flashed it at the host with her finger over the photo. The host barely glanced at the ID before sailing off to leave Nadia alone.

To buy herself time, Nadia ordered the least expensive drink on the menu, a light Pilsner beer. She sipped it slowly as she tried calling Shiloh's cell. No answer. She didn't leave a message. Her hands started shaking, then stopped again. The dog, Anubis, shoaled nervously around her ankles. The bartender looked at her strangely but said nothing.

By then she'd calmed down enough to feel something poking her from the seat of her jeans. Pulling it out, she examined the small piece of bent silver. Although it was twisted like a fishhook, the charm was still easily identifiable as the initial *J*.

J for Jasmine, Nadia thought, remembering her meeting earlier that day and what Shiloh and Bernadette said about Jasmine's bracelet. Nadia called the numbers she had for Bernadette Jenkins and Joe Arnold's house. She was half-relieved when none of them picked up. Nadia didn't know what she could say to explain.

Hey, I know I was only supposed to drop off Scarlet's flute, but we ended up going to look for Jackson down in the old subway tunnels instead. The good news is, we found him. Jeff and Jasmine Jenkins too. The bad news is that they and a bunch of other kids are now part of Simon's cult. They also grabbed Scarlet while we were running for our lives. Not sure what happened to her, but it can't be good. I barely got away. I'm sitting in a brewery in OTR, hoping nobody catches me using a fake ID, but too scared to leave.

She went over the message in her mind several times, trying to think of any possible way to make it sound less crazy. Several minutes later, when she figured out she couldn't, Nadia dialed Shiloh's cell again. She explained what happened as best she could until the voicemail cut her off. Then, she stepped outside into a crowd lingering on the sidewalk and called the police.

Saturday, October 14th, Morning

S hiloh Foley and Nadia Haas sat in her office in Mt. Adams. Cold, half mugs of coffee on the desk between them. Avoiding Shiloh's gaze, Nadia stared out the window. The fog coming in from the river was heavy and low, making the air thick with gray haze. Scarlet Arnold's dog, Anubis, slept at Nadia's feet. His tail curled protectively around his body.

"I'm not even going to ask what you were thinking," Shiloh said tersely. She too stared out the window, twisting her gold tree necklace and pressing the charm lightly to her lips in contemplation. "We both know that you should have known better. I don't think harping on it will improve anything. I'm just glad you're not hurt and that you weren't afraid to call and report what happened once you escaped."

"That probably won't save Scarlet though," Nadia replied. She avoided eye contact. "The police certainly took their sweet time getting down there. They didn't believe me at all when I first called it in. If I hadn't gotten a hold of you so that you could convince them, they'd still be doing nothing. Their disbelief made us lose hours." Nadia shrugged. "Typical. Cops never believe a young mixed-race woman when they try to say something weird is going on. They always just assume we're on drugs."

"I agree that their response was slow, for obvious reasons. That sucks," Shiloh said softly, getting up to retrieve the coffee pot. "Believe me, I had words with Schultz and his squad about it. At least they're on the way over there now. You shouldn't blame yourself or give up hope so easily. Scarlet might be found alive yet. On one hand, going down there with just the two of you and a dog was an impulsive mistake that put both of your lives in danger. On the other hand, it gave the police the break in the case that they needed. They'll be able to gather a lot of evidence. Enough to convict Simon and the rest as soon as they're caught. Even though Simon's crew will likely be gone by the time they arrive, there's still a pretty good chance that they won't harm Scarlet. Not severely, at least."

"What makes you say that?" Nadia asked. "Those people are seriously crazy. They were wearing butchered cats and drinking each other's blood."

Shiloh winced as she poured out a warm-up for each of their coffees. "Because it's not part of the plan. Simon appears to have everything quite carefully planned out, like he's the main character in this revenge drama. He doesn't kill on impulse. Otherwise, Jasmine Jenkins and all those other kids would have been dead before now. No," Shiloh mused, taking a sip of her rewarmed coffee. "Simon Bowles is a man who plays a very, very long game. He also seems to discriminate between those he chooses to kill and those he doesn't according to how willing they are to participate in his overall scheme. To me, I think whether Scarlet Arnold lives or dies depends on how much she hates her fathers, biological and legal."

Nadia frowned, making eye contact with Shiloh for the first time. "What does it matter if Scarlet hates her dads if Simon's planning on killing all of their parents anyway?"

"It all goes back to Simon's vision of himself as a Prophet," Shiloh answered. "A Prophet who makes his predictions come true by acting as a scourge. Like that quote from Hamlet that he left at Ellis's murder scene. The one about him being a scourge and minister. Simon sees himself as a judge who is not only passing judgment but also carrying out sentences of execution. Only it's not heavenly justice, but justice here on Earth. That is probably why he's also taking on the persona of Baphomet in his rituals. As above, so below. They took Simon's youth from him while maintaining an above-board appearance, so Simon's taking their children away and using them as tools of destruction as they work through his scheme underground."

"So, if Simon could persuade Scarlet to act out her hatred on her fathers or brothers, for example," Nadia posed, thinking aloud. "He would let her live. Because then she would be helping him administer this alleged justice, as Simon views it. That's super twisted."

"Simon Bowles is a very twisted man," Shiloh agreed. "But he's also a very astute judge of character. Think about how carefully he chooses, manipulates, or eliminates his victims. He sits back and watches these five families for years. Then, he singles out their weakest links. The things they were most ashamed of or insecure about. Simon probably knew that Lorelei Winter-Lang was the least insecure or able to be shamed because she was a successful model and had her whole life splashed across social media. That gave Simon nothing to work with, so she had to go. The other victims may have had little things here or there that they were hiding, like Jaya Khoury and Ellis Purcell. They were both in the closet because they were afraid of embarrassing their parents. Both were still basically good kids though, who didn't take hard drugs and who liked their parents enough to at least try to keep up with whatever expectations they had. So Simon had to eliminate them too. Then, you have those two popular girls, Reece Muller and Savannah Arnold. My guess, from what evidence we've gathered, is that those two were pretty close cases. They weren't above taking the bait and accepting his lure of a new allegedly performance-enhancing drug when it was offered. However, when it came time for them to have to follow up on the other part of it—killing their parents—they balked. Probably because they were their respective families' favorite kids, and they knew it. Thus, either Simon eliminated them or had some of the other kids do it."

"Which leaves all the less favored kids perfectly ready to be manipulated. Eager to try a new drug if they thought it would give them an edge, and when it didn't, they said to hell with it all and succumbed to whatever Simon wanted them to do. Because Simon made them feel special. Chosen. Seen and understood. In a way that their parents never did." Nadia finished.

"You've got it," Shiloh seconded. "Khalid Khoury and Jasmine Jenkins were both outside children of the Khourys' mess of a marriage. Riley Mueller lived in the shadow of her more popular twin sister, Reece. Allen Purcell's parents probably preferred his more talented younger brother, Ellis. As for Jefferson and Jackson Arnold, their father is a drunk and a bully who's only impressed by athleticism. I'm sure they could have turned against him with the right indoctrination fairly easily, if Simon emphasized how they'd never measure up to expectations."

"All of that makes perfect sense with the kids," Nadia reasoned. "But what about Veronica Arnold? If Simon's ultimate plan was to turn as many of the kids as possible against their parents by plying them with drugs and this weird demon-infused empowerment ideology to make them easier to manipulate, then why kill Veronica Arnold right away?"

"Her killing doesn't fit the mold," Shiloh conceded. "You're right about that. From the very beginning though, I've sensed that Ronni's death was an anomaly. That she was just in the wrong place at the wrong time. That happens sometimes when you're dealing with a violently insane person. They strike out at anyone who gets in their way. Veronica was already trying to distance herself from Joe and the rest of their crowd too, which should have put her even further out of harm's way. Perhaps Veronica was trying to track down her daughter. Perhaps we'll never know until we can get a confession out of Simon or the others once they've been arrested."

Just then, Shiloh's cell rang. It was Detective Schultz. The call was brief, and before it ended, Shiloh was already gathering her things into the red leather tote bag she always carried.

"They've found Scarlet," she announced to Nadia as she pressed to end the call. "Down near the entrance of the tunnel, by where you parked your car.

"Is she alive?" Nadia asked hopefully.

"Yes..." Shiloh replied slowly. "Schultz wants us to come down there immediately. Both of us. You especially. They've brought the bomb squad in. It's somewhat of a situation. They want someone to try to communicate with Scarlet nonverbally before they attempt to move her. Or your car."

"My car?" Nadia pressed for details. "What kind of situation? Scarlet isn't hurt, is she?"

"Um..." Shiloh mused. "Not yet, but you should mentally prepare yourself just in case. It's kind of difficult to explain. I'm not sure I understand what Schultz was describing myself, without seeing it. I guess we'll find out."

Twenty minutes later, Shiloh and Nadia arrived at the Liberty Street subway entrance. Pulling up as close as the police barrier would allow, Shiloh parked at the curb. Dozens of emergency personnel, both medical and police, milled about, speaking in hushed tones. A ring of news vans surrounded by reporters and camera operators buzzed like a crowd of anxious bees near the perimeter of the police barrier. As they approached,

Shiloh and Nadia could see what Detective Schultz was at a loss to explain fully on the phone.

Tied to the rearview mirror of Nadia's turquoise Prius with a long electrical cord was Jasmine's horse, Lyra. The same horse that Nadia saw in the tunnels the evening before. The horse was still covered in luminescent green paint, which shone eerily through the thick fog. Sitting on Lyra's back was a dark, shaggy figure. By the time they were at the edge of the yellow caution tape barrier set up around the scene, they could make out who the person was. Scarlet Arnold. Her face was smeared with blood. Around her shoulders was draped what Nadia recognized with horror was one of the long cloaks made of cat fur. Rough wooden signs with Bible verses on them hung from both her and the horse's necks. The girl said nothing and did not move. Nor did the horse, who had some lumpy blobs of something gray around its hooves. Motionless, both stared at them with wild, terrified eyes.

"Why is she still sitting there?" Nadia asked. "What's wrong with her?"

"The bomb squad and the rescue team are both still trying to decide how best to approach removing her from the horse. How to free the animal without breaking its legs or pulling the detonation cord." Schultz replied, motioning to the electrical cord that—it was easier to see on closer inspection—ran beneath the hood of the Prius. "The search team found them like this when they arrived on the scene first thing this morning. Scarlet can't move because she's both tied and glued to the animal. Her mouth's glued shut as well, so we've not been able to speak with her. Also, if you look closely," Schultz pointed at Lyra. "That's quick-set concrete around the horse's hooves. They've been cemented to the ground."

"Dear God!" Shiloh exclaimed. "It's like he's made a monument out of them. A monument that explodes if you try to move it. What verse is that hanging around her neck?"

"Ezekiel 14:22, I looked it up," Schultz replied. The detective read aloud from his phone screen, "*Yet there will be some survivors—sons and daughters who will be brought out of it. They will come to you, and when you see their conduct and their actions, you will be consoled regarding the disaster I have brought on Jerusalem—every disaster I have brought on it.*"

"Mean anything to you?" Schultz finished, looking first at Shiloh and then at Nadia.

"She's the survivor," Nadia replied, continuing to stare at Scarlet, mystified. "The daughter who is supposed to be the consolation for the disasters Simon has all planned out."

"It means Simon's incorporated her interruption as part of the plan," Shiloh added. "Scarlet and Lyra's public torture is a visual metaphor. Simon's version of Revelations Six. Death is riding on a pale horse when the hour of judgment is near. Simon allowed Scarlet to live so that she could be the one to tell the tale. A literal living monument to his vengeance on the men from St. Augustine's. She must have refused to be part of his plan, and he chose to incorporate her choice. Schultz," she said, turning to the detective, "I think Simon's going to act again very soon. Tonight. Maybe it's already in motion. We've got to warn them. All five men and what remains of their families are in imminent danger. This is a definite sign."

"I thought it might be something like that," Schultz nodded. "I'm getting to where I can figure out the sick bastard's symbolism too. We'll get on it right away, while the team is still working to free those poor things." The detective motioned toward Scarlet and Lyra.

Just then, the lead emergency tech came up to Schultz. "Sorry to interrupt, but we think we've got a plan. The bomb squad says there is a device beneath the car hood, wired to the battery, but it's stable. No timer, but it's got a motion sensor. So long as we don't try to move it or tug on the cord tied to the horse, we should be okay. They have a guy on the way who specializes in that kind of thing who can disarm it safely without detonation. With your permission, we'd like to call out an emergency large animal vet with a standing horse sling too. Once that's secured around the animal to keep her from falling and breaking her legs and the bomb is neutralized, we can cut the cord and sedate her. While the horse is under, we can get a stonemason to use a hand hammer and a small chisel to chip away around her hooves enough to get her removed from the ground for transport. Some solvents can be diluted enough to get the rest of it off her without causing chemical burns. I'm afraid they'll destroy any prints or other evidence though, so the forensic guys should get those off beforehand if they can."

"As for the girl," the tech looked back over her shoulder at Scarlet. "That's a little more complicated. You'll probably want to finish collecting everything you can of her here too. The removal is going to be messy. The team thinks she's glued onto the horse's back with quick-drying construction adhesive. We can get it off with mineral oil, most likely, with minimal damage to her skin or the animal's. However, we think it's best to transport them together after the horse is sedated and do that part at the vet facility. It may take a while, and the animal is sure to startle whenever it comes to. After all, it's been through a lot. The girl seems to be juiced up on whatever that super-drug cocktail is too. There's no telling what she'll do as we start peeling her off. The last thing we'd want is for either of them to start kicking and struggling too much. That could break both their backs or worse."

"Sounds complicated," Schultz replied, shaking his head. "I'm sure you know what's best. Go ahead. I'll gather all the guys and let them know."

The detective turned back to Shiloh and Nadia. "Looks like it's going to be a while before we're going to be able to get that poor girl's mouth unglued so that anyone can talk to her. In the meantime, would you two like to come with me? We've got some important warnings to deliver around. I'd like to have a couple more eyewitnesses along. Might help to persuade some of them to accept police protection."

"You mean, for getting Roman to accept it," Shiloh said. "Yeah, I follow you. We'll go."

"Why wouldn't Judge Mueller want police protection?" Nadia asked.

"Bad optics," Shiloh replied. "The election is next month. People see a bunch of cops swarming around his house and Joe's compound right across the street, and they'll talk. Talking that would inevitably lead to spreading rumors about the crime and cover-up that started it all. Which could destroy his public image and his potential for re-election."

"Him and all the rest of those guys," Detective Schultz seconded. "Don't you think that's part of Simon's plan too? To give them the choice between humiliation and scandal, a public death if you will, or holding onto their pride right up until it kills them?"

"I think everything is part of Simon Bowles's plan," Shiloh said. "Probably even the reactions we're having at this very moment. The worst part is, no matter how much we have figured it out, he's always one step ahead of us. I don't think there's much we can do to stop it."

Saturday, October 14th, Evening

"Absolutely not," Roman Mueller said, his arms crossed firmly over his chest. "We don't need police protection. This house has a fully stocked disaster bunker that I've maintained since I built it. Food, weaponry, gas masks, the works, with almost two thousand square feet of space, including the gym. Enough for up to ninety days, although I don't think it will take that long. Lunatics like these always slip up or burn out quickly."

Shiloh rolled her eyes. "I never had you pegged as a prepper, Roman." She glanced around Roman and Kimberly's sleek, minimalist living room and then back at the three generations of Mueller men sitting on the three-seat portion of their enormous, butter-soft leather pit sofa. "But I can kind of see it. I've always wondered why you had one of the smallest houses in the neighborhood. I thought it was perhaps because you were a politician trying to appear humble. I should have known better. It's all underground."

"Now is not the time for humor, Shiloh," Sarah Mueller stated primly. Her thin, frosted pink lips formed a tight horizontal line. Shiloh didn't look at her former mother-in-law, who sat on the two-seat portion of the desert-colored sofa next to Kimberly.

"Don't you think your constituents will notice that you're not sitting on the bench or campaigning three weeks before the election? Wouldn't it come across as more transparent and honest if the scandal did break that you were out there, being seen in the public eye and ready to answer for it?"

Detective Schultz suggested. It was the strategy that he and Shiloh agreed upon during the drive-over. Classic good cop, bad cop technique. Shiloh would try to bait Roman until he became frustrated enough to give up, while Schultz attempted to appeal to his self-preservative instincts.

"My son," Horace Muller said, emphasizing their relationship, "has nothing to answer for, nor anything to fear from this lunatic monster and his horde. Roman's constituents know that he's taken a leave of absence for bereavement on account of his daughter's death. They will understand and respect that. If her murderer and this cabal choose to attempt to defame him in the press during his time of grief by spilling their hallucinations all over the media, then let them go right ahead. The whole thing is an unmitigated lie. A blatant slander against the character of some of this city's finest men, concocted out of deep-seated jealousy. We've been a respected family in this city for generations. No one will believe them. Especially if the police don't juice everything up by hovering around as if they're the ones who've done something wrong."

"Actually," Nadia stated. "If what multiple witness accounts claim is true, then..."

"People of low stations will say anything to make their presence known," Sarah Muller snapped, her pale blue eyes cold. "It's a shame what this society has come to. The way people try to tear down those who've attempted to act as uplifting pillars of the community. People have no respect for authority these days."

Nadia stared at the old woman hard. Her dark eyes took in Sarah's stiff, white, collarless suit, triple-strand pearl necklace, and feathered hair sprayed into an immovable helmet. "Pillars fall, Ms. Mueller, when the ground they're built on decides they're no longer worth supporting."

Shiloh placed a light hand on the girl's arm. "In all seriousness, what my associate is trying to say is that regardless of what society as a whole is or is not doing, the fact remains that there is a credible, immediate threat to your family." She motioned to include all five Muellers sitting in the semi-circle. "They also pose a threat to four of your oldest friends and their families as well. If you agree to go with Detective Schultz, allow him and his team to escort you somewhere safe, out of the area, just until Simon and the rest are apprehended..."

"We could go to Daddy's," Kimberly interjected. "Daddy would take all of us into his home in Nashville. He's got a big ol' place up on the lake in Hendersonville. We could even bring the dogs. It's just for a few days, Roman," she pleaded, reaching for her youngest child's hand. Her lower lip began to tremble. "Think of RJ. They've already killed Reece and brainwashed Riley too. Won't you do it for him, Roman? If you won't do it for anyone else? For your son?"

Roman Muller looked at his father. Horace, his heavy white brows knit together like storm clouds, glanced down at his grandson, RJ. The boy sat still as a rabbit between his father and grandfather on the sofa. Horace Mueller closed his eyes and shook his head.

"Did anyone ask your opinion?" Roman said, his voice tense and threatening with anger. "If you want to go running back home to your redneck Daddy," he drew out the last word in a mock Southern twang, "then go ahead. But you will not be taking my son with you. He is a Mueller. And Muellers stand their ground."

Undeterred, Kimberly knelt in front of her youngest child. "RJ, honey... don't you want to go to Grandpa and Grandma's with me? Where it's safe?" She reached to take the boy's hands again. RJ withdrew back into the sofa and hid his face beneath his grandfather's arm.

Kimberly began to cry. Roman slapped her hard. She collapsed onto the hardwood floor.

"Don't try to turn my son against me, you redneck bitch," Roman fumed as the room went silent. "You've already ruined my daughters with all your permissive horseshit. One dead, and the other queer. Taken up with a bunch of devil worshippers. You had one job, to be a mother, and you couldn't do it. Go back where you belong, I'm done with you."

"Roman, I know this is a very stressful time," Detective Schultz began.

"Save it, Bruce," Roman snapped, his voice growing angrier by the second. "I think we're done here too. You can take her," he pointed at Kimberly, who was still lying in a sobbing heap on the floor. "But we're staying right here. I'll even save you the trip of going around to Joe, Raff, Kash, and Kyle because I'll call them myself. We're St. Augustine's men. We take care of our own. And if I hear so much as a word of any of this leaking to the press or see a single police cruiser going down that street," Roman pointed out the bay window of his living room, "I swear I will have your job. I will sue this city and any media outlet that picks up the story for every dime of money they have in defamation. Do I make myself clear?"

"As crystal," Detective Schultz replied, his jaw tight.

Kneeling together, Schultz and the women helped Kimberly up. Shiloh and Nadia went with her into the master wing of the house to help Kimberly pack a bag of clothes.

"Take everything important to you," Shiloh whispered to Kimberly. "I have a very bad feeling about this." Nodding but saying nothing, Kimberly emptied her jewelry armoire. She packed a second bag of photos and sentimental pieces from the shelves in her dressing room, topping off the overfilled second bag with several envelopes stuffed with cash that she produced from a shoebox. To Shiloh, it all seemed too organized. As if her sister-in-law had known such a night might come for a long time. She wondered how much abuse Kimberly had endured as Roman's wife. They left through the kitchen by a side door, taking Kimberly's dogs out of their enclosure behind the garage and putting them in the vehicle along with her bags. The rest of the Mueller family remained in the living room, silent and stoic on their leather sofas. Kimberly and Roman did not exchange goodbyes.

"I don't suppose there's anythin' you could do to watch over RJ, huh?" Kimberly asked as they drove away. She sat in the back seat, still sniffling and holding Pearl and Shadow protectively close to her on either side. "No drones or nothin'? Where if somethin' did happen, you'd see it right quick and could send in the SWAT team?"

"I wish there were," Schultz answered. "You heard what Mueller told us. We have to stand down. He doesn't want protection. We can only hope that the fortress he's built will hold."

"What about the others?" Nadia asked. "Surely at least one of them will have the common sense to know that it's best to have some kind of outside help."

"I'll call them," Schultz said as he circled past the Arnold compound on the way down the hill. "I'm pretty sure what the answer will be, though. Joe was always the deep pocket of that bunch, who funded their good time. Roman was the brains. They'll do whatever he says."

As their car pulled onto the freeway, Shiloh agreed with Detective Schultz. "When rich people close ranks, there is no such thing as common sense. Whether they live or die, whatever hill they choose to die on, they will die alone."

Saturday, October 14th, Night

While Roman Mueller and his family were arguing about why they did not need police protection, across town Dr. Akash Khoury was sitting down to dinner with his wife, Helen, and son, Khalid. Knowing that Saturday was their cook's night off, Khalid called his parents and offered to pick up some takeaway. Khalid painstakingly recorded his parents' very specific instructions for their meals. His mother's salmon was to be seared but rare inside. His father's wagyu steak was ordered Pittsburgh rare, and paired with asparagus grilled in EVOO, not butter. Deconstructed kale wedge salads for both, no cheese or bacon. Lemon garlic vinaigrette and gluten-free croutons on the side.

As he listened to them dictate their orders, phone propped casually between his ear and shoulder, Khalid decided that the best place to hide the poison would be inside the leaves of kale. The strong tang of lemon vinegar and olive oil, the only salad dressing his surgeon father permitted inside their home, would be enough to cover the bitter aftertaste of poison.

For himself, Khalid ordered a massive cheeseburger with extra bacon, loaded chili cheese fries, a giant-sized brownie with extra chocolate sauce, and a forty-ounce, full-sugar freestyle soda from the chain fast-food joint across the street from the fancy steakhouse that his parents favored. Growing up, Khalid Khoury was never allowed fast food, just as he'd never been allowed to go outside or get on the gaming console before he'd finished his homework. As a college freshman living in the dorms across town, Khalid devoured anything fried he could get his hands on for breakfast, lunch, and dinner. In the first two months of college, he'd already gained ten pounds. The muscles of his body, carefully sculpted by a strict diet and workout regimen decreed by his fitness-obsessed father, had grown softer after multiple weeks without training. Still, it had remained a quiet rebellion. Khalid had never eaten fast food in front of his parents before. He'd never been so bold.

His sister had, many times, but then she was his parents' favorite. In their eyes, Jaya was superior in every way to Khalid. Jaya was the valedictorian of her class, whereas Khalid only brought home a mix of A's and B's. His parents berated him that he'd never get into medical school with such mediocre grades. Jaya had been a regionally ranked gymnast, while Khalid only rode the bench as a B-team football player for his father's alma mater at St. Augustine. To his friends, Khalid was witty, and girls found him good-looking. He'd even managed to catch the attention of Lorelei Winter-Lang, a genuine model whose father his dad was friends with. Khalid thought that should have made his parents happy, but for some unexplained reason, his mother, Helen, was horrified. Not wanting to displease her, although he always felt that he did unintentionally, Khalid broke things off with Lorelei before they even got to second base. Khalid had not known, until after he met Simon, of his parents' infidelities.

He'd been adrift that fall semester until one night at a party. Khalid bumped into an attractive young Black woman server with long braids. She'd asked him his name, and when he told her, she smiled and asked if he was Dr. Khoury's son. When he'd said yes, she'd called him *Brother*, which puzzled Khalid at the time. Then, she slipped him a small envelope of paper filled with white powder and explained what it did. Going into the bathroom, Khalid slid the powder onto his tongue and leaned back against the cold, white-tiled wall. He felt its buzz kick in. When he looked in the mirror, his pupils were dilated wide and his eyes were glassy. At that moment, Khalid Khoury felt something he'd never experienced before. Freedom from the guilt of being alive.

As the room melted into a rainbow of colors, Khalid began to sweat profusely. He looked down at the paper in his hand. On it were written the words, *Like the world better as you see it now? Join us.* The message was followed by an address and signed in ink with a bold, backsloped script. *The Prophet of Eden Park.*

The next night, Khalid couldn't sleep. His mouth was dry no matter how much water he drank. His heart raced, and he couldn't stop sweating. On the third night, Khalid used the GPS on his phone to track down the address written on the paper. Everything after that fourth night was a blur of illusions and disillusionment.

On the way out of the steakhouse after picking up his parents' food, Khalid stopped in the bathroom. He pulled two paper packets out of his coat pocket. One, he poured half into each of his parents' salad dressing cups. The other he poured onto his tongue, just as he had that first night at the party. Driving back to Indian Hill, as the evening sky swirled around his dilated field of vision in a panorama of colors, he thought about the message on the paper.

Like the world better as you see it now?

Yes, Khalid thought, pulling into his parents' driveway. He liked it much better indeed.

An hour later, Khalid Khoury sat in the middle seat of the long mahogany table in his parents' formal dining room, calmly eating his loaded French fries. Both his mother and father had berated his food choice from the moment he pulled it out of the greasy paper bag. They were so involved in chastising their son that neither of them heard their cell phones ring when Judge Roman Muller attempted to call them. Both Dr. Khoury and his wife, Helen, insisted that no cell phones ever be brought to the dinner table.

Khalid heard their phones ring but said nothing. He simply took their meals out of the paper boxes that he'd transported them in, mixed the pre-poisoned dressing into their salad greens in a stainless-steel bowl under their watchful eyes, lest he commit the dreadful sin of pouring an entire container over them, and then placed the salads on their plates. The elder Khourys always ate dinner seated *Citizen Kane* style, with one at each end so that both were heads of the table.

When his mother, Helen, began choking halfway through her salad, Khalid still said nothing. He chewed his cheeseburger calmly as the man whom Khalid had supposed for eighteen years was his father rushed to her side. Within seconds, Akash began coughing too. Dr. Khoury begged Khalid to call 911. Instead, Khalid got up, slid his food over to Kash's place, knocked his father's meal off onto the floor, and sat down. Still chewing,

Khalid watched as his parents foamed at the mouth, vomited, and shook until they fell over onto the floor dead.

Finishing his chocolate brownie in no hurry, Khalid ran his finger around the inside of the plastic chocolate sauce cup, dipping out every last drop. Then, he wadded up the fast food wrappers and shoved them back into the bag. Khalid threw it onto the floor next to his father's untouched, perfectly seared hundred-dollar steak. Picking up the steak knife that he'd laid by his father's plate, Khalid went over to Akash's body and touched his wrist for a pulse. Feeling none, he cut into his wrist, letting Dr. Khoury's nutrient-rich blood flow into the cheap chocolate sauce cup. Last, taking a small paintbrush from inside his jacket pocket, Khalid dipped it into the cup and traced the verse onto his parents' starched white-linen tablecloth. *1 Corinthians 4:5.*

The next day, when police found the bodies of Dr. Akash Khoury and his wife, Helen Altman Khoury, they would look up the verse's meaning: *Judge nothing before the appointed time; wait until the Lord comes. He will bring to light what is hidden in darkness and will expose the motives of the heart.*

Meanwhile, out on the outskirts of the East Side of town at Lunken Airport, Kyle Lang was yelling at the mechanic of his private jet about why the plane wasn't ready for takeoff. Patiently, the mechanic explained again that somehow the fuel lines had been severed. All the plane's fuel had spilled out. They would have to wait for new lines to be delivered by overnight express, make the repairs, and then refuel. At the earliest, they would be able to inspect the plane again and take off in the morning.

"What kind of shitty excuse for airport security do you have in this dump anyway?" Kyle fumed. "Look, asshole, don't you know who I am? Me and my friend," he gestured at Rafferty Purcell, who stood behind him, deep in an anxious conversation with a short, skinny man who was wearing a black leather motorcycle jacket. "Just got a call from one of our buddies saying that some nutjob from high school was out to kill us. We gotta get outta town!"

"Hey mate," the skinny man said. "There's no need to get bent out of shape. I was just out here tonight checking on my plane. Tried to call, but for some reason, phone service was down, so I had the chauffeur bring me out. I wasn't planning on leaving until the morning. You can take my plane if you want. That twitchy new guy back there," he glanced over his shoulder down the terminal corridor but saw no one. "Anyway, the chap who was just here said it was already fueled up and ready to go."

Kyle looked stunned. "Why would you offer me your plane? Do I know you?"

The man ducked his head, whispering to himself. "Ah, no. I guess you wouldn't. Lori said you didn't care to keep track of who she was with. Guess she was right." He stuck out his hand. "My name's Robby Drystan. I'm with Cindervoid. We're an alternative rock and roll band. Pretty big in the UK. Or we were, until we broke up earlier this year, 'cause I couldn't get my shit together. I used to date your daughter, Lorelei, but I kinda fucked that up too. I'm sorry."

Feeling the intensity of the much larger man's stare, Robby became self-conscious. He ran a hand through his greasy, unwashed hair. "God, I'm making a mess of this. Anyway, I'd just flown into town to try to patch things up with Lori. I've been sober for ninety days. Got my red chip from AA and everything, so I gave her a call. Lori said it was okay if I wanted to try to talk in person, so I jumped at the chance. Turns out I was too late though."

"I think that's the best possible way to make amends," Rafferty Purcell interjected, cutting off the rest of Drystan's confession. "Kyle, I think we should take Robby up on his very generous offer." Purcell's angular face twisted into a wolfish smile as his beady black eyes flashed anxiously between the two men.

"Uh yeah, I guess," Kyle sputtered, his frustration ebbing at this unexpected turn of events. "If the ground crew says everything's a go, then I guess let's go. Gimme your number, kid. I'll have Raff here send you a wire transfer for the costs to get her back to you."

"Ah, don't worry about it," Robby replied. "Just happy to have kind of a chance to do something for Lori by way of helping her old man. She really missed you, you yanno? After you and her Ma split."

Robby stared at Kyle expectantly, as if expecting a response. Lang wasn't listening. "Oh yeah, yeah, kid," Lang mumbled as he and Purcell gathered their bags.

"Hey, are you going to be here a while?" Purcell asked.

"Dunno, maybe," Drystan shook his head. "I should go back to the hotel, but I've just been pretty down for the last few days. It's hard to get motivated for anything. For obvious reasons. It's just nice to be out somewhere for a bit."

"Oh well, I guess that's fine," Purcell said, dismissively. "If you were, I was going to tell you that if a woman shows up—heavyset, with dark curly hair and too much makeup on—looking for me, that's my ex-wife. Francine Altman. I told her why Kyle and I were flying out, and that she might want to check in on our other son, Allen. I haven't heard from him since the day after his brother, Ellis, well..." Purcell trailed off, then finished his thought. "Francine might come out here, even though I told her not to. I should have called her back about funeral arrangements, but I thought it was going to be at least a week until the police were ready. Anyway, if you see her, you can tell her we already left."

Drystan nodded and settled down into one of the padded chairs in the airport lounge as a transit worker carried Lang and Purcell away with their bags in a golf cart. Fifteen minutes later, they were settled into Robby Drystan's private plane, taxiing down the runway. Suddenly, the plane stopped.

"What the hell is wrong now?" Lang fumed.

"I'll go check," Purcell said. He unbuckled his seatbelt as a man in a flight attendant uniform stepped out from behind the curtain leading to the cockpit.

"No need," said the attendant. As his dark gaze met Purcell's, Rafferty could see that his oldest son's eyes were wide open and glassy. A flat, zombie mirror of Purcell's own.

"Allen!" Purcell exclaimed," "What are you doing here?"

Allen laughed. "Glad to hear that you remembered my name at least, *Dad*." The young man sneered at the last word. "I wanted my face to be the last thing you saw in this world."

Purcell had no chance to reply. At that moment, Allen pulled a canister of tear gas from his pocket. Pulling the pin, Allen Purcell hurled the container at his father and took off running the other way toward the cockpit.

The canister hit Rafferty Purcell in the face and exploded, blinding him. He screamed and staggered backward. Seeing what happened to his friend, Kyle Lang leaped to his feet and sprinted toward the back of the plane. The gas stung his skin and eyes. Lang made it to the bathroom and slammed the door shut. Trapped in the tiny, windowless space, he could see the noxious cloud beginning to creep beneath the door. Lang started to cough. He fumbled in his pockets for his cell to call 911, then realized he must have dropped it as he fled.

Back in the airport lounge, a large woman, expensively dressed in a purple crepe skirt suit that was at least one size too small and mismatched, with orange-tinted foundation layered heavily over her pockmarked face, tapped Robby Drystan on the shoulder.

"Excuse me young man, but have you seen my ex-husband?" The woman said, in a prim, self-important voice dripping with sarcasm. "Sharp-eyed, weasel-faced fellow with thinning dark curly hair? My name is Francine Altman. Formerly Purcell. My ex-husband, Rafferty, called and left the strangest message. He said he was in some kind of trouble and that he and his old football buddy, Kyle Lang, were going to try to catch a private flight out of Lunken Airport. I told him no sir, that he had to stay right here in town until we could finally sit down and make arrangements for our son Ellis's funeral. I know he's done everything he could for the last ten years to avoid me and the boys, but he simply cannot escape us this time. Rafferty has to learn that he must take responsibility for..."

By then, Robby Drystan had stopped listening. His attention was diverted out the window. He was watching a man. The same man with a twitchy, sweating weasel's face who'd told him earlier that his plane was already fueled and ready to go a day before he needed it. That man was running as fast as he could away from the craft. It was parked at the end of the runway.

"I think we need to get back, Mum," Drystan said. He stood up and began gently pushing Francine backward.

"Well, how rude!" she exclaimed. "Were you even listening to a word I said?"

At that moment, neither Francine Altman nor Robby Drystan heard anything else. As his private plane exploded, Robby fell on top of Francine, knocking her to the floor. Every window in the airport lounge blew inward with a deafening crash.

When the rescue crew arrived on the scene, charred scraps of cloth and paper still swirled around the smoldering wreckage. Paramedics found the unlikely pair of recovering alcoholic rocker Robby Drystan and fussy Midwestern philanthropist Francine Altman picking glass shards out of their hair like a pair of stunned chimpanzees. Temporarily deafened, but otherwise unharmed.

An hour later, the recovery team discovered a Bible verse scrawled in red spray paint near the end of the runway, from Second Peter 3:10. *The day of the Lord will come like a thief. The heavens will disappear with a roar; the elements will be destroyed by fire, and the earth and everything done in it will be laid bare.*

As Robby and Francine sat on the back of a firetruck at Lunken Airport, wrapped in blankets and giving official statements about the explosion they'd witnessed, Joe Arnold sat in the leather chair behind the desk at his home office across town in Indian Hill.

Joe was polishing his gun. A Marlin 1895 Big Loop, to be exact. The same rifle he'd used to shoot the ten-foot-tall Kodiak grizzly bear that now stared at him, stuffed and glassy-eyed, from across his study. Next to him on the mahogany desk where Joe Arnold propped his feet was a nearly empty bottle of scotch.

Joe had spoken to Roman Mueller about an hour before. It was a rambling and circular conversation from Joe's end because he was already half-drunk. Roman called his best friend first to warn him, right after his wife, Kimberly, left with the others. Joe had never liked Kimberly Tuttle, he claimed. Southern women were particularly shifty. Although he'd given all his kids' Southern names, Joe didn't trust the Southerners who lived in modern times—even if he did prefer country music to the rest of the noisy trash he'd heard on the radio lately. A lot of the early Presidents were from the South though, and Joe liked what they stood for. What Joe Arnold was, above all else, was one hundred percent American. No, Joe told Roman, he'd always thought he could do better than Kimberly. This was his chance. Joe had been considering moving down to Florida for a while anyway. Perhaps they could go together. Once they'd knocked out this Toilet Bowles lowlife, everything could go back to being better than it was before.

Joe declined Roman's offer to stay in the Mueller family's bunker. To Joe, that would have amounted to admitting he wasn't capable of protecting himself. Even though he wished he or his father had thought to put a bunker somewhere under their compound. That would have been some damn good thinking.

Joe also thought Roman was exaggerating. If Joe believed the entire story, that would mean his two oldest boys had been won over to ol' Toilet Bowles's version of the dark side. Jackson had always been a little funny,

Joe thought, but Jeff was a 100% straight arrow. Regardless, Joe Arnold didn't believe that his boys would fall for any such malarkey, no sir. That was worse than them becoming some kind of Socialist Commie dipshit like CNN was full of. His boys were raised better than that. Something that shameful was more than Joe Arnold, a man who always referred to himself in the third person by first and last name, could bear to think of.

And so Joe Arnold sat, full of whiskey and bravado, with his crocodile leather cowboy-booted feet propped up on his desk. Staring at the Kodiak and surrounded by a lifetime's worth of stuffed carcasses from his countless other conquests. Rifle in hand, Joe felt like a guy out of a Hemingway novel about some European civil war that he was supposed to have read in high school but never got around to. Still, it was a good image though, Joe thought, as he drained the last of the scotch from the bottle. Back to a wall and ready for anything. He was the man.

Joe Arnold considered calling the hospital to see how Scarlet was doing but decided against it. The girl had always been weird. She'd be completely screwed up beyond repair after what had happened if that part of Roman's story was true. Joe just couldn't deal with that at the moment. Better to let that little weasel Rafferty deal with her, Joe rationalized. Scarlet should have been Raff's problem the whole time anyway. Would have saved him a ton in head shrinker bills over the years.

As he pondered this, Joe Arnold heard a knocking on the window that looked out over the indoor pool. The same kind of knock his boys would make when they wanted him to come and watch a new dive they'd been working on. But Joe hadn't seen his boys in days. Puzzled, Joe got up out of his chair with difficulty. Dizzy in his alcoholic haze, he stumbled to open the window.

"Hey!" Joe called, setting his gun down and leaning it against the windowsill. "Are you guys down there? Where have you been?"

"No, Joe," a low, purringly menacing voice answered from across the room. A voice that Joe Arnold recognized. "It's me. Jasmine."

Joe Arnold spun around and tripped, knocking his rifle to the floor. He fell to his knees.

"Jazzy?" he asked, rubbing his eyes. Across the room, standing in the doorway, was what appeared to be a second bear. Next to the one that was his trophy. Yet, this bear was weird-looking. It was shaggy in all the wrong places, and the head was too long, like a goat's. Joe was confused. Hadn't

Roman said something about Jasmine when he'd called? Joe couldn't remember. He could barely stand up. "Where have you been, darlin'?"

"Around," Jasmine replied simply. As Joe watched, the weird, bear-like figure that spoke with Jasmine Jenkins's voice stepped further into the room. Two more similar shapes emerged.

"Hello, Dad," they replied in unison.

By this time, Joe Arnold was bewildered. "Jeff? Jackson? Is that you, boys? What the hell kind of getup do you all have on?"

None of them answered. Instead, before Joe Arnold had time to shoulder his gun, all three pounced on him at the same time. Slashing with machetes in both hands, his sons and Jasmine sliced Joe Arnold's body to ribbons. As he bled out, Jasmine took a bottle of scotch from Joe's well-stocked liquor cabinet and poured it over the body. Using his father's cigar lighter, Jackson set the corpse alight. The trio stood and watched as the flames engulfed him for several minutes before Jeff threw a heavy bearskin rug over Joe to put out the fire. The coroner's report the next day would say the man looked as if he'd been mauled by a bear, then roasted alive.

Scrawled on the custom mahogany desk behind the corpse would be yet another verse, Revelations 21:8, written in Joe's blood. *The cowardly, the unbelieving, the vile, the murderers, the sexually immoral, those who practice magic arts, the idolaters, and all liars—they will be consigned to the fiery lake of burning sulfur.*

When they finished, the three raided one of Joe's many unlocked gun cabinets. They took all they could carry.

"That was a lot of work," Jasmine said as the three trudged across the road to Roman Mueller's house. "With all those guns around, why couldn't we just have shot him?"

"That wouldn't have been right," Jefferson said, his blue eyes dancing wildly in his bloody face. "Remember what Dad always told us, Jackson?"

"That there's nothing more shameful than a man being shot by his own gun," Jackson replied, brandishing his father's Marlin 1895 rifle.

Finding this statement surprisingly funny, both young men crowed with laughter.

"Shut up, fools!" Jasmine scolded. Her eyes flashed crazily bright as sweat streamed down the sides of her face. "Put your robes back on. We've still got one left. Look!"

Saturday, October 14th, Midnight

Across the street, Riley Mueller stood beneath the camera posted over the front door of her parents' house. She was dressed normally, in a girlish cropped tee shirt, baggy low-rise jeans, and clunky white sneakers, not in gory robes like the other three. Gazing up into the camera with wide, drug-glazed eyes, she tucked her dishwater blonde, center-parted hair behind her ears and pleaded, in her most innocent voice.

"Dad, Mom, are you in there? It's Riley. I'm scared!" The girl looked over her shoulder in the direction from which Jasmine, Jackson, and Jeff were approaching slowly but still out of frame. "I think someone's following me. Please let me in!"

Downstairs in the bunker, Roman Muller watched his daughter on the CC monitor and swore under his breath. Recognizing his sister and terrified of everything happening around him, RJ began to cry. The boy wrapped himself into a ball and rocked back and forth on the floor.

"Don't do it, Roman," Horace Mueller hissed. "It's a trap. They're using her as bait to play on your sympathy. Remember what the detective said. Riley's been brainwashed. She's as good as dead already, no matter what you do."

"Your father is right," Sarah Mueller seconded. "Think about Patty Hearst. That girl who joined up with that, what was it called, Horace?"

"Symbionese Liberation Army," her husband replied.

"Yes," Sarah continued. "Those radical left-wing Communist people. They'll stop at nothing to brainwash any child from a good Christian conservative family. They prey on wayward young girls, especially. Just think about that no-good Charlie Manson. He got his start right here in Cincinnati, stealing cars. Took one right out of Eden Park with a local girl in it. He drove all the way to California with her. Right before he went crazy and started killing people."

"I didn't know that," Roman said, turning away from the screen toward his parents.

"Oh yeah," Horace replied. "Your grandfather, Virgil, was one of the judges who sent Manson to juvie once when he was a kid. If you read all that bullshit Manson put out about it later, he claimed to have been abused there, sexually. Claims that's what set him off, but I doubt it. Manson was a bad egg from the start. Illegitimate son, whose mother was a prostitute. The family was from West Virginia, so you know what kinds of people they were. Just pure white trash. People like that will always try to blame the justice system for punishing them when they go wrong. It's just their lack of character."

"Just like Simon," Roman breathed. "Oh God, what have I done?"

"Dad," RJ said, pulling on his father's pants leg from the floor. "Dad, what are those things coming up behind Riley?"

Roman glanced back up at the screen. No longer pounding on the door and begging to be let in, his daughter was now standing with her back to the camera, calmly talking to three figures. Completely concealed in shaggy fur robes, their heads were covered in masks of some sort, with faces that looked like goats. Each of them carried long guns in both hands. Although Roman couldn't make out what they were saying, it appeared that they were arguing. Then a fourth figure walked into frame. Dressed strangely, like the others, but with taller horns. He took one of the rifles from a companion. Finally, two more appeared and accepted guns as well, making six total. All of them gathered closer into a semicircle, leaving Riley out. She turned her worried face up toward the camera again. Her eyes pleaded silently to be let in.

"What are they saying?" Roman wondered aloud. He reached for the remote control, turning the volume up as high as it would go and leaning in so close to the screen that the end of his nose almost touched it. He watched as the ragged intruders raised their hands together, making some kind of strange sign.

Suddenly, the circle parted. The robed figures spun in unison and raised their rifles at Riley. The girl screamed as they fired. The sounds of her execution rang out around the Muellers' bunker. Roman leaped back from the monitor. RJ screamed and covered his ears. Horace and Sarah Mueller sat slack-jawed, too terrified to move.

Shoving Riley's body roughly out of the way, the attackers shot again, this time at the front door. The Muellers continued to watch in horror. There was a tremendous crash, the sound of the heavy, beveled glass breaking, followed by silence.

"They're inside," Roman whispered. He turned away from the screen. RJ whimpered and shook in fear. His grandmother Sarah frowned upon the boy disapprovingly. Stunned, Roman reached down to put his arms around his son.

"Well, let those bastards just try to get in here," Horace said smugly, crossing his arms over his chest as he leaned back into the sofa. "This bunker is a foot thick of concrete and reinforced steel rebar. Airtight too. The place could even survive a nuclear explosion. Of course, you've got to keep up with routine maintenance, like anything else. Glad I had the technician out just a few weeks ago to check the seal and reset the password."

Roman froze. "Dad, you told me that you changed the password by yourself."

"Eh, I tried, but you know how terrible I am with all that technical stuff," Horace replied. "I told her what to do and let the tech key it in."

"Dad, what did she look like?" Roman's face blanched.

"How would I remember that?" Horace scoffed. "They're just service people. Some Black girl, I think. They let women do just about everything nowadays."

Across the room, six soft beeps chirped from the keypad next to the bunker door. As the automatic lock clicked and the door swung open, four men in blood-crusted fur cloaks and goat masks burst through. Rifles drawn, they shot and killed every member of the Mueller family within seconds. Following instructions, they were in the process of stalking room by room through the remainder of the bunker looking for anyone else potentially hiding when they heard the six beeps sound again. Suddenly, all the lights went out, and the airlock door slammed shut.

"Stupid rich boys," Jasmine Jenkins said, taking off her mask at the top of the stairs. Shaking out her long braids, she punched in the code to turn off the oxygen return system that provided ventilation to the bunker. With a whir and a clunk, she heard the system shut down. According to the clock, they had exactly sixty minutes of air if they remained still before they began to suffocate. Less if they tried to fight their way out, Jasmine thought, as she could feel the slight reverberation of their pounding on the inside of the airlock door.

Peeling back her disgusting robe, Jasmine pulled out a can of blood-red spray paint. She shook it up and wrote the citation of the final verse that Simon had chosen on the heavy steel. Although it would take days before they could drill through the foot-thick concrete walls and recover the gas-bloated bodies from inside the Mueller family bunker, police arriving on the scene would decipher the ominous meaning of the Bible verse on the door almost immediately. It was from Isaiah 34:4.

All the stars in the sky will be dissolved, and the heavens will roll up like a scroll; all the starry hosts will fall like withered leaves from the vine, like shriveled figs from the fig tree.

Upstairs, Jasmine told Simon that everything was complete. He congratulated her and handed Jasmine a small envelope filled with white powder. Her eyes sparkled as she unfolded the paper and poured its contents onto her tongue. Stepping over the bullet-riddled body of Riley Mueller on the way out, they left the door open.

Walking down the unlit street past the Arnold compound, they did not hear a sound. If any neighbors saw anything suspicious that night and attempted to call the police, they'd immediately be put on hold and then disconnected. Until the discovery of his friends' charred bodies in the private plane wreckage at the airport brought in the FAA the following morning, Judge Roman Mueller's orders for a complete police stand down were followed perfectly.

When they neared the black van parked behind the Arnold compound, Simon asked Jasmine to wait while he retrieved something. Suspecting nothing, Jasmine stood patiently surveying the Arnold estate. According to Simon's promise, Joe Arnold's compound would soon be hers. By drugging Scarlet but allowing her to live after they'd killed the remainder of her family, Simon claimed, they'd created a situation in which someone would have to step in as her guardian. Most likely, Jasmine's sister Bernadette would be appointed. Simon felt certain that Bernie would be so overjoyed to have her sister back that they could easily persuade her to share the wealth. After that, it wouldn't take long before they could find a way for Jasmine to take the estate from Bernadette and Scarlet completely.

It felt good, Jasmine thought, to finally have a man as intelligent and thorough as Simon including her in his plans. Looking out for her, without demanding any sexual favors. That had never happened to Jasmine before in her entire life. True, she and Simon had some violent disagreements in the past, but those were before he'd revealed the entire plan to her. What Jasmine had done for Simon, what they'd done together, proved her allegiance. To Simon, the Prophet, and their Lord Baphomet. She had earned it, Jasmine thought. The right to be chosen, respected, and rewarded. It was about damn time.

Simon walked back around the van and stopped. His arms were at his sides, and he stood in the shadow of the vehicle. Jasmine could not see the rifle in Simon's left hand.

"Stop right there," Simon said. "Don't move. I want to take a mental picture of you right now as you are. In your moment of triumph, celebrated as the Queen you deserve to be."

Jasmine tossed her long braids to one side and rolled her shoulders back. She posed, fierce-faced in the moonlight. Her eyes gleamed bright, wild gold, like a lioness in the dark.

Simon raised the rifle and fired one shot. Jasmine Jenkins fell dead on Joe Arnold's back lawn. Wiping the rifle down carefully with a sanitizing cloth to remove all traces of himself, Simon laid the gun down on top of Jasmine's body. He returned swiftly to the van.

"The pretty ones always think they're special," Simon said to himself as he drove away. "Vanity and flattery. Gets them every time."

Wednesday, October 18th, Afternoon

Shiloh Foley did not learn about the St. Augustine's Massacre, as the events came to be known in the press, until the Sunday morning after they happened. On that Saturday night, she'd attended the Cincinnati Shakespeare Company's new contemporary interpretation of *Hamlet* with Laurence Blake in the leading role. Shiloh and her friends new and old, Nadia Haas, Joanne Blake, Bernadette Jenkins, Frida Jiminez, Kimberly Mueller, and Detective Bruce Schultz with his wife, Kaley, made up the entire front row. The arrangement had been Shiloh's idea, to try to take Kimberly's mind off her final argument with Roman. Detective Schultz insisted that none of the women go home alone that evening. Since Shiloh, Nadia, and Joanne already had tickets for the preview night, it wasn't difficult for Laurie to ask for a few more, all things considered.

After their unsuccessful attempt to persuade Roman and the other men to accept police protection left Kimberly with no place to go on short notice, the women decided to rent a group of rooms all on the same floor at the 21c Hotel downtown. Detective Schultz agreed. Not only was it a high-visibility location, but also it was a quick walk from the main police headquarters. That made it easy to switch out a couple of officers every six hours to keep them under surveillance while still allowing them room to move around a bit.

By the second night, Nadia had made arrangements to take a leave of absence from Xavier and go stay with her dad in New York. Laurie had moved several bags of his things from his apartment downtown to stay with his mother, Joanne, in Norwood, until things blew over. Frida's school also gave her administrative leave, which she used to go visit family in California. When Scarlet was released from the hospital on Tuesday, Bernadette decided it wouldn't be a bad idea to drive her up to the lake country and stay around Traverse City for a few days, perhaps to visit Interlochen. She thought that it might be good for the girl's mental health to have a glimpse of what the future might hold for her while the police continued to finish out the investigation of her family compound, the entirety of which was declared a crime scene. Before she left, Bernadette attempted to pay Shiloh for her time in the search for her sister, but Shiloh declined. She told Bernadette to save her money and to consider moving someplace new instead.

Kimberly remained until Wednesday morning to identify the bodies of her family as they were recovered from the Mueller home and bunker. Shiloh was relieved that Kimberly's father, Nashville attorney Cliff Tuttle, came up to be with his daughter during the difficult time. Holding up about as well as anyone could expect of a person in her situation, Kimberly returned with her father and her dogs to Tennessee immediately after the Wednesday morning inquest.

Thus, by Wednesday afternoon, Shiloh Foley found herself alone, once again wandering the downstairs art gallery at the 21c. The exhibition, a series based around a theme of the supernatural, was intriguing, but it made her long to be outside, in the real natural world again. To follow the paths she'd walked countless times, stopping to speak to the trees and animals and to let the power of the outdoors, the one force that had never failed to ground her emotions and steady her soul, heal her once more. Shiloh couldn't remember the last time she'd been cooped up indoors for three days at a stretch, with people hovering over her every move, unless she'd had the flu. Also, the vet had called to say that William was healing well enough to be taken home. Getting restless, Shiloh called Detective Schultz and asked if he thought it would be okay if she checked out that day. He agreed if she promised to pick up her cat, run whatever errands she needed, and then go over to her father PJ's house to spend the night, at least through the weekend. Despite three days of an all-out manhunt for Simon Bowles Tierney, the police had still turned up nothing. Although most everyone on the force supposed he'd fled the city, Detective Schultz still didn't want to take any chances. Now that Shiloh's client's part in the case had come to a close, Schultz made it clear that Shiloh was to steer clear of the rest and let the police take over.

After picking up a still-sleeping William from the vet, Shiloh breezed through the Athleta store and Joseph-Beth Books at Rookwood shopping center for a couple of workout outfits and some light reading material. A book of New England ghost stories by an author she'd never heard of, Hazel Goodnight, caught her eye. Since she was discouraged from returning to her office in Mt. Adams for the week, Shiloh supposed that she'd spend most of her time at the gym and trying to occupy her mind with something other than the search for Simon. All things considered, a book about hauntings seemed weirdly appropriate.

As a last-minute impulse, she bought a bouquet of white roses at Whole Foods to take up to Ethan's grave in Spring Grove. Part of her routine, ever since her husband's death, had been to take him flowers almost every Sunday. Due to the case, she'd missed the last two Sundays in a row. A first since Ethan's passing, Shiloh realized.

This is how it begins, she thought sadly. *First two weeks, then three. A month. Then before I know it, I'm moving somewhere else, and he's gone forever.*

Getting back into the car with the flowers, Shiloh fought back tears. Hearing her, William awoke and yawned, stretching his long front legs across the center console of the Forester. The cat's bright green eyes glowed up at Shiloh inquisitively as if to ask, *Are you okay, Mommy?*

"Oh sweetheart," Shiloh sighed as she smoothed the cat's fur and put the car into reverse. "I'm the one who should be asking you that. I know neither of us is okay yet. But we will be."

Driving past the gates of Spring Grove Cemetery and slowly pulling up the circular drive to the Mueller family plot, Shiloh thought about all the thousands of people buried there. Spring Grove was the largest non-military cemetery in the United States. Billionaires, Civil War generals, bootleggers, and even the guy who supposedly inspired the billboard with the all-seeing eyes of Dr. T.J. Eckleberg in Fitzgerald's *The Great Gatsby*. The Mueller family plot was in this older part of the cemetery, in Section 54 between the Lawler Sphinx and the Groff Pyramid, both of which had been considered controversial at the time of their installation due to their allegedly pagan iconography. Although her former in-laws had despised them as being too flashy and attention-seeking, Shiloh found them wonderfully unique. She'd always appreciated the peaceful beauty of the unconventional cemetery. As a teen, she had often visited the Egyptian-styled monuments before she'd ever heard of Ethan Mueller or his family, just to marvel at what types of interesting people might have requested them built over their final resting places.

Shiloh parked near the curb and left her once-more sleeping cat in the vehicle with the windows cracked. She carried the bouquet of white roses to Ethan's grave, an unobtrusive single stone tablet with only his name, dates, and the phrase, *Beloved Son and Brother*, on it. Putting down her red tote bag, she sat cross-legged on the ground below the footstone and closed her eyes. Inhaling slowly the smell of fresh-cut grass and dusty leaves, and with each exhale feeling the knots of tension in her neck and shoulders begin to relax and release. The air was completely still, and no birds sang.

"There's no place for you here, you know," a voice whispered behind her. A light, dreamy voice, like that of a child. Shiloh's heart stopped. Although she'd never heard the voice speaking instead of singing before, she could feel, with every fiber of her being, who it belonged to. The range of options available and the seconds she had to choose between them flashed through her mind. Shiloh opened her eyes and stared blankly at her husband's tombstone.

"I mean that literally," the high-toned voice continued, as Simon Bowles Tierney stepped out from behind an oak tree and into the waning afternoon sunlight. He pointed at the series of gravestones surrounding Ethan's. "There are only four spaces left, and there should be six Muellers already down at the county morgue. I guess they'll put the girls elsewhere. There perhaps," Simon pointed to an emptier patch of grass several sections over. "Females in general seem to be of secondary importance to their family. If I were you, I'd move away."

"How did you know I was here?" Shiloh asked, trying not to look at him.

"Today?" Simon's already airy voice went up with the question. "I didn't. It was a happy accident. I've been coming here my whole life. Most recently for the same reason as you." Noticing that Shiloh was avoiding his gaze, Simon walked around in front and inclined his head downward toward Ethan's tombstone.

Shiloh could not help but look at him. The filthy trench coat, worn over a faded black button-down and baggy cotton slacks with heavy-soled workman's boots, seemed to emphasize the emaciated frame of the man wearing them. His long, pale face was streaked with deep, ugly claw marks. *William's claw marks*, Shiloh thought. Over his right eye, Shiloh saw that Simon wore a plain black leather patch. *The vet was right. My cat clawed his eye out.*

"However," Simon said, pointing at her tote bag. "I would caution you against carrying an open tote bag in the future, Ms. Foley. Especially since you tend to leave it cluttered with papers so that you cannot see the bottom. You never know when someone might want to slip something in there. Something that would help them follow you around."

"That was *you*?" Shiloh said, the realization of the otherwise unremarkable memory dawning on her. "That night at Sundry & Vice. The drunk who knocked my bag over and then ran off." She reached for her bag, internally cursing herself for never cleaning it out.

"I wouldn't make any sudden moves, Ms. Foley," Simon said. He reached inside his trench coat with an eerie calmness and pulled out a long, straight-handled machete. He held it slack by his side in his left hand. "Yes, I slipped one of those tracking dots in your bag, but it's been there for a while now. That was how I knew when to enter your house to search for the journals, because you'd gone to your father's place on the other side of the river. You can toss it away as soon as you leave here, and I will no longer be any the wiser regarding your whereabouts. Although," Simon cocked his slender head to the side. "I don't think I needed it after all. You are too much a creature of habit, Ms. Foley. Of routine. I know routines are recommended by all the best grief therapists, or so I've read." He winked at her with his good eye before continuing. "But they can also be very limiting. Even dangerous. It's better to shake things up now and then. Let the wheel of fate spin on."

Shiloh's initial impulse to flee began to ebb away. *If he was going to attack me, he would have done so by now*, she thought. *He wants something else.*

"So you read all of my journals?" Shiloh said cautiously. "When you broke into my house and cut poor William's tail off."

"I thought it was only fair," Simon replied, slipping the knife back into his coat. "A tail for an eye. Besides, you'd read *my* journals. I saw you. And Ethan's. A lot can be learned from what one chooses to confess or doesn't, even to the untamed universe of a blank page. There's a certain freedom to be gained by it. A purgation and release so that one can begin anew. Don't you agree, Ms. Foley?"

Aware that Simon was leading the conversation like a skilled defense attorney but unable to disagree, Shiloh nodded.

"And what I learned, Ms. Foley," Simon continued. "From reading your journals and following you more closely, is that you have nothing truly terrible to confess. You seem like a rather good person. A light magician, in contrast to my darkness. Although I feel that all of us truly exist in some shade of gray. For that reason, I would say that I was sorry for dragging you into this whole revenge drama of mine. Except for the fact that you weren't truly harmed by it, I don't think. I mean, your cat was, I suppose, and you seem to care for the animal a rather extraordinary amount. But that is your own chosen misfortune, Ms. Foley, to love something so ephemeral as a cat. Of course, one might argue that all love is ephemeral, but truly, loving something that can only live for a decade or two is an invitation for heartbreak. Plus, if I'm being completely honest," Simon looked at her directly with his one good eye. "And I do want to be completely honest with you, Ms. Foley. I hate cats."

That's what he wants, Shiloh thought, her mind flooding with relief. *He wants to confess. If I just play along and listen, perhaps he will let me go.*

"Why do you hate cats?" Shiloh asked, trying her best to remain calm and to seem as if she were just having a normal conversation.

Simon grinned, revealing a too-white pair of oversized dentures beneath his crooked nose. "Because they're too much like me!" He cackled, a crackling, labored wheeze of a laugh. Then, to Shiloh's surprise, he plopped down to sit on Ethan's headstone.

"An alley cat will do anything to survive. Fight anything. Eat anything. Even its own kind. Like a cannibal. I suppose it started that day my mother left that last bag of food out for me and then disappeared. She'd been taken in for a psychiatric evaluation, but I didn't know that. I was just a child. I had that one sack of burgers and fries to last me who knows how long. I was little, but I already knew how to ration food out, so that's what I was doing. Trying to make whatever I had left in that sack last as long as I could. But when I came back to where I'd stashed it and saw those cats had eaten every bite of it... well. That was the last straw. I killed every one of them I could get my hands on. Been doing so ever since. Tried to eat a few. I wouldn't recommend it. They're only any good for the fur, and it's rangy at best. But no, wait..."

Simon stopped himself. "That's not completely true, Ms. Foley. Stray cats are good for something else too. They're good for disposing of trash. That's why I fed my mother to them." Here, he paused again, cackling as if he thought it was the funniest joke in the world and expected some kind of big reaction from Shiloh for such a shocking statement.

She tried her best not to give it to him. "You fed your mother to a bunch of stray cats?" she repeated, as steadily as she could.

"Well, yes," Simon admitted, plainly disappointed at her calmness. "When they let her out of the nut house in Athens as it was closing, I was in high school. By then, I'd had some bad things happen to me. You know," he glanced at her for affirmation before continuing. "But I was on the upswing. I was at St. Aug's. I was doing well academically. I'd made a friend." Simon patted Ethan's tombstone. "So I was kinda hoping that maybe the gods were through with making me go through whatever I needed to in this lifetime to prove myself worthy of happiness. I was hoping that maybe my mother would come out better and be able to live a normal life."

Pausing, Simon shook his head. "But no. She was even worse. Went right back to everything she'd been doing wrong before. Taking drugs. Trying to turn tricks but failing. Living in the tunnels. I went down there to see her a couple of times. She seemed to be in a pretty bad way, but I didn't know what to do. The third time I went down there, she was dead. Had been for quite some time. Stinking. I should have felt sorry for her, but I've never really felt sympathy for anyone except myself. Instead, I felt angry. Very, very angry. Angry that for a while, she'd left me alone, and I'd started to have some things. But then she came back and stole them. Just like those cats stole my food. That's when I first learned about finishing the circle. I let the cats have her. As above, so below. If you cause others pain, the judgment will always find you. I made a bunch of little cuts on her arms and legs and chopped the flesh up so it was nice and juicy and easy to get to. Then I went and got the biggest, rangiest tomcat I could find. Stuffed him in a sack and then sicced him on her. You should have seen that old thing. He went to town. I didn't go back for weeks after that, but when I did, I knew he must have told all his carnivorous friends. There was nothing left of her but bones with gnaw marks all over them."

"What did you do with the bones?" Shiloh asked, again trying not to seem as if what Simon was saying was affecting her at all even though she felt sick to her stomach.

"I don't know," Simon shrugged. "I didn't go back to the tunnels for many years afterwards, because that was my sophomore year at St. Aug's. Some other really bad stuff happened to me then." A tremor ran over Simon's body. He suddenly stopped talking, and his facial expression went slack as his head drooped forward.

Oh God, you've got to keep him up, keep him talking, or you'll never get out of here alive, Shiloh's mind raced as she struggled to turn on her lawyer brain. "Changing the subject a bit, have you ever loved anyone, Simon?"

"Loved anyone?" Simon repeated, his words slurring now, almost as if he were drunk, even though Shiloh could tell he was sober. "Yes. I loved someone once, very much." His facial muscles regained a more normal composure as he patted Ethan's headstone.

"You loved the same person I loved," Shiloh said. Simon nodded.

"The same way?" Shiloh hinted. Simon nodded again.

"Both ways," he added. "All the ways. Even after he lied."

"Yes, I know," Shiloh said softly. "Ethan never got over it, you know? Abandoning you. The guilt about it ruined his whole life. He loved you too, Simon. Not in the same way. Not in all the ways that you did, but I know that Ethan loved you. You can't regret something that you've done to someone that much and for that long if you never loved them. You saw that, didn't you? When you read his journals?"

"I read it, yes," Simon replied, his tone gentle and childlike once more. "But you have to understand, I was angry with him too. Angry for so very, very long. More than I was even with the ones who'd done it, in the end."

"Because you felt Ethan betrayed you," Shiloh suggested. "That's why you killed him, didn't you, Simon? That's what you've been trying to confess to me all this time we've been sitting here, isn't it?"

"I didn't mean to," Simon said. "Or maybe for a moment, I did. All my life, I've been angry. Most of the time, I can control it. The thing that triggers it most is when people break promises. When they lie or when they just don't turn out to be what they claim to be."

He sighed heavily and stood up again. "I claim to be a Prophet, but what I really am is a planner. Prophecy is just a fancy name for a plan that other people hear you make and choose to believe in. Plans are the simpler promises people make to themselves. That's how I've learned to manage my anger. Making prophecies to avenge myself and then plans to carry them out. However, I also found out very early in life that to fulfill plans, to be able to keep the promises you make to yourself, you need money. And that's one thing I've never done, Ms. Foley. Lie to myself. So I found any way I could to make enough money to keep making plans and keep pushing that anger down. It was still there though, waiting until that day last summer."

"The day that Ethan was shot," Shiloh said, purposefully using the passive voice.

"Yes," Simon replied. "I knew Jasmine was a liar from the day I met her. When she first came to me to buy because she'd heard the word on the street about the new drugs I was compounding that people couldn't get anywhere else. But I needed her. I needed a way into that group. The group of old St. Augustine's boys who'd shut me out, until they decided to attack. To finish out this plan that I'd had for years, I watched them. They acted as if nothing had ever happened. Like they'd never tried to destroy me even more completely than I'd already been. I watched them build lives out of lies for years. I saw how much their children and their wives hated them because the people who try to love you and can't are the ones who have seen you for who you truly are. Finally, I got to the point that I was sick of hearing all their secondhand lies. I made a plan that they had to go, and I started telling it to others close enough to them who believed it. Then it became a prophecy, you see, because that's what a prophecy is. A plan that one man makes and others choose to believe in. Since all of it was an idea I'd come up with there in the park, I started calling myself the Prophet of Eden Park."

He studied the setting sun. "Jasmine and I were arguing that day. I'd told her too much, in hopes of getting her more invested, but I misjudged her. I thought she was tougher. I thought Jasmine was more like me, but she wasn't. She wanted out. She wasn't interested in vengeance against a world that was never made for her. She only wanted more money, more admirers, and more drugs. The things my mother wanted. The things all shallow, spoiled people want but don't expect to have to pay for if they're attractive enough. Jasmine wasn't as brave at first as she pretended to be. I should have known. Another lie. Her deception made me angry. I would have killed her that day. I tried to kill her."

"But Ethan intervened," Shiloh finished. "I understand."

"No, not quite," Simon said. "I promised that I'd be completely truthful, and I will. At that moment, Jasmine and I were fighting and Ethan stepped between us. For just one instant, I hated him too. Hated him for finally interfering when he'd run away so long ago. Hated him just as much as I did all the rest of them. Hated him for daring to feel good and self-righteous only when it suited him. Hated him for looking at me, but never seeing me. And so I shot him."

"You can't hate someone you've never loved," Shiloh said. "If it means anything to you, you have my forgiveness. Not for all the rest of it, but for Ethan. Just that part."

"I don't care about the rest of it," Simon replied nonchalantly. "For them, all I have to say is that the judgment they deserved found them. As it says in Romans 6:23, the wages of sin are death. The ouroboros devours itself." He motioned to the sky and earth simultaneously.

"Do you really believe all of that?" Shiloh asked. "As above, so below, and the rest of it? Or was it just part of the plan? The prophecy that you needed to justify making it happen?"

Simon smiled. "Both. I named my company Zauber. Do you know what that word means in German?"

Shiloh shook her head.

"Magic," Simon replied. "I am a seeker, just like you, Ms. Foley. As I'm sure you are aware from my history, there was no truth available for me to find in the religion in which I was raised. There, I found only pain. Lies and more lies. Thus, I sought out other forces to believe in that are just as powerful, if not more so. So far, they have never lied to me. They have never hurt me. They have served me better, so I have continued to serve them. And if those whom I work out my prophecies through need a bit of theatrics to be won over to the cause of justice, who am I to deny them a magic show?"

"That makes sense, I guess," Shiloh reasoned. Slowly, without any sudden movements, she stood up. "I think I'm going to go now, but before I do, I need to ask you three more questions."

Simon stared at her expectantly.

"First, is that your father's coat?" Shiloh's voice was timid. The question was partly genuine curiosity and partly a distraction move in their verbal game of chess.

The brow above Simon's remaining eye arched slightly. "I think you already know the answer to that question, Ms. Foley," he replied with a slight grin. "I am a sentimental man."

"Okay," Shiloh breathed, slightly relieved by his amusement and the fact that she had caught him off guard. "Second question. Are you done? Killing people, I mean."

"For now, yes," Simon answered plainly. "I have played out my role as scourge and minister. I have paid the men of St. Augustine's the wages of their sins. This plan, my prophecy, is almost completed. My next prophecy is that I will leave here and never return. I plan to go as soon as tomorrow, if possible."

"Okay," Shiloh replied, processing his answer carefully. She didn't like his inclusion of the word *almost* or any of the other contingencies. "Third and final question. Will I see you again? As in, will you keep following me around? No offense, but I'd rather not keep looking over my shoulder for the rest of my life. I'd like to believe you are a man of your word. That if you say you won't, then you won't."

Simon smiled again. "Because I loved him once, I will let the one he loved go. I shall suffer so that a witch may live. You have my word that if you say nothing about our meeting today to anyone, you will not see me again. Ever. Unless you need me. Someday, you might. Then you'd have to be the one making the call. From time to time, everyone needs a friend."

"What's that supposed to mean?" Shiloh asked.

Simon did not answer. He turned his back to Shiloh and strolled away, humming. The tune seemed familiar, but her mind was reeling too much to place it. Shiloh walked to her car and put her hand on the door. Then, she hesitated. As he was almost out of sight over the hill, Simon called back to her.

"Go!" he shouted. "And don't come back across the river tonight after sunset!"

Shiloh didn't argue. When she got in her car, she looked up the time for sunset on her phone. Seven minutes after seven. Then she glanced at the clock. It was almost six. She'd promised to meet her father to drop off William and get him situated and then go out for dinner at some new place that had just opened at Newport on the Levee. That was her father's way. Feed a person dinner and make them feel better. To Shiloh, it was as good a plan as any.

On the way there, Shiloh dumped the contents of her tote bag into her lap. Sure enough, hidden under the flotsam of energy bar wrappers and old mail was a tracker dot. As she drove over the river, she stayed in the lane closest to the guardrail and threw it as hard as she could out into the water.

An hour later, Shiloh and her father, P.J., sat on the back patio of the new Latin fusion restaurant at the Levee, waiting for her brother and his wife, who were always late. Although she was burning to tell P.J. what had happened at Spring Grove Cemetery that afternoon, Shiloh kept her promise. It was easy to do, with so much other news to discuss.

Perusing the drink menu, a new type of spicy margarita with a hot seasoning salt rim caught her eye. "Ring of Fire," Shiloh said to the server. "That's a funny name; I'll have one of those." Then, it hit her. The song that Simon was humming as he walked away. The abandoned subway tunnels that formed a ring around the city. The fire circle that Nadia had told her about in Simon's ritual. The explosives rigged to Scarlet and Lyra. Simon's last words of warning to her not to go back over the river after sunset. The Ouroboros. At that moment, Shiloh knew exactly what Simon was going to do. Equally, she knew she could say nothing about it. She could only watch and wait as the wheel of his judgment completed its final circle.

"Hey, y'all," Shiloh's brother, Three-Pete, said as he and his wife sat down. "Say Shi, I don't know if you're ready to take on another case yet, but I do have one for you."

"Really?" Shiloh asked absently as she dipped a chip in some salsa and stared across the river. It was almost sunset. "What is it?"

"Okay," Three-Pete began, winding up with excitement as he spoke. "Do you remember the other day when I was on the phone with that other antiques dealer down in Wilmington? Nora Hewitt? She has that big deal going for those billionaires down on the coast who are remodeling some of the old Charleston mansions?"

"Vaguely, yes. Go on," Shiloh replied, not paying attention as she continued to scan the riverfront. Anxious, she twirled her golden tree necklace, winding and unwinding its chain.

"Well," Three-Pete continued. "The daughter of one of those billionaire clients was murdered last night. Really weird situation. They found her body lying on top of the grave of the girl who was supposed to have been the inspiration for Annabel Lee. You know, like the Edgar Allan Poe poem?"

"That is weird," Shiloh replied, looking at her brother for the first time. "What does it have to do with me?"

"They found a bunch of strange spiritual messages too," Three-Pete said. "We were just talking about it on the phone. All the local private detectives are spooked by it. That, and the fact that it involves some of the richest old families in town. Since all the regular locals are afraid to touch the case, they've called in an outside paranormal investigator. She's supposed to figure out if there's anything to all the evil spell-looking stuff. Try to quiet some rumors."

"That's a hard job if she's legit," Shiloh said. "I wish her good luck with that one. People in general are very superstitious. However, they're also too skeptical. When they finally see something that should reasonably make them believe there are other forces and entities out there in the universe that are real, they refuse to believe it. What's her name?"

"I think Nora said her name was Dr. Hazel Goodnight," Three-Pete replied. "She's some kind of writer and a professor, too. All of it sounded like the kind of case you just wrapped up with, so I gave her your number and told her to give you a call. I figure if nothing else, you'd at least get a little time on the beach in the off-season."

"Can't beat that," PJ said as the server returned with their drinks. "Getting paid just to go down to the beach at this time of year."

As Shiloh accepted hers from the tray, a series of booms came from across the river. The ground and table shook from the reverberation as a dark ring of smoke began to mushroom into the sky across the river on the Cincinnati side.

"What the hell was that?" P.J. yelled. "An earthquake? Terrorists?"

"It sounded like the end of days," Three-Pete said.

"Close," Shiloh said, taking a sip of her drink. "More like the end of a prophecy."

"What prophecy is that?" her brother asked.

"Second Peter, I think," Shiloh said. Her father and brother looked at her curiously at the mention of their names. "On the final day of the Judgment, the Lord will come like a thief in the night, all the evil deeds done on earth will be exposed, the heavens will roar, and the wicked will be consumed by fire."

"Well, there must be a whole lot of wickedness going on over there," P.J. said, pulling his glasses out of his pocket and straining to see over his bifocals. "Looks like there's a ring of fire around the entire city."

"That's pretty heavy stuff, Sis," Three-Pete replied. "What made you think of that verse?"

"Not what, but who," Shiloh sighed. "The Prophet of Eden Park."

Acknowledgements

Cincinnati is a city haunted by hidden history that has subtly morphed into national folklore. Much of it, from the abandoned subway tunnels to the graveyards beneath Music Hall, lies literally underground. Other tales are shadowed in cultural guilt halfway between legend and truth. George Remus, Cincinnati bootlegger, acquaintance of F. Scott Fitzgerald, and inspiration for Jay Gatsby, shot his wife in Eden Park on the way to divorce court. Then, he pioneered the temporary insanity defense by acting as his own attorney. Infamous serial killer Charles Manson, a Cincinnati native, was allegedly swapped for a pitcher of beer in a local bar by his mother. Later, he practiced his rhetoric by dressing as Jesus and wandering around Eden Park swigging tequila and spouting philosophy, before ultimately stealing a car and heading for California. Across town, true stories of the horrors committed at Sedamsville Rectory remain among the city's shameful secrets that have ironically made it one of America's most frequently filmed ghost hunting spots. Despite all of this, Cincinnati remains the American metro in which the fewest number of native born residents ever leave. As a non-native who will forever be an outsider, I acknowledge that living there gave me the opportunity to ponder its suspicious insularity and allowed me to write a book that considers how systemic silencing can create monsters.

As always, I remain grateful to my editor, Raigan Nickle, for diligently dissecting the details of this story and its large cast of characters. Also, I greatly appreciate my cover designer, Marta Obucina, for her patience and artistry. Last, I send all my love to my partner Andrew, and my cat, Jim Nightshade. Thank you both for listening and understanding.

About the Author

Vivian Catfield is the pen name of Dr. Candace Ursula Grissom. She holds a PhD in English from Middle Tennessee State University, an MFA in Creative Writing from Sewanee: The University of the South, and a BS in Music Business, also from MTSU, among other degrees. Born in North Alabama, she lived in Murfreesboro, Tennessee for many years. Currently, she resides in Cincinnati, Ohio with her partner Andrew and her cat Jim Nightshade. Outside of literature, her interests include acting, exploring haunted history, and spending time outdoors. Prophet of Eden Park is her third novel. If you enjoyed it, please consider checking out her first two novels, Keys in the Dust and Looking Glass Theory.

Also by Vivian Catfield

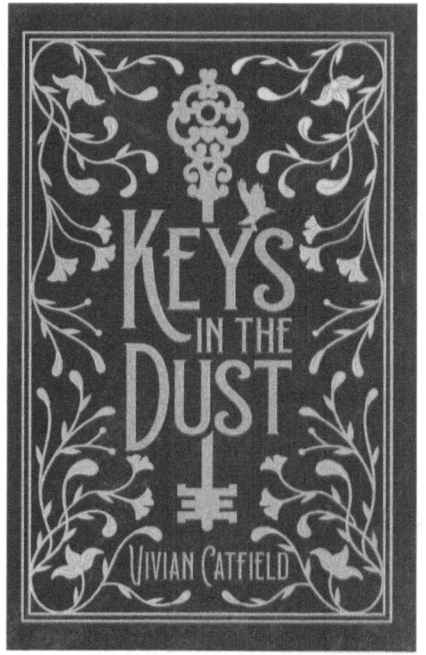

What if one silver key could unlock your power—and your destiny?

Willow Todd never expected a mysterious key to lead her to Rookes College, a hidden school of elemental witchcraft on an island shrouded in a magickal glamor. As a Spirit witch, Willow enters a world of natural magick, sisterhood, and ancient traditions—where students bond with animal familiars and harness the power of Earth, Air, Fire, Water, and Spirit. But Rookes isn't just a sanctuary. A deadly hurricane is coming, threatening to destroy both the island and the balance of the Otherworld. Guided by mentors inspired by historical heroines, Willow and her coven must raise a Cone of Power to defend their home. As Willow's magickal gifts awaken, so does her connection to Elliott—a mysterious Spirit witch with a broken past. Together, they'll discover that love, nature, and unity may be the most powerful magick of all.

Also by Vivian Catfield

What would you change if you could live your life over again?

Following her husband's death, Nora Hewitt seeks a new beginning by opening an interior design firm in Wilmington, North Carolina. However, Nora's entrepreneurial dreams are shattered after she acquires a set of haunted mirrors. Eerie, inexplicable events lead her to befriend a ghost hunter, revealing a forgotten world beyond the glass. When her sister vanishes, Nora must confront her family's tragic history: secret paranormal experiments, her father's alleged suicide, and her husband's mysterious death. Guided by restless spirits, including a past-life lover, Nora races to save her sister, while embracing her power as a woman alone.

Also by Vivian Catfield

Which wolf will win the battle raging inside of you?

On the eve of the Colorado Gold Rush, Mae Ulrich, a strong-willed, progressive heiress from Maine, leaves her home with dreams of starting a frontier school. Plagued by prophetic nightmares of vicious beasts, Mae's idealism is destroyed when she uncovers a ruthless plot to steal Native American lands and gold. Traveling west with a saloon keeper and a fur trader, Mae bonds with a mysterious cowboy and a gifted student. When a violent attack forces Mae to confront her fears, her shocking connection to the beasts is revealed. Embracing her inner darkness, Mae fights for justice in a gold-hungry nation, questioning the costs of change in a brutal pre-Civil War America.

www.ingramcontent.com/pod-product-compliance
Lightning Source LLC
Chambersburg PA
CBHW052036240626
47153CB00006B/2108